F
SILV

PENGU

A DEATH

Daniel Silva is also the author of the bestselling thrillers *The Unlikely Spy*, *The Mark of the Assassin*, *The Marching Season*, *The Kill Artist*, *The English Assassin* and *The Confessor*. The *Washington Post* ranks him as 'among the best of the younger American spy novelists' and he is regularly compared to Graham Green and John le Carré. He lives in Washington, DC. *A Death in Vienna* completes the trilogy of novels (*The English Assassin* and *The Confessor*) which deals with the various repercussions of the Holocaust.

A DEATH IN VIENNA

DANIEL SILVA

PENGUIN BOOKS

PENGUIN BOOKS

Published by the Penguin Group
Penguin Books Ltd, 80 Strand, London WC2R 0RL, England
Penguin Group (USA) Inc., 375 Hudson Street, New York, New York 10014, USA
Penguin Group (Canada), 10 Alcorn Avenue, Toronto, Ontario, Canada M4V 3B2
(a division of Pearson Penguin Canada Inc.)
Penguin Ireland, 25 St Stephen's Green, Dublin 2, Ireland (a division of Penguin Books Ltd)
Penguin Group (Australia), 250 Camberwell Road,
Camberwell, Victoria 3124, Australia (a division of Pearson Australia Group Pty Ltd)
Penguin Books India Pvt Ltd, 11 Community Centre,
Panchsheel Park, New Delhi – 110 017, India
Penguin Group (NZ), cnr Airborne and Rosedale Roads,
Albany, Auckland 1310, New Zealand (a division of Pearson New Zealand Ltd)
Penguin Books (South Africa) (Pty) Ltd, 24 Sturdee Avenue,
Rosebank 2196, South Africa

Penguin Books Ltd, Registered Offices: 80 Strand, London WC2R 0RL, England

www.penguin.com

First published in the United States of America by G. P. Putnam's Sons 2004
First published in Great Britain in Penguin Books 2005
8

Printed in England by Clays Ltd, St Ives plc

Dedicated to those who give the murderers
and their accomplices no peace,
To my friend and editor, Neil Nyren,
And, as always, to my wife, Jamie, and
my children, Lily and Nicholas

In a place where wood is chopped, splinters must fall, and there is no avoiding this.

—SS-GRUPPENFÜHRER HEINRICH MÜLLER
HEAD OF THE GESTAPO

We're not in the Boy Scouts. If we'd wanted to be in the Boy Scouts, we would have joined the Boy Scouts.

—RICHARD HELMS
FORMER CIA DIRECTOR

PART ONE

THE MAN FROM CAFÉ CENTRAL

1

VIENNA

THE OFFICE IS hard to find, and intentionally so. Located near the end of a narrow, curving lane, in a quarter of Vienna more renowned for its nightlife than its tragic past, the entrance is marked only by a small brass plaque bearing the inscription WARTIME CLAIMS AND INQUIRIES. The security system, installed by an obscure firm based in Tel Aviv, is formidable and highly visible. A camera glowers menacingly from above the door. No one is admitted without an appointment and a letter of introduction. Visitors must pass through a finely tuned magnetometer. Purses and briefcases are inspected with unsmiling efficiency by one of two disarmingly pretty girls. One is called Reveka, the other Sarah.

Once inside, the visitor is escorted along a claustrophobic corridor lined with gunmetal-gray filing cabinets, then into a large typically Viennese chamber with pale floors, a high ceiling, and bookshelves bowed beneath the weight of countless volumes and file folders. The donnish clutter is appealing, though some are unnerved by the green-tinted bulletproof windows overlooking the melancholy courtyard.

The man who works there is untidy and easily missed. It is his special talent. Sometimes, as you enter, he is standing atop a library ladder rummaging for a book. Usually he is seated at his desk, wreathed in cigarette smoke, peering at the stack of paperwork and files that never seems to diminish. He takes a moment to finish a sentence or jot a loose minute in the margin of a document, then he rises and extends his tiny hand, his quick brown eyes flickering over you. "Eli Lavon," he says modestly as he shakes your hand, though everyone in Vienna knows who runs Wartime Claims and Inquiries.

Were it not for Lavon's well-established reputation, his appearance—a shirtfront chronically smeared with ash, a shabby burgundy-colored cardigan with patches on the elbows and a tattered hem—might prove disturbing. Some suspect he is without sufficient means; others imagine he is an ascetic or even slightly mad. One woman who wanted help winning restitution from a Swiss bank concluded he was suffering from a permanently broken heart. How else to explain that he had never been married? The air of bereavement that is sometimes visible when he thinks no one is looking? Whatever the visitor's suspicions, the result is usually the same. Most cling to him for fear he might float away.

He points you toward the comfortable couch. He asks the girls to hold his calls, then places his thumb and forefinger together and tips them toward his mouth. *Coffee, please.* Out of earshot the girls quarrel about whose turn it is. Reveka is an Israeli from Haifa, olive-skinned and black-eyed, stubborn and fiery. Sarah is a well-heeled American Jew from the Holocaust studies program at Boston University, more cerebral than Reveka and therefore more patient. She is not above resorting to deception or even outright lies to avoid a chore she believes is beneath her. Reveka, honest and temperamental, is easily outmaneuvered, and so it is usually Reveka who joylessly plunks a silver tray on the coffee table and retreats in a sulk.

Lavon has no set formula for how to conduct his meetings. He permits the visitor to determine the course. He is not averse to answering questions about himself and, if pressed, explains how it came to be that one of Israel's most talented young archaeologists chose to sift through the unfinished business of the Holocaust rather than the troubled soil of his homeland. His willingness to discuss his past, however, goes only so far. He does not tell visitors that, for a brief period in the early 1970s, he worked for Israel's notorious secret service. Or that he is still regarded as the finest street surveillance artist the service has ever produced. Or that twice a year, when he returns to Israel to see his aged mother, he visits a highly secure facility north of Tel Aviv to share some of his secrets with the next generation. Inside the service he is still referred to as "the Ghost." His mentor, a man called Ari Shamron, always said that Eli Lavon could disappear while shaking your hand. It was not far from the truth.

He is quiet around his guests, just as he was quiet around the men he stalked for Shamron. He is a chain smoker, but if it bothers the guest he will refrain. A polyglot, he listens to you in whatever language you prefer. His gaze is sympathetic and steady, though behind his eyes it is sometimes possible to detect puzzle pieces sliding into place. He prefers to hold all questions until the visitor has completed his case. His time is precious, and he makes decisions quickly. He knows when he can help. He knows when it is better to leave the past undisturbed.

Should he accept your case, he asks for a small sum of money to finance the opening stages of his investigation. He does so with noticeable embarrassment, and if you cannot pay he will waive the fee entirely. He receives most of his operating funds from donors, but Wartime Claims is hardly a profitable enterprise and Lavon is chronically strapped for cash. The source of his funding has been a contentious issue in certain circles of Vienna, where he is reviled as a troublesome outsider financed by international Jewry, always sticking his nose into places it doesn't belong. There are many in Austria who would like Wartime Claims to close its doors for good. It is because of them that Eli Lavon spends his days behind green bulletproof glass.

On a snow-swept evening in early January, Lavon was alone in his office, hunched over a stack of files. There were no visitors that day. In fact it had been many days since Lavon had accepted appointments, the bulk of his time being consumed by a single case. At seven o'clock, Reveka poked her head through the door. "We're hungry," she said with typical Israeli bluntness. "Get us something to eat." Lavon's memory, while impressive, did not extend to food orders. Without looking up from his work, he waved his pen in the air as though he were writing—*Make me a list, Reveka.*

A moment later, he closed the file and stood up. He looked out his window and watched the snow settling gently onto the black bricks of the courtyard. Then he pulled on his overcoat, wrapped a scarf twice around his neck, and placed a cap atop his thinning hair. He walked down the hall to the room where the girls worked. Reveka's desk was a skyline of German military files; Sarah, the eternal graduate student, was concealed behind a stack of books. As usual, they were quarreling. Reveka wanted Indian from a take-away just on the other side of the Danube Canal; Sarah craved pasta from an Italian café on the Kärntnerstrasse. Lavon, oblivious, studied the new computer on Sarah's desk.

"When did that arrive?" he asked, interrupting their debate.

"This morning."

"Why do we have a new computer?"

"Because you bought the old one when the Hapsburgs still ruled Austria."

"Did I authorize the purchase of a new computer?"

The question was not threatening. The girls managed the office. Papers were placed beneath his nose, and usually he signed them without looking.

"No, Eli, you didn't approve the purchase. My father paid for the computer."

Lavon smiled. "Your father is a generous man. Please thank him on my behalf."

The girls resumed their debate. As usual it resolved in Sarah's favor. Reveka wrote out the list and threatened to pin it to Lavon's sleeve. Instead, she stuffed it into his coat pocket for safekeeping and gave him a little shove to send him on his way. "And don't stop for a coffee," she said. "We're starving."

It was almost as difficult to leave Wartime Claims and Inquiries as it was to enter. Lavon punched a series of numbers into a keypad on the wall next to the entrance. When the buzzer sounded, he pulled open the interior door and stepped into the security chamber. The outer door would not open until the inner door had been closed for ten seconds. Lavon put his face to the bulletproof glass and peered out.

On the opposite side of the street, concealed in the shadows at the entrance of a narrow alleyway, stood a heavy-shouldered figure with a fedora hat and mackintosh raincoat. Eli Lavon could not walk the streets of Vienna, or any other city for that matter, without ritualistically checking his tail and recording faces that appeared too many times in too many disparate situations. It was a professional affliction. Even from a distance, and even in the poor light, he knew that he had seen the figure across the street several times during the last few days.

He sorted through his memory, almost as a librarian would sort through a card index, until he found references to previous sightings. *Yes, here it is. The Judenplatz, two days ago. It was you who was following me after I had coffee with that reporter from the States.* He returned to the index and found a second reference. The window of a bar along the Sterngasse. Same man, without the fedora hat, gazing casually over his pilsner as Lavon hurried through a biblical deluge after a perfectly wretched day at the office. The third reference took him a bit longer to locate, but he found it nonetheless. The Number Two streetcar, evening rush. Lavon is pinned against the doors by a florid-faced Viennese who smells of bratwurst and apricot schnapps. Fedora has somehow managed to find a seat and is calmly cleaning his nails with his ticket stub. He is a man who enjoys cleaning things, Lavon had thought at the time. Perhaps he cleans things for a living.

Lavon turned round and pressed the intercom. No response. *Come on, girls.* He pressed it again, then looked over his shoulder. The man in the fedora and mackintosh coat was gone.

A voice came over the speaker. *Reveka.*

"Did you lose the list already, Eli?"

Lavon pressed his thumb against the button.

"Get out! *Now!*"

A few seconds later, Lavon could hear the trample of footfalls in the corridor. The girls appeared before him, separated by a wall of glass. Reveka coolly punched in the code. Sarah stood by silently, her eyes locked on Lavon's, her hand on the glass.

He never remembered hearing the explosion. Reveka and Sarah were engulfed in a ball of fire, then were swept away by the blast wave. The door blew outward. Lavon was lifted like a child's toy, arms spread wide, back arched like a gymnast. His flight was dreamlike. He felt himself turning over and over again. He had no memory of impact. He knew only that he was lying on his back in snow, in a hailstorm of broken glass. "My girls," he whispered as he slid slowly into blackness. "My beautiful girls."

2

VENICE

IT WAS A small terra-cotta church, built for a poor parish in the *sestière* of Cannaregio. The restorer paused at the side portal beneath a beautifully proportioned lunette and fished a set of keys from the pocket of his oilskin coat. He unlocked the studded oaken door and slipped inside. A breath of cold air, heavy with damp and old candle wax, caressed his cheek. He stood motionless in the half-light for a moment, then headed across the intimate Greek Cross nave, toward the small Chapel of Saint Jerome on the right side of the church.

The restorer's gait was smooth and seemingly without effort. The slight outward bend to his legs suggested speed and surefootedness. The face was long and narrow at the chin, with a slender nose that looked as if it had been carved from wood. The cheekbones were wide, and there was a hint of the Russian steppes in the restless green eyes. The black hair was cropped short and shot with gray at the temples. It was a face of many possible national origins, and the restorer possessed the linguistic gifts to put it to good use. In Venice, he was known as Mario Delvecchio. It was not his real name.

The altarpiece was concealed behind a tarpaulin-draped scaffold. The restorer took hold of the aluminum tubing and climbed silently upward. His work platform was as he had left it the previous afternoon: his brushes and his palette, his pigments and his medium. He switched on a bank of fluorescent lamps. The painting, the last of Giovanni Bellini's great altarpieces, glowed under the intense lighting. At the left side of the image stood Saint Christopher, the Christ Child straddling his shoulders. Opposite stood Saint Louis of Toulouse, a crosier in hand, a bishop's miter atop his head, his shoulders draped in a cape of red and gold brocade. Above it all, on a second parallel plane, Saint Jerome sat before an open Book of Psalms, framed by a vibrant blue sky streaked with gray-brown clouds. Each saint was separated from the other, alone before God, the isolation so complete it was almost painful to observe. It was an astonishing piece of work for a man in his eighties.

The restorer stood motionless before the towering panel, like a fourth figure rendered by Bellini's skilled hand, and allowed his mind to float away into the landscape. After a moment he poured a puddle of Mowolith 20 medium onto his palette, added pigment, then thinned the mixture with Arcosolve until the consistency and intensity felt right.

He looked up again at the painting. The warmth and richness of the colors had led the art historian Raimond Van Marle to conclude the hand of Titian was clearly in evidence. The restorer believed Van Marle, with all due respect, was sadly mistaken. He had retouched works by both artists and knew their brushwork like the sun lines around his own eyes. The altarpiece in the Church of San Giovanni Crisostomo was Bellini's and Bellini's alone. Besides, at the time of its production, Titian was desperately attempting to replace Bellini as Venice's most important painter. The restorer sincerely doubted Giovanni would have invited the young headstrong Titian to assist in so important a commission. Van Marle, had he done his homework, would have saved himself the embarrassment of so ludicrous an opinion.

The restorer slipped on a pair of Binomags and focused on the rose-colored tunic of Saint Christopher. The painting had suffered from decades of neglect, wild temperature swings, and the continuous onslaught of incense and candle smoke. Christopher's garments had lost much of their original luster and were scarred by the islands of *pentimenti* that had pushed their way to the surface. The restorer had been granted authority to carry out an aggressive repair. His mission was to restore the painting to its original glory. His challenge was to do so without making it look as though it had been churned out by a counterfeiter. In short, he wished to come and go leaving no trace of his presence, to make it appear as if the retouching had been performed by Bellini himself.

For two hours, the restorer worked alone, the silence broken only by the shuffle of feet outside in the street and the rattle of rising aluminum storefronts. The interruptions began at ten o'clock with the arrival of the renowned Venetian altar cleaner, Adrianna Zinetti. She poked her head around the restorer's shroud and wished him a pleasant morning. Annoyed, he raised his magnifying visor and peered down over the edge of his platform. Adrianna had positioned herself in such a way that it was impossible to avoid gazing down the front of her blouse at her extraordinary breasts. The restorer nodded solemnly, then watched her slither up her scaffolding with feline assurance. Adrianna knew he was living with another woman, a Jewess from the old ghetto, yet she still flirted with him at every opportunity, as if one more suggestive glance, or one more "accidental" touch, would be the one to topple his defenses. Still, he envied the simplicity with which she viewed the world. Adrianna loved art and Venetian food and being adored by men. Little else mattered to her.

A young restorer called Antonio Politi came next, wearing sunglasses and looking hung over, a rock star arriving for yet another interview he wished to cancel. Antonio did not bother to wish the restorer good morning. Their dislike was mutual. For the Crisostomo project, Antonio had been assigned Sebastiano del Piombo's main altarpiece. The restorer believed the boy was not ready for the piece, and each evening, before leaving the church, he secretly scaled Antonio's platform to inspect his work.

Francesco Tiepolo, the chief of the San Giovanni Crisostomo project, was the last to arrive, a shambling, bearded figure, dressed in a flowing white shirt and silk scarf round his thick neck. On the streets of Venice, tourists mistook him for Luciano Pavarotti. Venetians rarely made such a mistake, for Francesco Tiepolo ran the most successful restoration company in the entire Veneto region. Among the Venetian art set, he was an institution.

"*Buongiorno,*" Tiepolo sang, his cavernous voice echoing high in the central dome. He seized the restorer's platform with his large hand and gave it one violent shake. The restorer peered over the side like a gargoyle.

"You almost ruined an entire morning's work, Francesco."

"That's why we use isolating varnish." Tiepolo held up a white paper sack. "*Cornetto?*"

"Come on up."

Tiepolo put a foot on the first rung of the scaffolding and pulled himself up. The restorer could hear the aluminum tubing straining under Tiepolo's enormous weight. Tiepolo opened the sack, handed the restorer an almond *cornetto,* and took one for himself. Half of it disappeared in one bite. The restorer sat on the edge of the platform with his feet dangling over the side. Tiepolo stood before the altarpiece and examined his work.

"If I didn't know better, I would have thought old Giovanni slipped in here last night and did the inpainting himself."

"That's the idea, Francesco."

"Yes, but few people have the gifts to actually pull it off." The rest of the *cornetto* disappeared into his mouth. He brushed powdered sugar from his beard. "When will it be finished?"

"Three months, maybe four."

"From my vantage point, three months would be better than four. But heaven forbid I should rush the great Mario Delvecchio. Any travel plans?"

The restorer glared at Tiepolo over the *cornetto* and slowly shook his head. A year earlier, he had been forced to confess his true name and occupation to Tiepolo. The Italian had preserved that trust by never revealing the information to another soul, though from time to time, when they were alone, he still asked the restorer to speak a few words of Hebrew, just to remind himself that the legendary Mario Delvecchio truly was an Israeli from the Valley of Jezreel named Gabriel Allon.

A sudden downpour hammered on the roof of the church. From atop the platform, high in the apse of the chapel, it sounded like a drum roll. Tiepolo raised his hands toward the heavens in supplication.

"Another storm. God help us. They say the *acqua alta* could reach five feet. I still haven't dried out from the last one. I love this place, but even I don't know how much longer I can take it."

It had been a particularly difficult season for high water. Venice had flooded more than fifty times, and three months of winter still remained. Gabriel's house had been inundated so many times that he'd moved everything off the ground floor and was installing a waterproof barrier around his doors and windows.

"You'll die in Venice, just like Bellini," Gabriel said. "And I'll bury you beneath a cypress tree on San Michele, in an enormous crypt befitting a man of your achievements."

Tiepolo seemed pleased with this image, even though he

knew that, like most modern Venetians, he would have to suffer the indignity of a mainland burial.

"And what about you, Mario? Where will you die?"

"With a bit of luck, it will be at the time and place of my own choosing. That's about the best a man like me can hope for."

"Just do me one favor."

"What's that?"

Tiepolo gazed at the scarred painting. "Finish the altarpiece before you die. You owe it to Giovanni."

THE FLOOD SIRENS atop the Basilica San Marco cried out a few minutes after four o'clock. Gabriel hurriedly cleaned his brushes and his palette, but by the time he'd descended his scaffolding and crossed the nave to the front portal, the street was already running with several inches of floodwater.

He went back inside. Like most Venetians, he owned several pairs of rubber Wellington boots, which he stored at strategic points in his life, ready to be deployed at a moment's notice. The pair he kept in the church were his first. They'd been lent to him by Umberto Conti, the master Venetian restorer with whom Gabriel had served his apprenticeship. Gabriel had tried countless times to return them, but Umberto would never take them back. *Keep them, Mario, along with the skills I've given you. They will serve you well, I promise.*

He pulled on Umberto's faded old boots and cloaked himself in a green waterproof poncho. A moment later he was wading through the shin-deep waters of the Salizzada San Giovanni Crisostomo like an olive-drab ghost. In the Strada Nova, the wooden gangplanks known as *passerelle* had yet to be laid down by the city's sanitation workers—a bad sign, Gabriel knew, for it meant the flooding was forecast to be so severe the *passerelle* would float away.

By the time he reached the Rio Terrà San Leonardo, the water was nearing his boot tops. He turned into an alley, quiet except for the sloshing of the waters, and followed it to a temporary wooden footbridge spanning the Rio di Ghetto Nuovo. A ring of unlit apartment houses loomed before him, notable because they were taller than any others in Venice. He waded through a swamped passageway and emerged into a large square. A pair of bearded yeshiva students crossed his path, tiptoeing across the flooded square toward the synagogue, the fringes of their *tallit katan* dangling against their trouser legs. He turned to his left and walked to the doorway at No. 2899. A small brass plaque read COMUNITÀ EBRÀICA DI VENEZIA: JEWISH COMMUNITY OF VENICE. He pressed the bell and was greeted by an old woman's voice over the intercom.

"It's Mario."

"She's not here."

"Where is she?"

"Helping out at the bookstore. One of the girls was sick."

He entered a glass doorway a few paces away and lowered his hood. To his left was the entrance of the ghetto's modest museum; to the right an inviting little bookstore, warm and brightly lit. A girl with short blond hair was perched on a stool behind the counter, hurriedly cashing out the register before the setting of the sun made it impossible for her to handle money. Her name was Valentina. She smiled at Gabriel and pointed the tip of her pencil toward the large floor-to-ceiling window overlooking the canal. A woman was on her hands and knees, soaking up water that had seeped through the allegedly watertight seals around the glass. She was strikingly beautiful.

"I told them those seals would never hold," Gabriel said. "It was a waste of money."

Chiara looked up sharply. Her hair was dark and curly and shimmering with highlights of auburn and chestnut. Barely constrained by a clasp at the nape of her neck, it spilled riotously about her shoulders. Her eyes were caramel and flecked with gold. They tended to change color with her mood.

"Don't just stand there like an idiot. Get down here and help me."

"Surely you don't expect a man of my talent—"

The soaking white towel, thrown with surprising force and accuracy, struck him in the center of the chest. Gabriel wrung it out into a bucket and knelt next to her. "There's been a bombing in Vienna," Chiara whispered, her lips pressed to Gabriel's neck. "He's here. He wants to see you."

THE FLOODWATERS LAPPED against the street entrance of the canal house. When Gabriel opened the door, water rippled across the marble hall. He surveyed the damage, then wearily followed Chiara up the stairs. The living room was in heavy shadow. An old man stood in the rain-spattered window overlooking the canal, as motionless as a figure in the Bellini. He wore a dark business suit and silver necktie. His bald head was shaped like a bullet; his face, deeply tanned and full of cracks and fissures, seemed to be fashioned of desert rock. Gabriel went to his side. The old man did not acknowledge him. Instead, he contemplated the rising waters of the canal, his face set in a fatalistic frown, as though he were witnessing the onset of the Great Flood come to destroy the wickedness of man. Gabriel knew that Ari Shamron was about to inform him of death. Death had joined them in the beginning, and death remained the foundation of their bond.

3

VENICE

IN THE CORRIDORS and conference rooms of the Israeli intelligence services, Ari Shamron was a legend. Indeed, he was the service made flesh. He had penetrated the courts of kings, stolen the secrets of tyrants, and killed the enemies of Israel, sometimes with his bare hands. His crowning achievement had come on a rainy night in May 1960, in a squalid suburb north of Buenos Aires, when he leapt from the back of a car and seized Adolf Eichmann.

In September 1972, Prime Minister Golda Meir had ordered

him to hunt down and assassinate the Palestinian terrorists who had kidnapped and murdered eleven Israelis at the Munich Olympic Games. Gabriel, then a promising student at the Bezalel Academy of Art in Jerusalem, reluctantly joined Shamron's venture, fittingly code-named Wrath of God. In the Hebrew-based lexicon of the operation, Gabriel was an *Aleph*. Armed only with a .22-caliber Beretta, he had quietly killed six men.

Shamron's career had not been an unbroken ascent to greater glory. There had been deep valleys along the way and mistaken journeys into operational wasteland. He developed a reputation as a man who shot first and worried about the consequences later. His erratic temperament was one of his greatest assets. It struck fear into friends and enemies alike. For some politicians, Shamron's volatility was too much to bear. Rabin often avoided his calls, fearing the news he might hear. Peres thought him a primitive and banished him into the Judean wilderness of retirement. Barak, when the Office was foundering, had rehabilitated Shamron and brought him back to right the ship.

Officially he was retired now, and his beloved Office was in the hands of a thoroughly modern and conniving technocrat called Lev. But among many quarters, Shamron would always be the *Memuneh*, the one in charge. The current prime minister was an old friend and fellow traveler. He'd given Shamron a vague title and just enough authority to make a general nuisance of himself. There were some at King Saul Boulevard who swore that Lev was secretly praying for Shamron's rapid demise—and that Shamron, stubborn and steel-willed Shamron, was keeping himself alive merely to torment him.

Now, standing before the window, Shamron calmly told Gabriel what he knew about the events in Vienna. A bomb had exploded the previous evening inside Wartime Claims and Inquiries. Eli Lavon was in a deep coma in the intensive care ward of the Vienna General Hospital, the odds of survival one in two at best. His two research assistants, Reveka Gazit and Sarah Greenberg, had been killed in the blast. An offshoot of bin Laden's Al Qaeda organization, a shadowy group called the Islamic Fighting Cells, had claimed responsibility. Shamron spoke to Gabriel in his murderously accented English. Hebrew was not permitted in the Venice canal house.

Chiara brought coffee and rugelach to the sitting room and settled herself between Gabriel and Shamron. Of the three, only Chiara was currently under Office discipline. Known as a *bat leveyha*, her work involved posing as the lover or spouse of a case officer in the field. Like all Office personnel, she was trained in the art of physical combat and in the use of weaponry. The fact that she had scored higher than the great Gabriel Allon on her final firing range exam was a source of some tension in their household. Her undercover assignments often required a certain intimacy with her partner, such as showing affection in restaurants and nightclubs and sharing the same bed in hotel rooms or safe flats. Romantic relationships between case officers and escort agents were officially forbidden, but Gabriel knew that the close living quarters and natural stress of the field often drew them together. Indeed, he had once had an affair with his *bat leveyha* while in Tunis. She'd been a beautiful Marseilles Jew named Jacqueline Delacroix, and the affair had nearly destroyed his marriage. Gabriel, when Chiara was away, often pictured her in the bed of another man. Though not prone to jealousy, he secretly looked forward to the day King Saul Boulevard decided she was too overexposed for fieldwork.

"Who *exactly* are the Islamic Fighting Cells?" he asked.

Shamron made a face. "They're small-time operators mainly, active in France and a couple of other European countries. They enjoy setting fire to synagogues, desecrating Jewish cemeteries, and beating up Jewish children on the streets of Paris."

"Was there anything useful in the claim of responsibility?"

Shamron shook his head. "Just the usual drivel about the plight of the Palestinians and the destruction of the Zionist entity. It warns of continuous attacks against Jewish targets in Europe until Palestine is liberated."

"Lavon's office was a fortress. How did a group that usually uses Molotov cocktails and spray-paint cans manage to get a bomb inside Wartime Claims and Inquiries?"

Shamron accepted a cup from Chiara. "The Austrian Staatspolizei aren't sure yet, but they believe it may have been concealed in a computer delivered to the office earlier that day."

"Do we believe the Islamic Fighting Cells have the ability to conceal a bomb in a computer and smuggle it into a secure building in Vienna?"

Shamron stirred sugar violently into his coffee and slowly shook his head.

"So who did it?"

"Obviously, I'd like to know the answer to that question."

Shamron removed his coat and rolled up his shirtsleeves. The message was unmistakable. Gabriel looked away from Shamron's hooded gaze and thought of the last time the old man had sent him to Vienna. It was January 1991. The Office had learned that an Iraqi intelligence agent operating from the city was planning to direct a string of terrorist attacks against Israeli targets to coincide with the first Persian Gulf War. Shamron had ordered Gabriel to monitor the Iraqi and, if necessary, take preemptive action. Unwilling to endure another long separation from his family, Gabriel had brought his wife, Leah, and young son, Dani, along with him. Though he didn't realize it, he had walked into a trap laid by a Palestinian terrorist named Tariq al-Hourani.

Gabriel, lost in thought for a long moment, finally looked up at Shamron. "Have you forgotten that Vienna is the forbidden city for me?"

Shamron lit one of his foul-smelling Turkish cigarettes and placed the dead match in the saucer next to his teaspoon. He pushed his eyeglasses onto his forehead and folded his arms. They were still powerful, braided steel beneath a thin layer of sagging suntanned skin. So were the hands. The gesture was one Gabriel had seen many times before. Shamron the unmovable. Shamron the indomitable. He'd struck the same pose after dispatching Gabriel to Rome to kill for the first time. He'd been an old man even then. Indeed, he'd never really been young at all. Instead of chasing girls on the beach at Netanya, he'd been a unit commander in the Palmach, fighting the first battle in Israel's war without end. His youth had been stolen from him. In turn he had stolen Gabriel's.

"I volunteered to go to Vienna myself, but Lev wouldn't hear of it. He knows that because of our regrettable history there, I'm something of a pariah. He reckoned the Staatspolizei would be more forthcoming if we were represented by a less polarizing figure."

"So your solution is to send *me*?"

"Not in any official capacity, of course." These days Shamron did almost nothing in an official capacity. "But I would feel much more comfortable if someone I trusted was keeping an eye on things."

"We have Office personnel in Vienna."

"Yes, but they report to Lev."

"He *is* the chief."

Shamron closed his eyes, as if he were being reminded of a painful subject. "Lev has too many other problems at the moment to give this the attention it deserves. The boy emperor in Damascus is making troublesome noises. The mullahs of Iran are trying to build Allah's bomb, and Hamas is turning children into bombs and detonating them on the streets of Tel Aviv and Jerusalem. One minor bombing in Vienna is not going to get the attention it deserves, even though the target was Eli Lavon."

Shamron stared compassionately at Gabriel over the rim of his coffee cup. "I know you have no desire to go back to Vienna, especially after another bombing, but your friend is lying in a Viennese hospital fighting for his life! I would think you'd like to know who put him there."

Gabriel thought of the half-completed Bellini altarpiece in the church of San Giovanni Crisostomo and could feel it slipping away from him. Chiara had turned away from Shamron and was eyeing him intently. Gabriel avoided her gaze.

"If I went to Vienna," he said quietly, "I would need an identity."

Shamron shrugged, as if to say there were ways—*obvious*

ways, dear boy—of getting around a small problem such as cover. Gabriel had expected this would be Shamron's response. He held out his hand.

Shamron opened his briefcase and handed over a manila envelope. Gabriel lifted the flap and poured the contents on the coffee table: airline tickets, a leather billfold, a well-traveled Israeli passport. He opened the cover of the passport and saw his own face staring back at him. His new name was Gideon Argov. He'd always liked the name Gideon.

"What does Gideon do for a living?"

Shamron inclined his head toward the billfold. Among the usual items—credit cards, a driver's license, a health-club and video-club membership—he found a business card:

GIDEON ARGOV

WARTIME CLAIMS AND INQUIRIES

17 MENDELE STREET

JERUSALEM 92147

5427618

Gabriel looked up at Shamron. "I didn't know Eli had an office in Jerusalem."

"He does now. Try the number."

Gabriel shook his head. "I believe you. Does Lev know about this?"

"Not yet, but I plan on telling him once you're safely on the ground in Vienna."

"So we're deceiving the Austrians *and* the Office. That's impressive, even for you, Ari."

Shamron gave a sheepish smile. Gabriel opened the airline jacket and examined his travel itinerary.

"I don't think it would be a good idea for you to travel directly to Vienna from here. I'll accompany you back to Tel Aviv in the morning—separate seats, of course. You'll turn around and catch the afternoon flight into Vienna."

Gabriel lifted his gaze and stared at Shamron, his expression dubious. "And if I'm recognized at the airport and dragged into a room for some special Austrian attention?"

"That's always a possibility, but it *has* been thirteen years. Besides, you've been to Vienna recently. I recall a meeting we had in Eli's office last year concerning an imminent threat to the life of His Holiness Pope Paul the Seventh."

"I have been back to Vienna," Gabriel conceded, holding up the false passport. "But never like this, and never through the airport."

Gabriel spent a long moment appraising the false passport with his restorer's eye. Finally he closed the cover and slipped it into his pocket. Chiara stood and walked out of the room. Shamron watched her go, then looked at Gabriel.

"It seems I've managed to disrupt your life once again."

"Why should this time be any different?"

"Do you want me to talk to her?"

Gabriel shook his head. "She'll get over it," he said. "She's a professional."

THERE WERE MOMENTS of Gabriel's life, fragments of time, which he rendered on canvas and hung in the cellar of his subconscious. To this gallery of memory he added Chiara as he saw her now, seated astride his body, bathed in a Rembrandt light from the streetlamps beyond their bedroom window, a satin duvet bunched at her hips, her breasts bared. Other images intruded. Shamron had opened the door to them, and Gabriel, as always, was powerless to push them back. There was Wadal Adel Zwaiter, a skinny intellectual in a plaid jacket, whom Gabriel had killed in the foyer of an apartment house in Rome. There was Ali Abdel Hamidi, who had died by Gabriel's hand in a Zurich alley, and Mahmoud al-Hourani, older brother of Tariq al-Hourani, whom Gabriel had shot through the eye in Cologne as he lay in the arms of a lover.

A mane of hair fell across Chiara's breasts. Gabriel reached up and gently pushed it away. She looked at him. It was too dark to see the color of her eyes, but Gabriel could sense her thoughts. Shamron had trained him to read the emotions of others, just as Umberto Conti had taught him to mimic the Old Masters. Gabriel, even in the arms of a lover, could not suspend his ceaseless search for the warning signs of betrayal.

"I don't want you to go to Vienna." She placed her hands on Gabriel's chest. Gabriel could feel his heart beating against the cool skin of her palm. "It's not safe for you there. Of all people, Shamron should know that."

"Shamron is right. It was a long time ago."

"Yes, it was, but if you go there and start asking questions about the bombing, you'll rub up against the Austrian police and security services. Shamron is using you to keep his hand in the game. He doesn't have your best interests in mind."

"You sound like a Lev man."

"It's you I care about." She bent down and kissed his mouth. Her lips tasted of blossom. "I don't want you to go to Vienna and become lost in the past." After a moment's hesitation, she added, "I'm afraid I'll lose you."

"To who?"

She lifted the duvet to her shoulders and covered her breasts. Leah's shadow fell between them. It was Chiara's intention to let her into the room. Chiara only talked about Leah in bed, where she believed Gabriel would not lie to her. Gabriel's entire life was a lie; with his lovers he was always painfully honest. He could make love to a woman only if she knew that he had killed men on behalf of his country. He never told lies about Leah. He considered it his duty to speak honestly of her, even to the women who had taken her place in his bed.

"Do you have any idea how hard this is for me?" Chiara asked. "Everyone knows about Leah. She's an Office legend, just like you and Shamron. How long am I supposed to live with the fear that one day you'll decide you can't do this anymore?"

"What do you want me to do?"

"Marry me, Gabriel. Stay in Venice and restore paintings. Tell Shamron to leave you alone. You have scars all over your body. Haven't you given enough to your country?"

He closed his eyes. Before him opened a gallery door. Reluctantly he passed through to the other side and found himself on a street in the old Jewish quarter of Vienna with Leah and Dani at his side. They have just finished dinner, snow is falling. Leah is on edge. There had been a television in the bar of the restaurant, and all the meal they had watched Iraqi missiles raining down on Tel Aviv. Leah is anxious to return home and telephone her mother. She rushes Gabriel's ritual search of his car's undercarriage. *Come on, Gabriel, hurry. I want to talk to my mother. I want to hear the sound of her voice.* He rises, straps Dani into his car seat, and kisses Leah. Even now he can still taste the olives on her mouth. He turns and starts back to the cathedral, where, as part of his cover, he is restoring an altarpiece depicting the martyrdom of Saint Stephen. Leah turns the key. The engine hesitates. Gabriel spins round and screams at her to stop, but Leah can't see him because the windshield is dusted with snowfall. She turns the key again. . . .

He waited for the images of fire and blood to dissolve into blackness; then he told Chiara what she wanted to hear. When he returned from Vienna, he would go to see Leah in the hospital and explain to her that he had fallen in love with another woman.

Chiara's face darkened. "I wish there were some other way."

"I have to tell her the truth," Gabriel said. "She deserves nothing less."

"Will she understand?"

Gabriel shrugged his shoulders. Leah's affliction was psychotic depression. Her doctors believed the night of the bombing played without break in her memory like a loop of videotape. It left no room for impressions or sound from the real world. Gabriel often wondered what Leah saw of him on that night. Did she see him walking away toward the spire of the cathedral, or could she feel him pulling her blackened body from the fire? He was certain of only one thing. Leah would not speak to him. She had not spoken a single word to him in thirteen years.

"It's for me," he said. "I have to say the words. I have to tell her the truth about you. I have nothing to be ashamed of, and I'm certainly not ashamed of you."

Chiara lowered the duvet and kissed him feverishly. Gabriel could feel tension in her body and taste arousal on her breath. Afterward he lay beside her, stroking her hair. He could not sleep, not the night before a journey back to Vienna. But there was something else. He felt as though he had just committed an act of sexual betrayal. It was as if he had just been inside another man's woman. Then he realized that, in his mind, he was already Gideon Argov. Chiara, for the moment, was a stranger to him.

4

VIENNA

"PASSPORT, PLEASE."

Gabriel slid it across the countertop, the emblem facing down. The officer glanced wearily at the scuffed cover and thumbed the folio pages until he located the visa. He added another stamp—with more violence than was necessary, Gabriel thought—and handed it over without a word. Gabriel dropped the passport into his coat pocket and set out across the gleaming arrivals hall, towing a rolling suitcase behind him.

Outside, he took his place in line at the taxi stand. It was bitterly cold, and there was snow in the wind. Snatches of Viennese-accented German reached his ears. Unlike many of his countrymen, the mere sound of spoken German did not set him on edge. German was his first language and remained the language of his dreams. He spoke it perfectly, with the Berlin accent of his mother.

He moved to the front of the queue. A white Mercedes slid forward to collect him. Gabriel memorized the registration number before sliding into the back seat. He placed the bag on the seat and gave the driver an address several streets away from the hotel where he'd booked a room.

The taxi hurtled along the motorway, through an ugly industrial zone of factories, power plants, and gasworks. Before long, Gabriel spotted the floodlit spire of St. Stephen's Cathedral, looming over the Innere Stadt. Unlike most European cities, Vienna had remained remarkably unspoiled and free of urban blight. Indeed, little about its appearance and lifestyle had changed from a century earlier, when it was the administrative center of an empire stretching across central Europe and the Balkans. It was still possible to have an afternoon cake and cream at Demel's or to linger over coffee and a journal at the Landtmann or Central. In the Innere Stadt, it was best to forsake the automobile and move about by streetcar or on foot along the glittering pedestrian boulevards lined with Baroque and Gothic architecture and exclusive shops. Men still wore loden-cloth suits and feathered Tyrolean caps; women still found it fashionable to wear a dirndl. Brahms had said he stayed in Vienna because he preferred to work in a village. It was still a village, thought Gabriel, with a village's contempt for change and a village's resentment of outsiders. For Gabriel, Vienna would always be a city of ghosts.

They came to the Ringstrasse, the broad boulevard encircling the city center. The handsome face of Peter Metzler, the candidate for chancellor from the far-right Austrian National Party, grinned at Gabriel from the passing lamp posts. It was election season, and the avenue was hung with hundreds of campaign posters. Metzler's well-funded campaign had clearly spared no expense. His face was everywhere, his gaze unavoidable. So was his campaign slogan: *Eine Neue Ordnung Für Ein Neues Österreich*!: *A New Order for a New Austria*! The Austrians, thought Gabriel, were incapable of subtlety.

Gabriel left the taxi near the state opera house and walked a short distance to a narrow street called the Weihburggasse. It appeared no one was following him, though from experience he knew expert watchers were almost impossible to detect. He entered a small hotel. The concierge, upon seeing his Israeli passport, adopted a posture of bereavement and murmured a few sympathetic words about "the terrible bombing in the Jewish Quarter." Gabriel, playing the role of Gideon Argov, spent a few minutes chatting with the concierge in German before climbing the stairs to his room on the second floor. It had wood floors the color of honey and French doors overlooking a darkened interior courtyard. Gabriel drew the curtains and left the bag on the bed in plain sight. Before leaving, he placed a telltale in the doorjamb that would signal whether the room had been entered in his absence.

He returned to the lobby. The concierge smiled as if they had not seen each other in five years instead of five minutes. Outside it had begun to snow. He walked the darkened streets of the Innere Stadt, checking his tail for surveillance. He paused at shop windows to glance over his shoulder, ducked into a public telephone and pretended to place a call while scanning his surroundings. At a newsstand he bought a copy of *Die Presse*, then, a hundred meters farther on, dropped it into a rubbish bin. Finally, convinced he was not being followed, he entered the Stephansplatz U-Bahn station.

He had no need to consult the brightly lit maps of the Vienna transport system, for he knew it from memory. He purchased a ticket from a vending machine, then passed through the turnstile and headed down to the platform. He boarded a carriage and memorized the faces around him. Five stops later, at the Westbahnhof, he transferred to a northbound train on the U6 line. Vienna General Hospital had its own station stop. An escalator bore him slowly upward to a snowy quadrangle, a few paces from the main entrance at Währinger Gürtel 18-20.

A hospital had occupied this plot of ground in west Vienna for more than three hundred years. In 1693, Emperor Leopold I, concerned by the plight of the city's destitute, had ordered the construction of the Home for the Poor and Invalid. A century later, Emperor Joseph II renamed the facility the General Hospital for the Sick. The old building remained, a few streets over on the Alserstrasse, but around it had risen a modern university hospital complex spread over several city blocks. Gabriel knew it well.

A man from the embassy was sheltering in the portico, beneath an inscription that read: *SALUTI ET SOLATIO AEGRORUM:* TO HEAL AND COMFORT THE SICK. He was a small, nervous-looking diplomat called Zvi. He shook Gabriel's hand and, after briefly examining his passport and business card, expressed his sorrow over the death of his two colleagues.

They stepped into the main lobby. It was deserted except for an old man with a sparse white beard, sitting at one end of a couch with his ankles together and his hat on his knees, like a traveler waiting for a long-delayed train. He was muttering to himself. As Gabriel walked past, the old man looked up and their eyes met briefly. Then Gabriel entered a waiting elevator, and the old man disappeared behind a pair of sliding doors.

When the elevator doors opened on the eighth floor, Gabriel was greeted by the comforting sight of a tall, blond Israeli wearing a two-piece suit and a wire in his ear. At the entrance of the intensive care unit stood another security man. A third, small and dark and dressed in an ill-fitting suit, was outside the door of Eli's room. He moved aside so Gabriel and the diplomat could enter. Gabriel stopped and asked why he wasn't being searched.

"You're with Zvi. I don't need to search you."

Gabriel held up his hands. "Search me."

The security man tilted his head and consented. Gabriel recognized the frisk pattern. It was by the book. The crotch search was more intrusive than necessary, but then Gabriel had it coming. When it was over, he said, "Search everyone who comes into this room."

Zvi, the embassy man, watched the entire scene. Clearly, he no longer believed the man from Jerusalem was Gideon Argov of Wartime Claims and Inquiries. Gabriel didn't much care. His friend was lying helpless on the other side of the door. Better to ruffle a few feathers than to let him die because of complacency.

He followed Zvi into the room. The bed was behind a glass partition. The patient didn't look much like Eli, but then Gabriel wasn't surprised. Like most Israelis, he had seen the toll a bomb can take on a human body. Eli's face was concealed behind the mask of a ventilator, his eyes bound by gauze, his head heavily bandaged. The exposed portion of his cheeks and jaw showed the aftereffects of glass exploding into his face.

A nurse with short black hair and very blue eyes was checking the intravenous drip. She looked into the visitors' room and briefly held Gabriel's gaze before resuming her work. Her eyes betrayed nothing.

Zvi, after giving Gabriel a moment to himself, walked over to the glass and brought him up to date on his colleague's condition. He spoke with the precision of a man who had watched too many medical dramas on television. Gabriel, his eyes fastened on Eli's face, heard only half of what the diplomat was saying—enough to realize that his friend was near death, and that, even if he lived, he might never be the same.

"For the moment," Zvi said in conclusion, "he's being kept alive by the machines."

"Why are his eyes bandaged?"

"Glass fragments. They were able to get most of them, but he still has a half-dozen or so lodged in his eyes."

"Is there a chance he'll be blind?"

"They won't know until he regains consciousness," Zvi said. Then he added pessimistically, "*If* he regains consciousness."

A doctor came into the room. He looked at Gabriel and Zvi and nodded once briskly, then opened the glass door and stepped into the ward. The nurse moved away from the bedside, and the doctor assumed her place. She came around the end of the bed and stood before the glass. For a second time, her eyes met Gabriel's, then she drew the curtain closed with a sharp jerk of her wrist. Gabriel walked into the hall, followed by Zvi.

"You all right?"

"I'll be fine. I just need a minute to myself."

The diplomat went back inside. Gabriel clasped his hands behind his back, like a soldier at ease, and drifted slowly along the familiar corridor. He passed the nurses' station. The same trite Vienna streetscape hung next to the window. The smell was the same, too—the smell of disinfectant and death.

He came to a half-open door bearing the number 2602-C. He pushed it gently with his fingertips, and the door swung silently open. The room was dark and unoccupied. Gabriel glanced over his shoulder. There were no nurses about. He slipped inside and closed the door behind him.

He left the lights off and waited for his eyes to grow accustomed to the dark. Soon the room came into focus: the empty bed, the bank of silent monitors, the vinyl-covered chair. The most uncomfortable chair in all of Vienna. He'd spent ten nights in that chair, most of them sleepless. Only once had Leah regained consciousness. She'd asked about Dani, and Gabriel unwisely told her the truth. Tears spilled onto her ruined cheeks. She never spoke to him again.

"You're not supposed to be in here."

Gabriel, startled, turned quickly around. The voice belonged to the nurse who'd been at Eli's side a moment earlier. She spoke to him in German. He responded in the same language.

"I'm sorry, I just—"

"I know what you're doing." She allowed a silence to fall between them. "I remember you."

She leaned against the door and folded her arms. Her head fell to one side. Were it not for her baggy nurse's uniform and the stethoscope hanging around her neck, Gabriel would have thought she was flirting with him.

"Your wife was the one who was involved in the car bombing a few years back. I was a young nurse then, just starting out. I took care of her at night. You don't remember?"

Gabriel looked at her for a moment. Finally, he said, "I believe you're mistaken. This is my first time in Vienna. And I've never been married. I'm sorry," he added hastily, heading toward the door. "I shouldn't have been in here. I just needed a place to gather my thoughts."

He moved past her. She put her hand on his arm.

"Tell me something," she said. "Is she alive?"

"Who?"

"Your wife, of course."

"I'm sorry," he said firmly, "but you have me confused with someone else."

She nodded—*As you wish.* Her blue eyes were damp and shining in the half-light.

"He's a friend of yours, Eli Lavon?"

"Yes, he is. A very close friend. We work together. I live in Jerusalem."

"*Jerusalem,*" she repeated, as though she liked the sound of the word. "I would like to visit Jerusalem sometime. My friends think I'm crazy. You know, the suicide bombers, all the other things . . ." Her voice trailed off. "I still want to go."

"You should," Gabriel said. "It's a wonderful place."

She touched his arm a second time. "Your friend's injuries are severe." Her tone was tender, tinged with sorrow. "He's going to have a very tough time of it."

"Is he going to live?"

"I'm not allowed to answer questions like that. Only the doctors can offer a prognosis. But if you want my opinion, spend some time with him. Tell him things. You never know, he might be able to hear you."

HE STAYED FOR another hour, staring at Eli's motionless figure through the glass. The nurse returned. She spent a few minutes checking Eli's vital signs, then motioned for Gabriel to come inside the room. "It's against the rules," she said conspiratorially. "I'll stand watch at the door."

Gabriel didn't speak to Eli, just held his bruised and swollen hand. There were no words to convey the pain he felt at seeing another loved one lying in a Viennese hospital bed. After five minutes, the nurse came back, laid her hand on Gabriel's shoulder, and told him it was time to leave. Outside, in the corridor, she said her name was Marguerite. "I'm working tomorrow night," she said. "I'll see you then, I hope."

Zvi had left; a new team of guards had come on duty. Gabriel rode the elevator down to the lobby and went outside. The night had turned bitterly cold. He shoved his hands into his coat pockets and quickened his pace. He was about to head down the escalator into the U-Bahn station when he felt a hand on his arm. He turned around, expecting to see Marguerite, but instead found himself face to face with the old man who'd been talking to himself in the lobby when Gabriel arrived.

"I heard you speaking Hebrew to that man from the embassy." His Viennese German was frantically paced, his eyes wide and damp. "You're Israeli, yes? A friend of Eli Lavon's?" He didn't wait for an answer. "My name is Max Klein, and this is all my fault. Please, you must believe me. This is all my fault."

5

VIENNA

MAX KLEIN LIVED a streetcar ride away, in a graceful old district just beyond the Ringstrasse. His was a fine old Biedermeier apartment building with a passageway leading to a big interior courtyard. The courtyard was dark, lit only by the soft glow of lights burning in the apartments overhead. A second passageway gave onto a small, neat foyer. Gabriel glanced at the tenant list. Halfway down he saw the words: *M. KLEIN—3B*. There was no elevator. Klein clung to the wood banister as he climbed stubbornly upward, his feet heavy on the well-trodden runner. On the third-floor landing were two wooden doors with peepholes. Gravitating toward the one on the right, Klein removed a set of keys from his coat pocket. His hand shook so badly the keys jingled like a percussion instrument.

He opened the door and went inside. Gabriel hesitated just beyond the threshold. It had occurred to him, sitting next to Klein on the streetcar, that he had no business meeting with anyone under circumstances such as these. Experience and hard lessons had taught him that even an obviously Jewish octogenarian had to be regarded as a potential threat. Any anxiety Gabriel was feeling quickly evaporated, however, as he watched Klein turn on practically every light in the apartment. It was not the action of a man laying a trap, he thought. Max Klein was frightened.

Gabriel followed him into the apartment and closed the door. In the bright light, he finally got a good look at him. Klein's red, rheumy eyes were magnified by a pair of thick black spectacles. His beard, wispy and white, no longer concealed the dark liver spots on his cheeks. Gabriel knew, even before Klein told him, that he was a survivor. Starvation, like bullets and fire, leaves scars. Gabriel had seen different versions of the face in his farming town in the Jezreel Valley. He had seen it on his parents.

"I'll make tea," Klein announced before disappearing through a pair of double doors into the kitchen.

Tea at midnight, thought Gabriel. It was going to be a long evening. He went to the window and parted the blinds. The snow had stopped for now, and the street was empty. He sat down. The room reminded him of Eli's office: the high Biedermeier ceiling, the haphazard way in which the books lay on the shelves. Elegant, intellectual clutter.

Klein returned and placed a silver tea service on a low table. He sat down opposite Gabriel and regarded him silently for a moment. "You speak German very well," he said finally. "In fact, you speak it like a Berliner."

"My mother was from Berlin," Gabriel said truthfully, "but I was born in Israel."

Klein studied him carefully, as if he too were looking for the scars of survival. Then he lifted his palms quizzically, an invitation to fill in the blanks. Where was she? How did she survive? Was she in a camp or did she get out before the madness?

"They stayed in Berlin and were eventually deported to the camps," Gabriel said. "My grandfather was a rather well-known painter. He never believed that the Germans, a people he believed were among the most civilized on earth, would go as far as they did."

"What was your grandfather's name?"

"Frankel," Gabriel said, again veering toward the truth. "Viktor Frankel."

Klein nodded slowly in recognition of the name. "I've seen his work. He was a disciple of Max Beckmann, was he not? Extremely talented."

"Yes, that's right. His work was declared degenerate by the Nazis early on and much of it was destroyed. He also lost his job at the art institute where he was teaching in Berlin."

"But he stayed." Klein shook his head. "No one believed it could happen." He paused a moment, his thoughts elsewhere. "So what happened to them?"

"They were deported to Auschwitz. My mother was sent to the women's camp at Birkenau and managed to survive for more than two years before she was liberated."

"And your grandparents?"

"Gassed on arrival."

"Do you remember the date?"

"I believe it was January 1943," Gabriel said.

Klein covered his eyes.

"Is there something significant about that date, Herr Klein?"

"Yes," Klein said absently. "I was there the night those Berlin transports arrived. I remember it very well. You see, Mr. Argov, I was a violinist in the Auschwitz camp orchestra. I played music for devils in an orchestra of the damned. I serenaded the condemned as they trudged slowly toward the gas."

Gabriel's face remained placid. Max Klein was clearly a man suffering from enormous guilt. He believed he bore some responsibility for the deaths of those who had filed past him on the way to the gas chambers. It was madness, of course. He was no more guilty than any of the Jews who had toiled in the slave labor factories or in the fields of Auschwitz in order to survive one more day.

"But that's not the reason you stopped me tonight at the hospital. You wanted to tell me something about the bombing at Wartime Claims and Inquiries?"

Klein nodded. "As I said, this is all my doing. I'm the one responsible for the deaths of those two beautiful girls. I'm the reason your friend Eli Lavon is lying in that hospital bed near death."

"Are you telling me *you* planted the bomb?" Gabriel's tone

was intentionally heavy with incredulity. The question was meant to sound preposterous.

"Of course not!" Klein snapped. "But I'm afraid I set in motion the events that led others to place it there."

"Why don't you just tell me everything you know, Herr Klein? Let me judge who's guilty."

"Only God can judge," Klein said.

"Perhaps, but sometimes even God needs a little help."

Klein smiled and poured tea. Then he told the story from the beginning. Gabriel bided his time and didn't rush the proceedings along. Eli Lavon would have played it the same way. "For the old ones, memory is like a stack of china," Lavon always said. "If you try to pull a plate from the middle, the whole thing comes crashing down."

THE APARTMENT HAD belonged to his father. Before the war, Klein had lived there along with his parents and two younger sisters. His father, Solomon, was a successful textile merchant, and the Kleins lived a charmed upper-middle-class existence: afternoon strudels at the finest Vienna coffeehouses, evenings at the theater or the opera, summers at the modest family villa in the south. Young Max Klein was a promising violinist—*Not quite ready for the symphony or the opera, mind you, Mr. Argov, but good enough to find work in smaller Viennese chamber orchestras.*

"My father, even when he was tired from working all day, rarely missed a performance." Klein smiled for the first time at the memory of his father watching him play. "The fact that his son was a Viennese musician made him extremely proud."

Their idyllic world had come to an abrupt end on March 12, 1938. It was a Saturday, Klein remembered, and for the overwhelming majority of Austrians, the sight of Wehrmacht troops marching through the streets of Vienna had been a cause for celebration. *For the Jews, Mr. Argov . . . for us, only dread.* The worst fears of the community were quickly realized. In Germany, the assault on the Jews had been a gradual undertaking. In Austria, it was instantaneous and savage. Within days, all Jewish-owned businesses were marked with red paint. Any non-Jew who entered was assaulted by Brownshirts and SS. Many were forced to wear placards that declared: *I, Aryan swine, have bought in a Jewish shop.* Jews were forbidden to own property, to hold a job in any profession or to employ someone else, to enter a restaurant or a coffeehouse, to set foot in Vienna's public parks. Jews were forbidden to possess typewriters or radios, because those could facilitate communication with the outside world. Jews were dragged from their homes and their synagogues and beaten on the streets.

"On March 14, the Gestapo broke down the door of this very apartment and stole our most prized possessions: our rugs, our silver, our paintings, even our Shabbat candlesticks. My father and I were taken briefly into custody and forced to scrub sidewalks with boiling water and a toothbrush. The rabbi from our synagogue was hurled into the street and his beard torn from his face while a crowd of Austrians looked on and jeered. I tried to stop them, and I was nearly beaten to death. I couldn't be taken to a hospital, of course. That was forbidden by the new anti-Jewish laws."

In less than a week, the Jewish community of Austria, one of the most vital and influential in all of Europe, was in tatters: community centers and Jewish societies shut down, leaders in jail, synagogues closed, prayer books burned on bonfires. On April 1, a hundred prominent public figures and businessmen were deported to Dachau. Within a month, five hundred Jews had chosen to kill themselves rather than face another day of torment, including a family of four who lived next door to the Kleins. "They shot themselves, one at a time," Klein said. "I lay in my bed and listened to the whole thing. A shot, followed by sobs. Another shot, more sobs. After the fourth shot, there was no one left to cry, no one but me."

More than half the community decided to leave Austria and emigrate to other lands. Max Klein was among them. He obtained a visa to Holland and traveled there in 1939. In less than a year, he would find himself under the Nazi jackboot once more. "My father decided to remain in Vienna," Klein said. "He believed in the law, you see. He thought that if he just adhered to the law, things would be fine, and the storm would eventually pass. It got worse, of course, and when he finally decided to leave, it was too late."

Klein tried to pour himself another cup of tea, but his hand was shaking violently. Gabriel poured it for him and gently asked what had become of his parents and two sisters.

"In the autumn of 1941, they were deported to Poland and confined in the Jewish ghetto in Lodz. In January 1942, they were deported one final time, to the Chelmno extermination camp."

"And you?"

Klein's head fell to one side—*And me?* Same fate, different ending. Arrested in Amsterdam in June 1942, detained in the Westerbork transit camp, then sent east, to Auschwitz. On the rail platform, half-dead from thirst and hunger, a voice. A man in prison clothing is asking whether there are any musicians on the arriving train. Klein latches onto the voice, a drowning man seizing a lifeline. *I'm a violinist,* he tells the man in stripes. *Do you have an instrument?* He holds up a battered case, the only thing he had brought from Westerbork. *Come with me. This is your lucky day.*

"My lucky day," Klein repeated absently. "For the next two and a half years, while more than a million go up in smoke, my colleagues and I play music. We play on the selection ramp to help the Nazis create the illusion that the new arrivals have come to a pleasant place. We play as the walking dead file into the disrobing chambers. We play in the yard during the endless roll calls. In the morning, we play as the slaves file out to work, and in the afternoon, when they stagger back to their barracks with death in their eyes, we are playing. We even play before executions. On Sundays, we play for the Kommandant and his staff. Suicide continuously thins our ranks. Soon I'm the one working the crowd on the ramp, looking for musicians to fill the empty chairs."

One Sunday afternoon—*It is sometime in the summer of 1942, but I'm sorry, Mr. Argov, I cannot recall the exact date*—Klein is walking back to his barracks after a Sunday concert. An SS officer comes up from behind and knocks him to the ground. Klein gets to his feet and stands at attention, avoiding the SS man's gaze. Still, he sees enough of the face to realize that he has met the man once before. It was in Vienna, at the Central Office for Jewish Emigration, but on that day he'd been wearing a fine gray suit and standing at the side of none other than Adolf Eichmann.

"The Sturmbannführer told me that he would like to conduct an experiment," Klein said. "He orders me to play Brahms's Sonata No. 1 for Violin and Piano in G Major. I take my violin from its case and begin to play. An inmate walks past. The Sturmbannführer asks him to please name the piece I am playing. The inmate says he does not know. The Sturmbannführer draws his sidearm and shoots the inmate through the head. He finds another inmate and poses the same question. *What piece is this fine violinist playing?* And on it goes for the next hour. Those who can answer the question correctly are spared. Those who can't, he shoots through the head. By the time he's finished, fifteen bodies are lying at my feet. When his thirst for Jewish blood is quenched, the man in black smiles and walks away. I lay down with the dead and said mourner's Kaddish for them."

KLEIN LAPSED INTO a long silence. A car hissed past in the street. Klein lifted his head and began to speak again. He was not quite ready to make the connection between the atrocity at Auschwitz and the bombing of Wartime Claims and Inquiries, though by now Gabriel had a clear sense of where the story was headed. He continued chronologically, one china plate at a time, as Lavon would have said. Survival at Auschwitz. Liberation. His return to Vienna . . .

The community had numbered 185,000 before the war, he said. Sixty-five thousand had perished in the Holocaust. Seventeen hundred broken souls stumbled back into Vienna in 1945, only to be greeted by open hostility and a new wave of anti-Semitism. Those who'd emigrated at the point of a German gun were discouraged from returning. Demands for financial restitution were met by silence or were sneeringly referred to Berlin. Klein, returning to his home in the Second District, found an Austrian family living in the flat. When he asked them to leave, they refused. It took a decade to finally pry them loose. As for his father's textile business, it was gone for good, and no restitution ever made. Friends encouraged him to go to Israel or America. Klein refused. He vowed to stay on in Vienna, a living, breathing, walking memorial to those who had been driven out or murdered in the death camps. He left his violin behind at Auschwitz and never played again. He earned his living as a clerk in a dry-goods store, and later as an insurance salesman. In 1995, on the fiftieth anniversary of the war's end, the government agreed to pay surviving Austrian Jews approximately six thousand dollars each. Klein showed Gabriel the check. It had never been cashed.

"I didn't want their money," he said. "Six thousand dollars? For what? My mother and father? My two sisters? My home? My possessions?"

He tossed the check onto the table. Gabriel sneaked a glance at his wristwatch and saw it was two-thirty in the morning.

Klein was closing in, circling his target. Gabriel resisted the impulse to give him a nudge, fearing that the old man, in his precarious state, might stumble and never regain his footing.

"Two months ago, I stop for coffee at the Café Central. I'm given a lovely table next to a pillar. I order a Pharisäer." He paused and raised his eyebrows. "Do you know a Pharisäer, Mr. Argov? Coffee with whipped cream, served with a small glass of rum." He apologized for the liquor. "It was the late afternoon, you see, and cold."

A man enters the café, tall, well-dressed, a few years older than Klein. *An Austrian of the old school, if you know what I mean, Mr. Argov.* There's an arrogance in his walk that causes Klein to lower his newspaper. The waiter rushes across the floor to greet him. The waiter is wringing his hands, hopping from foot to foot like a schoolboy who needs to piss. *Good evening, Herr Vogel. I was beginning to think we wouldn't see you today. Your usual table? Let me guess: an Einspänner? And how about a sweet? I'm told the Sachertorte is lovely today, Herr Vogel . . .*

And then the old man speaks a few words, and Max Klein feels his spine turn to ice. It is the same voice that ordered him to play Brahms at Auschwitz, the same voice that calmly asked Klein's fellow inmates to identify the piece or face the consequences. And here was the murderer, prosperous and healthy, ordering an Einspänner and a Sachertorte at the Central.

"I felt as though I was going to be sick," Klein said. "I threw money on the table and stumbled into the street. I looked once through the window and saw the monster named Herr Vogel reading his newspaper. It was as if the encounter never happened at all."

Gabriel resisted the impulse to ask how, after so long, Klein could be so certain that the man from Café Central was the same man who'd been at Auschwitz sixty years earlier. Whether Klein was right or not was not as important as what happened next.

"What did you do about it, Herr Klein?"

"I became quite the regular customer at the Café Central. Soon, I too was greeted by name. Soon, I too had a regular table, right next to the honorable Herr Vogel. We began to wish each other good afternoon. Sometimes, while we read our newspapers, we would chat about politics or world events. Despite his age, his mind was very sharp. He told me he was a businessman, an investor of some sort."

"And when you'd learned as much as you could by having coffee next to him, you went to see Eli Lavon at Wartime Claims and Inquiries?"

Klein nodded slowly. "He listened to my story and promised to look into it. In the meantime, he asked me to stop going to the Central for coffee. I was reluctant. I was afraid he was going to slip away again. But I did as your friend asked."

"And then?"

"A few weeks went by. Finally I received a call. It was one of the girls from the office, the American one named Sarah. She informed me that Eli Lavon had some news to report to me. She asked me to come to the office the next morning at ten o'clock. I told her I would be there, and I hung up the telephone."

"When was that?"

"The same day of the bombing."

"Have you told any of this to the police?"

Klein shook his head. "As you might expect, Mr. Argov, I'm

not fond of Austrian men in uniform. I am also well aware of my country's rather shoddy record when it comes to the prosecution of war criminals. I kept silent. I went to the Vienna General Hospital and watched the Israeli officials coming and going. When the ambassador came, I tried to approach him but I was pushed away by his security men. So I waited until the right person came along. You seemed like him. Are you the right person, Mr. Argov?"

THE APARTMENT HOUSE across the street was nearly identical to the one where Max Klein lived. On the second floor a man stood in the darkened window with a camera pressed to his eye. He focused the telephoto lens on the figure striding through the passageway of Klein's building and turning into the street. He snapped a series of photographs, then lowered the camera and sat down in front of the tape recorder. In the darkness it took him a moment to find the PLAY button.

"So I waited until the right person came along. You seemed like him. Are you the right person, Mr. Argov?"

"Yes, Herr Klein. I'm the right person. Don't worry, I'm going to help you."

"None of this would have happened if it weren't for me. Those girls are dead because of me. Eli Lavon is in that hospital because of me."

"That's not true. You did nothing wrong. But given what's taken place, I'm concerned about your safety."

"So am I."

"Has anyone been following you?"

"Not that I can tell, but I'm not sure I would know it if they were."

"Have you received any threatening telephone calls?"

"No."

"Has anyone at all tried to contact you since the bombing?"

"Just one person, a woman named Renate Hoffmann."

STOP. REWIND. PLAY.

"Just one person, a woman named Renate Hoffmann."

"Do you know her?"

"No, I've never heard of her."

"Did you speak to her?"

"No, she left a message on my machine."

"What did she want?"

"To talk."

"Did she leave a number?"

"Yes, I wrote it down. Hold on a minute. Yes, here it is. Renate Hoffmann, five-three-three-one-nine-zero-seven."

STOP. REWIND. PLAY.

"Renate Hoffmann, five-three-three-one-nine-zero-seven."

STOP.

6

VIENNA

THE COALITION FOR a Better Austria had all the trappings of a noble yet ultimately hopeless cause. It was located on the second floor of a dilapidated old warehouse in the Twentieth District, with sooty windows overlooking a railyard. The workspace was open and communal and impossible to heat properly. Gabriel, arriving the following morning, found most of the youthful staff wearing thick sweaters and woolen caps.

Renate Hoffmann was the group's legal director. Gabriel had telephoned her earlier that morning, posing as Gideon Argov from Jerusalem, and told her about his encounter the previous evening with Max Klein. Renate Hoffmann had hastily agreed to a meeting with him, then broken the connection, as if she were reticent to discuss the matter on the telephone.

She had a cubicle for an office. When Gabriel was shown inside, she was on the telephone. She pointed toward an empty chair with the tip of a chewed pen. A moment later, she concluded the conversation and stood to greet him. She was tall and better dressed than the rest of the staff: black sweater and skirt, black stockings, flat-soled black shoes. Her hair was flaxen and did not reach her square, athletic shoulders. Parted on the side, it fell naturally toward her face, and she was holding back a troublesome forelock with her left hand as she shook hands firmly with Gabriel with her right. She wore no rings on her fingers, no makeup on her attractive face, and no scent other than tobacco. Gabriel guessed that she was not yet thirty-five.

They sat down again, and she asked a series of curt, lawyerly questions. How long have you known Eli Lavon? How did you find Max Klein? How much did he tell you? When did you arrive in Vienna? With whom have you met? Have you discussed the matter with the Austrian authorities? With officials from the Israeli embassy? Gabriel felt a bit like a defendant in the dock, yet his responses were as polite and accurate as possible.

Renate Hoffmann, her cross-examination complete, regarded him skeptically for a moment. Then she stood suddenly and pulled on a long, gray overcoat with very square shoulders.

"Let's take a walk."

Gabriel looked out the soot-smudged windows and saw that it was sleeting. Renate Hoffman shoved some files into a leather bag and slung it over her shoulder. "Trust me," she said, sensing his apprehension. "It's better if we walk."

RENATE HOFFMANN, ON the icy footpaths of the Augarten, explained to Gabriel how she had become Eli Lavon's most important asset in Vienna. After graduating at the top of her class from Vienna University, she had gone to work for the Austrian state prosecutor's office, where she had served exceptionally for seven years. Then, five years ago, she'd resigned, telling friends and colleagues that she longed for the freedom of private practice. In truth, Renate Hoffman had decided she could no longer work for a government that showed less concern about justice than about protecting the interests of the state and its most powerful citizens.

It was the Weller case that forced her hand. Weller was a Staatspolizei detective with a fondness for torturing confessions out of prisoners and administering justice personally when a proper trial was deemed too inconvenient. Renate Hoffmann tried to bring charges against him after a Nigerian asylum-seeker died in his custody. The Nigerian had been bound and gagged and there was evidence he had been struck repeatedly and choked. Her superiors had sided with Weller and dropped the case.

Weary of fighting the establishment from the inside, Renate Hoffman had concluded that the battle was better waged from without. She'd started a small law firm in order to pay the bills but devoted most of her time and energy to the Coalition for a Better Austria, a reformist group dedicated to shaking the country out of its collective amnesia about its Nazi past. Simultaneously she also formed a quiet alliance with Eli Lavon's Wartime Claims and Inquiries. Renate Hoffmann still had friends inside the bureaucracy, friends who were willing to do favors for her. These friends gave her access to vital government records and archives that were closed to Lavon.

"Why the secrecy?" Gabriel asked. "The reluctance to talk on the telephone? The long walks in the park when the weather is perfectly dreadful?"

"Because this is Austria, Mr. Argov. Needless to say, the work we do is not popular in many quarters of Austrian society, just as Eli's wasn't." She caught herself using the past tense and quickly apologized. "The extreme right in this country doesn't like us, and they're well represented in the police and security services."

She brushed some sleet pellets from a park bench and they both sat down. "Eli came to me about two months ago. He told me about Max Klein and the man he'd seen at Café Central: Herr Vogel. I was skeptical, to say the least, but I decided to check it out, as a favor to Eli."

"What did you find?"

"His name is Ludwig Vogel. He's the chairman of something called Danube Valley Trade and Investment Corporation. The firm was founded in the early sixties, a few years after Austria emerged from the postwar occupation. He imported foreign products into Austria and served as an Austrian front man and facilitator for companies wishing to do business here, especially German and American companies. When the Austrian economy took off in the 1970s, Vogel was perfectly positioned to take full advantage of the situation. His firm provided venture capital for hundreds of projects. He now owns a substantial stake in many of Austria's most profitable corporations."

"How old is he?"

"He was born in a small village in Upper Austria in 1925 and baptized in the local Catholic church. His father was an ordinary laborer. Apparently, the family was quite poor. A younger brother died of pneumonia when Ludwig was twelve. His mother died two years later of scarlet fever."

"Nineteen twenty-five? That would make him only seventeen years old in 1942, far too young to be a Sturmbannführer in the SS."

"That's right. And according to the information I uncovered about his wartime past, he *wasn't* in the SS."

"What sort of information?"

She lowered her voice and leaned closer to him. Gabriel smelled morning coffee on her breath. "In my previous life, I sometimes found it necessary to consult files stored in the Austrian Staatsarchiv. I still have contacts there, the kind of people who are willing to help me under the right circumstances. I called on one of those contacts, and this person was kind enough to photocopy Ludwig Vogel's Wehrmacht service file."

"Wehrmacht?"

She nodded. "According to the Staatsarchiv documents, Vogel was conscripted in late 1944, when he was nineteen, and sent to Germany to serve in defense of the Reich. He fought the Russians in the battle of Berlin and managed to survive. During the final hours of the war, he fled west and surrendered to the Americans. He was interned at a U.S. Army detention facility south of Berlin, but managed to escape and make his way back to Austria. The fact that he escaped from the Americans didn't seem to count against him, because from 1946 until the State Treaty of 1955, Vogel was a civilian employee of the American occupation authority."

Gabriel looked over at her sharply. "The Americans? What kind of work did he do?"

"He started as a clerk at headquarters and eventually worked as a liaison officer between the Americans and the fledgling Austrian government."

"Married? Children?"

She shook her head. "A lifelong bachelor."

"Has he ever been in trouble? Financial irregularities of any kind? Civil suits? Anything?"

"His record is remarkably clean. I have another friend at the Staatspolizei. I had him run a check on Vogel. He came up with nothing, which in a way is quite remarkable. You see, almost every prominent citizen in Austria has a Staatspolizei file. But not Ludwig Vogel."

"What do you know about his politics?"

Renate Hoffmann spent a long moment surveying her surroundings before answering. "I asked that same question to some contacts I have on some of the more courageous Viennese newspapers and magazines, the ones that refuse to toe the government line. It turns out Ludwig Vogel is a major financial supporter of the Austrian National Party. In fact, he's practically bankrolled the campaign of Peter Metzler himself." She paused for a moment to light a cigarette. Her hand was shaking with cold. "I don't know if you've been following our campaign here, but unless things change dramatically in the next three weeks, Peter Metzler is going to be the next chancellor of Austria."

Gabriel sat silently, absorbing the information he had just been told. Renate Hoffmann took a single puff of her cigarette and tossed it into a mound of dirty snow.

"You asked me why we were going out in weather like this, Mr. Argov. Now you know."

SHE STOOD without warning and started walking. Gabriel got to his feet and followed after her. *Steady yourself,* he thought. An interesting theory, a tantalizing set of circumstances, but there was no proof and one enormous piece of exculpatory evidence. According to the files in the Staatsarchiv, Ludwig Vogel couldn't possibly be the man Max Klein had accused him of being.

"Is it possible Vogel knew Eli was investigating his past?"

"I've considered that," Renate Hoffman said. "I suppose someone at the Staatsarchiv or the Staatspolizei might have tipped him off about my search."

"Even if Ludwig Vogel really was the man Max Klein saw at Auschwitz, what's the worst that could happen to him now, sixty years after the crime?"

"In Austria? Precious little. When it comes to prosecuting war criminals, Austria's record is shameful. In my opinion, it was practically a safe haven for Nazi war criminals. Have you ever heard of Doctor Heinrich Gross?"

Gabriel shook his head. Heinrich Gross, she said, was a doctor at the Spiegelgrund clinic for handicapped children. During the war, the clinic served as a euthanasia center where the Nazi doctrine of eradicating the "pathological genotype" was put into practice. Nearly eight hundred children were murdered there. After the war, Gross went on to a distinguished career as a pediatric neurologist. Much of his research was carried out on brain tissue he had taken from victims of Spiegelgrund, which he kept stored in an elaborate "brain library." In 2000, the Austrian federal prosecutor finally decided it was time to bring Gross to justice. He was charged with complicity in nine of the murders carried out at Spiegelgrund and brought to trial.

"One hour into the proceedings, the judge ruled that Gross was suffering from the early stages of dementia and was in no condition to defend himself in a court of law," Renate Hoffman said. "He suspended the case indefinitely. Doctor Gross stood, smiled at his lawyer, and walked out of the courtroom. On the courthouse steps, he spoke to reporters about his case. It was quite clear that Doctor Gross was in complete control of his mental faculties."

"Your point?"

"The Germans are fond of saying that only Austria could convince the world that Beethoven was an Austrian and Hitler was a German. We like to pretend that we were Hitler's first victim instead of his willing accomplice. We choose not to remember that Austrians joined the Nazi party at the same rate as our German cousins, or that Austria's representation in the SS was disproportionately high. We choose not to remember that Adolf

Eichmann was an Austrian, or that eighty percent of his staff was Austrian, or that seventy-five percent of his death camp commandants were *Austrian.*" She lowered her voice. "Doctor Gross was protected by Austria's political elite and judicial system for decades. He was a member in good standing of the Social Democratic party, and he even served as a court forensic psychiatrist. Everyone in the Viennese medical community knew the source of the good doctor's so-called brain library, and everyone knew what he had done during the war. A man like Ludwig Vogel, even if he were exposed as a liar, could expect the same treatment. The chances of him ever facing trial in Austria for his crimes would be *zero.*"

"Suppose he knew about Eli's investigation? What would he have to fear?"

"Nothing, other than the embarrassment of exposure."

"Do you know where he lives?"

Renate Hoffmann pushed a few stray hairs beneath the band of her beret and looked at him carefully. "You're not thinking about trying to meet with him, are you, Mr. Argov? Under the circumstances, that would be an incredibly foolish idea."

"I just want to know where he lives."

"He has a house in the First District, and another in the Vienna woods. According to real estate records, he also owns several hundred acres and a chalet in Upper Austria."

Gabriel, after taking a glance over his shoulder, asked Renate Hoffmann if he could have a copy of all the documents she'd collected. She looked down at her feet, as if she'd been expecting the question.

"Tell me something, Mr. Argov. In all the years I worked

with Eli, he never once mentioned the fact that Wartime Claims and Inquiries had a Jerusalem branch."

"It was opened recently."

"How convenient." Her voice was thick with sarcasm. "I'm in possession of those documents illegally. If I give them to an agent of a foreign government, my position will be even more precarious. If I give them to you, am I giving them to an agent of a foreign government?"

Renate Hoffmann, Gabriel decided, was a highly intelligent and street-smart woman. "You're giving them to a friend, Miss Hoffmann, a friend who will do absolutely nothing to compromise your position."

"Do you know what will happen if you're arrested by the Staatspolizei while in possession of confidential Staatsarchiv files? You'll spend a long time behind bars." She looked directly into his eyes. "And so will I, if they find out where you got them."

"I don't intend to be arrested by the Staatspolizei."

"No one ever does, but this is Austria, Mr. Argov. Our police don't play by the same rules as their European counterparts."

She reached into her handbag, withdrew a manila envelope, and handed it to Gabriel. It disappeared into the opening of his jacket and they kept walking.

"I don't believe you're Gideon Argov from Jerusalem. That's why I gave you the file. There's nothing more I can do with it, not in this climate. Promise me you'll tread carefully, though. I don't want the Coalition and its staff to suffer the same fate as Wartime Claims." She stopped walking and turned briefly to face him. "And one more thing, Mr. Argov. Please don't call me again."

THE SURVEILLANCE VAN was parked on the edge of the Augarten, on the Wasnergasse. The photographer sat in the back, concealed behind one-way glass. He snapped one final shot as the subjects separated, then downloaded the pictures to a laptop computer and reviewed the images. The one that showed the envelope changing hands had been shot from behind. Nicely framed, well lit, a thing of beauty.

7

VIENNA

ONE HOUR LATER, in an anonymous neo-Baroque building on the Ringstrasse, the photograph was delivered to the office of a man named Manfred Kruz. Contained in an unmarked manila envelope, it was handed to Kruz without comment by his attractive secretary. As usual he was dressed in a dark suit and white shirt. His placid face and sharp cheekbones, combined with his habitual somber dress, gave him a cadaverous air that unnerved underlings. His Mediterranean features—the nearly black hair, the olive skin, and coffee-colored eyes—had given rise to rumors within the service that a gypsy or perhaps even a Jew lurked in his lineage. It was a libel, advanced by his legion of enemies, and Kruz did not find it amusing. He was not popular among the troops, but then he didn't much care. Kruz was well-connected: lunch with the minister once a week, friends among the wealthy and the political elite. Make an enemy of Kruz and you could find yourself writing parking tickets in the backwoods of Carinthia.

His unit was known officially as Department Five, but among senior Staatspolizei officers and their masters at the Interior Ministry, it was referred to simply as "Kruz's gang." In moments of self-aggrandizement, a misdemeanor to which Kruz willingly pleaded guilty, he imagined himself the protector of all things Austrian. It was Kruz's job to make certain that the rest of the world's problems didn't seep across the borders into the tranquil *Österreich*. Department Five was responsible for counterterrorism, counter-extremism, and counter-intelligence. Manfred Kruz possessed the power to bug offices and tap telephones, to open mail and conduct physical surveillance. Foreigners who came to Austria looking for trouble could expect a visit from one of Kruz's men. So could native-born Austrians whose political activities diverged from the prescribed lines. Little took place inside the country that he didn't know about, including the recent appearance in Vienna of an Israeli who claimed to be a colleague of Eli Lavon from Wartime Claims and Inquiries.

Kruz's innate mistrust of people extended to his personal secretary. He waited until she had left the room before prizing open the envelope and shaking the print onto his blotter. It fell facedown. He turned it over, placed it in the sharp white light of his halogen lamp, and carefully examined the image. Kruz was not interested in Renate Hoffmann. She was the subject of regular surveillance by Department Five, and Kruz had spent more time than he cared to remember studying surveillance photographs and listening to transcripts of proceedings inside the premises of the Coalition for a Better Austria. No, Kruz was more interested in the dark, compact figure walking at her side, the man who called himself Gideon Argov.

After a moment he stood and worked the tumbler on the wall safe behind his desk. Inside, wedged between a stack of case files and a bundle of scented love letters from a girl who worked in payroll, was a videotape of an interrogation. Kruz glanced at the date on the adhesive label—JANUARY 1991—then inserted the tape into his machine and pressed the play button.

The shot rolled for a few frames before settling into place. The camera had been mounted high in the corner of the interrogation room, where the wall met the ceiling, so that it looked down upon the proceedings from an oblique angle. The image was somewhat grainy, the technology a generation old. Pacing the room with a menacing slowness was a younger version of Kruz. Seated at the interrogation table was the Israeli, his hands blackened by fire, his eyes by death. Kruz was quite certain it was the same man who was now calling himself Gideon Argov. Uncharacteristically, it was the Israeli, not Kruz, who posed the first question. Now, as then, Kruz was taken aback by the perfect German, spoken in the distinctive accent of a Berliner.

"Where's my son?"

"I'm afraid he's dead."

"What about my wife?"

"Your wife has been severely injured. She needs immediate medical attention."

"Then why isn't she getting it?"

"We need to know some information first before she can be treated."

"Why isn't she being treated now? Where is she?"

"Don't worry, she's in good hands. We just need some questions answered."

"Like what?"

"You can begin by telling us who you really are. And please, don't lie to us anymore. Your wife doesn't have much time."

"I've been asked my name a hundred times! You know my name! My God, get her the help she needs."

"We will, but first tell us your name. Your real name, this time. No more aliases, pseudonyms, or cover names. We haven't the time, not if your wife is going to live."

"My name is Gabriel, you bastard!"

"Is that your first name or your last?"

"My first."

"And your last?"

"Allon."

"Allon? That's a Hebrew name, is it not? You're Jewish. You are also, I suspect, Israeli."

"Yes, I'm Israeli."

"If you are an Israeli, what are you doing in Vienna with an Italian passport? Obviously, you're an agent of Israeli intelli-

gence. Who do you work for, Mr. Allon? What are you doing here?"

"Call the ambassador. He'll know who to contact."

"We'll call your ambassador. And your foreign minister. And your prime minister. But right now, if you want your wife to get the medical treatment she so desperately needs, you're going to tell us who you work for and why you're in Vienna."

"Call the ambassador! Help my wife, goddamn it!"

"Who do you work for!"

"You know who I work for! Help my wife. Don't let her die!"

"Her life is in your hands, Mr. Allon."

"You're dead, you motherfucker! If my wife dies tonight, you're dead. Do you hear me? You're fucking dead!"

The tape dissolved to a blizzard of silver and black. Kruz sat for a long time, unable to take his eyes from the screen. Finally he switched his telephone to secure and dialed a number from memory. He recognized the voice that greeted him. They exchanged no pleasantries.

"I'm afraid we have a problem."

"Tell me."

Kruz did.

"Why don't you arrest him? He's in this country illegally on a forged passport, and in violation of an agreement made between your service and his."

"And then what? Hand him over to the state prosecutor's office so they can put him on trial? Something tells me he might want to use a platform like that to his advantage."

"What are you suggesting?"

"Something a bit more subtle."

"Consider the Israeli your problem, Manfred. Deal with it."

"And what about Max Klein?"

The line went dead. Kruz hung up the phone.

IN A QUIET backwater of the Stephansdom Quarter, in the very shadow of the cathedral's north tower, there is a lane too narrow for anything but pedestrian traffic. At the head of the lane, on the ground floor of a stately old Baroque house, there is a small shop that sells nothing but collector-quality antique clocks. The sign over the door is circumspect, the shop hours unpredictable. Some days it does not open for business at all. There are no employees other than the owner. To one set of exclusive clients, he is known as Herr Gruber. To another, the Clockmaker.

He was short of stature and muscular in build. He preferred pullovers and loose-fitting tweed jackets, because formal shirts and ties did not fit him particularly well. He was bald, with a fringe of cropped gray hair, and his eyebrows were thick and dark. He wore round spectacles with tortoise-shell frames. His hands were larger than most in his field, but dexterous and highly skilled.

His workshop was as orderly as an operating room. On the worktable, in a pool of clean light, lay a 200-year-old Neuchatel wall clock. The three-part case, decorated in floral-patterned cameos, was in perfect condition, as was the enamel dial with Roman numerals. The Clockmaker had entered the final stages of an extensive overhaul of the two-train Neuchatel movement.

The finished piece would fetch close to ten thousand dollars. A buyer, a collector from Lyon, was waiting.

The bell at the front of the shop interrupted the Clockmaker's work. He poked his head around the door frame and saw a figure standing outside in the street, a motorcycle courier, his wet leather jacket gleaming with rain like a seal's skin. There was a package under his arm. The Clockmaker went to the door and unlocked it. The courier handed over the package without a word, then climbed onto the bike and sped away.

The Clockmaker locked the door again and carried the package to his worktable. He unwrapped it slowly—indeed, he did almost everything slowly—and lifted the cover of a cardboard packing case. Inside lay a Louis XV French wall clock. Quite lovely. He removed the casing and exposed the movement. The dossier and photograph were concealed inside. He spent a few minutes reviewing the document, then concealed it inside a large volume entitled *Carriage Clocks in the Age of Victoria.*

The Louis XV had been delivered by the Clockmaker's most important client. The Clockmaker did not know his name, only that he was wealthy and politically connected. Most of his clients shared those two attributes. This one was different, though. A year ago he'd given the Clockmaker a list of names, men scattered from Europe to the Middle East to South America. The Clockmaker was steadily working his way down the list. He'd killed a man in Damascus, another in Cairo. He'd killed a Frenchman in Bordeaux and a Spaniard in Madrid. He'd crossed the Atlantic in order to kill two wealthy Argentines. One name remained on the list, a Swiss banker in Zurich. The

Clockmaker had yet to receive the final signal to proceed against him. The dossier he'd received tonight was a new name, a bit closer to home than he preferred, but hardly a challenge. He decided to accept the assignment.

He picked up the telephone and dialed.

"I received the clock. How quickly do you need it done?"

"Consider it an emergency repair."

"There's a surcharge for emergency repairs. I assume you're willing to pay it?"

"How much of a surcharge?"

"My usual fee, plus half."

"For this job?"

"Do you want it done, or not?"

"I'll send over the first half in the morning."

"No, you'll send it *tonight.*"

"If you insist."

The Clockmaker hung up the telephone as a hundred chimes simultaneously tolled four o'clock.

8

VIENNA

GABRIEL HAD NEVER been fond of Viennese coffeehouses. There was something in the smell—the potion of stale tobacco smoke, coffee, and liqueur—that he found offensive. And although he was quiet and still by nature, he did not enjoy sitting for long periods, wasting valuable time. He did not read in public, because he feared old enemies might be stalking him. He drank coffee only in the morning, to help him wake, and rich desserts made him ill. Witty conversation annoyed him, and listening to the conversations of others, especially pseudo-intellectuals, drove him to near madness. Gabriel's private hell would be a room where he would be forced to listen to a discussion of art led by people who knew nothing about it.

It had been more than thirty years since he had been to Café Central. The coffeehouse had proven to be the setting for the final stage of his apprenticeship for Shamron, the portal between the life he'd led before the Office and the twilight world he would inhabit after. Shamron, at the end of Gabriel's training period, had devised one more test to see whether he was ready for his first assignment. Dropped at midnight on the outskirts of Brussels, paperless and without a centime in his pocket, he had been ordered to meet an agent the next morning in the Leidseplein in Amsterdam. Using stolen money and a passport he'd taken from an American tourist, he'd managed to arrive on the morning train. The agent he found waiting was Shamron. He relieved Gabriel of the passport and his remaining money, then told him to be in Vienna the following afternoon, dressed in different clothes. They met on a bench in the Stadtpark and walked to the Central. At a table next to a tall, arched window, Shamron had given Gabriel an airline ticket to Rome and the key to an airport locker where he would find a Beretta pistol. Two nights later, in the foyer of an apartment house in the Piazza Annabaliano, Gabriel had killed for the first time.

Then, as now, it was raining when Gabriel arrived at Café Central. He sat on a leather banquette and placed a stack of German-language newspapers on the small, round table. He ordered a Schlagobers, black coffee topped with whipped cream. It came on a silver tray with a glass of iced water. He opened the first newspaper, *Die Presse*, and began to read. The bombing at Wartime Claims and Inquiries was the lead story. The Interior Minister was promising swift arrests. The political right was demanding harsher immigration measures to prevent Arab terrorists, and other troublesome elements, from crossing Austria's borders.

Gabriel finished the first newspaper. He ordered another Schlagobers and opened a magazine called *Profil.* He looked around the café. It was rapidly filling with Viennese office workers stopping for a coffee or a drink on the way home from work. Unfortunately none bore even a remote resemblance to Max Klein's description of Ludwig Vogel.

By five o'clock, Gabriel had drunk three cups of coffee and was beginning to despair of ever seeing Ludwig Vogel. Then he noticed that his waiter was wringing his hands with excitement and shifting his weight from foot to foot. Gabriel followed the line of the waiter's gaze and saw an elderly gentleman coming through the door—*An Austrian of the old school, if you know what I mean, Mr. Argov.* Yes, I do, thought Gabriel. *Good afternoon, Herr Vogel.*

HIS HAIR WAS nearly white, deeply receded, and combed very close to his scalp. His mouth was small and taut, his clothing expensive and elegantly worn: gray flannel trousers, a double-breasted blazer, a burgundy-colored ascot. The waiter helped him off with his overcoat and led him to a table, just a few feet from Gabriel's.

"An Einspänner, Karl. Nothing more."

Confident, baritone, a voice used to giving orders.

"Can I tempt you with a Sachertorte? Or an apple strudel? It's very fresh tonight."

A weary shake of the head, once to the left, once to the right.

"Not today, Karl. Just coffee."

"As you wish, Herr Vogel."

Vogel sat down. At that same instant, two tables away, his bodyguard sat, too. Klein hadn't mentioned the bodyguard. Perhaps he hadn't noticed him. Perhaps he was a new addition. Gabriel forced himself to look down at his magazine.

The seating arrangements were far from optimal. As luck would have it, Vogel was facing Gabriel directly. A more oblique angle would have allowed Gabriel to observe him without fear of being noticed. What's more, the bodyguard was seated just behind Vogel, his eyes on the move. Judging from the bulge in the left side of his suit jacket, he was carrying a weapon in a shoulder holster. Gabriel considered changing tables but feared it would arouse Vogel's suspicion, so he stayed put and sneaked glances at him over the top of his magazine.

And on it went for the next forty-five minutes. Gabriel finished the last of his reading material and started in on *Die Presse* again. He ordered a fourth Schlagobers. At some point he became aware that he too was being watched, not by the bodyguard but by Vogel himself. A moment later, he heard Vogel say, "It's damned cold tonight, Karl. How about a small glass of brandy before I leave?"

"Of course, Herr Vogel."

"And one for the gentlemen at that table over there, Karl."

Gabriel looked up and saw two pairs of eyes studying him, the small, dull eyes of the fawning waiter, and Vogel's, which were blue and bottomless. His small mouth had curled into a humorless smile. Gabriel didn't know quite how to react, and Ludwig Vogel was clearly enjoying his discomfort.

"I was just leaving," Gabriel said in German, "but thank you very much."

"As you wish." Vogel looked at the waiter. "Come to think of it, Karl, I think I'll be going, too."

Vogel stood suddenly. He handed the waiter a few bills, then walked to Gabriel's table.

"I offered to buy you a brandy because I noticed you were looking at me," Vogel said. "Have we ever met before?"

"No, I don't think so," Gabriel said. "And if I was looking at you, I meant nothing by it. I just enjoy looking at faces in Viennese coffeehouses." He hesitated, then added, "One never knows whom one might run into."

"I couldn't agree more." Another humorless smile. "Are you sure we've never met before? Your face seems very familiar to me."

"I sincerely doubt it."

"You're new to the Central," Vogel said with certainty. "I come here every afternoon. You might say I'm Karl's best customer. I know I've never seen you here before."

"I usually take my coffee at Sperl."

"Ah, Sperl. Their strudel is good, but I'm afraid the sound of the billiards tables intrudes on my concentration. I must say, I'm fond of the Central. Perhaps we'll see each other again."

"Perhaps," Gabriel said noncommittally.

"There was an old man who used to come here often. He was about my age. We used to have lovely conversations. He hasn't come for some time. I hope he's all right. When one is old, things have a way of going wrong very quickly."

Gabriel shrugged. "Maybe he's just moved on to another coffeehouse."

"Perhaps," Vogel said. Then he wished Gabriel a pleasant evening and walked into the street. The bodyguard followed discreetly after him. Through the glass, Gabriel saw a Mercedes sedan slide forward. Vogel shot one more glance in Gabriel's direction before lowering himself into the back seat. Then the door closed and the car sped away.

Gabriel sat for a moment, turning over the details of the unexpected encounter. Then he paid his check and walked into the frigid evening. He knew he had just been sent a warning. He also knew that his time in Austria was limited.

THE AMERICAN WAS the last to depart Café Central. He paused in the doorway to turn up the collar of his Burberry overcoat, doing his best to avoid looking like a spy, and watched the Israeli disappear into the darkened street. Then he turned and headed in the opposite direction. It had been an interesting afternoon. A ballsy move on Vogel's part, but then that was Vogel's style.

The embassy was in the Ninth District, a bit of a trek, but the American decided it was a good night for walking. He liked walking in Vienna. It suited him. He'd wanted nothing more than to be a spy in the city of spies and had spent his youth preparing himself. He'd studied German at his grandmother's knee and Soviet policy with the brightest minds in the field at Harvard. After graduation, the doors to the Agency were thrown open to him. Then the Empire crumbled and a new threat rose from the sands of the Middle East. Fluent German and a graduate degree from Harvard didn't count for much in the new Agency. Today's stars were human action figures who could live off worms and grubs and walk a hundred miles with some hill tribesman without complaining of so much as a blister. The American had got Vienna, but the Vienna that awaited him had lost her old importance. She was suddenly just another European backwater, a cul-de-sac, a place to quietly end a career, not launch one.

Thank God for the Vogel affair. It had livened things up a bit, even if it was only temporary.

The American turned into the Boltzmanngasse and paused at the formidable security gate. The Marine guard checked his identification card and permitted him to enter. The American had official cover. He worked in Cultural. It only reinforced his feelings of obsolescence. A spy, working with Cultural cover in Vienna. How perfectly quaint.

He rode the lift up to the fourth floor and paused at a door with a combination lock. Behind it was the nerve center of the Agency's Vienna station. The American sat down before a computer, logged on, and tapped out a brief cable to Headquarters. It was addressed to a man named Carter, the deputy director for operations. Carter hated chatty cables. He'd ordered the American to find out one simple piece of information. The American had done it. The last thing Carter needed was a blow-by-blow account of his harrowing exploits at Café Central. Once it might have sounded compelling. Not anymore.

He typed five words—*Avraham is in the game*—and fired it into the secure ether. He waited for a response. To pass the time, he worked on an analysis of the upcoming election. He doubted it would be required reading on the seventh floor at Langley.

His computer beeped. He had a message waiting. He clicked on it, and words appeared on the screen.

Keep Elijah under watch.

The American hastily tapped out another message: *What if Elijah leaves town?*

Two minutes later: *Keep Elijah under watch.*

The American logged off. He put aside the report on the election. He was back in the game, at least for now.

GABRIEL SPENT THE rest of that evening at the hospital. Marguerite, the night nurse, came on duty an hour after he arrived. When the doctor had completed his examination, she permitted him to sit at Eli's bedside. For a second time, she suggested Gabriel talk to him, then she slipped from the room to give him a few moments of privacy. Gabriel didn't know what to say, so he leaned close to Eli's ear and whispered to him in Hebrew about the case: Max Klein, Renate Hoffmann, Ludwig Vogel . . . Eli lay motionless, his head bandaged, his eyes bound. Later, in the corridor, Marguerite confided to Gabriel that there had been no improvement in Eli's condition. Gabriel sat in the adjoining waiting room for another hour, watching Eli through the glass, then took a taxi back to his hotel.

In his room he sat down at the desk and switched on the lamp. In the top drawer he found a few sheets of hotel stationery and a pencil. He closed his eyes for a moment and pictured Vogel as he had seen him that afternoon in Café Central.

"Are you sure we've never met before? Your face seems very familiar to me."

"I sincerely doubt it."

Gabriel opened his eyes again and started sketching. Five minutes later, Vogel's face was staring up at him. *What might he have looked like as a young man?* He began to sketch again. He thickened the hair, removed the hoods and crinkles from the eyes. He smoothed the furrows from the forehead, tightened the skin on the cheeks and along the jawline, erased the deep troughs leading from the base of the nose to the corners of the small mouth.

Satisfied, he placed the new sketch next to the first. He began a third version of the man, this time with the high-collared tunic and peaked cap of an SS man. The image, when it was complete, set fire to the skin of his neck.

He opened the file Renate Hoffmann had given him and read the name of the village where Vogel had his country house. He located the village on a tourist map he found in the desk drawer, then dialed a rental car office and reserved a car for the morning.

He carried the sketches to the bed and, with his head propped on the pillow, stared at the three different versions of Vogel's face. The last, the one of Vogel in the uniform of the SS, seemed vaguely familiar to him. He had the nagging sensation he had seen the man someplace before. After an hour, he sat up and carried the sketches into the bathroom. Standing at the sink, he burned the images in the same order he had sketched them: Vogel as prosperous Viennese gentleman, Vogel fifty years younger, Vogel as SS murderer . . .

9

VIENNA

THE FOLLOWING MORNING Gabriel went shopping in the Kärntnerstrasse. The sky was a dome of pale blue streaked with alabaster. Crossing the Stephansplatz, he was nearly toppled by the wind. It was an Arctic wind, chilled by the fjords and glaciers of Norway, strengthened by the icy plains of Poland, and now it was hammering against the gates of Vienna like a barbarian horde.

He entered a department store, glanced at the directory, and rode the escalator up to the floor that sold outerwear. There he selected a dark blue ski jacket, a thick fleece pullover, heavy gloves, and waterproof hiking boots. He paid for his things and went out again, strolling the Kärntnerstrasse with a plastic bag in each hand, checking his tail.

The rental car office was a few streets away from his hotel. A silver Opel station wagon awaited him. He loaded the bags into the back seat, signed the necessary papers, and sped away. He drove in circles for a half-hour, looking for signs of surveillance, then made his way to the entrance of the A1 motorway and headed west.

The clouds thickened gradually, the morning sun vanished. By the time he reached Linz, it was snowing heavily. He stopped at a gas station and changed into the clothing he'd bought in Vienna, then pulled back onto the A1 and made the final run into Salzburg.

It was midafternoon when he arrived. He left the Opel in a car park and spent the remainder of the afternoon wandering the streets and squares of the old city, playing the part of a tourist. He climbed the carved steps leading up the Mönchsberg and admired the view of Salzburg from the height of the church steeples. Then it was over to the Universitätsplatz to see the Baroque masterpieces of Fischer von Erlach. When darkness fell, he went back down to the old city and dined on Tyrolean ravioli in a quaint restaurant with hunting trophies on the dark-paneled walls.

By eight o'clock, he was behind the wheel of the Opel again, heading east out of Salzburg into the heart of the Salzkammergut. The snowfall grew heavier as the highway climbed steadily into the mountains. He passed through a village called

Hof on the southern shore of the Fuschlsee; then, a few miles farther on, he came to the Wolfgangsee. The town for which it was named, St. Wolfgang, stood on the opposite shore of the lake. He could just make out the shadowed spire of the Pilgrimage Church. He remembered it contained one of the finest Gothic altarpieces in all of Austria.

In the sleepy village of Zichenbach, he made a right turn into a narrow lane that rose sharply up the slope of the mountain. The town fell away behind him. There were cottages along the road, with snow-covered roofs and smoke curling from the chimneys. A dog ran out from one of them and barked as Gabriel passed.

He drove across a one-lane bridge, then slowed to a stop. The road seemed to have given up in exhaustion. A narrower path, barely wide enough to accommodate a car, continued into a birch forest. About thirty meters farther on was a gate. He shut down the engine. The deep silence of the forest was oppressive.

He removed the flashlight from the glove compartment and climbed out. The gate was shoulder-high and fashioned of old timber. A sign warned that the property on the other side was private and that hunting and hiking were strictly *verboten* and punishable by fines and imprisonment. Gabriel put a foot on the middle slat, hauled himself over the top, and dropped into the downy blanket of snow on the other side.

He switched on the flashlight, illuminating the path. It rose at a sharp incline and curved off to the right, disappearing behind a wall of birch. There were no footprints and no tire tracks. Gabriel doused the light and hesitated a moment while his eyes grew accustomed to the darkness, then started walking again.

Five minutes later, he came upon a large clearing. At the top of the clearing, about a hundred meters away, stood the house, a traditional alpine chalet, very large, with a pitched roof and eaves that hung well beyond the outer walls of the structure. He paused for a moment, listening for any sign his approach had been detected. Satisfied, he circled the clearing, keeping to the tree line. The house was in complete darkness, no lights burning inside, none on the exterior. There were no vehicles.

He stood for a moment, debating whether he should commit a crime on Austrian soil by breaking into the house. The unoccupied chalet represented a chance to peer into Vogel's life, a chance that would surely not come his way again anytime soon. He was reminded of a recurring dream. Titian wishes to consult with Gabriel on a restoration, but Gabriel keeps putting Titian off because he's hopelessly behind schedule and can't take the time for a meeting. Titian is terribly offended and rescinds the offer in a rage. Gabriel, alone before a limitless canvas, forges on without the master's help.

He started across the clearing. A glance over his shoulder confirmed what he already knew—he was leaving an obvious trail of human footprints leading from the edge of the trees to the back of the house. Unless it snowed again soon, the tracks would remain visible for anyone to see. *Keep moving. Titian is waiting.*

He arrived at the rear of the chalet. The length of the exterior wall was stacked with firewood. At the end of the woodpile was a door. Gabriel tried the latch. Locked, of course. He removed his gloves and took out the thin metal strip that he habitually carried in his wallet. He worked it gently inside the keyhole until he felt the mechanism give way. Then he turned the latch and stepped inside.

HE SWITCHED ON the flashlight and found he was standing in a mudroom. Three pairs of Wellington boots stood at attention against the wall. A loden-cloth coat hung from a hook. Gabriel searched the pockets: some loose change, a wadded handkerchief, crinkled by an old man's dried phlegm.

He stepped through a doorway and was confronted by a flight of stairs. He climbed swiftly upward, flashlight in hand, until he came to another door. This one was unlocked. Gabriel eased it open. The groan of the dry hinges echoed in the vast silence of the house.

He found himself in a pantry, which looked as though it had been looted by an army in retreat. The shelves were nearly bare and covered in a fine layer of dust. The adjoining kitchen was a combination of modern and traditional: German-made appliances with stainless-steel fronts, cast-iron pots hanging over a large open hearth. He opened the refrigerator: a half-drunk bottle of Austrian white wine, a lump of cheese green with mold, a few jars of ancient condiments.

He walked through a dining room into a large great room. He played the light around the room and stopped when it fell upon an antique writing table. There was one drawer. Warped by the cold, it was wedged tightly shut. Gabriel pulled hard and nearly tore it off the runners. He shone the light inside: pens and pencils, rusted paper clips, a stack of business stationery from Danube Valley Trade and Investment, personal stationery: *From the desk of Ludwig Vogel . . .*

Gabriel closed the drawer and shone the light on the surface of the desk. In a wooden paper tray was a stack of correspondence. He leafed through the pages: a few private letters, documents that appeared to be related to Vogel's business dealings. Attached to some of the documents were memoranda, all written in the same spidery script. He seized the papers, folded them in half, and pushed them down the front of his jacket.

The telephone was equipped with a built-in answering machine and digital display. The clock was set to the wrong time. Gabriel lifted the cover, exposing a pair of minicassettes. It had been his experience that telephone machines never completely erased tapes and that much valuable information was often left behind, easily accessible to a technician with proper equipment. He removed the cassettes and slipped them into his pocket. Then he closed the lid and pressed the redial button. There was a burst of dial tone, followed by the dissonant song of the automatic dialer. The number flashed across the display window: *5124124.* A Vienna number. Gabriel committed it to memory.

The next sound was the one-note ring of an Austrian telephone, followed by a second. Before the line could ring a third time, a man picked up.

"Hello . . . hello . . . Who's there? Ludwig, is that you? Who is this?"

Gabriel reached down and severed the connection.

HE MOUNTED THE main staircase. How long did he have before the man at the other end of the line realized his mistake? How quickly could he marshal his forces and mount a counterattack? Gabriel could almost hear a clock ticking.

At the top of the stairs was an alcovelike foyer, furnished as a small seating area. Next to the chair was a stack of books, and resting on the books was an empty snifter. On each side of the alcove was a doorway leading to a bedroom. Gabriel entered the one to his right.

The ceiling was at an angle, reflecting the pitch of the roof. The walls were bare except for a large crucifix hanging over the unmade bed. The alarm clock on the nightstand flashed *12:00 . . . 12:00 . . . 12:00 . . .* Coiled snakelike in front of the clock was a black-beaded rosary. A television set stood on a pedestal at the foot of the bed. Gabriel dragged his gloved fingertip across the screen and left a dark line in the dust.

There was no closet, only a large Edwardian-style wardrobe. Gabriel opened the door and played his flashlight around the interior: stacks of neatly folded sweaters, jackets, dress shirts, and trousers hanging from the rod. He pulled open a drawer. Inside was a felt-lined jewelry case: tarnished cufflinks, signet rings, an antique watch with a cracked black leather band. He turned over the watch and examined the backing. *To Erich, in adoration, Monica.* He picked up one of the rings, a heavy gold signet adorned with an eagle. It too was engraved, in tiny script that ran along the interior of the band: *1005, well done, Heinrich.* Gabriel slipped the watch and the signet ring into his pocket.

He left the bedroom, pausing in the alcove. A glance through the window showed no movement in the drive. He entered the second bedroom. The air was heavy with the unmistakable scent of attar of roses and lavender. A pale, soft rug covered the floor; a flowered eiderdown quilt lay over the bed. The Edwardian wardrobe was identical to the one in the first bedroom, except the doors were mirrored. Inside, Gabriel found the clothing of a woman. Renate Hoffmann had told him Vogel was a lifelong bachelor. So whom did the clothes belong to?

Gabriel went to the bedside table. A large leather-bound Bible stood atop a lace cloth. He picked it up by the spine and vigorously thumbed the pages. A photograph fluttered to the floor. Gabriel examined it by flashlight. It showed a woman, a teen-aged boy, and a middle-aged man, seated on a blanket in an alpine meadow in summer. They were all smiling for the camera. The woman had her arm around the man's shoulder. Even though it had been taken thirty or forty years ago, it was clear the man was Ludwig Vogel. And the woman? *To Erich, in adoration, Monica.* The boy, handsome and neatly groomed, looked oddly familiar.

He heard a sound outside, a muffled rumble, and hurried over to the window. He parted the curtain and saw a pair of headlights rising slowly through the trees.

GABRIEL SLIPPED THE photograph into his pocket and hurried down the staircase. The great room already was lit by the glow of the vehicle's headlights. He retraced his path—across the kitchen, through the pantry, down the back stairs—until he found himself in the mudroom once more. He could hear footfalls on the floor above him; someone was in the house. He eased the door open and slipped out, closing it quietly behind him.

He walked around to the front of the house, keeping beneath the eaves. The vehicle, a four-wheel-drive sport utility, was parked a few meters from the front door. The headlamps were burning and the driver's-side door hung open. Gabriel could hear the electronic pinging of an alarm. The keys were still in the ignition. He crept over to the vehicle, removed the keys, and hurled them into the darkness.

He crossed the meadow and started down the slope of the mountain. With the heavy boots and thick snow, it was something from his nightmares. The cold air clawed at his throat. As he rounded the final bend in the path, he saw that the gate was open and a man was standing next to his car, shining a flashlight through the window.

Gabriel did not fear a confrontation with one man. Two, however, was another thing altogether. He decided to go on the offensive, before the one up at the house could make his way down the mountain. He shouted in German, "You there! What do you think you're doing with my car?"

The man turned around and shone his flashlight toward Gabriel. He made no movement that suggested he was reaching for a gun. Gabriel kept running, playing the role of an outraged motorist whose car has been violated. Then he removed the flashlight from his coat pocket and swung it toward the man's face.

He raised his hand defensively, and the blow was absorbed by his heavy coat. Gabriel let go of the flashlight and kicked the man hard on the inside of his knee. He groaned in pain and threw a wild punch. Gabriel stepped away, easily avoiding it, careful not to lose his footing in the snow. His opponent was a large man, some six inches taller than Gabriel and at least fifty pounds heavier. If things deteriorated into a wrestling match, the outcome would be thrown into question.

The man threw another wild punch, a roundhouse that glanced off the front of Gabriel's chin. He ended up off balance, leaning over to the left, with his right arm down. Gabriel seized the arm and stepped forward. He drew back his elbow and drove it twice into the man's cheekbone, careful to avoid the killing zone in front of the ear. The man collapsed into the snow, dazed. Gabriel hit him in the head with the flashlight for good measure, and the man fell unconscious.

Gabriel looked over his shoulder and saw that there was no one on the track. He unzipped the man's jacket and searched for a billfold. He found one in an interior breast pocket. Inside was an identification badge. The name did not concern him; the affiliation did. The man lying unconscious in the snow was a Staatspolizei officer.

Gabriel resumed his search of the unconscious man and found, in the breast pocket of his jacket, a small leather-bound policeman's notepad. Written on the first page, in childlike block letters, was the registration number for Gabriel's rental car.

10

VIENNA

NEXT MORNING, GABRIEL made two telephone calls upon his return to Vienna. The first was to a number located inside the Israeli embassy. He identified himself as Kluge, one of his many telephone names, and said he was calling to confirm an appointment with a Mr. Rubin in Consular. After a moment the voice at the other end of the line said, "The Opernpassage—do you know it?"

Gabriel indicated, with some irritation, that he did. The

Opernpassage was a dingy, pedestrian thoroughfare beneath the Karlsplatz.

"Enter the passage from the north," the voice said. "Halfway down, on your right side, you'll see a hat shop. Walk past that shop at precisely ten o'clock."

Gabriel broke the connection, then dialed Max Klein's apartment in the Second District. There was no answer. He hung the receiver back on the hook and stood for a moment, wondering where Klein could be.

He had ninety minutes until his meeting with the courier. He decided to use the time productively by ridding himself of the rental car. The situation had to be handled carefully. Gabriel had taken the Staatspolizei officer's notebook. If by some chance the policeman had managed to remember the registration number after being knocked unconscious, it would have taken him only minutes to trace the car to the rental agent in Vienna, and then to an Israeli named Gideon Argov.

Gabriel crossed the Danube and drove around the modern United Nations complex, looking for a parking space on the street. He found one, about a five-minute walk from the U-Bahn station, and pulled in. He raised the hood and loosened the battery cables, then climbed behind the wheel and turned the key. Greeted by silence, he closed the hood and walked away.

From a phone booth in the U-Bahn station he called the rental car office to inform them that their Opel had broken down and needed to be collected. He permitted a note of indignation to creep into his voice, and the attendant at the other end of the line was highly apologetic. There was nothing in the clerk's voice to indicate the company had been contacted by the police concerning a burglary the previous evening in the Salzkammergut.

A train rolled into the station. Gabriel hung up and boarded the last carriage. Fifteen minutes later, he was entering the Opernpassage—from the north, just as the man from the embassy had instructed. It was filled with morning commuters spilling from the Karlsplatz U-Bahn station, the air thick with the stench of fast food and cigarettes. An Albanian with drugged eyes asked Gabriel for a euro to buy food. Gabriel slipped past without a word and made his way toward the hatter.

The man from the embassy was coming out as Gabriel approached. Blond and blue-eyed, he wore a mackintosh raincoat with a scarf wrapped tightly around his throat. A plastic bag bearing the name of the hatter hung from his right hand. They were known to each other. His name was Ben-Avraham.

They walked side by side toward the exit at the other end of the passage. Gabriel handed over an envelope containing all the material he had gathered since his arrival in Austria: the dossier given to him by Renate Hoffmann, the watch and the ring taken from Ludwig Vogel's armoire, the photograph concealed in the Bible. Ben-Avraham slipped the envelope into the plastic bag.

"Get it home," Gabriel said. "Quickly."

Ben-Avraham nodded tersely. "And the receiving party at King Saul Boulevard?"

"It's not going to King Saul Boulevard."

Ben-Avraham raised an eyebrow suggestively. "You know the rules. Everything goes through Headquarters."

"Not this," Gabriel said, nodding toward the plastic bag. "It goes to the Old Man."

They reached the end of the passage. Gabriel turned and started in the opposite direction. Ben-Avraham followed after him. Gabriel could see what he was thinking. Should he violate a petty Office dictum and risk the wrath of Lev—who loved nothing more than enforcing petty Office dictums—or should he perform a small favor for Gabriel Allon and Ari Shamron? Ben-Avraham's deliberation did not last long. Gabriel had not expected it would. Lev was not the type to inspire personal devotion among his troops. Lev was the man of the hour, but Shamron was the *Memuneh*, and the *Memuneh* was eternal.

Gabriel, with a sideways movement of his eyes, sent Ben-Avraham on his way. He spent ten minutes pacing the length of the Opernpassage, searching for any sign of surveillance, then went back up to the street. From a public telephone he tried Max Klein's number a second time. There was still no answer.

He climbed on a passing streetcar and rode it around the city center to the Second District. It took him a few moments to find Klein's address. In the foyer, he pressed the buzzer for the apartment but received no response. The caretaker, a middle-aged woman in a flowered frock, poked her head from her apartment and eyed Gabriel suspiciously.

"Who are you looking for?"

Gabriel answered truthfully.

"He usually goes to the synagogue in the morning. Have you tried there?"

The Jewish Quarter was just on the other side of the Danube Canal, a ten-minute walk at most. As usual, the synagogue was under guard. Gabriel, despite his passport, had to pass through a magnetometer before being admitted. He took a *kippah* from the basket and covered his head before entering the sanctuary. A few elderly men were praying near the *bimah.* None of them was Max Klein. In the foyer he asked the security guard whether he'd seen Klein that morning. The guard shook his head and suggested Gabriel try the community center.

Gabriel walked next door and was admitted by a Russian Jew named Natalia. Yes, she told him, Max Klein often spends his morning at the center, but she hadn't seen him today. "Sometimes, the old ones have coffee at the Café Schottenring," she said. "It's at Number Nineteen. You might find him there."

There was indeed a group of elderly Viennese Jews having coffee at the Café Schottenring, but Klein wasn't one of them. Gabriel asked if he'd been there that morning, and six gray heads shook in unison.

Frustrated, he walked back across the Danube Canal to the Second District and returned to Klein's apartment building. He pressed the buzzer and once again received no response. Then he knocked on the door of the caretaker's apartment. Seeing Gabriel for a second time, her face turned suddenly grave.

"Wait here," she said. "I'll get the key."

THE CARETAKER UNLOCKED the door and, before stepping across the threshold, called out Klein's name. Hearing no reply, they went inside. The curtains were drawn, the sitting room was in heavy shadow.

"Herr Klein?" she called out again. "Are you here? Herr Klein?"

Gabriel opened the double doors leading to the kitchen and

peered inside. Max Klein's dinner was sitting on the small table, untouched. He walked down the hallway, pausing once to peer into the empty bathroom. The bedroom door was locked. Gabriel hammered on it with his fist and called Klein's name. There was no response.

The caretaker came to his side. They looked at each other. She nodded. Gabriel seized the latch with both hands and drove his shoulder into the door. The wood splintered, and he stumbled into the bedroom.

Here, as in the sitting room, the curtains were drawn. Gabriel ran his hand along the wall, groping in the gloom until he found a switch. A small bedside lamp threw a cone of light on the figure lying on the bed.

The caretaker gasped.

Gabriel eased forward. Max Klein's head was covered by a clear plastic bag, and a gold-braided cord was wrapped around his neck. His eyes stared at Gabriel through the fogged plastic.

"I'll call the police," the caretaker said.

Gabriel sat at the end of the bed and buried his face in his hands.

IT TOOK TWENTY minutes for the first police to arrive. Their apathetic manner suggested an assumption of suicide. In a way this was fortunate for Gabriel, because suspicion of foul play would have significantly altered the nature of the encounter. He was interviewed twice, once by the uniformed officers who had first responded to the call, then again by a Staatspolizei detective called Greiner. Gabriel said his name was Gideon Argov and that he worked for the Jerusalem office of Wartime Claims and Inquiries. That he had come to Vienna after the bombing to be with his friend Eli Lavon. That Max Klein was an old friend of his father, and that his father suggested he look up Klein and see how the old man was getting on. He didn't mention his meeting with Klein two nights earlier, nor did he inform the police of Klein's suspicions about Ludwig Vogel. His passport was examined, as was his business card. Telephone numbers were written in small black notebooks. Condolences were offered. The caretaker made tea. It was all very polite.

Shortly after noon, a pair of ambulance attendants came to collect the body. The detective handed Gabriel a card and told him he was free to leave. Gabriel went out into the street and walked around the corner. In a shadowed alleyway, he leaned against the sooty bricks and closed his eyes. A suicide? No, the man who had survived the horrors of Auschwitz had not committed suicide. He had been murdered, and Gabriel couldn't help but feel that he was partly to blame. He'd been a fool to leave Klein unprotected.

He started back toward his hotel. The images of the case played out in his mind like fragments of an unfinished painting: Eli Lavon in his hospital bed, Ludwig Vogel in the Café Central, the Staatspolizei man in the Salzkammergut, Max Klein lying dead with a plastic bag over his head. Each incident was like another weight being added to the pan of a scale. The balance was about to tip, and Gabriel suspected he would be the next victim. It was time to leave Austria while he still could.

He entered his hotel and asked the desk clerk to prepare his bill, then walked upstairs to his room. His door, despite the Do

Not Disturb sign hanging from the latch, was ajar, and he could hear voices emanating from inside. He eased it open with his fingertips. Two men in plainclothes were in the process of lifting the mattress off the box spring. A third, clearly their superior, was sitting at the desk watching the proceedings like a bored fan at a sporting contest. Seeing Gabriel standing at the door, he stood slowly and put his hands on his hips. The last weight had just been added to the pan.

"Good afternoon, Allon," said Manfred Kruz.

11

VIENNA

IF YOU'RE CONSIDERING the possibility of escape, you'll find all the exits blocked and a very large man at the bottom of the stairs who'll relish the opportunity to subdue you." Kruz's body was turned slightly. He gazed at Gabriel, fencerlike, over one shoulder and held up his palm in a placatory gesture. "There's no need for this to get out of hand. Come inside and close the door."

His voice was the same, underpowered and unnaturally calm, an undertaker helping a grieving relative to select a casket. He had aged in thirteen years—there were a few more wrinkles around his cunning mouth and a few more pounds on his slender frame—and, based on his well-cut clothing and arrogant demeanor, he had been promoted. Gabriel kept his gaze focused on Kruz's dark eyes. He could feel the presence of another man at his back. He stepped across the threshold and swung the door shut behind him. He heard a heavy thud, then a curse muttered in German. Kruz held up a palm again. This time it was a command for Gabriel to stop.

"Are you armed?"

Gabriel shook his head wearily.

"Do you mind if I put my mind at ease?" Kruz asked. "You do have something of a reputation."

Gabriel raised his hands above his shoulders. The officer who'd been behind him in the hall entered the room and conducted the search. It was professional and very thorough, starting with the neck and ending with the ankles. Kruz seemed disappointed by the results.

"Remove your coat and empty your pockets."

Gabriel hesitated and was spurred on with a painful jab to the kidney. He unzipped his coat and handed it to Kruz, who searched the pockets and felt the lining for a false compartment.

"Turn out the pockets of your trousers."

Gabriel complied. The result was a few coins and the stub of a streetcar ticket. Kruz looked at the two officers holding the mattress and ordered them to reassemble the bed. "Mr. Allon is a professional," he said. "We're not going to find anything."

The officers plopped the mattress back onto the box spring.

Kruz, with a wave of his hand, told them to leave the room. He sat down again at the desk and pointed toward the bed.

"Make yourself comfortable."

Gabriel remained standing.

"How long have you been in Vienna?"

"You tell me."

Kruz acknowledged the professional compliment with a terse smile. "You arrived on a flight from Ben-Gurion Airport the night before last. After checking into this hotel, you proceeded to Vienna General Hospital, where you spent several hours with your friend Eli Lavon."

Kruz fell silent. Gabriel wondered how much else Kruz knew about his activities in Vienna. Did he know about the meetings with Max Klein and Renate Hoffmann? His encounter with Ludwig Vogel at the Café Central and his excursion to Salzkammergut? Kruz, if he did know more, was unlikely to say. He was not the kind to tip his hand for no reason. Gabriel imagined him a cold and emotionless gambler.

"Why didn't you arrest me earlier?"

"I haven't arrested you now." Kruz lit a cigarette. "We were prepared to overlook your violation of our agreement because we assumed you'd come to Vienna to be at the side of your injured friend. But it quickly became apparent that you intended to conduct a private investigation of the bombing. For obvious reasons, I cannot allow that."

"Yes," Gabriel agreed, "for obvious reasons."

Kruz spent a moment contemplating the smoke rising from the ember of his cigarette. "We had an agreement, Mr. Allon. Under no circumstances were you to return to this country.

You're not welcome here. You're not supposed to be here. I don't care if you're upset about your friend Eli Lavon. This is our investigation, and we don't need any help from you or your service."

Kruz looked at his watch. "There's an El Al flight leaving in three hours. You're going to be on it. I'll keep you company while you pack your bags."

Gabriel looked around at his clothing strewn across the floor. He lifted the lid of his suitcase and saw that the lining had been cut away. Kruz shrugged his shoulders—*What did you expect?* Gabriel bent down and started picking up his belongings. Kruz looked out the French doors and smoked.

After a moment, Kruz asked, "Is she still alive?"

Gabriel turned slowly around and fixed his gaze on Kruz's small, dark eyes. "Are you referring to my wife?"

"Yes."

Gabriel shook his head slowly. "Don't speak about my wife, Kruz."

Kruz smiled humorlessly. "You're not going to start making threats again, are you, Allon? I might be tempted to take you into custody for a more thorough questioning about your activities here."

Gabriel said nothing.

Kruz crushed out his cigarette. "Pack your bags, Allon. You don't want to miss your plane."

PART TWO

THE HALL OF NAMES

12

JERUSALEM

THE LIGHTS OF Ben-Gurion Airport pricked the darkness of the Coastal Plain. Gabriel leaned his head against the window and watched the runway rising slowly to meet him. The tarmac shone like glass in the night rain. As the plane slowed to a stop, Gabriel spotted the man from King Saul Boulevard, sheltering beneath an umbrella at the foot of the stairs. He made certain he was the last passenger to leave the plane.

They entered the terminal through a special doorway used

by senior government officials and visiting dignitaries. The man from headquarters was a disciple of Lev, corporate and high-tech, with a boardroom bearing and a belief that men of the field were simply blunt objects to be manipulated by higher beings. Gabriel walked one step ahead of him.

"The boss wants to see you."

"I'm sure he does, but I haven't slept in two days, and I'm tired."

"The boss doesn't care if you're tired. Who the hell do you think you are, Allon?"

Gabriel, even in the sanctuary of Ben-Gurion Airport, did not appreciate the use of his real name. He wheeled around. The headquarters man held up his palms in surrender. Gabriel turned and kept walking. The headquarters man had the good sense not to follow.

Outside, rain was hammering against the pavement. Lev's doing, no doubt. Gabriel sought shelter beneath the taxi stand and thought about where to go. He had no residence in Israel; the Office was his only home. Usually he stayed at a safe flat or Shamron's villa in Tiberias.

A black Peugeot turned into the traffic circle. The weight of the armor made it ride low on the heavy-duty suspension. It stopped in front of Gabriel, the bulletproof rear window slid down. Gabriel smelled the bitter, familiar scent of Turkish tobacco. Then he saw the hand, liver-spotted and blue-veined, gesturing wearily for him to come out of the rain.

THE CAR LURCHED forward even before Gabriel could close the door. Shamron was never one for standing still. He crushed out his cigarette for Gabriel's sake and lowered the windows for a few seconds in order to clear the air. When the windows were closed again, Gabriel told him of Lev's hostile reception. He spoke to Shamron in English at first; then, remembering where he was, he switched to Hebrew.

"Apparently, he wants to have a word with me."

"Yes, I know," Shamron said. "He'd like to see me as well."

"How did he find out about Vienna?"

"It seems Manfred Kruz paid a courtesy call on the embassy after your deportation and threw something of a fit. I'm told it wasn't pretty. The Foreign Ministry is furious, and the entire top floor of King Saul Boulevard is baying for my blood—and yours."

"What can they do to me?"

"Nothing, which is why you're my perfect accomplice—that and your obvious talents, of course."

The car sped out of the airport and turned onto the highway. Gabriel wondered why they were heading toward Jerusalem, but was too exhausted to care. After a while, they began to climb into the Judean Mountains. Soon the car was filled with the scent of eucalyptus and wet pine. Gabriel looked out the rain-spattered window and tried to remember the last time he had set foot in his country. It was after he had hunted down Tariq al-Hourani. He'd spent a month in a safe flat just outside the walls of the Old City, recovering from a bullet wound in his chest. That was more than three years ago. He realized that the threads that bound him to this place were fraying. He wondered whether he, like Francesco Tiepolo, would die in Venice and suffer the indignity of a mainland burial.

"Something tells me Lev and the Foreign Ministry are going

to be *slightly* less annoyed with me when they find out what's inside this." Shamron held up an envelope. "Looks like you were a very busy boy during your brief stay in Vienna. Who's Ludwig Vogel?"

Gabriel, his head propped against the window, told Shamron everything, beginning with his encounter with Max Klein, and ending with his tense confrontation with Manfred Kruz in his hotel room. Shamron was soon smoking again, and though Gabriel could not see his face clearly in the back of the darkened limousine, the old man was actually smiling. Umberto Conti may have given Gabriel the tools to become a great restorer, but Shamron was responsible for his flawless memory.

"No wonder Kruz was so anxious to get you out of Austria," Shamron said. "The Islamic Fighting Cells?" He emitted a burst of derisive laughter. "How convenient. The government accepts the claim of responsibility and sweeps the affair under the rug as an act of Islamic terror on Austrian soil. That way the trail doesn't get too close to Austrians—or to Vogel and Metzler, especially so near to the election."

"But what about the documents from the Staatsarchiv? According to them, Ludwig Vogel is squeaky clean."

"So why did he plant a bomb in Eli's office and murder Max Klein?"

"We don't know if he did either one of those things."

"True, but the facts certainly suggest that's a possibility. We might not be able to prove it in court, but the story would sell a lot of newspapers."

"You're suggesting a leak?"

"Why don't we light a fire under Vogel and see how he reacts?"

"Bad idea," Gabriel said. "Remember Waldheim and the revelations about his Nazi past? They were dismissed as foreign agitation and outside interference in Austrian affairs. Ordinary Austrians closed ranks around him, as did the Austrian authorities. The affair also raised the level of anti-Semitism inside the country. A leak, Ari, would be a very bad idea."

"So what do you suggest we do?"

"Max Klein was convinced that Ludwig Vogel was an SS man who committed an atrocity at Auschwitz. According to the documents in the Staatsarchiv, Ludwig Vogel was too young to be that man—and he was in the Wehrmacht, not the SS. But assume for argument's sake that Max Klein was right."

"That would mean that Ludwig Vogel is someone else."

"Exactly," Gabriel said. "So let's find out who he really is."

"How do you intend to do that?"

"I'm not sure," Gabriel said, "but the things in that envelope, in proper hands, might yield some valuable clues."

Shamron nodded thoughtfully. "There's a man at Yad Vashem who you should see. He'll be able to help you. I'll set up an appointment first thing in the morning."

"There's one more thing, Ari. We need to get Eli out of Vienna."

"My thoughts exactly." Shamron removed the telephone from the console and pressed a Speed-dial button. "This is Shamron. I need to speak to the prime minister."

YAD VASHEM, located atop Mount Herzel in the western portion of Jerusalem, is Israel's official memorial to the six million who perished in the Shoah. It is also the world's foremost center for Holocaust research and documentation. The library contains more than one hundred thousand volumes, the largest and most complete collection of Holocaust literature in the world. Stored in the archives are more than fifty-eight million pages of original documents, including thousands of personal testimonies, written, dictated, or videotaped by survivors of the Shoah in Israel and around the world.

Moshe Rivlin was expecting him. A rotund, bearded academic, he spoke Hebrew with a pronounced Brooklyn accent. His special area of expertise resided not with the victims of the Shoah but with its perpetrators—the Germans who served the Nazi death machine and the thousands of non-German helpers who willingly and enthusiastically took part in the destruction of Europe's Jews. He served as a paid consultant for the U.S. Justice Department's Office of Special Investigations, compiling documentary evidence against accused Nazi war criminals and scouring Israel for living witnesses. When he was not searching the archives of Yad Vashem, Rivlin could usually be found among the survivors, looking for someone who remembered.

Rivlin led Gabriel inside the archives building and into the main reading room. It was a surprisingly cramped space, brightly lit by large floor-to-ceiling windows overlooking the hills of west Jerusalem. A pair of scholars sat hunched over open books; another stared transfixed into the screen of a microfilm reader. When Gabriel suggested something a bit more private, Rivlin led him into a small side room and closed the thick glass door. The version of events Gabriel provided was well sanitized, but thorough enough so that nothing important was lost in translation. He showed Rivlin all the material he had gathered in Austria: the Staatsarchiv file, the photograph, the wristwatch, and the ring. When Gabriel pointed out the inscription on the inside of the band, Rivlin read it and looked up sharply.

"Amazing," he whispered.

"What does it mean?"

"I have to gather some documents from the archives." Rivlin stood. "It's going to take a little time."

"How long?"

The archivist shrugged. "An hour, maybe a little less. Have you ever been to the memorials?"

"Not since I was a schoolboy."

"Take a walk." Rivlin patted Gabriel's shoulder. "Come back in an hour."

GABRIEL WALKED ALONG a pine-shaded footpath and descended the stone passage into the darkness of Children's Memorial. Five candles, reflected infinitely by mirrors, created the illusion of a galaxy of stars, while a recorded voice read the names of the dead.

He emerged back into the brilliant sunlight and walked to the Hall of Remembrance, where he stood motionless before the eternal flame, flickering amid black basalt engraved with some of history's most infamous names: Treblinka, Sobibor, Majdanek, Bergen-Belsen, Chelmo, Auschwitz. . . .

In the Hall of Names, there were no flames or statues, just countless file folders filled with Pages of Testimony, each bearing the story of a martyr: name, place and date of birth, name of parents, place of residence, profession, place of death. A gentle woman named Shoshanna searched the computer database and located the Pages of Testimony for Gabriel's grandparents, Viktor and Sarah Frankel. She printed them out and handed them sadly over to Gabriel. At the bottom of each page was the name of the person who had supplied the information: Irene Allon, Gabriel's mother.

He paid a small surcharge for the printouts, two shekels for each, and walked next door to the Yad Vashem Art Museum, home of the largest collection of Holocaust art in the world. As he roamed the galleries, he found it nearly impossible to fathom the undying human spirit that managed to produce *art* under conditions of starvation, slavery, and unimaginable brutality. Suddenly, his own work seemed trivial and utterly without meaning. *What did dead saints in a museum of a church have to do with anything?* Mario Delvecchio, arrogant, egotistical Mario Delvecchio, seemed entirely irrelevant.

In the final room was a special exhibit of children's art. One image seized him like a choke hold, a charcoal sketch of an androgynous child, cowering before the gigantic figure of an SS officer.

He glanced at his watch. An hour had passed. He left the art museum and hurried back to the archives to hear the results of Moshe Rivlin's search.

HE FOUND RIVLIN pacing anxiously in the sandstone forecourt of the archives building. Rivlin seized Gabriel by the arm and led him inside to the small room where they had met an hour before. Two thick files awaited them. Rivlin opened the first and handed Gabriel a photograph: Ludwig Vogel, in the uniform of an SS Sturmbannführer.

"It's Radek," Rivlin whispered, unable to contain his excitement. "I think you may have actually found Erich *Radek*!"

13

VIENNA

HERR KONRAD BECKER, of Becker & Puhl, Talstrasse 26, Zurich, arrived in Vienna that same morning. He cleared passport control with no delay and made his way to the arrivals hall, where he located the uniformed driver clutching a cardboard sign that read HERR BAUER. The client insisted on the added precaution. Becker did not like the client—nor was he under any illusions about the source of the account—but such was the nature of private Swiss banking, and Herr Konrad Becker was a true believer. If capitalism were a religion, Becker would be a leader of an extremist sect. In Becker's learned opinion, man possessed the divine right to make money unfettered by government regulation and to conceal it wherever and however he pleased. Avoidance of taxation was not a choice but a moral duty. Inside the secretive world of Zurich banking, he was known for absolute discretion. It was the reason Konrad Becker had been entrusted with the account in the first place.

Twenty minutes later, the car drew to a stop in front of a graystone mansion in the First District. On Becker's instructions, the driver tapped the horn twice and, after a brief delay, the metal gate swung slowly open. As the car pulled into the drive, a man stepped out of the front entrance and descended the short flight of steps. He was in his late forties, with the build and swagger of a downhill racer. His name was Klaus Halder.

Halder opened the car door and led Becker into the entrance hall. As usual, he asked the banker to open his briefcase for inspection. Then it was the rather degrading Leonardo pose, arms and legs spread wide, for a thorough going over with a handheld magnetometer.

Finally he was escorted into the drawing room, a formal Viennese parlor, large and rectangular, with walls of rich yellow, and crown molding painted the color of clotted cream. The furniture was Baroque and covered in rich brocade. An ormolu clock ticked softly on the mantel. Each piece of furniture, each lamp and decorative object, seemed to complement its neighbor and the room as a whole. It was the room of a man who clearly possessed money and taste in equal amounts.

Herr Vogel, the client, was seated beneath a portrait that appeared, in the opinion of Herr Becker, to have been painted by Lucas Cranach the Elder. He rose slowly and extended his hand. They were a mismatched pair: Vogel, tall and Germanic, with his bright blue eyes and white hair; Becker, short and bald with a cosmopolitan assurance born of the varied nature of his clientele. Vogel released the banker's hand and gestured toward an empty chair. Becker sat down and produced a leather-bound ledger from his attaché case. The client nodded gravely. He was never one for small talk.

"As of this morning," Becker said, "the total value of the account stands at two and a half billion dollars. Roughly one billion of that is cash, equally divided between dollars and euros. The rest of the money is invested—the usual fare, securities and bonds, along with a substantial amount of real estate. In preparation for the liquidation and dispersal of the account, we are in the process of selling off the real estate holdings. Given the state of the global economy, it's taking longer than we had hoped."

"When will that process be complete?"

"Our target date is the end of the month. Even if we should fall short of our goal, dispersal of the monies will commence immediately upon receipt of the letter from the chancellor's office. The instructions are very specific on this point. The letter must be hand-delivered to my office in Zurich, not more than one week after the chancellor is sworn in. It must be on the official stationery of the chancellery and above the chancellor's signature."

"I can assure you the chancellor's letter will be forthcoming."

"In anticipation of Herr Metzler's victory, I've begun the difficult task of tracking down all those who are due payment. As you know, they are scattered from Europe to the Middle East, to South America and the United States. I've also had contact with the head of the Vatican Bank. As you might expect, given the current financial state of the Holy See, he was very pleased to take my call."

"And why not? A quarter of a billion dollars is a great deal of money."

From the banker, a vigilant smile. "Yes, but not even the Holy Father will know the true source of the money. As far as the Vatican is concerned, it is from a wealthy donor who wishes to remain anonymous."

"And then there's your share," said Vogel.

"The *bank's* share is one hundred million dollars, payable upon dispersal of all the funds."

"One hundred million dollars, plus all the transaction fees you've collected over the years and the percentage you take from the annual profit. The account has made you an extremely wealthy man."

"Your comrades provided generously for those who assisted them in this endeavor." The banker closed the ledger with a muffled thump. Then he folded his hands and stared at them thoughtfully for a moment before speaking. "But I'm afraid there have been some unexpected . . . *complications.*"

"What sort of complications?"

"It seems that several of those who were to receive money have died recently under mysterious circumstances. The latest was the Syrian. He was murdered in a gentlemen's club in Istanbul, in the arms of a Russian prostitute. The girl was murdered, too. A terrible scene."

Vogel shook his head sadly. "The Syrian would have been advised to avoid such places."

"Of course, as the bearer of the account number and password, you will maintain control of any funds that cannot be dispersed. That is what the instructions stipulate."

"How fortunate for me."

"Let us hope that the Holy Father does not suffer a similar accident." The banker removed his eyeglasses and inspected the lenses for impurities. "I feel compelled to remind you, Herr Vogel, that I am the only person with the authority to disperse the funds. In the event of my death, authority would pass to my partner, Herr Puhl. Should I die under violent or mysterious circumstances, the account will remain frozen until the circumstances of my death are determined. If the circumstances cannot be determined, the account will be rendered dormant. And you know what happens to dormant accounts in Switzerland."

"Eventually, they become the property of the bank itself."

"That's correct. Oh, I suppose you could mount a court challenge, but that would raise a number of embarrassing questions about the provenance of the money—questions that the Swiss banking industry, and the government, would rather not have aired in public. As you might imagine, such an inquiry would be uncomfortable for all involved."

"Then for my sake, please take care, Herr Becker. Your continued good health and safety are of the utmost importance to me."

"I'm so pleased to hear that. I look forward to receiving the chancellor's letter."

The banker returned the account ledger to his attaché case and closed the lid.

"I'm sorry, but there is one more formality that slipped my mind. When discussing the account, it's necessary for you to tell me the account number. For the record, Herr Vogel, will you recite it for me now?"

"Yes, of course." Then, with Germanic precision: "Six, two, nine, seven, four, three, five."

"And the password?"

"One, zero, zero, five."

"Thank you, Herr Vogel."

TEN MINUTES LATER, Becker's car stopped outside the Ambassador Hotel. "Wait here," the banker said to the driver. "I won't be more than a few minutes."

He crossed the lobby and rode the elevator to the fourth floor. A tall American in a wrinkled blazer and striped tie admitted him into Room 417. He offered Becker a drink, which the banker refused, then a cigarette, which he also declined. Becker never touched tobacco. Maybe he would start.

The American held out his hand toward the briefcase. Becker handed it over. The American lifted the lid and pried loose the false leather lining, exposing the microcassette recorder. Then he removed the tape and placed it into a small playback machine. He pressed REWIND, then PLAY. The sound quality was remarkable.

"For the record, Herr Vogel, will you recite it for me now?"

"Yes, of course. Six, two, nine, seven, four, three, five."

"And the password?"

"One, zero, zero, five."

"Thank you, Herr Vogel."

STOP.

The American looked up and smiled. The banker looked as though he had just been caught betraying his wife with her best friend.

"You've done very well, Herr Becker. We're grateful."

"I've just committed more violations of the Swiss banking secrecy laws than I can count."

"True, but they're shitty laws. And besides, you still get a hundred million dollars. *And* your bank."

"But it's not my bank any longer, is it? It's *your* bank now."

The American sat back and folded his arms. He didn't insult Becker with a denial.

14

JERUSALEM

GABRIEL HAD NO idea who Erich Radek was. Rivlin told him.

Erich Wilhelm Radek had been born in 1917 in the village of Alberndorf, thirty miles north of Vienna. The son of a police officer, Radek had attended a local gymnasium and showed a marked aptitude for mathematics and physics. He won a scholarship to attend the University of Vienna, where he studied engineering and architecture. According to university records, Radek was a gifted student who received high marks. He was also active in right-wing Catholic politics.

In 1937, he applied for membership in the Nazi Party. He was accepted and assigned the party number 57984567. Radek also became affiliated with the Austrian Legion, an illegal Nazi paramilitary organization. In March 1938, at the time of the Anschluss, he applied to join the SS. Blond and blue-eyed, with a lean athletic build, Radek was declared "pure Nordic" by the SS Racial Commission and, after a painstaking check of his ancestry, was deemed to be free of Jewish and other non-Aryan blood and accepted into the elite brotherhood.

"This is a copy of Radek's party file and the questionnaires he filled out at the time of his application. It comes from the Berlin Documentation Center, the largest repository of Nazi and SS files in the world." Rivlin held up two photographs, one a straight-on shot, the other a profile. "These are his official SS photographs. Looks like our man, doesn't it?"

Gabriel nodded. Rivlin returned the photographs to the file and continued his history lesson:

By November of 1938, Radek had forsaken his studies and was working at the Central Office for Jewish Emigration, the Nazi institution that waged a campaign of terror and economic deprivation against Austria's Jews designed to compel them to leave the country "voluntarily." Radek made a favorable impression on the head of the Central Office, who was none other than Adolf Eichmann. When Radek expressed a desire to go to Berlin, Eichmann agreed to help. Besides, Eichmann was ably assisted in Vienna by a young Austrian Nazi named Aloïs Brunner, who would eventually be implicated in the deportations and murders of 128,000 Jews from Greece, France, Romania, and Hungary. In May 1939, on Eichmann's recommendation, Radek was transferred to the Reich Security Main Office in Berlin, where he was assigned to the *Sicherheitsdienst*, the Nazi security service known as the SD. He soon found himself working directly for the SD's notorious chief, Reinhard Heydrich.

In June 1941, Hitler launched Operation Barbarossa, the invasion of the Soviet Union. Erich Radek was given command of SD operations in what became known as the Reichskommissariat Ukraine, a large swatch of the Ukraine that included the regions of Volhynia, Zhitomir, Kiev, Nikolayev, Tauria, and Dnepropetrovsk. Radek's responsibilities included field security and antipartisan operations. He also created the collaborationist Ukrainian Auxiliary Police and controlled their activities.

During preparations for Barbarossa, Hitler had secretly ordered Heinrich Himmler to exterminate the Jews of the Soviet Union. As the Wehrmacht rolled across Soviet territory, four Einsatzgruppen mobile killing units followed closely behind. Jews were rounded up and transported to isolated sites—usually located near antitank ditches, abandoned quarries, or deep ravines—where they were murdered by machine-gun fire and hastily buried in mass graves.

"Erich Radek was well aware of the activities of the Einsatzgruppen units in the Reichskommissariat," Rivlin said. "It was, after all, his turf. And he was no bureaucratic desk murderer. By all accounts, Radek actually enjoyed watching Jews being murdered by the thousands. But his most significant contribution to the Shoah still lay ahead."

"What was that?"

"You have the answer to that question in your pocket. It's engraved on the inside of that ring you took from the house in Upper Austria."

Gabriel dug the ring from his pocket and read the inscription: *1005, well done, Heinrich.*

"I suspect that *Heinrich* is none other than Heinrich Müller, the chief of the Gestapo. But for our purposes, the most important information contained in the inscription are those four numbers at the beginning: one, zero, zero, five."

"What do they mean?"

Rivlin opened the second file. It was labeled: AKTION 1005.

IT BEGAN, oddly enough, with a complaint from the neighbors.

Early in 1942, spring runoff exposed a series of mass graves in the Warthegau district of western Poland along the Ner River. Thousands of corpses floated to the surface, and a horrible stench spread for miles around the site. A German living nearby sent an anonymous letter to the Foreign Office in Berlin complaining about the situation. Alarm bells sounded. The graves contained the remains of thousands of Jews murdered by the mobile gas vans then being used at the Chelmno extermination camp. The Final Solution, Nazi Germany's most closely guarded secret, was in danger of being exposed by snowmelt.

The first reports of the mass killings of Jews had already begun reaching the outside world, thanks to a Soviet diplomatic cable that alerted the Allies to the horrors being carried out by German forces on Polish and Soviet soil. Martin Luther, who handled "Jewish affairs" on behalf of the German Foreign Office, knew that the exposed graves near Chelmno represented a serious threat to the secrecy of the Final Solution. He forwarded a copy of the anonymous letter to Heinrich Müller of the Gestapo and requested immediate action.

Rivlin had a copy of Müller's response to Martin Luther. He laid it on the table, turned it so Gabriel could see, and pointed at the relevant passage:

> The anonymous letter sent to the Foreign Office concerning the apparent solution of the Jewish question in the Warthegau district, which was submitted by you to me on 6 February 1942, I immediately transmitted for proper treatment. The results will be forthcoming in due course. In a place where wood is chopped, splinters must fall, and there is no avoiding this.

Rivlin pointed to the citations in the upper left-hand corner of the memo: *IV B4 43/42 gRs [1005]*.

"Adolf Eichmann almost certainly received a copy of Müller's response to Martin Luther. You see, Eichmann's department of the Reich Security Main Office appears in the address line. The numbers '43/42' represent the date: the forty-third day of 1942, or February twenty-eighth. The initials *g-R-s* signify that the matter is *Geheime Reichssache,* a top-secret Reich matter. And here, in brackets at the end of the line, are the four numbers that would eventually be used as the code name for the top-secret *Aktion,* one, zero, zero, five."

Rivlin returned the memo to the file.

"Shortly after Müller sent that letter to Martin Luther, Erich Radek was relieved of his command in the Ukraine and transferred back to the Reich Security Main Office in Berlin. He was assigned to Eichmann's department and embarked on a period of intense study and planning. You see, concealing the greatest case of mass murder in history was no small undertaking. In June, he returned to the east, operating under Müller's direct authority, and went to work."

Radek established the headquarters of his *Sonderkommando* 1005 in the Polish city of Lodz, about fifty miles southeast of the Chelmno death camp. The exact address was *Geheime Reichssache* and unknown except to a few senior SS figures. All correspondence was routed through Eichmann's department in Berlin.

Radek settled on cremation as the most effective method of disposing of the bodies. Burning had been attempted before, usually with flamethrowers, but with unsatisfactory results. Radek put his engineering training to good use, devising a method of burning corpses two thousand at a time in towering aerodynamic pyres. Thick wooden beams, twenty-three to twenty-seven feet in length, were soaked in petrol and placed atop cement blocks. The corpses were layered between the beams—bodies, beams, bodies, beams, bodies. . . . Petrol-soaked kindling was placed at the base of the structure and set ablaze. When the fire died down, the charred bones would be crushed by heavy machinery and dispersed.

The dirty work was done by Jewish slave laborers. Radek organized the Jews into three teams, one team to open the burial pits, a second to carry the corpses from the pits to the pyre, and a third to sift the ashes for bones and valuables. At the conclusion of each operation, the terrain was leveled and replanted to conceal what had taken place there. Then the slaves were murdered and disposed of. In that way the secrecy of *Aktion* 1005 was preserved.

When work was completed at Chelmno, Radek and his *Sonderkommando* 1005 headed to Auschwitz to clean out the rapidly filling burial pits there. By the end of the summer of 1942, serious contamination and health problems had arisen at Belzec, Sobibor, and Treblinka. Wells near the camps, which supplied drinking water to guards and nearby Wehrmacht units, had been contaminated by the proximity of the mass graves. In some cases, the thin layer of covering soil had burst open, and noxious odors were spewing into the air. At Treblinka, the SS and Ukrainian murderers hadn't even bothered to bury all the bodies. On the day camp commandant Franz Stangl arrived to take up his post, it was possible to smell Treblinka from twenty miles away. Bodies littered the road to the camp, and piles of putrefying bodies greeted him on the rail platform. Stangl complained that he couldn't start work at Treblinka until someone cleaned up the mess. Radek ordered the burial pits to be opened and the bodies burned.

In the spring of 1943, the advance of the Red Army compelled Radek to turn his attention from the extermination camps of Poland to the killing sites farther east, in occupied Soviet territory. Soon he was back on his home turf in the Ukraine. Radek knew where the bodies were buried, quite literally, because two years earlier he had coordinated the operations of the Einsatzgruppen killing squads. In late summer, the *Sonderkom-*

mando 1005 moved from the Ukraine to Byelorussia, and by September, it was active in the Baltic states of Lithuania and Latvia, where entire Jewish populations had been wiped out.

Rivlin closed the file and pushed it away in disgust.

"We'll never know how many bodies Radek and his men disposed of. The crime was far too enormous to conceal completely, but *Aktion* 1005 managed to efface much of the evidence and make it virtually impossible after the war to arrive at an accurate estimate of the dead. So thorough was Radek's work that, in some cases, the Polish and Soviet commissions investigating the Shoah could find *no* traces of the mass graves. At Babi Yar, Radek's cleanup was so complete that, after the war, the Soviets were able to turn it into a park. And now, unfortunately, the lack of physical remains of the dead has given inspiration to the lunatic fringe who claim the Holocaust never happened. Radek's actions haunt us to this day."

Gabriel thought of the Pages of Testimony in the Hall of Names, the only gravestones for millions of victims.

"Max Klein swore that he saw Ludwig Vogel at Auschwitz in summer or early autumn of 1942," Gabriel said. "Based on what you've told me, that's entirely possible."

"Indeed, assuming, of course, that Vogel and Radek are in fact the same man. Radek's *Sonderkommando* 1005 was definitely active in Auschwitz in 1942. Whether Radek was there or not on a given day is probably impossible to prove."

"How much do we know about what happened to Radek after the war?"

"Not much, I'm afraid. He attempted to flee Berlin disguised as a Wehrmacht corporal. He was arrested on suspicion of being an SS man and was interned at the Mannheim POW camp. Sometime in early 1946, he escaped. After that, it's a mystery. It appears he managed to get out of Europe. There were alleged sightings in all the usual places—Syria, Egypt, Argentina, Paraguay—but nothing reliable. The Nazi hunters were after big fish like Eichmann, Bormann, Mengele, and Müller. Radek managed to fly below the radar. Besides, the secret of *Aktion* 1005 was so well kept that the subject barely arose at the Nuremberg trials. No one really knew much about it."

"Who ran Mannheim?"

"It was an American camp."

"Do we know how he managed to escape Europe?"

"No, but we should assume that he had help."

"The ODESSA?"

"It might have been the ODESSA, or one of the other secret Nazi aid networks." Rivlin hesitated, then said, "Or it might have been a highly public and ancient institution based in Rome that operated the most successful Ratline of the postwar period."

"The Vatican?"

Rivlin nodded. "The ODESSA couldn't hold a candle to the Vatican when it came to financing and running an escape route from Europe. Because Radek was an Austrian, he would almost certainly have been assisted by Bishop Hudal."

"Who's Hudal?"

"Aloïs Hudal was an Austrian native, an anti-Semite, and a fervent Nazi. He used his position as rector of the Pontificio

Santa Maria dell'Anima, the German seminary in Rome, to help hundreds of SS officers escape justice, including Franz Stangl, the commandant of Treblinka."

"What kind of assistance did he provide them?"

"For starters, a Red Cross passport in a new name and an entrance visa to a country far away. He also gave them a bit of pocket money and paid for their passage."

"Did he keep records?"

"Apparently so, but his papers are kept under lock and key at the Anima."

"I need everything you have on Bishop Aloïs Hudal."

"I'll assemble a file for you."

Gabriel picked up Radek's photograph and looked at it carefully. There was something familiar about the face. It had been clawing at him throughout Rivlin's briefing. Then he thought of the charcoal sketches he'd seen that morning at the Holocaust art museum, the child cowering before an SS monster, and he knew at once where he'd seen Radek's face before.

He stood suddenly, toppling his chair.

"What's wrong?" Rivlin asked.

"I know this man," Gabriel said, eyes on the photo.

"How?"

Gabriel ignored the question. "I need to borrow this," he said. Then, without waiting for Rivlin's answer, he slipped out the door and was gone.

15

JERUSALEM

IN THE OLD days he would have taken the fast road north through Ramallah, Nablus, and Jenin. Now, even a man with the survival skills of Gabriel would be foolhardy to attempt such a run without an armored car and battle escort. So he took the long way round, down the western slope of the Judean Mountains toward Tel Aviv, up the Coastal Plain to Hadera, then northeast, through the Mount Carmel ridge, to El Megiddo: Armageddon.

The valley opened before him, stretching from the Samarian

hills in the south to the slopes of the Galilee in the north, a green-brown patchwork of row crops, orchards, and forestlands planted by the earliest Jewish settlers in Mandate Palestine. He headed toward Nazareth, then east, to a small farming town on the edge of the Balfour Forest called Ramat David.

It took him a few minutes to find the address. The bungalow that had been built for the Allons had been torn down and replaced by a California-style sandstone rambler with a satellite dish on the roof and an American-made minivan in the front drive. As Gabriel looked on, a soldier stepped from the front door and walked briskly across the front lawn. Gabriel's memory flashed. He saw his father, making the same journey on a warm evening in June, and though he had not realized it then, it would be the last time Gabriel would ever see him alive.

He looked at the house next door. It was the house where Tziona had lived. The plastic toys littering the front lawn indicated that Tziona, unmarried and childless, did not live there anymore. Still, Israel was nothing if not an extended, quarrelsome family, and Gabriel was confident the new occupants could at least point him in the right direction.

He rang the bell. The plump young woman who spoke Russian-accented Hebrew did not disappoint him. Tziona was living up in Safed. The Russian woman had a forwarding address.

JEWS HAD BEEN living in the center of Safed since the days of antiquity. After the expulsion from Spain in 1492, the Ottoman Turks allowed many more Jews to settle there, and the city flourished as a center of Jewish mysticism, scholarship, and art. During the war of independence, Safed was on the verge of falling to superior Arab forces when the besieged community was reinforced by a platoon of Palmach fighters, who stole into the city after making a daring night crossing from their garrison on Mount Canaan. The leader of the Palmach unit negotiated an agreement with Safed's powerful rabbis to work over Passover to reinforce the city's fortifications. His name was Ari Shamron.

Tziona's apartment was in the Artists' Quarter, at the top of a flight of cobblestone steps. She was an enormous woman, draped in a white caftan, with wild gray hair and so many bracelets that she clanged and clattered when she threw her arms around Gabriel's neck. She drew him inside, into a space that was both a living room and potter's studio, and sat him down on the stone terrace to watch the sunset over the Galilee. The air smelled of burning lavender oil.

A plate of bread and hummus appeared, along with olives and a bottle of Golan wine. Gabriel relaxed instantly. Tziona Levin was the closest thing to a sibling he had. She had cared for him when his mother was working or was too sick from depression to get out of bed. Some nights he would climb out his window and steal next door into Tziona's bed. She would caress and hold him in a way his mother never could. When his father was killed in the June war, it was Tziona who wiped away his tears.

The rhythmic, hypnotic sound of *Ma'ariv* prayers floated up from a nearby synagogue. Tziona added more lavender oil to the lamp. She talked of the *matsav:* the situation. Of the fighting in the Territories and the terror in Tel Aviv and Jerusalem. Of friends lost to the *shaheed* and friends who had given up trying to find work in Israel and had moved to America instead.

Gabriel drank his wine and watched the fiery sun sink into the Galilee. He was listening to Tziona, but his thoughts were of his mother. It had been nearly twenty years since her death, and in the intervening time, he had found himself thinking of her less and less. Her face, as a young woman, was lost to him, stripped of pigment and abraded, like a canvas faded by time and exposure to corrosive elements. Only her death mask could he conjure. After the tortures of cancer, her emaciated features had settled into an expression of serenity, like a woman posing for a portrait. She seemed to welcome death. It had finally given her deliverance from the torments raging inside her memory.

Had she loved him? Yes, he thought now, but she had surrounded herself with walls and battlements that he could never scale. She was prone to melancholia and violent mood swings. She did not sleep well at night. She could not show pleasure on festive occasions and could not partake of rich food and drink. She wore a bandage always on her left arm, over the faded numbers tattooed into her skin. She referred to them as her mark of Jewish weakness, her emblem of Jewish shame.

Gabriel had taken up painting to be closer to her. She soon resented this as an unwarranted intrusion on her private world; then, when his talents matured and began to challenge hers, she begrudged his obvious gifts. Gabriel pushed her to new heights. Her pain, so visible in life, found expression in her work. Gabriel grew obsessed with the nightmarish imagery that flowed from her memory onto her canvases. He began to search for the source.

In school he had learned of a place called Birkenau. He asked her about the bandage she wore habitually on her left arm, about the long-sleeved blouses she wore, even in the furnace like heat of the Jezreel Valley. He asked what had happened to her during the war, what had happened to his grandparents. She refused at first, but finally, under his steady onslaught of questions, she relented. Her account was hurried and reluctant; Gabriel, even in youth, was able to detect the note of evasion and more than a trace of guilt. Yes, she had been in Birkenau. Her parents had been murdered there on the day they arrived. She had worked. She had survived. That was all. Gabriel, hungry for more details about his mother's experience, began to concoct all manner of scenarios to account for her survival. He too began to feel ashamed and guilty. Her affliction, like a hereditary disorder, was thus passed on to the next generation.

The matter was never discussed again. It was as if a steel door had swung shut, as if the Holocaust had never happened. She fell into a prolonged depression and was bedridden for many days. When finally she emerged, she retreated to her studio and began to paint. She worked relentlessly, day and night. Once Gabriel peered through the half-open door and found her sprawled on the floor, her hands stained by paint, trembling before a canvas. That canvas was the reason he had come to Safed to see Tziona.

The sun was gone. It had grown cold on the terrace. Tziona drew a shawl around her shoulders and asked Gabriel if he ever intended to come home. Gabriel mumbled something about needing to work, like Tziona's friends who had moved to America.

"And who are you working for these days?"

He didn't rise to the challenge. "I restore Old Master paintings. I need to be where the paintings are. In Venice."

"*Venice,*" she said derisively. "Venice is a museum." She raised her wineglass toward the Galilee. "This is real life. *This* is art. Enough of this restoration. You should be devoting all your time and energy to your own work."

"There's no such thing as my own work. That went out of me a long time ago. I'm one of the best art restorers in the world. That's good enough for me."

Tziona threw up her hands. Her bracelets clattered like wind chimes. "It's a lie. You're a lie. You're an artist, Gabriel. Come to Safed and find your art. Find *yourself.*"

Her prodding was making him uncomfortable. He might have told her there was now a woman involved, but that would have opened a whole new front that Gabriel was anxious to avoid. Instead, he allowed a silence to fall between them, which was filled by the consoling sound of *Ma'ariv.*

"What are you doing in Safed?" she finally asked. "I know you didn't come all the way up here for a lecture from your *Doda* Tziona."

He asked whether Tziona still had his mother's paintings and sketches.

"Of course, Gabriel. I've been keeping them all these years, waiting for you to come and claim them."

"I'm not ready to take them off your hands yet. I just need to see them."

She held a candle to his face. "You're hiding something from me, Gabriel. I'm the only person in the world who can tell when you're keeping secrets. It was always that way, especially when you were a boy."

Gabriel poured himself another glass of wine and told Tziona about Vienna.

SHE PULLED OPEN the door of the storeroom and yanked down on the drawstring of the overhead light. The closet was filled floor to ceiling with canvases and sketches. Gabriel began leafing through the work. He'd forgotten how gifted his mother was. He could see the influence of Beckmann, Picasso, Egon Schiele, and of course her father, Viktor Frankel. There were even variations on themes Gabriel had been exploring in his own work at the time. His mother had expanded on them, or, in some cases, utterly demolished them. She had been breathtakingly talented.

Tziona pushed him aside and came out with a stack of canvases and two large envelopes filled with sketches. Gabriel crouched on the stone floor and examined the works while Tziona looked on over his shoulder.

There were images of the camps. Children crowded into bunks. Women slaving over machinery in the factories. Bodies stacked like cordwood, waiting to be hurled into the fire. A family huddled together while the gas gathered round them.

The final canvas depicted a solitary figure, an SS man dressed head-to-toe in black. It was the painting he had seen that day in his mother's studio. While the other works were dark and abstract, here she strove for realism and revelation. Gabriel found himself marveling at her impeccable draftsmanship and brushwork before his eyes finally settled on the face of the subject. It belonged to Erich Radek.

TZIONA MADE a bed for Gabriel on the living room couch and told him the midrash of the broken vessel.

"Before God created the world, there was only God. When God decided to create the world, God pulled back in order to create a space for the world. It was in that space that the universe was formed. But now, in that space, there was no God. God created Divine Sparks, light, to be placed back into God's creation. When God created light, and placed light inside of Creation, special containers were prepared to hold it. But there was an accident. A cosmic accident. The containers broke. The universe became filled with sparks of God's divine light and shards of broken containers."

"It's a lovely story," Gabriel said, helping Tziona tuck the ends of a sheet beneath the couch cushions. "But what does it have to do with my mother?"

"The midrash teaches us that until the sparks of God's light are gathered together, the task of creation will not be complete. As Jews, this is our solemn duty. We call it *Tikkun Olam:* Repair of the World."

"I can restore many things, Tziona, but I'm afraid the world is too broad a canvas, with far too much damage."

"So start small."

"How?"

"Gather your mother's sparks, Gabriel. And punish the man who broke her vessel."

THE FOLLOWING MORNING, Gabriel slipped out of Tziona's apartment without waking her and crept down the cobblestone steps in the shadowless gray light of dawn with the portrait of Radek beneath his arm. An Orthodox Jew, on his way to morning prayer, thought him a madman and shook his fist in anger. Gabriel loaded the painting into the trunk of the car and headed out of Safed. A bloodred sunrise broke over the ridge. Below, on the valley floor, the Sea of Galilee turned to fire.

He stopped in Afula for breakfast and left a message on Moshe Rivlin's voice mail, warning him that he was coming back to Yad Vashem. It was late morning by the time he arrived. Rivlin was waiting for him. Gabriel showed him the canvas.

"Who painted it?"

"My mother."

"What was her name?"

"Irene Allon, but her German name was Frankel."

"Where was she?"

"The women's camp at Birkenau, from January 1943 until the end."

"The death march?"

Gabriel nodded. Rivlin seized Gabriel by the arm and said, "Come with me."

RIVLIN PLACED GABRIEL at a table in the main reading room of the archives and sat down before a computer terminal. He entered the words "Irene Allon" into the database and drummed his stubby fingers impatiently on the keyboard while waiting for a response. A few seconds later, he scribbled five numbers onto a piece of scratch paper and without a word to Gabriel disappeared through a doorway leading to the storerooms of the archives. Twenty minutes later, he returned and placed a document on the table. Behind a clear plastic cover were the words YAD VASHEM ARCHIVES in both Hebrew and English, along with a file number: 03/812. Gabriel carefully lifted the plastic cover and turned to the first page. The heading made him feel suddenly cold: THE TESTIMONY OF IRENE ALLON, DELIVERED MARCH 19, 1957. Rivlin placed a hand on his shoulder and slipped out of the room. Gabriel hesitated a moment, then looked down and began to read.

16

THE TESTIMONY OF IRENE ALLON: MARCH 19, 1957

I will not tell all the things I saw. I cannot. I owe this much to the dead. I will not tell you all the unspeakable cruelty we endured at the hands of the so-called master race, nor will I tell you the things that some of us did in order to survive just one more day. Only those who lived through it will ever understand what it was truly like, and I will not humiliate the dead one last time. I will only tell you the things that I did, and the things that were done to me. I spent two years in Auschwitz-Birkenau, two years to the very day, almost precisely two years to the hour. My name is Irene Allon. I used to be called Irene Frankel. This is what I witnessed in January 1945, on the death march from Birkenau.

To understand the misery of the death march, you must first know something of what came before. You've heard the story from others. Mine is not so different. Like all the others, we came by train. Ours set out from Berlin in the middle of the night. They told us we were going to the east, to work. We believed them. They told us it would be a proper carriage with seats. They assured us we would be given food and water. We believed them. My father, the painter Viktor Frankel, had packed a sketchpad and some pencils. He had been fired from his teaching position and his work had been declared "degenerate" by the Nazis. Most of his paintings had been seized and burned. He hoped the Nazis would allow him to resume his work in the east.

Of course, it was not a proper carriage with seats, and there was no food or water. I do not remember precisely how long the journey lasted. I lost count of how many times the sun rose and set, how many times we traveled in and out of the darkness. There was no toilet, only one bucket—one bucket for sixty of us. You can imagine the conditions we endured. You can imagine the unbearable smell. You can imagine the things some of us resorted to when our thirst pushed us over the edge of insanity. On the second day, an old woman standing next to me died. I closed her eyes and prayed for her. I watched my mother, Hannah Frankel, and waited for her to die, too. Nearly half our car was dead by the time the train finally screeched to a stop. Some prayed. Some actually thanked God the journey was finally over.

For ten years we had lived under Hitler's thumb. We had suffered the Nuremberg Laws. We had lived the nightmare of Kristallnacht. We had watched our synagogues burn. Even so, I was not prepared for the sight that greeted me when the bolts slid back and the doors were finally thrown open. I saw a towering, tapered redbrick chimney, belching thick smoke. Below the chimney was a building, aglow with a raging, leaping flame. There was a terrible smell on the air. We could not identify it. It lingers in my nostrils to this day. There was a sign over the rail platform. Auschwitz. I knew then that I had arrived in hell.

"Juden, raus, raus!" An SS man cracks a whip across my thigh. "Get out of the car, *Juden*." I jump onto the snow-covered platform. My legs, weak from many days of standing, buckle beneath me. The SS man cracks his whip again, this time across my shoulders. The pain is like nothing I have ever felt before. I get to my feet. Somehow, I manage not to cry out. I try to help my mother down from the car. The SS man pushes me away. My father jumps onto the platform and collapses. My mother too. Like me, they are whipped to their feet.

Men in striped pajamas clamber onto the train and start tossing out our luggage. I think, Who are these crazy people trying to steal the meager possessions they had permitted us to bring? They look like men from an insane asylum, shaved heads, sunken faces, rotten teeth. My father turns to an SS officer and says, "Look there, those people are taking our things. Stop them!" The SS officer calmly replies that our luggage is not being stolen, just removed for sorting. It would be sent along, once we'd been assigned housing. My father thanks the SS man.

With clubs and whips they separate us, men from women,

and instruct us to form neat rows of five. I did not know it then, but I will spend much of the next two years standing or marching in neat rows of five. I am able to maneuver myself next to my mother. I try to hold her hand. An SS man brings his club down on my arm, severing my grasp. I hear music. Somewhere, a chamber orchestra is playing Schubert.

At the head of the line is a table and a few SS officers. One in particular stands out. He has black hair and skin the color of alabaster. He wears a pleasant smile on his handsome face. His uniform is neatly pressed, his riding boots shine in the bright lights of the rail platform. Kid gloves cover his hands, spotless and white. He is whistling "The Blue Danube Waltz." To this day, I cannot bear to hear it. Later, I will learn his name. His name is Mengele, the chief doctor of Auschwitz. It is Mengele who decides who is capable of work and who will go immediately to the gas. Right and left, life and death.

My father steps forward. Mengele, whistling, glances at him, then says pleasantly, "To the left, please."

"I was assured I would be going to a family camp," my father says. "Will my wife be coming with me?"

"Is that what you wish?"

"Yes, of course."

"Which one is your wife?"

My father points to my mother. Mengele says, "You there, get out of line and join your husband on the left. Hurry, please, we haven't got all night."

I watch my parents walk away to the left, following the others. Old people and small children, that's who goes to the left. Young and healthy are being sent to the right. I step forward to face the beautiful man in his spotless uniform. He looks me up and down, seems pleased, and wordlessly points to the right.

"But my parents went to the left."

The Devil smiles. There is a gap between his two front teeth. "You'll be with them soon enough, but trust me, for now, it's better you go to the right."

He seems so kind, so pleasant. I believe him. I go to the right. I look over my shoulder for my parents, but they have been swallowed by the mass of filthy, exhausted humanity trudging quietly toward the gas in neat rows of five.

I cannot possibly tell you everything that took place during the next two years. Some of it I cannot remember. Some of it I have chosen to forget. There was a merciless rhythm to Birkenau, a monotonous cruelty that ran on a tight and efficient schedule. Death was constant, yet even death became monotonous.

We are shorn, not just our heads, but everywhere, our arms, our legs, even our pubic hair. They don't seem to care that the shears are cutting our skin. They don't seem to hear our screams. We are assigned a number and tattooed on our left arm, just below the elbow. I cease to be Irene Frankel. Now I am a tool of the Reich known as 29395. They spray us with disinfectant, they give us prison clothing made from heavy rough wool. Mine smells of sweat and blood. I try not to breathe too deeply. Our "shoes" are wooden blocks with leather straps. We cannot walk in them. Who could? We are given a metal bowl and are ordered to carry it at all times. Should we misplace our bowl, we are told we will be shot immediately. We believe them.

We are taken to a barracks not fit for animals. The women who await us are something less than human. They are starving, their stares are vacant, their movements slow and listless. I wonder how long it will be before I look like them. One of these half-humans points me toward an empty bunk. Five girls crowd onto a wooden shelf with only a bit of bug-infested straw for bedding. We introduce ourselves. Two are sisters, Roza and Regina. The others are called Lene and Rachel. We are all German. We have all lost our parents on the selection ramp. We form a new family that night. We hold each other and pray. None of us sleeps.

We are awakened at four o'clock the next morning. I will wake at four o'clock every morning for the next two years, except on those nights when they order a special nighttime roll call and make us stand at attention in the freezing yard for hours on end. We are divided into kommandos and sent out to work. Most days, we march out into the surrounding countryside to shovel and sift sand for construction or to work in the camp agricultural projects. Some days we build roads or move stone from place to place. Not a single day passes that I am not beaten: a blow with a club, a whip across my back, a kick in the ribs. The offense can be dropping a stone or resting too long on the handle of my shovel. The two winters are bitterly cold. They give us no extra clothing to protect us from the weather, even when we are working outside. The summers are miserably hot. We all contract malaria. The mosquitoes do not discriminate between German masters and Jewish slaves. Even Mengele comes down with malaria.

They do not give us enough food to survive, only enough so that we would starve slowly and still be of service to the Reich. I lose my period, then I lose my breasts. Before long, I too look like one of the half-humans I'd seen that first day in Birkenau. For breakfast, it's gray water they call "tea." For lunch, rancid soup, which we eat in the place where we are working. Sometimes, there might be a small morsel of meat. Some of the girls refuse to eat it because it is not kosher. I do not abide by the dietary laws while I am at Auschwitz-Birkenau. There is no God in the death camps, and I hate God for abandoning us to our fate. If there is meat in my bowl, I eat it. For supper, we are given bread. It is mostly sawdust. We learn to eat half the bread at night and save the rest for the morning so that we have something in our stomachs before we march to the fields to work. If you collapse at work, they beat you. If you cannot get up, they toss you onto the back of a flatbed and carry you to the gas.

This is our life in the women's camp of Birkenau. We wake. We remove the dead from their bunks, the lucky ones who perish peacefully in their sleep. We drink our gray tea. We go to roll call. We march out to work in neat rows of five. We eat our lunch. We are beaten. We come back to camp. We go to roll call. We eat our bread, we sleep and wait for it all to begin again. They make us work on Shabbat. On Sundays, their holy day, there is no work. Every third Sunday, they shave us. Everything runs on a schedule. Everything except the selections.

We learn to anticipate them. Like animals, our survival senses are highly tuned. The camp population is the most reliable warning sign. When the camp is too full, there will be a selection. There is never a warning. After roll call, we are ordered to line up on the Lagerstrasse to await our turn before Mengele and his selection team, to await our chance to prove we are still capable of work, still worthy of life.

The selections take an entire day. They give us no food and nothing to drink. Some never make it to the table where Mengele plays god. They are "selected" by the SS sadists long before. A brute named Taube enjoys making us do "exercises" while we wait so we will be strong for the selectors. He forces us to do push-ups, then orders us to put our faces in the mud and stay there. Taube has a special punishment for any girl who moves. He steps on her head with all his weight and crushes her skull.

Finally, we stand before our judge. He looks us up and down, takes note of our number. Open your mouth, Jew. Lift your arms. We try to look after our health in this cesspool, but it is impossible. A sore throat can mean a trip to the gas. Salves and ointments are too precious to waste on Jews, so a cut on the hand can mean the gas the next time Mengele is culling the population.

If we pass visual inspection, our judge has one final test. He points toward a ditch and says, "Jump, Jew." I stand before the ditch and gather my last reserves of strength. Land on the other side and I will live, at least until the next selection. Fall in, and I will be tossed onto the back of a flatbed and driven to the gas. The first time I go through this madness, I think: I am a German-Jewish girl from Berlin from a good family. My father was a renowned painter. Why am I jumping this trench? After that, I think of nothing but reaching the other side and landing on my feet.

Roza is the first of our new family to be selected. She has the misfortune of being very sick with malaria at the time of a big selection, and there is no way to conceal it from Mengele's expert eyes. Regina begs the Devil to take her too, so that her sister will not have to die alone in the gas. Mengele smiles, revealing his gapped teeth. "You'll go soon enough, but you can work a little longer first. Go to the right." For the only time in my life, I am glad not to have a sister.

Regina stops eating. She doesn't seem to notice when they

beat her at work. She has crossed over the line. She is already dead. At the next big selection, she waits patiently on the endless line. She endures Taube's "exercises" and keeps her face in the mud so he will not crush her skull. When finally she reaches the selection table, she flies at Mengele and tries to stab him through the eye with the handle of her spoon. An SS man shoots her in the stomach.

Mengele is clearly frightened. "Don't waste any gas on her! Throw her into the fire alive! Up the chimney with her!"

They toss Regina into a wheelbarrow. We watch her go and pray she dies before she reaches the crematorium.

In the autumn of 1944, we begin hearing the Russian guns. In September, the camp's air raid sirens sound for the first time. Three weeks later they sound again, and the camp's antiaircraft guns fire their first shots. That same day, the Sonderkommando at Crematorium IV revolt. They attack their SS guards with pickaxes and hammers and manage to set fire to their barracks and the crematoria before being machine-gunned. A week later, bombs fall into the camp itself. Our masters show signs of stress. They no longer look so invincible. Sometimes they even look a little frightened. This gives us a certain pleasure and a modicum of hope. The gassings stop. They still kill us, but they have to do it themselves. Selected prisoners are shot in the gas chambers or near Crematorium V. Soon they begin dismantling the crematoria. Our hope of survival increases.

The situation deteriorates throughout that autumn and winter. Food is in short supply. Each day, many women collapse and die of starvation and exhaustion. Typhus takes a terrible toll. In December, Allied bombs fall on the I.G. Farben synthetic fuel and rubber plant. A few days later, the Allies strike again, but this time several bombs fall on an SS sickbay barracks inside Birkenau. Five SS are killed. The guards grow more irritable, more unpredictable. I avoid them. I try to make myself invisible.

The New Year comes, 1944 turns to 1945. We can sense Auschwitz is dying. We pray it will be soon. We debate what to do. Should we wait for the Russians to free us? Should we try to escape? And if we manage to get across the wire? Where will we go? The Polish peasants hate us just as much as the Germans. We wait. What else can we do?

In mid-January, I smell smoke. I look out the barracks door. Bonfires are raging all over the camps. The smell is different. For the first time, they're not burning people. They're burning paper. They're burning the evidence of their crimes. The ash drifts over Birkenau like snowfall. I smile for the first time in two years.

On January 17, Mengele leaves. The end is near. Shortly after midnight, there is a roll call. We are told the entire Auschwitz camp is being evacuated. The Reich still requires our bodies. The healthy will evacuate on foot. The sick will stay behind to meet their fate. We fall into rank and march out in neat rows of five.

At one o'clock in the morning, I pass through the gates of hell for the last time, two years to the day after my arrival, almost two years to the hour. I am not free yet. I have one more test to endure.

The snowfall is heavy and relentless. In the distance we can hear the thunder of an artillery duel. We walk, a seemingly endless chain of half-humans, dressed in our striped rags and our clogs. The shooting is as relentless as the snow. We try to count the shots. One hundred . . . two hundred . . . three . . . four . . . five. . . . We stop counting after that. Each shot represents one more life extinguished, one more murder. We number several thousand when we set out. I fear we will all be dead before we reach our destination.

Lene walks on my left, Rachel on my right. We dare not stumble. Those who stumble are shot on the spot and thrown into a ditch. We dare not fall out of formation and lag behind. Those who do are shot, too. The road is littered with the dead. We step over them and pray we do not falter. We eat snow to quench our thirst. There is nothing we can do about the horrible cold. A woman takes pity on us and throws boiled potatoes. Those foolish enough to pick them up are shot dead.

We sleep in barns or in abandoned barracks. Those who cannot rise quickly enough when awakened are shot dead. My hunger seems to be eating a hole in my stomach. It is much worse than the hunger of Birkenau. Somehow, I summon the strength to keep placing one foot in front of the other. Yes, I want to survive, but it is also a matter of defiance. They want me to fall so they can shoot me. I want to witness the destruction of their thousand-year Reich. I want to rejoice in its death, just as the Germans rejoiced in ours. I think of Regina, flying at Mengele during the selection, trying to kill him with her spoon. Regina's courage gives me strength. Each step is rebellion.

On the third day, at nightfall, he comes for me. He is on horseback. We are sitting in the snow at the side of the road, resting. Lene is leaning on me. Her eyes are closed. I fear she is finished. Rachel presses snow to her lips to revive her. Rachel is the strongest. She had practically carried Lene all that afternoon.

He looks at me. He is a Sturmbannführer in the SS. After twelve years of living under the Nazis, I have learned to recognize their insignia. I try to make myself invisible. I turn my head and tend to Lene. He yanks on the reins of his horse and maneuvers himself into position so he can look at me some more. I wonder what he sees in me. Yes, I was a pretty girl once, but I am hideous now, exhausted, filthy, sick, a walking skeleton. I cannot bear my own smell. I know that if I interact with him, it will end badly. I put my head on my knees and feign sleep. He is too smart for that.

"You there," he calls.

I look up. The man on horseback is pointing directly at me.

"Yes, you. Get on your feet. Come with me."

I stand up. I am dead. I know it. Rachel knows it, too. I can see it in her eyes. She has no more tears to cry.

"Remember me," I whisper as I follow the man on horseback into the trees.

Thankfully, he does not ask me to walk far, just to a spot a few meters from the side of the road, where a large tree had fallen. He dismounts and tethers his horse. He sits down on the fallen tree and orders me to sit next to him. I hesitate. No SS man has ever asked such a thing. He pats the tree with the palm of his hand. I sit, but several inches farther away than he had commanded. I am afraid, but I am also humiliated by my smell. He slides closer. He stinks of alcohol. I'm done for. It's only a question of time.

I look straight ahead. He removes his gloves, then touches my face. In two years at Birkenau, no SS man had ever touched me. Why is this man, a Sturmbannführer, touching me now? I have endured many torments, but this is by far the worst. I look straight ahead. My flesh is ablaze.

"Such a shame," he says. "Were you very beautiful once?"

I can think of nothing to say. Two years at Birkenau has taught me that in situations like these, there is never a right answer. If I answer yes, he'll accuse me of Jewish arrogance and kill me. If I answer no, he'll kill me for lying.

"I'll share a secret with you. I've always been attracted to Jewesses. If you ask me, we should have killed the men and utilized the women for our own enjoyment. Did you have a child?"

I think of all the children I saw going to the gas at Birkenau. He demands a response by squeezing my face between his thumb and fingers. I close my eyes and try not to cry out. He repeats the question. I shake my head, and he releases his grip.

"If you're able to survive the next few hours, you might someday have a child. Will you tell this child about what happened to you during the war? Or will you be too ashamed?"

A child? How could a girl in my position ever contemplate giving birth to a child? I have spent the last two years simply trying to survive. A child is beyond my comprehension.

"Answer me, Jew!"

His voice is suddenly harsh. I feel the situation is about to spin out of control. He takes hold of my face again and turns it toward him. I try to look away, but he shakes me, compelling me to look into his eyes. I have no strength to resist. His face is instantly chiseled into my memory. So is the sound of his voice and his Austrian-accented German. I hear it still.

"What will you tell your child about the war?"

What does he want to hear? What does he want me to say?

He squeezes my face. "Speak, Jew! What will you tell your child about the war?"

"The truth, Herr Sturmbannführer. I'll tell my child the truth."

Where these words come from, I do not know. I only know that if I am to die, I will die with a modicum of dignity. I think again of Regina, flying at Mengele armed with a spoon.

He relaxes his grip. The first crisis seems to have passed. He exhales heavily, as if exhausted by his long day of work, then removes a flask from the pocket of his greatcoat and takes a long pull. Thankfully, he does not offer me any. He returns the flask to his pocket and lights a cigarette. He does not offer me a cigarette. I have tobacco and liquor, he is telling me. You have nothing.

"The truth? What is the truth, Jew, as you see it?"

"Birkenau is the truth, Herr Sturmbannführer."

"No, my dear, Birkenau is not the truth. Birkenau is a rumor. Birkenau is an invention by enemies of the Reich and Christianity. It is Stalinist, atheist propaganda."

"What about the gas chambers? The crematoria?"

"These things did not exist at Birkenau."

"I saw them, Herr Sturmbannführer. We all saw them."

"No one is going to believe such a thing. No one is going to believe it's possible to kill so many. Thousands? Surely, the death of thousands is possible. After all, this was war. Hundreds of thousands? Perhaps. But millions?" He draws on his cigarette. "To tell you the truth, I saw it with my own eyes, and even I cannot believe it."

A shot crackles through the forest, then another. Two more girls gone. The Sturmbannführer takes another long pull at his flask of liquor. Why is he drinking? Is he trying to keep warm? Or is he steeling himself before he kills me?

"I'm going to tell you what you're going to say about the

war. You're going to say that you were transferred to the east. That you had work. That you had plenty of food and proper medical care. That we treated you well and humanely."

"If that is the truth, Herr Sturmbannführer, then why am I a skeleton?"

He has no answer, except to draw his pistol and place it against my temple.

"Recite to me what happened to you during the war, Jew. You were transferred to the east. You had plenty of food and proper medical care. The gas chambers and the crematoria are Bolshevik-Jewish inventions. Say those words, Jew."

I know there is no escaping this situation with my life. Even if I say the words, I am dead. I will not say them. I will not give him the satisfaction. I close my eyes and wait for his bullet to carve a tunnel through my brain and release me from my torment.

He lowers the gun and calls out. Another SS man comes running. The Sturmbannführer orders him to stand guard over me. He leaves and walks back through the trees to the road. When he returns, he is accompanied by two women. One is Rachel. The other is Lene. He orders the SS man to leave, then places the gun to Lene's forehead. Lene looks directly into my eyes. Her life is in my hands.

"Say the words, Jew! You were transferred to the east. You had plenty of food and proper medical care. The gas chambers and the crematoria are Bolshevik-Jewish lies."

I cannot allow Lene to be killed by my silence. I open my mouth to speak, but before I can recite the words, Rachel shouts, "Don't say it, Irene. He's going to kill us anyway. Don't give him the pleasure."

The Sturmbannführer removes the gun from Lene's head and places it against Rachel's. "You say it, Jewish bitch."

Rachel looks him directly in the eye and remains silent.

The Sturmbannführer pulls his trigger, and Rachel falls dead into the snow. He places the gun against Lene's head, and once again commands me to speak. Lene slowly shakes her head. We say goodbye with our eyes. Another shot, and Lene falls next to Rachel.

It is my turn to die.

The Sturmbannführer points the gun at me. From the road comes the sound of shouting. *Raus! Raus!* The SS are prodding the girls to their feet. I know my walk is over. I know I am not leaving this place with my life. This is where I will fall, at the side of a Polish road, and here I will be buried, with no *mazevoth* to mark my grave.

"What will you tell your child about the war, Jew?"

"The truth, Herr Sturmbannführer. I'll tell my child the truth."

"No one will believe you." He holsters his pistol. "Your column is leaving. You should join them. You know what happens to those who fall behind."

He mounts his horse and jerks on the reins. I collapse in the snow next to the bodies of my two friends. I pray for them and beg their forgiveness. The end of the column passes by. I stagger out of the trees and fall into place. We walk that entire night, in neat rows of five. I shed tears of ice.

Five days after walking out of Birkenau, we come to a train station in the Silesian village of Wodzislaw. We are herded onto open coal cars and travel through the night, exposed to the vicious January weather. The Germans had no need to waste any more of their precious ammunition on us. The cold kills half of the girls on my car alone.

We arrive at a new camp, Ravensbrück, but there is not enough food for the new prisoners. After a few days, some of us move on, this time by flatbed truck. I end my odyssey in a camp in Neüstadt Glewe. On May 2, 1945, we wake to discover that our SS tormentors have fled the camp. Later that day, we are liberated by American and Russian soldiers.

It has been twelve years. Not a day passes that I don't see the faces of Rachel and Lene—and the face of the man who murdered them. Their deaths weigh heavily upon me. Had I recited the Sturmbannführer's words, perhaps they would be alive and I would be lying in an unmarked grave next to a Polish road, just another nameless victim. On the anniversary of their murders, I say mourner's Kaddish for them. I do this out of habit but not faith. I lost my faith in God in Birkenau.

My name is Irene Allon. I used to be called Irene Frankel. In the camp I was known as prisoner number 29395, and this is what I witnessed in January 1945, on the death march from Birkenau.

17

TIBERIAS, ISRAEL

IT WAS SHABBAT. Shamron ordered Gabriel to come to Tiberias for supper. As Gabriel drove slowly along the steeply sloped drive, he looked up at Shamron's terrace and saw gaslights dancing in the wind from the lake—and then he glimpsed Shamron, the eternal sentinel, pacing slowly amid the flames. Gilah, before serving them food, lit a pair of candles in the dining room and recited the blessing. Gabriel had been raised in a home without religion, but at that moment he thought the sight of Shamron's wife, her eyes closed, her hands drawing the candlelight toward her face, was the most beautiful he'd ever seen.

Shamron was withdrawn and preoccupied during the meal and in no mood for small talk. Even now he would not speak of his work in front of Gilah, not because he didn't trust her, but because he feared she would stop loving him if she knew all the things he had done. Gilah filled the long silences by talking about her daughter, who'd moved to New Zealand to get away from her father and was living with a man on a chicken farm. She knew Gabriel was somehow linked to the Office but suspected nothing of the true nature of his work. She thought him a clerk of some sort who spent a great deal of time abroad and enjoyed art.

She served them coffee and a tray of cookies and dried fruit, then cleared the table and saw to the dishes. Gabriel, over the sound of running water and clinking china emanating from the kitchen, brought Shamron up to date. They spoke in low voices, with the Shabbat candles flickering between them. Gabriel showed him the files on Erich Radek and *Aktion* 1005. Shamron held the photograph up to the candlelight and squinted, then pushed his reading glasses onto his bald head and settled his hard gaze on Gabriel once more.

"How much do you know about what happened to my mother during the war?"

Shamron's calculated look, delivered over the rim of a coffee cup, made it plain there was nothing he did not know about Gabriel's life, including what had happened to his mother during the war. "She was from Berlin," Shamron said. "She was deported to Auschwitz in January 1943 and spent two years in the women's camp at Birkenau. She left Birkenau on a death march. Unlike thousands of others, she managed to survive and was liberated by Russian and American troops at Neüstadt Glewe. Am I forgetting anything?"

"Something happened to her on the death march, something she would never discuss with me." Gabriel held up the photograph of Erich Radek. "When Rivlin showed me this at Yad Vashem, I knew I'd seen the face somewhere before. It took me awhile to remember, but finally I did. I saw it when I was a boy, on canvases in my mother's studio."

"Which is why you went to Safed, to see Tziona Levin."

"How do you know?"

Shamron sighed and sipped his coffee. Gabriel, unnerved, told Shamron about his second visit to Yad Vashem that morning. When he placed the pages of his mother's testimony on the table, Shamron's eyes remained fixed on Gabriel's face. And then Gabriel realized that Shamron had read it before. The *Memuneh* knew about his mother. The *Memuneh* knew everything.

"You were being considered for one of the most important assignments in the history of the Office," Shamron said. His voice contained no trace of remorse. "I needed to know everything I could about you. Your army psychological profile described you as a lone wolf, egotistical, with the emotional coldness of a natural killer. My first visit with you provided confirmation of this, though I also found you unbearably rude and clinically shy. I wanted to know why you were the way you were. I thought your mother might be a good place to start."

"So you looked up her testimony at Yad Vashem?"

He closed his eyes and nodded once.

"Why didn't you ever say anything to me?"

"It wasn't my place," Shamron said without sentiment. "Only your mother could tell you about such a thing. She obviously carried a terrible burden of guilt until the day she died. She didn't want you to know. She wasn't alone. There were many survivors, just like your mother, who could never bring themselves to truly confront their memories. In the years after the war, before you were born, it seemed as though a wall of silence had been erected in this country. *The Holocaust?* It was discussed endlessly. But those who actually endured it tried desperately to bury their memories and move on. It was another form of survival. Unfortunately, their pain was passed on to the next generation, the sons and daughters of the survivors. People like Gabriel Allon."

Shamron was interrupted by Gilah, who poked her head into the room and asked whether they needed more coffee. Shamron held up his hand. Gilah understood they were discussing work and slipped back into the kitchen. Shamron folded his arms on the table and leaned forward.

"Surely you must have suspected she'd given testimony. Why didn't that natural curiosity of yours lead you to Yad Vashem to have a look for yourself?" Shamron, greeted only by Gabriel's silence, answered the question for himself. "Because, like all children of survivors, you were always careful not to disturb your mother's fragile emotional state. You were afraid that if you pushed too hard, you might send her into a depression from which she might never return?" He paused. "Or was it because you feared what you might find? Were you actually *afraid* to know the truth?"

Gabriel looked up sharply but made no reply. Shamron contemplated his coffee for a moment before speaking again.

"To be honest with you, Gabriel, when I read your mother's testimony, I knew that you were perfect. You work for me because of her. She was incapable of loving you completely. How could she? She was afraid she would lose you. Everyone she'd ever loved had been taken from her. She lost her parents on the selection ramp and the girls she befriended at Birkenau were taken from her because she would not say the words an SS Sturmbannführer wanted her to say."

"I would have understood if she'd tried to tell me."

Shamron slowly shook his head. "No, Gabriel, no one can truly understand. The guilt, the shame. Your mother managed to find her way in this world after the war, but in many ways her life ended that night on the side of a Polish road." He brought his palm down on the table, hard enough to rattle the remaining dishes. "So what do we do? Do we wallow in self-pity, or do we keep working and see if this man is truly Erich Radek?"

"I think you know the answer to that."

"Does Moshe Rivlin think it's possible Radek was involved in the evacuation of Auschwitz?"

Gabriel nodded. "By January 1945, the work of *Aktion* 1005 was largely complete, since all of the conquered territory in the east had been overrun by the Soviets. It's possible he went to Auschwitz to demolish the gas chambers and crematoria and prepare the remaining prisoners for evacuation. They were, after all, witnesses to the crime."

"Do we know how this piece of filth managed to get out of Europe after the war?"

Gabriel told him Rivlin's theory, that Radek, because he was an Austrian Catholic, had availed himself of the services of Bishop Aloïs Hudal in Rome.

"So why don't we follow the trail," Shamron said, "and see if it leads back to Austria again?"

"My thoughts exactly. I thought I'd start in Rome. I want to have a look at Hudal's papers."

"So would a lot of other people."

"But they don't have the private number of the man who lives on the top floor of the Apostolic Palace."

Shamron shrugged. "This is true."

"I need a clean passport."

"Not a problem. I have a very good Canadian passport you can use. How's your French these days?"

"Pas mal, mais je dois pratiquer l'accent d'un Quebecois."

"Sometimes, you frighten even me."

"That's saying something."

"You'll spend the night here and leave for Rome tomorrow. I'll take you to Lod. On the way we'll stop at the American Embassy and have a chat with the local head of station."

"About what?"

"According to the file from the Staatsarchiv, Vogel worked for the Americans in Austria during the occupation period. I've asked our friends in Langley to have a look through their files and see if Vogel's name pops up. It's a long shot, but maybe we'll get lucky."

Gabriel looked down at his mother's testimony: *I will not tell all the things I saw. I cannot. I owe this much to the dead. . . .*

"Your mother was a very brave woman, Gabriel. That's why I chose you. I knew you came from excellent stock."

"She was much braver than I am."

"Yes," Shamron agreed. "She was braver than all of us."

BRUCE CRAWFORD'S REAL occupation was one of the worst-kept secrets in Israel. The tall, patrician American was the chief of the CIA's Tel Aviv station. Declared to both the Israeli government and the Palestinian Authority, he often served as a conduit between the two warring sides. Seldom was the night Crawford's telephone didn't ring at some hideous hour. He was tired, and looked it.

He greeted Shamron just inside the gates of the embassy on Haraykon Street and escorted him into the building. Crawford's office was large and, for Shamron's taste, overdecorated. It seemed the office of a corporate vice president rather than the lair of a spy, but then that was the American way. Shamron sank into a leather chair and accepted a glass of chilled water with lemon from a secretary. He considered lighting a Turkish cigarette, then noticed the NO SMOKING sign prominently displayed on the front of Crawford's desk.

Crawford seemed in no hurry to get down to the matter at hand. Shamron had expected this. There was an unwritten rule among spies: when one asks a friend for a favor, one must be prepared to sing for his supper. Shamron, because he was technically out of the game, could offer nothing tangible, only the advice and the wisdom of a man who had made many mistakes.

Finally, after an hour, Crawford said, "About that Vogel thing."

The American's voice trailed off. Shamron, taking note of the tinge of failure in Crawford's voice, leaned forward in his chair expectantly. Crawford played for time by removing a paper clip from his special magnetic dispenser and industriously straightening it.

"We had a look through our own files," Crawford said, his gaze downward at his work. "We even sent a team out to Maryland to dig through the Archives annex. I'm afraid we struck out."

"Struck out?" Shamron considered the use of American sports colloquialisms inappropriate for a business so vital as espionage. Agents, in Shamron's world, did not strike out, fumble the ball, or make slam dunks. There was only success or failure, and the price of failure, in a neighborhood like the Middle East, was usually blood. "What does this mean *exactly*?"

"It means," Crawford said pedantically, "that our search produced nothing. I'm sorry, Ari, but sometimes, that's the way it goes with these things."

He held up his straightened paper clip and examined it carefully, as though proud of his accomplishment.

GABRIEL WAS WAITING IN the back seat of Shamron's Peugeot.

"How did it go?"

Shamron lit a cigarette and answered the question.

"Do you believe him?"

"You know, if he'd told me that they'd found a routine personnel file or a security clearance background report, I might have believed him. But *nothing*? Who does he think he's talking to? I'm insulted, Gabriel. I truly am."

"You think the Americans know something about Vogel?"

"Bruce Crawford just confirmed it for us." Shamron glared at his stainless-steel watch. "Damn! It took him an hour to screw up the nerve to lie to me, and now you're going to miss your flight."

Gabriel looked down at the telephone in the console. "Do it," he murmured. "I dare you."

Shamron snatched up the telephone and dialed. "This is Shamron," he snapped. "There's an El Al flight leaving Lod for Rome in thirty minutes. It has just developed a mechanical problem that will require a one-hour delay in its departure. Understand?"

TWO HOURS LATER, Bruce Crawford's telephone purred. He brought the receiver to his ear. He recognized the voice. It was the surveillance man he had assigned to follow Shamron. A dangerous game, following the former chief of the Office on his own soil, but Crawford was under orders.

"After he left the embassy, he went to Lod."

"What was he doing at the airport?"

"Dropping off a passenger."

"Did you recognize him?"

The surveillance man indicated that he did. Without mentioning the passenger's name, he managed to communicate the fact that the man in question was a noteworthy Office agent, recently active in a central European city.

"Are you sure it was him?"

"No doubt about it."

"Where was he going?"

Crawford, after hearing the answer, severed the connection. A moment later, he was seated before his computer, punching out a secure cable to Headquarters. The text was direct and terse, just the way the addressee liked it.

Elijah is heading to Rome. Arrives tonight on El Al flight from Tel Aviv.

18

ROME

GABRIEL WANTED TO meet the man from the Vatican someplace other than his office on the top floor of the Apostolic Palace. They settled on Piperno, an old restaurant on a quiet square near the Tiber, a few streets over from the ancient Jewish ghetto. It was the kind of December afternoon only Rome can produce, and Gabriel, arriving first, arranged for a table outside in a patch of warm, brilliant sunlight.

A few minutes later, a priest entered the square and headed

toward the restaurant at a determined clip. He was tall and lean and as handsome as an Italian movie idol. The cut of his black clerical suit and Roman collar suggested that, while chaste, he was not without personal or professional vanity. And with good reason. Monsignor Luigi Donati, the private secretary of His Holiness Pope Paul VII, was arguably the second most powerful man in the Roman Catholic Church.

There was a cold toughness about Luigi Donati that made it difficult for Gabriel to imagine him baptizing babies or anointing the sick in some dusty Umbrian hilltown. His dark eyes radiated a fierce and uncompromising intelligence, while the stubborn set of his jaw revealed that he was a dangerous man to cross. Gabriel knew this to be true from direct experience. A year earlier, a case had led him to the Vatican and into Donati's capable hands, and together they had destroyed a grave threat to Pope Paul VII. Luigi Donati owed Gabriel a favor. Gabriel was betting Donati was a man who paid his debts.

Donati was also a man who enjoyed nothing more than whiling away a few hours at a sunlit Roman café. His demanding style had won him few friends within the Curia and, like his boss, he slipped the bonds of the Vatican whenever possible. He had seized Gabriel's invitation to lunch like a drowning man grasping hold of a lifeline. Gabriel had the distinct impression Luigi Donati was desperately lonely. Sometimes Gabriel wondered whether Donati regretted the life he had chosen.

The priest lit a cigarette with a gold executive lighter. "How's business?"

"I'm working on another Bellini. The Crisostomo altarpiece."

"Yes, I know."

Before becoming Pope Paul VII, Cardinal Pietro Lucchesi had been the Patriarch of Venice. Luigi Donati had been at his side. His ties to Venice remained strong. There was little that happened in his old archdiocese that he didn't know about.

"I trust Francesco Tiepolo is treating you well."

"Of course."

"And Chiara?"

"She's well, thank you."

"Have you two given any consideration to . . . *formalizing* your relationship?"

"It's complicated, Luigi."

"Yes, but what isn't?"

"You know, for a moment there, you actually sounded like a priest."

Donati threw back his head and laughed. He was beginning to relax. "The Holy Father sends his regards. He says he's sorry he couldn't join us. Piperno is one of his favorite restaurants. He recommends we start with the *filetti di baccalà.* He swears it's the best in Rome."

"Does infallibility extend to appetizer recommendations?"

"The pope is infallible only when he is acting as the supreme teacher on matters of faith and morals. I'm afraid the doctrine does not extend to fried codfish fillets. But he does have a good deal of worldly experience in these matters. If I were you, I'd go with the *filetti.*"

The white-jacketed waiter appeared. Donati handled the ordering. The frascati began to flow, and Donati's mood mellowed like the soft afternoon. He spent the next few minutes regaling Gabriel with Curial gossip and stories of backstairs brawling and court intrigue. It was all very familiar. The Vatican was not much different from the Office. Finally, Gabriel guided the conversation round to the topic that had brought him and Donati together in the first place: the role of the Roman Catholic Church in the Holocaust.

"How is the work of the Historical Commission coming along?"

"As well as can be expected. We're supplying the documents from the Secret Archives, they're doing the analysis with as little interference from us as possible. A preliminary report of their findings is due in six months. After that, they'll start work on a multivolume history."

"Any indications which way the preliminary report is going to go?"

"As I said, we're trying to let the historians work with as little interference from the Apostolic Palace as possible."

Gabriel shot Donati a dubious glance over his wineglass. Were it not for the monsignor's clerical suit and Roman collar, Gabriel would have assumed he was a professional spy. The notion that Donati didn't have at least two sources on the Commission staff was insulting. Gabriel, between sips of frascati, expressed this view to Monsignor Donati. The priest confessed.

"All right, let's say I'm not completely in the dark about the Commission."

"And?"

"The report will take into account the enormous pressures on

Pius, yet even so, I'm afraid it will not paint a terribly flattering portrait of his actions, or of the actions of the national churches in central and eastern Europe."

"You sound nervous, Luigi."

The priest leaned forward over the table and seemed to choose his next words carefully. "We've opened a Pandora's box, my friend. Once a process like this is set in motion, it's impossible to predict where it will end and what other areas of the Church it will affect. The liberals have seized on the Holy Father's actions and are pleading for more: a Third Vatican Council. The reactionaries are screaming heresy."

"Anything serious?"

Again, the monsignor took an inordinate amount of time before answering. "We're picking up some very serious rumblings from some reactionaries in the Languedoc region of France—the sort of reactionaries who believe Vatican Two was the work of the Devil and that every pope since John the Twenty-third has been a heretic."

"I thought the Church was full of people like that. I had my own run-in with a friendly group of prelates and laymen called Crux Vera."

Donati smiled. "I'm afraid this group is cut from the same cloth, except, unlike Crux Vera, they don't have a power base inside the Curia. They're outsiders, barbarians beating at the gates. The Holy Father has very little control over them, and things have started to heat up."

"Let me know if there's something I can do to help."

"Be careful, my friend, I might take you up on that."

The *filetti di baccalà* arrived. Donati squeezed lemon juice over the plate and popped one of the fillets into his mouth whole. He washed down the fish with a drink of the frascati and sat back in his chair, his handsome features set in a look of pure contentment. For a priest working in the Vatican, the temporal world offered few delights more tantalizing than lunch on a sun-washed Roman square. He started on another *filetti* and asked Gabriel what he was doing in town.

"I guess you could say I'm working on a matter related to the work of the Historical Commission."

"How so?"

"I have reason to suspect that shortly after the war ended, the Vatican may have helped a wanted SS man named Erich Radek escape Europe."

Donati stopped chewing, his face suddenly serious. "Be careful with the terms you use and the assumptions you make, my friend. It's quite possible this man Radek received help from someone in Rome, but it wasn't the *Vatican.*"

"We believe it was Bishop Hudal of the Anima."

The tension in Donati's face eased. "Unfortunately, the good bishop did help a number of fugitive Nazis. There's no denying that. What makes you think he helped this man Radek?"

"An educated guess. Radek was an Austrian Catholic. Hudal was rector of the German seminary in Rome and father confessor to the German and Austrian community. If Radek came to Rome looking for help, it would make sense that he would turn to Bishop Hudal."

Donati nodded in agreement. "I can't argue with that. Bishop Hudal was interested in protecting fellow citizens of his country from what he believed were the vengeful intentions of the Allied victors. But that doesn't mean that he knew that Erich Radek was a war criminal. How could he know? Italy was flooded with millions of displaced persons after the war, all of them looking for help. If Radek came to Hudal and told him a sad story, it's likely he would have been given sanctuary and help."

"Shouldn't Hudal have asked a man like Radek why he was on the run?"

"Perhaps he should have, but you're being naïve if you assume that Radek would have answered the question truthfully. He would have lied, and Bishop Hudal would have had no way of knowing otherwise."

"A man doesn't become a fugitive for no reason, Luigi, and the Holocaust was no secret. Bishop Hudal should have realized he was helping war criminals escape justice."

Donati waited to respond while the waiter served a pasta course. "What you have to understand is that there were many organizations and individuals at the time who assisted refugees, inside the Church and outside. Hudal wasn't the only one."

"Where did he get the money to finance his operation?"

"He claimed it all came from the accounts of the seminary."

"And you believe that? Each SS man Hudal assisted required pocket money, passage on a ship, a visa, and a new life in a foreign country, not to mention the cost of providing them sanctuary in Rome until they could be shipped off. Hudal is thought to have helped *hundreds* of SS men in this way. That's a lot of money, Luigi—hundreds of thousands of dollars. I find it hard to believe the Anima had that kind of spare change lying around."

"So you're assuming he was given money by someone," Donati said, expertly twirling pasta onto his fork. "Someone like the Holy Father, for example."

"The money had to come from somewhere."

Donati laid down his fork and folded his hands thoughtfully. "There is evidence to suggest that Bishop Hudal *did* receive Vatican funds to pay for his refugee work."

"They weren't *refugees,* Luigi. Not all of them, at least. Many of them were guilty of unspeakable crimes. Are you telling me Pius had no idea Hudal was helping wanted war criminals escape justice?"

"Let us just say that, based on available documentary evidence and testimony from surviving witnesses, it would be very difficult to prove that charge."

"I didn't know you'd studied Canon Law, Luigi." Gabriel repeated the question, slowly, with a prosecutorial emphasis on the relevant words. "Did the pope know Hudal was helping war criminals escape justice?"

"His Holiness opposed the Nuremberg trials because he believed they would only serve to further weaken Germany and embolden the Communists. He also believed the Allies were after vengeance and not justice. It's quite possible the Holy Father knew Bishop Hudal was helping Nazis and that he approved. Proving that contention, however, is another matter." Donati aimed the prongs of his fork at Gabriel's untouched pasta. "You'd better eat that before it gets cold."

"I'm afraid I've lost my appetite."

Donati plunged his fork into Gabriel's pasta. "So what is this Radek fellow alleged to have done?"

Gabriel gave a brief synopsis of Sturmbannführer Erich

Radek's illustrious SS career, beginning with his work for Adolf Eichmann's Jewish emigration office in Vienna and concluding with his command of *Aktion* 1005. By the end of Gabriel's account, Donati too had lost his appetite.

"Did they really believe they could conceal all the evidence of a crime so enormous?"

"I'm not sure whether they believed it was possible, but they succeeded to a large extent. Because of men like Erich Radek, we'll never know how many people *really* perished in the Shoah."

Donati contemplated his wine. "What is it you want to know about Bishop Hudal's assistance to Radek?"

"We can assume that Radek needed a passport. For that, Hudal would have turned to the International Red Cross. I want to know the name on that passport. Radek would have also needed a place to go. He would have needed a visa." Gabriel paused. "I know it was a long time ago, but Bishop Hudal kept records, didn't he?"

Donati nodded slowly. "Bishop Hudal's private papers are stored in the archives of the Anima. As you might expect, they are sealed."

"If there's anyone in Rome who can unseal them, it's you, Luigi."

"We can't just barge into the Anima and ask to see the bishop's papers. The current rector is Bishop Theodor Drexler, and he's no fool. We'd need an excuse—a cover story, as they say in your trade."

"We have one."

"What's that?"

"The Historical Commission."

"You're suggesting we tell the rector that the Commission has requested Hudal's papers?"

"Precisely."

"And if he balks?"

"Then we name-drop."

"And who are you supposed to be?"

Gabriel reached into his pocket and produced a laminated identification card, complete with a photograph.

"Shmuel Rubenstein, professor of comparative religion at Hebrew University in Jerusalem." Donati handed the card back to Gabriel and shook his head. "Theodor Drexler is a brilliant theologian. He'll want to engage you in a discussion—perhaps something about the common roots of the two oldest religions in the western world. I'm quite confident you'll fall flat on your face, and the bishop will see right through your little act."

"It's your job to see that doesn't happen."

"You overestimate my abilities, Gabriel."

"Call him, Luigi. I need to see Bishop Hudal's papers."

"I will, but first, I have one question. *Why?*"

Donati, having heard Gabriel's answer, dialed a number on his mobile phone and asked to be connected to the Anima.

19

ROME

THE CHURCH OF Santa Maria dell'Anima is located in the Centro Storico, just to the west of the Piazza Navona. For four centuries it has been the German church in Rome. Pope Adrian VI, the son of a German shipbuilder from Utrecht and the last non-Italian pope before John Paul II, is buried in a magnificent tomb just to the right of the main altar. The adjoining seminary is reached from the Via della Pace, and it was there, standing in the cold shadows of the forecourt, where they met Bishop Theodor Drexler the following morning.

Monsignor Donati greeted him in excellent Italian-accented German, and introduced Gabriel as "the learned Professor Shmuel Rubenstein from Hebrew University." Drexler offered his hand at such an angle that for an instant Gabriel wasn't sure whether to shake it or kiss the ring. After a brief hesitation, he gave it one firm pump. The skin was as cool as church marble.

The rector led them upstairs into an unpresumptuous book-lined office. His soutane rustled as he settled himself into the largest chair in the seating area. His large gold pectoral cross shone in the sunlight slanting through the tall windows. He was short and well-fed, nearing seventy, with a gossamer halo of white hair and extremely pink cheeks. The corners of his tiny mouth were lifted perpetually into a smile—even now, when he was clearly unhappy—and his pale blue eyes sparkled with a condescending intelligence. It was a face that could comfort the sick and put the fear of God into a sinner. Monsignor Donati had been right. Gabriel would have to watch his step.

Donati and the bishop spent a few minutes exchanging pleasantries about the Holy Father. The bishop informed Donati that he was praying for the pontiff's continued good health, while Donati announced that His Holiness was extraordinarily pleased with Bishop Drexler's work at the Anima. He referred to the bishop as "Your Grace" as many times as possible. By the end of the exchange, Drexler was so buttered up that Gabriel feared he might slide off his chair.

When Monsignor Donati finally got around to the purpose of

their visit to the Anima, Drexler's mood darkened swiftly, as if a cloud had passed before the sun, though his smile remained firmly in place.

"I fail to see how a polemical investigation into Bishop Hudal's work for German refugees after the war will aid the healing process between Roman Catholics and Jews." His voice was soft and dry, his German Viennese-accented. "A fair and balanced investigation of Bishop Hudal's activities would reveal that he helped a good many Jews as well."

Gabriel leaned forward. It was time for the learned professor from Hebrew University to insert himself into the conversation. "Are you saying, Your Grace, that Bishop Hudal hid Jews during the Rome roundup?"

"Before the roundup and after. There were many Jews living within the walls of the Anima. Baptized Jews, of course."

"And those who weren't baptized?"

"They couldn't be hidden *here*. It wouldn't have been proper. They were sent elsewhere."

"Forgive me, Your Grace, but how exactly did one tell a baptized Jew from an ordinary Jew?"

Monsignor Donati crossed his leg and carefully smoothed the crease in his trouser leg, a signal to cease and desist in this line of inquiry. The bishop drew a breath and answered the question.

"They might have been asked a few simple questions about matters of faith and Catholic doctrine. They might have been asked to recite the Lord's Prayer or the Ave Maria. Usually, it became apparent quite quickly who was telling the truth and who was lying in order to gain sanctuary at the seminary."

A knock at the door accomplished Luigi Donati's goal of ending the exchange. A young novice entered the room, bearing a silver tray. He poured tea for Donati and Gabriel. The bishop drank hot water with a thin slice of lemon.

When the boy was gone, Drexler said, "But I'm sure you're not interested in Bishop Hudal's efforts to shield Jews from the Nazis, are you, Professor Rubenstein? You're interested in the assistance he gave to German officers after the war?"

"Not German officers. Wanted SS war criminals."

"He didn't *know* they were criminals."

"I'm afraid that defense strains credulity, Your Grace. Bishop Hudal was a committed anti-Semite and a supporter of Hitler's regime. Does it not make sense that he would willingly help Austrians and Germans after the war, regardless of the crimes they had committed?"

"His opposition to Jews was theological in nature, not social. As for his support of the Nazi regime, I offer no defense. Bishop Hudal is condemned by his own words and his writings."

"And his *car*," Gabriel added, putting Moshe Rivlin's file to good use. "Bishop Hudal flew the flag of the united Reich on his official limousine. He made no secret of where his sympathies lay."

Drexler sipped his lemon water and turned his frozen gaze on Donati. "Like many others within the Church, I had my concerns about the Holy Father's Historical Commission, but I kept those concerns to myself out of respect for His Holiness. Now it seems the Anima is under the microscope. I must draw the line. I will not have the reputation of this great institution dragged through the mud of history."

Monsignor Donati pondered his trouser leg for a moment,

then looked up. Beneath the calm exterior, the papal secretary was seething at the rector's insolence. The bishop had pushed; Donati was about to push back. Somehow, he managed to keep his voice to a chapel murmur.

"Regardless of your concerns on this matter, Your Grace, it is the Holy Father's desire that Professor Rubenstein be granted access to Bishop Hudal's papers."

A deep silence hung over the room. Drexler fingered his pectoral cross, looking for an escape hatch. There was none; resignation was the only honorable course of action. He toppled his king.

"I have no wish to defy His Holiness on this matter. You leave me no choice but to cooperate, Monsignor Donati."

"The Holy Father will not forget this, Bishop Drexler."

"Nor will I, Monsignor."

Donati flashed an ironic smile. "It is my understanding that the bishop's personal papers remain here at the Anima."

"That is correct. They are stored in our archives. It will take a few days to locate them all and organize them in such a fashion that they can be read and understood by a scholar such as Professor Rubenstein."

"How very thoughtful of you, Your Grace," said Monsignor Donati, "but we'd like to see them *now*."

HE LED THEM down a corkscrew stone stairway with timeworn steps as slick as ice. At the bottom of the stairs was a heavy oaken door with cast-iron fittings. It had been built to withstand a battering ram but had proved no match for a clever priest from the Veneto and the "professor" from Jerusalem.

Bishop Drexler unlocked the door and shouldered it open. He groped in the gloom for a moment, then threw a switch that made a sharp, echoing snap. A series of overhead lights burst on, buzzing and humming with the sudden flow of electricity, revealing a long subterranean passage with an arched stone ceiling. The bishop silently beckoned them forward.

The vault had been constructed for smaller men. The diminutive bishop could walk the passage without altering his posture. Gabriel had only to dip his head to avoid the light fixtures, but Monsignor Donati, at well over six feet in height, was forced to bend at the waist like a man suffering from severe curvature of the spine. Here resided the institutional memory of the Anima and its seminary, four centuries' worth of baptismal records, marriage certificates, and death notices. The records of the priests who'd served here and the students who'd studied within the walls of the seminary. Some of it was stored in pinewood file cabinets, some in crates or ordinary cardboard boxes. The newer additions were kept in modern plastic file containers. The smell of damp and rot was pervasive, and from somewhere in the walls came the trickle of water. Gabriel, who knew something about the detrimental effects of cold and damp on paper, rapidly lost hope of finding Bishop Hudal's papers intact.

Near the end of the passage was a small, catacomblike side chamber. It contained several large trunks, secured by rusted padlocks. Bishop Drexler had a ring of keys. He inserted one into the first lock. It wouldn't turn. He struggled for a moment before finally surrendering the keys to "Professor Rubenstein," who had no problem prying open the old locks.

Bishop Drexler hovered over them for a moment and offered to assist in their search of the documents. Monsignor Donati patted him on the shoulder and said they could manage on their own. The portly little bishop made the sign of the cross and padded slowly away down the arched passageway.

IT WAS GABRIEL, two hours later, who found it. Erich Radek had arrived at the Anima on March 3, 1948. On May 24, the Pontifical Commission for Assistance, the Vatican's refugee aid organization, issued Radek a Vatican identity document bearing the number 9645/99 and the alias "Otto Krebs." That same day, with the help of Bishop Hudal, Otto Krebs used his Vatican identification to secure a Red Cross passport. The following week he was issued an entrance visa by the Arab Republic of Syria. He purchased second-class passage with money given to him by Bishop Hudal and set sail from the Italian port of Genoa in late June. Krebs had five hundred dollars in his pocket. A receipt for the money, bearing Radek's signature, had been kept by Bishop Hudal. The final item in the Radek file was a letter, with a Syrian stamp and Damascus postmark, that thanked Bishop Hudal and the Holy Father for their assistance and promised that one day the debt would be repaid. It was signed Otto Krebs.

20

ROME

BISHOP DREXLER LISTENED to the audio tape one final time, then dialed the number in Vienna.

"I'm afraid we have a problem."

"What sort of problem?"

Drexler told the man in Vienna about the visitors to the Anima that morning: Monsignor Donati and a professor from Hebrew University in Jerusalem.

"What did he call himself?"

"Rubenstein. He claimed to be a researcher on the Historical Commission."

"He was no professor."

"I gathered that, but I was hardly in a position to challenge his bona fides. Monsignor Donati is a very powerful man within the Vatican. There's only one more powerful, and that's the heretic he works for."

"What were they after?"

"Documentation about assistance given by Bishop Hudal to a certain Austrian refugee after the war."

There was a long silence before the man posed his next question.

"Have they left the Anima?"

"Yes, about an hour ago."

"Why did you wait so long to telephone?"

"I was hoping to provide you with some information that can be put to good use."

"Can you?"

"Yes, I believe so."

"Tell me."

"The professor is staying at the Cardinal Hotel on the Via Giulia. And he's checked into the room in the name of René Duran, with a Canadian passport."

"I NEED YOU to collect a clock in Rome."

"When?"

"Immediately."

"Where is it?"

"There's a man staying at the Cardinal Hotel on the Via Giulia. He's registered in the name of René Duran, but sometimes he's using the name of Rubenstein."

"How long will he be in Rome?"

"Unclear, which is why you need to leave now. There's an Alitalia flight leaving for Rome in two hours. A business-class seat has been reserved in your name."

"If I'm traveling by plane, I won't be able to bring the tools I'll need for the repair. I'll need someone to supply me those tools in Rome."

"I have just the man." He recited a telephone number, which the Clockmaker committed to memory. "He's very professional, and most important, extremely discreet. I wouldn't send you to him otherwise."

"Do you have a photograph of this gentleman, Duran?"

"It will be coming over your fax machine momentarily."

The Clockmaker hung up the phone and switched off the lights at the front of the shop. Then he entered his workshop and opened a storage cabinet. Inside was a small overnight bag, containing a change of clothing and a shaving kit. The fax machine rang. The Clockmaker pulled on an overcoat and hat while the face of a dead man eased slowly into view.

21

ROME

GABRIEL TOOK A table inside Doney the following morning to have coffee. Thirty minutes later, a man entered and went to the bar. He had hair like steel wool and acne scars on his broad cheeks. His clothing was expensive but worn poorly. He drank two espressos rapid-fire and kept a cigarette working the entire time. Gabriel looked down at his *La Repùbblica* and smiled. Shimon Pazner had been the Office man in Rome for five years, yet he had still not lost the prickly exterior of a Negev settler.

Pazner paid his bill and went to the toilet. When he came out, he was wearing sunglasses, the signal that the meeting was on. He headed through the revolving door, paused on the pavement of the Via Veneto, then turned right and started walking. Gabriel left money on the table and followed after him.

Pazner crossed the Corso d'Italia and entered the Villa Borghese. Gabriel walked a little farther along the Corso and entered the park at another point. He met Pazner on a tree-lined footpath and introduced himself as René Duran of Montreal. Together they walked toward the Galleria. Pazner lit a cigarette.

"Word is you had a close shave up in the Alps the other night."

"Word travels fast."

"The Office is like a Jewish sewing circle, you know that. But you have a bigger problem. Lev has laid down the law. Allon is off limits. Allon, should he come knocking on your door, is to be turned into the street." Pazner spat at the ground. "I'm here out of loyalty to the Old Man, not you, Monsieur *Duran*. This had better be good."

They sat on a marble bench in the forecourt of the Galleria Borghese and looked in opposite directions for watchers. Gabriel told Pazner about the SS man Erich Radek who had traveled to Syria under the name Otto Krebs. "He didn't go to Damascus to study ancient civilization," Gabriel said. "The Syrians let him in for a reason. If he was close to the regime, he might show up in the files."

"So you want me to run a search and see if we can place him in Damascus?"

"Exactly."

"And how do you expect me to request this search without Lev and Security finding out about it?"

Gabriel looked at Pazner as though he found the question insulting. Pazner retreated. "All right, let's say I might have a girl in Research who can have a quiet look through the files for me."

"Just one girl?"

Pazner shrugged and tossed his cigarette onto the gravel. "It still sounds like a long shot to me. Where are you staying?"

Gabriel told him.

"There's a place called La Carbonara on the northern end of the Campo dei Fiori, near the fountain."

"I know it."

"Be there at eight o'clock. There'll be a reservation in the name of Brunacci for eight-thirty. If the reservation is for two, that means the search was a bust. If it's for four, come to the Piazza Farnese."

ON THE OPPOSITE bank of the Tiber, in a small square a few paces from St. Anne's Gate, the Clockmaker sat in the cold late-afternoon shadows of an outdoor café, sipping a cappuccino. At the next table, a pair of cassocked priests were engaged in animated conversation. The Clockmaker, though he spoke no Italian, assumed them to be Vatican bureaucrats. A hunchbacked alley cat threaded its way between the Clockmaker's legs and begged for food. He trapped the animal between his ankles and squeezed, slowly increasing the pressure, until the cat let out a strangled howl and scampered off. The priests looked up in disapproval; the Clockmaker left money on the table and walked away. Imagine, cats in a café. He was looking forward to concluding his business in Rome and returning to Vienna.

He walked along the edge of Bernini's Colonnade and paused for a moment to peer down the broad Via della Conciliazione toward the Tiber. A tourist thrust a disposable camera toward him and pleaded, in some indecipherable Slavic tongue, for the Clockmaker to take his photograph in front of the Vatican. The Austrian wordlessly pointed toward his wristwatch, indicating he was late for an appointment, and turned his back.

He crossed the large, thunderous square just beyond the opening in the Colonnade. It bore the name of a recent pope. The Clockmaker, though he had few interests other than antique timepieces, knew that this pope was a rather controversial figure. He found the intrigue swirling about him rather amusing. So he did not help the Jews during the war. Since when was it the responsibility of a pope to help Jews? They were, after all, the enemies of the Church.

He turned into the mouth of a narrow street, leading away from the Vatican toward the base of the Janiculum park. It was deeply shadowed and lined with ocher-colored buildings covered in a powdery dust. The Clockmaker walked the cracked pavement, searching for the address he had been given earlier that morning by telephone. He found it but hesitated before entering. Stenciled to the sooty glass were the words ARTICOLI RELIGIOSI. Below, in smaller letters, was the name GIUSEPPE MONDIANI. The Clockmaker consulted the slip of paper where he'd written the address. Number 22 Via Borgo Santo Spirito. He had come to the right place.

He pressed his face to the glass. The room on the other side was cluttered with crucifixes, statues of the Virgin, carvings of long-dead saints, rosaries and medals, all certified to have been blessed by *il papa* himself. Everything seemed to be covered with the fine, flourlike dust from the street. The Clockmaker, though raised in a strict Austrian Catholic home, wondered what would compel a person to pray to a statue. He no longer believed in God or the Church, nor did he believe in fate, divine intervention, an afterlife, or luck. He believed men controlled the course of their lives, just as the wheelwork of a clock controlled the motion of the hands.

He pulled open the door and stepped inside, accompanied by the tinkle of a small bell. A man emerged from a back room, dressed in an amber V-neck sweater with no shirt beneath and tan gabardine trousers that no longer held a crease. His limp, thinning hair was waxed into place atop his head. The Clockmaker, even from several paces away, could smell his offensive aftershave. He wondered whether the men of the Vatican knew their blessed religious articles were being dispensed by so reprehensible a creature.

"May I help you?"

"I'm looking for Signor Mondiani."

He nodded, as if to say the Clockmaker had found the man he was looking for. A watery smile revealed the fact that he was missing several teeth. "You must be the gentleman from Vienna," Mondiani said. "I recognize your voice."

He held out his hand. It was spongy and damp, just as the Clockmaker had feared. Mondiani locked the front door and hung a sign in the window that said, in English and Italian, that the shop was now closed. Then he led the Clockmaker through a doorway and up a flight of rickety wooden stairs. At the top of the steps was a small office. The curtains were drawn, and the air was heavy with the scent of a woman's perfume. And something else, sour and ammonia-like. Mondiani gestured toward the couch. The Clockmaker looked down; an image flashed before his eyes. He remained standing. Mondiani shrugged his narrow shoulders—*As you wish.*

The Italian sat down at his desk, straightened some papers, and smoothed his hair. It was dyed an unnatural shade of orange-black. The Clockmaker, balding with a salt-and-pepper fringe, seemed to be making him more self-conscious than he already was.

"Your colleague from Vienna said you required a weapon." Mondiani pulled open a desk drawer, removed a dark item with a flat metallic finish, and laid it reverently on his coffee-stained desk blotter, as though it were a sacred relic. "I trust you'll find this satisfactory."

The Clockmaker held out his hand. Mondiani placed the weapon in his palm.

"As you can see, it's a Glock nine-millimeter. I trust you're familiar with the Glock. After all, it is an Austrian-made weapon."

The Clockmaker raised his eyes from the weapon. "Has this been blessed by the Holy Father, like the rest of your inventory?"

Mondiani, judging from his dark expression, did not find the remark humorous. He reached into the open drawer once again and produced a box of ammunition.

"Do you require a second cartridge?"

The Clockmaker did not intend to get into a gunfight, but still, one always felt better with a loaded spare cartridge in one's hip pocket. He nodded; a second appeared on the blotter.

The Clockmaker broke open the box of ammunition and began thumbing rounds into the cartridges. Mondiani asked whether he required a silencer. The Clockmaker, his gaze down, nodded in the affirmative.

"Unlike the weapon itself, this is not manufactured in Austria. It was made right here," Mondiani said with excessive pride. "In Italy. It is very effective. The gun will emit little more than a whisper when fired."

The Clockmaker held the silencer to his right eye and peered through the barrel. Satisfied with the craftsmanship, he placed it on the desk, next to the other things.

"Do you require anything else?"

The Clockmaker reminded Signor Mondiani that he had requested a motorbike.

"Ah yes, the *motorino,*" Mondiani said, holding a set of keys aloft. "It's parked outside the shop. There are two helmets, just as you requested, different colors. I chose black and red. I hope that's satisfactory."

The Clockmaker glanced at his watch. Mondiani took the hint and moved things along. On a steno pad, with a chewed pencil, he prepared the invoice.

"The weapon is clean and untraceable," he said, the pencil scratching across the paper. "I suggest you drop it into the Tiber when you're finished. The Polizia di Stato will never find it there."

"And the motorbike?"

Stolen, said Mondiani. "Leave it in a public place with the keys in the ignition—a busy piazza, for example. I'm sure that within a few minutes, it will find a new home."

Mondiani circled the final figure and turned the pad around so the Clockmaker could see. It was in euros, thank God. The Clockmaker, despite the fact he was a businessman himself, had always loathed making transactions in lire.

"Rather steep, is it not, Signore Mondiani?"

Mondiani shrugged and treated the Clockmaker to another hideous smile. The Clockmaker picked up the silencer and screwed it carefully into the end of the barrel. "This charge here," the Clockmaker said, tapping the steno pad with the forefinger of his free hand. "What is that for?"

"That is my brokerage fee." Mondiani managed to say this with a completely straight face.

"You've charged me three times as much for the Glock as I would pay in Austria. That, Signor Mondiani, is your brokerage fee."

Mondiani folded his arms defiantly. "It is the *Italian* way. Do you want your weapon or not?"

"Yes," said the Clockmaker, "but at a reasonable price."

"I'm afraid that's the going rate in Rome at the moment."

"For an Italian, or just for foreigners?"

"It might be better if you took your business elsewhere." Mondiani held out his hand. It was trembling. "Give me the gun, please, and see yourself out."

The Clockmaker sighed. Perhaps it was better this way. Signor Mondiani, despite the assurances of the man from Vienna, was hardly the type to inspire trust. The Clockmaker, in a swift movement, rammed a cartridge into the Glock and chambered the first round. Signor Mondiani's hands came up defensively. The shots pierced his palms before striking his face. The Clockmaker, as he slipped out of the office, realized that Mondiani had been honest about at least one thing. The gun, when fired, emitted little more than a whisper.

HE LET HIMSELF out of the shop and locked the door behind him. It was nearly dark now; the dome of the Basilica had receded into the blackening sky. He inserted the key into the ignition of the motorbike and started the engine. A moment later he was speeding down the Via della Conciliazione toward the mud-colored walls of the Castel San Angelo. He sped across the Tiber, then made his way through the narrow streets of Centro Storico, until he came to the Via Giulia.

He parked outside the Cardinal Hotel, removed his helmet, and went into the lobby, then turned to the right and entered a small, catacomblike bar with walls fashioned of ancient Roman granite. He ordered a Coke from the bartender—he was confident he could accomplish this feat without betraying his Austrian-German accent—and carried the drink to a small table adjacent to the passageway between the lobby and the bar. To pass the time, he snacked on pistachio nuts and leafed through a stack of Italian newspapers.

At seven-thirty a man stepped out of the elevator: short dark hair, gray at the temples, very green eyes. He left his room key at the front desk and went into the street.

The Clockmaker finished his Coke, then went outside. He

swung his leg over Signor Mondiani's *motorino* and started the engine. The black helmet was hanging by its strap from the handlebars. The Clockmaker removed the red helmet from the rear storage compartment and put it on, then placed the black one into the compartment and closed the lid.

He looked up and watched the figure of the green-eyed man retreating steadily into the darkness of the Via Giulia. Then he pulled back on the throttle and eased slowly after him.

22

ROME

THE RESERVATION AT La Carbonara was for four. Gabriel walked to the Piazza Farnese and found Pazner waiting near the French Embassy. They walked to Al Pompière and took a quiet table in the back. Pazner ordered red wine and polenta and handed Gabriel a plain envelope.

"It took some time," Pazner said, "but eventually they found a reference to Krebs in a report about a Nazi named Aloïs Brunner. Know much about Brunner?"

He was a top aide to Eichmann, Gabriel replied, a deportation expert, highly skilled in the art of herding Jews into ghettos and then to the gas chambers. He'd worked with Eichmann on the deportation of the Austrian Jews. Later in the war, he handled deportations in Salonika and Vichy France.

Pazner, clearly impressed, impaled a piece of polenta. "And after the war he escaped to Syria, where he lived under the name George Fischer and served as a consultant to the regime. For all intents and purposes, the modern Syrian intelligence and security services were built by Aloïs Brunner."

"Was Krebs working for him?"

"So it would seem. Open the envelope. And, by the way, be sure you treat that report with the respect it deserves. The man who filed it paid a very high price. Take a look at the agent's code name."

"MENASHE" WAS THE code name of a legendary Israeli spy named Eli Cohen. Born in Egypt in 1924, Cohen had emigrated to Israel in 1957 and immediately volunteered to work for Israeli intelligence. His psychological testing produced mixed results. The profilers found him highly intelligent and blessed with an extraordinary memory for detail. But they also discovered a dangerous streak of "exaggerated self-importance" and predicted Cohen would take unnecessary risks in the field.

Cohen's file gathered dust until 1960, when increasing tension along the Syrian border led the men of Israeli intelligence to decide they desperately needed a spy in Damascus. A long search of candidates produced no suitable prospects. Then the search was broadened to include those who had been rejected for other reasons. Cohen's file was opened once more, and before long, he found himself being prepared for an assignment that would ultimately end in his death.

After six months of intensive training, Cohen, posing as Kamal Amin Thabit, was sent to Argentina to construct his cover story: a successful Syrian businessman who had lived abroad his entire life and wanted only to move to his homeland. He ingratiated himself with the large Syrian expatriate community of Buenos Aires and developed many important friendships, including one with Major Amin al-Hafez, who would one day become the president of Syria.

In January 1962, Cohen moved to Damascus and opened an import-export business. Armed with introductions from the Syrian community in Buenos Aires, he quickly became a popular figure on the Damascus social and political scene, developing friendships with high-level members of the military and the ruling Ba'ath party. Syrian army officers took Cohen on tours of military facilities and even showed him the fortifications on the strategic Golan Heights. When Major al-Hafez became president, there was speculation that "Kamal Amin Thabit" might be in line for a cabinet post, perhaps even the Ministry of Defense.

Syrian intelligence had no idea that the affable Thabit was in reality an Israeli spy who was sending a steady stream of reports to his masters across the border. Urgent reports were sent via coded Morse radio transmissions. Longer and more detailed reports were written in invisible ink, hidden in crates of damascene furniture, and shipped to an Israeli front in Europe. Intelligence provided by Cohen gave Israeli military planners a remarkable window on the political and military situation in Damascus.

In the end, the warnings about Cohen's penchant for risk proved correct. He grew reckless in his use of the radio, transmitting at the same time each morning or sending multiple transmissions in a single day. He sent greetings to his family and bemoaned Israel's defeat in an international football match. The Syrian security forces, armed with the latest Soviet-made radio detection gear, starting looking for the Israeli spy in Damascus. They found him on January 18, 1965, bursting into his apartment while he was sending a message to his controllers in Israel. Cohen's hanging, in May 1965, was broadcast live on Syrian television.

Gabriel read the first report by the light of a flickering table candle. It had been sent through the European channel in May 1963. Contained within a detailed report on internal Ba'ath party politics and intrigue was a paragraph devoted to Aloïs Brunner:

> I met "Herr Fischer" at a cocktail party hosted by a senior figure in the Ba'ath party. Herr Fischer was not looking particularly well, having recently lost several fingers on one hand to a letter bomb in Cairo. He blamed the attempt on his life on vengeful Jewish filth in Tel Aviv. He claimed that the work he was doing in Egypt would more than settle his account with the Israeli agents who had tried to murder him. Herr Fischer was accompanied that evening by a man called Otto Krebs. I had never seen Krebs before. He was tall and blue-eyed, very Germanic in appearance, unlike Brunner. He drank whiskey heavily and seemed a vulnerable sort, a man who might be blackmailed or turned by some other method.

"That's it?" Gabriel asked. "One sighting at a cocktail party?"

"Apparently so, but don't be discouraged. Cohen gave you one more clue. Look at the next report."

Gabriel looked down and read it.

> I saw "Herr Fischer" last week at a reception at the Ministry of Defense. I asked him about his friend, Herr Krebs. I told him that Krebs and I had discussed a business venture and I was disappointed that I had not heard back from him. Fischer said that was not surprising, since Krebs had recently moved to Argentina.

Pazner poured Gabriel a glass of wine. "I hear Buenos Aires is lovely this time of year."

GABRIEL AND PAZNER separated in the Piazza Farnese, then Gabriel walked alone on the Via Giulia toward his hotel. The night had turned colder, and it was very dark in the street. The deep silence, combined with the rough paving stones beneath his feet, made it possible for him to imagine Rome as it had been a century and a half earlier, when the men of the Vatican still ruled supreme. He thought of Erich Radek, walking this very street, waiting for his passport and his ticket to freedom.

But was it really Radek who had come to Rome?

According to Bishop Hudal's files, Radek had come to the Anima in 1948 and had left soon after as Otto Krebs. Eli Cohen had placed "Krebs" in Damascus as late as 1963. Then Krebs reportedly moved on to Argentina. The facts had exposed a glaring and perhaps irreconcilable contradiction in the case against

Ludwig Vogel. According to the documents in the Staatsarchiv, Vogel was living in Austria by 1946, working for the American occupation authority. If that were true, then Vogel and Radek couldn't possibly be the same man. How then to explain Max Klein's belief that he had seen Vogel at Birkenau? The ring Gabriel had taken from Vogel's chalet in Upper Austria? *1005, well done, Heinrich*... The wristwatch? *To Erich, in adoration, Monica*... Had another man come to Rome in 1948 posing as Erich Radek? And if so, *why*?

Many questions, thought Gabriel, and only one possible trail to follow: *Fischer said that was not surprising, since Krebs had recently moved to Argentina.* Pazner was right. Gabriel had no choice but to continue the search in Argentina.

The heavy silence was shattered by the insectlike buzz of a *motorino*. Gabriel glanced over his shoulder as the bike rounded a corner and turned into the Via Giulia. Then it accelerated suddenly and sped directly toward him. Gabriel stopped walking and removed his hands from his coat pockets. He had a decision to make. Stand his ground like a normal Roman or turn and run? The decision was made for him, a few seconds later, when the helmeted rider reached into the front of his jacket and drew a silenced pistol.

GABRIEL LUNGED INTO a narrow street as the gun spit three tongues of fire. Three rounds struck the cornerstones of a building. Gabriel lowered his head and started to run.

The *motorino* was traveling too fast to make the turn. It skidded past the entrance of the street, then wobbled around in an awkward circle, allowing Gabriel a few critical seconds to put some distance between himself and his attacker. He turned right, onto a street that ran parallel to the Via Giulia, then made a sudden left. His plan was to head for the Corso Vittorio Emanuale II, one of Rome's largest thoroughfares. There would be traffic on the street and pedestrians on the pavements. On the Corso he could find a place to conceal himself.

The whine of the *motorino* grew louder. Gabriel glanced over his shoulder. The bike was still following him and closing the distance at an alarming rate. He threw himself into a headlong sprint, hands clawing at the air, breath harsh and ragged. The headlamp fell upon him. He saw his own shadow on the paving stones in front of him, a flailing madman.

A second bike entered the street directly in front of him and skidded to a halt. The helmeted rider drew a weapon. So this is how it would be—a trap, two killers, no hope of escape. He felt like a target in a shooting gallery, waiting to be toppled.

He kept running, into the light. His arms rose, and he glimpsed his own hands, contorted and taut, the hands of a tormented figure in an Expressionist painting. He realized he was shouting. The sound echoed from the stucco and brickwork of the surrounding buildings and vibrated within his own ears, so that he could no longer hear the sound of the motorbike at his back. An image flashed before his eyes: his mother at the side of a Polish road with Erich Radek's gun to her temple. Only then did he realize he was screaming in German. The language of his dreams. The language of his nightmares.

The second assassin leveled the weapon, then lifted the visor of the helmet.

Gabriel could hear the sound of his own name.

"Get down! Get down! *Gabriel!*"

He realized it was the voice of Chiara.

He threw himself to the street.

Chiara's shots sailed overhead and struck the oncoming *motorino.* The bike veered out of control and slammed into the side of a building. The assassin catapulted over the handlebars and tumbled along the paving stones. The gun came to rest a few feet from Gabriel. He reached for it.

"No, Gabriel! Leave it! *Hurry!*"

He looked up and saw Chiara holding out her hand to him. He climbed on the back of the *motorino* and clung childlike to her hips as the bike roared up the Corso toward the river.

SHAMRON HAD A rule about safe flats: there was to be no physical contact between male and female agents. That evening, in an Office flat in the north of Rome, near a lazy bend in the Tiber, Gabriel and Chiara violated Shamron's rule with an intensity born of the fear of death. Only afterward did Gabriel bother to ask Chiara how she had found him.

"Shamron told me you were coming to Rome. He asked me to watch your back. I agreed, of course. I have a very personal interest in your continued survival."

Gabriel wondered how he had failed to notice he was being tailed by a five-foot-ten-inch Italian goddess, but then, Chiara Zolli was very good at her work.

"I wanted to join you for lunch at Piperno," she said mischievously. "I didn't think it was a terribly good idea."

"How much do you know about the case?"

"Only that my worst fears about Vienna turned out to be true. Why don't you tell me the rest?"

Which he did, beginning with his flight from Vienna and concluding with the information he had picked up earlier that night from Shimon Pazner.

"So who sent that man to Rome to kill you?"

"I think it's safe to assume it was the same person who engineered the murder of Max Klein."

"How did they find you here?"

Gabriel had been asking himself that same question. His suspicions fell upon the rosy-cheeked Austrian rector of the Anima, Bishop Theodor Drexler.

"So where are we going next?" Chiara asked.

"*We?*"

"Shamron told me to watch your back. You want me to disobey a direct order from the *Memuneh?*"

"He told you to watch me in Rome."

"It was an open-ended assignment," she replied, her tone defiant.

Gabriel lay there for a moment, stroking her hair. Truth was, he could use a traveling companion and a second pair of eyes in the field. Given the obvious risks involved, he would have preferred someone other than the woman he loved. But then, she had proven herself a valuable partner.

There was a secure telephone on the bedside table. He dialed Jerusalem and woke Moshe Rivlin from a heavy sleep. Rivlin gave him the name of a man in Buenos Aires, along with a telephone number and an address in the *barrio* San Telmo. Then

Gabriel called Aerolineas Argentinas and booked two business-class seats on a flight the following evening. He hung up the receiver. Chiara rested her cheek against his chest.

"You were shouting something back there in that alley when you were running toward me," she said. "Do you remember what you were saying?"

He couldn't. It was as if he had awakened unable to recall the dreams that disturbed his sleep.

"You were calling out to her," Chiara said.

"Who?"

"Your mother."

He remembered the image that had flashed before his eyes during that mind-bending flight from the man on the *motorino.* He supposed it was indeed possible he had been calling out to his mother. Since reading her testimony he had been thinking of little else.

"Are you sure it was Erich Radek who murdered those poor girls in Poland?"

"As sure as one *can* be sixty years after the fact."

"And if Ludwig Vogel is actually Erich Radek?"

Gabriel reached up and switched off the lamp.

23

ROME

THE VIA DELLA Pace was deserted. The Clockmaker stopped at the gates of the Anima and shut down the engine of the *motorino.* He reached out, his hand trembling, and pressed the button of the intercom. There was no reply. He rang the bell again. This time an adolescent voice greeted him in Italian. The Clockmaker, in German, asked to see the rector.

"I'm afraid it's not possible. Please telephone in the morning to make an appointment, and Bishop Drexler will be happy to see you. *Buonanotte*, signore."

The Clockmaker leaned hard on the intercom button. "I was told to come here by a friend of the bishop's from Vienna. It's an emergency."

"What was the man's name?"

The Clockmaker answered the question truthfully.

A silence, then: "I'll be down in a moment, signore."

The Clockmaker opened his jacket and examined the puckered wound just below his right clavicle. The heat of the round had cauterized the vessels near the skin. There was little blood, just an intense throbbing and the chills of shock and fever. A small-caliber weapon, he guessed, most likely a .22. Not the kind of weapon to inflict serious internal damage. Still, he needed a doctor to remove the round and thoroughly clean the wound before sepsis set in.

He looked up. A cassocked figure appeared in the forecourt and warily approached the gate—a novice, a boy of perhaps fifteen, with the face of an angel. "The rector says it is not convenient for you to come to the seminary at this time," the novice said. "The rector suggests that you find somewhere else to go tonight."

The Clockmaker drew his Glock and pointed it at the angelic face.

"Open the gate," he whispered. "*Now.*"

"YES, BUT WHY did you have to send him here?" The bishop's voice rose suddenly, as if he were warning a congregation of souls about the dangers of sin. "It would be better for all involved if he left Rome immediately."

"He can't travel, Theodor. He needs a doctor and a place to rest."

"I can see that." His eyes settled briefly on the figure seated on the opposite side of his desk, the man with salt-and-pepper hair and the heavy shoulders of a circus strongman. "But you must realize that you're placing the Anima in a terribly compromising position."

"The position of the Anima will look much worse if our friend Professor Rubenstein is successful."

The Bishop sighed heavily. "He can remain here for twenty-four hours, not a minute more."

"And you'll find him a doctor? Someone discreet?"

"I know just the fellow. He helped me a couple of years ago when one of the boys got into a bit of a scrape with a Roman tough. I'm sure I can count on his discretion in this matter, though a bullet wound is hardly an everyday occurrence at a seminary."

"I'm sure you'll think of some way to explain it. You have a very nimble mind, Theodor. May I speak with him a moment?"

The bishop held out the receiver. The Clockmaker grasped it with a bloodstained hand. Then he looked up at the prelate and, with a sideways nod of his head, sent him fleeing from his own office. The assassin brought the telephone to his ear. The man from Vienna asked what had gone wrong.

"You didn't tell me the target was under protection. That's what went wrong."

The Clockmaker then described the sudden appearance of the second person on a motorcycle. There was a moment of silence on the line, then the man from Vienna spoke in a confessional tone.

"In my rush to dispatch you to Rome, I neglected to relay an important piece of information about the target. In retrospect, that was a miscalculation on my part."

"An important piece of information? And what might that be?"

The man from Vienna acknowledged that the target was once connected to Israeli intelligence. "Judging from the events tonight in Rome," he said, "those connections remain as strong as ever."

For the love of God, thought the Clockmaker. *An Israeli agent?* It was no minor detail. He had a good mind to return to Vienna and leave the old man to deal with the mess himself. He decided instead to turn the situation to his own financial advantage. But there was something else. Never before had he failed to execute the terms of a contract. It wasn't just a question of professional pride and reputation. He simply didn't think it was wise to leave a potential enemy lying about, especially an enemy connected with an intelligence service as ruthless as Israel's. His shoulder began to throb. He looked forward to putting a bullet into that stinking Jew. *And* his friend.

"My price for this assignment just went up," the Clockmaker said. "Substantially."

"I expected that," replied the man from Vienna. "I will double the fee."

"Triple," countered the Clockmaker, and after a moment's hesitation, the man from Vienna consented.

"But can you locate him again?"

"We hold one significant advantage."

"What's that?"

"We know the trail he's following, and we know where he's going next. Bishop Drexler will see that you get the necessary treatment for your wound. In the meantime, get some rest. I'm quite confident you'll be hearing from me again shortly."

24

BUENOS AIRES

ALFONSO RAMIREZ SHOULD have been dead long ago. He was, without a doubt, one of the most courageous men in Argentina and all of Latin America. A crusading journalist and writer, he had made it his life's work to chip away at the walls surrounding Argentina and its murderous past. Considered too controversial and dangerous to be employed by Argentine publications, he published most of his work in the United States and Europe. Few Argentines, beyond the political and financial elite, ever read a word Ramirez wrote.

He had experienced Argentine brutality firsthand. During the Dirty War, his opposition to the military junta had landed him in jail, where he spent nine months and was nearly tortured to death. His wife, a left-wing political activist, was kidnapped by a military death squad and thrown alive from an airplane into the freezing waters of the South Atlantic. Were it not for the intervention of Amnesty International, Ramirez would certainly have suffered the same fate. Instead, he was released, shattered and nearly unrecognizable, to resume his crusade against the generals. In 1983, they stepped aside, and a democratically elected civilian government took their place. Ramirez helped prod the new government into putting dozens of army officers on trial for crimes committed during the Dirty War. Among them was the captain who'd thrown Alfonso Ramirez's wife into the sea.

In recent years, Ramirez had devoted his considerable skills to exposing another unpleasant chapter of Argentine history that the government, the press, and most of its citizenry had chosen to ignore. Following the collapse of Hitler's Reich, thousands of war criminals—German, French, Belgian, and Croatian—had streamed into Argentina, with the enthusiastic approval of the Perón government and the tireless assistance of the Vatican. Ramirez was despised in Argentine quarters where the influence of the Nazis still ran deep, and his work had proven to be just as hazardous as investigating the generals. Twice his office had been firebombed, and his mail contained so many letter bombs that the postal service refused to handle it. Were it not for Moshe Rivlin's introduction, Gabriel doubted Ramirez would have agreed to meet with him.

As it turned out, Ramirez readily accepted an invitation to lunch and suggested a neighborhood café in San Telmo. The café had a black-and-white checkerboard floor with square wooden tables arranged in no discernible pattern. The walls were whitewashed and fitted with shelves lined with empty wine bottles. Large doors opened onto the noisy street, and there were tables on the pavement beneath a canvas awning. Three ceiling fans stirred the heavy air. A German shepherd lay at the foot of the bar, panting. Gabriel arrived on time at two-thirty. The Argentine was late.

January is high summer in Argentina, and it was unbearably hot. Gabriel, who'd been raised in the Jezreel Valley and spent summers in Venice, was used to heat, but only a few days removed from the Austrian Alps, the contrast in climate took his body by surprise. Waves of heat rose from the traffic and flowed through the open doors of the café. With each passing truck, the temperature seemed to rise a degree or two. Gabriel kept his sunglasses on. His shirt was plastered to his spinal cord.

He drank cold water and chewed on a lemon rind, looking into the street. His gaze settled briefly on Chiara. She was sipping a Campari and soda and nibbling listlessly at a plate of empanada. She wore short pants. Her long legs stretched into the sunlight, and her thighs were beginning to burn. Her hair was twisted into a haphazard bun. A trickle of perspiration was inching its way down the nape of her neck, into her sleeveless blouse. Her wristwatch was on her left hand. It was a prearranged signal. Left hand meant that she had detected no surveillance, though Gabriel knew that even an agent of Chiara's skill would be hard-pressed to find a professional in the midday crowds of San Telmo.

Ramirez didn't arrive until three. He made no apology for being late. He was a large man, with thick forearms and a dark beard. Gabriel looked for the scars of torture but found none. His voice, when he ordered two steaks and a bottle of red wine, was affable and so loud it seemed to rattle the bottles on the shelves. Gabriel wondered whether steak and red wine was a wise choice, given the intense heat. Ramirez looked as though he found the question deeply scandalous. "Beef is the one thing about this country that's true," he said. "Besides, the way the economy is going—" The rest of his remark was drowned out by the rumble of a passing cement truck.

The waiter placed the wine on the table. It came in a green bottle with no label. Ramirez poured two glasses and asked Gabriel the name of the man he was looking for. Hearing the answer, the Argentine's dark eyebrows furrowed in concentration.

"Otto Krebs, eh? Is that his real name, or an alias?"

"An alias."

"How can you be sure?"

Gabriel handed over the documents he'd taken from the Santa Maria dell'Anima in Rome. Ramirez pulled a pair of greasy reading glasses from his shirt pocket and thrust them onto his face. Having the documents out in plain sight made Gabriel nervous. He cast a glance in Chiara's direction. The wristwatch was still on her left hand. Ramirez, when he looked up from the papers, was clearly impressed.

"How did you get access to the papers of Bishop Hudal?"

"I have a friend at the Vatican."

"No, you have a very *powerful* friend at the Vatican. The only man who could get Bishop Drexler to willingly open Hudal's papers is *il papa* himself!" Ramirez raised his wineglass in Gabriel's direction. "So, in 1948, an SS officer named Erich Radek comes to Rome and staggers into the arms of Bishop Hudal. A few months later, he leaves Rome as Otto Krebs and sets sail for Syria. What else do you know?"

The next document Gabriel laid on the wooden tabletop produced a similar look of astonishment from the Argentine journalist.

"As you can see, Israeli intelligence placed the man now known as Otto Krebs in Damascus as late as 1963. The source is very good, none other than Aloïs Brunner. According to Brunner, Krebs left Syria in 1963 and came here."

"And you have reason to believe he still might be here?"

"That's what I need to find out."

Ramirez folded his heavy arms and eyed Gabriel across the table. A silence fell between them, filled by the hot drone of traffic from the street. The Argentine smelled a story. Gabriel had anticipated this.

"So how does a man named René Duran from Montreal get his hands on secret documents from the Vatican *and* the Israeli intelligence service?"

"Obviously, I have good sources."

"I'm a very busy man, Monsieur Duran."

"If it's money you want—"

The Argentine held up his palm in an admonitory gesture.

"I don't want your money, Monsieur Duran. I can make my own money. What I want is the story."

"Obviously, press coverage of my investigation would be something of a hindrance."

Ramirez looked insulted. "Monsieur Duran, I'm confident I have much more experience pursuing men like Erich Radek than you do. I know when to investigate quietly and when to write."

Gabriel hesitated a moment. He was reluctant to enter into a *quid pro quo* with the Argentine journalist, but he also knew that Alfonso Ramirez might prove to be a valuable friend.

"Where do we start?" Gabriel asked.

"Well, I suppose we should find out whether Aloïs Brunner was telling the truth about his friend Otto Krebs."

"Meaning, did he ever come to Argentina?"

"Exactly."

"And how do we do that?"

Just then the waiter appeared. The steak he placed in front of Gabriel was large enough to feed a family of four. Ramirez smiled and started sawing away.

"*Bon appétit*, Monsieur Duran. Eat! Something tells me you're going to need your strength."

ALFONSO RAMIREZ DROVE the last surviving Volkswagen Sirocco in the western hemisphere. It might have been dark blue once; now the exterior had faded to the color of pumice. The windshield had a crack down the center that looked like a bolt of lightning. Gabriel's door was bashed in, and it required much of his depleted reservoir of strength to pry it open. The air conditioner no longer worked, and the engine roared like a prop plane.

They sped along the broad Avenida 9 de Julio with the windows down. Scraps of notepaper swirled around them. Ramirez seemed not to notice, or to care, when several pages were sucked out into the street. It had grown hotter with the late afternoon. The rough wine had left Gabriel with a headache. He turned his face toward the open window. It was an ugly boulevard. The façades of the graceful old buildings were scarred by an endless parade of billboards hawking German luxury cars and American soft drinks to a populace whose money was suddenly worthless. The limbs of the shade trees hung drunkenly beneath the onslaught of pollution and heat.

They turned toward the river. Ramirez looked into the rearview mirror. A life of being pursued by military thugs and Nazi sympathizers had left him with well-honed street instincts.

"We're being followed by a girl on a motor scooter."

"Yes, I know."

"If you knew, why didn't you say anything?"

"Because she works for me."

Ramirez took a long look into the mirror.

"I recognize those thighs. That girl was at the café, wasn't she?"

Gabriel nodded slowly. His head was pounding.

"You're a very interesting man, Monsieur Duran. And very lucky, too. She's beautiful."

"Just concentrate on your driving, Alfonso. She'll watch your back."

Five minutes later, Ramirez parked on a street running along the edge of the harbor. Chiara sped past, then swung round and parked in the shade of a tree. Ramirez killed the engine. The sun beat mercilessly on the roof. Gabriel wanted out of the car, but the Argentine wanted to brief him first.

"Most of the files dealing with Nazis in Argentina are kept under lock and key in the Information Bureau. They're still officially off-limits to reporters and scholars, even though the traditional thirty-year blackout period expired long ago. Even if we could get into the storerooms of the Information Bureau, we probably wouldn't find much. By all accounts, Perón had the most damaging files destroyed in 1955, when he was run out of office in a coup."

On the other side of the street, a car slowed, and the man behind the wheel took a long look at the girl on the motorbike. Ramirez saw it, too. He watched the car in his rearview mirror for a moment before resuming.

"In 1997, the government created the Commission for the Clarification of Nazi Activities in Argentina. It faced a serious problem from the beginning. You see, in 1996, the government burned all the damaging files still in its possession."

"Why create a commission in the first place?"

"They wanted credit for trying, of course. But in Argentina, the search for the truth can only go so far. A real investigation would have demonstrated the true depth of Perón's complicity in the postwar Nazi exodus from Europe. It would also have revealed the fact that many Nazis continue to live here. Who knows? Maybe your man, too."

Gabriel pointed at the building. "So what's this?"

"The Hotel de Immigrantes, first stop for the millions of immigrants who came to Argentina in the nineteenth and twentieth centuries. The government housed them here, until they could find work and a place to live. Now, the Immigration Office uses the building as a storage facility."

"For what?"

Ramirez opened the glove box and removed rubber surgical gloves and paper sterile masks. "It's not the cleanest place in the world. I hope you're not afraid of rats."

Gabriel lifted the latch and threw his shoulder against the door. Across the street, Chiara killed the engine of her motorbike and settled in for the wait.

A BORED POLICEMAN stood watch at the entrance. A girl in uniform sat before a rotating fan at the registrar's desk, reading a fashion magazine. She slid the logbook across the dusty desk. Ramirez signed and added the time. Two laminated tags with alligator clips appeared. Gabriel was No. 165. He affixed the badge to the top of his shirt pocket and followed Ramirez toward the elevator. "Two hours till closing time," the girl called out, then she turned another page of her magazine.

They boarded a freight elevator. Ramirez pulled the screen shut and pressed the button for the top floor. The elevator swayed slowly upward. A moment later, when they shuddered to a stop, the air was so hot and thick with dust it was difficult to breathe. Ramirez pulled on his gloves and mask. Gabriel followed suit.

The space they entered was roughly two city blocks long, and filled with endless ranks of steel shelves sagging beneath the weight of wooden crates. Gulls were flying in and out of the broken windows. Gabriel could hear the scratching of tiny clawed feet and the mewing of a catfight. The smell of dust and decaying paper seeped through the protective mask. The subterranean archive of the Anima in Rome seemed a paradise compared to this squalid place.

"What are these?"

"The things Perón and his spiritual successors in the Menem government didn't think to destroy. This room contains the immigration cards filled out by every passenger who disembarked at the Port of Buenos Aires from the 1920s to the 1970s. One floor down are the passenger manifests from every ship. Mengele, Eichmann, they all left their fingerprints here. Maybe Otto Krebs, too."

"Why is it such a mess?"

"Believe it or not, it used to be worse. A few years ago, a brave soul named Chela alphabetized the cards year by year. They call this the Chela room now. The immigration cards for 1963 are over here. Follow me." Ramirez paused and pointed toward the floor. "Watch out for the catshit."

They walked half a city block. The immigration cards for 1963 filled several dozen of the steel shelves. Ramirez located the wooden boxes containing cards with passengers whose last name began with *K*, then he removed them from the shelf and placed them carefully on the floor. He found four immigrants with the last name Krebs. None had the first name Otto.

"Could it be misfiled?"

"Of course."

"Is it possible someone removed it?"

"This is Argentina, my friend. Anything is possible."

Gabriel leaned against the shelves, dejected. Ramirez returned the immigration cards to the box, and the box to its place on the steel shelf. Then he looked at his watch.

"We have an hour and forty-five minutes till they close up for the night. You work forward from 1963, I'll work backward. Loser buys the drinks."

A THUNDERSTORM MOVED down from the river. Gabriel, through a broken window, glimpsed heat lightning flickering amid the cranes of the waterfront. The heavy cloud blocked out the late-day sun. Inside the Chela room it became nearly impossible to see. The rain began like an explosion. It swept through the gaping windows and soaked the precious files. Gabriel, the restorer, pictured running ink, images forever lost.

He found the immigration cards of three more men named Krebs, one in 1965, two more in 1969. None bore the first name Otto. The darkness slowed the pace of his search to a crawl. In order to read the immigration cards, he had to lug the boxes near a window, where there was still some light. There he would crouch, his back to the rain, fingers working.

The girl from the registrar's desk wandered up and gave them a ten-minute warning. Gabriel had only searched through 1972. He didn't want to come back tomorrow. He quickened his pace.

The storm ceased as suddenly as it began. The air was cooler and washed clean. It was quiet, except for the sound of rainwater gurgling in the gutters. Gabriel kept searching: 1973 . . . 1974 . . . 1975 . . . *1976*. . . . No more passengers named Krebs. Nothing.

The girl returned, this time to chase them out for the night. Gabriel carried his last crate back to the shelf, where he found Ramirez and the girl chatting away in Spanish.

"Anything?" Gabriel asked.

Ramirez shook his head.

"How far did you get?"

"All the way. You?"

Gabriel told him. "Think it's worth coming back tomorrow?"

"Probably not." He put his hand on Gabriel's shoulder. "Come on, I'll buy you a beer."

The girl collected their laminated badges and accompanied them down in the freight elevator. The windows of the Sirocco had been left open. Gabriel, depressed by failure, sat on the sodden car seat. The thunderous roar of the engine shattered the quiet of the street. Chiara followed as they drove away. Her clothing was drenched from the rain.

Two blocks from the archives, Ramirez reached into his shirt pocket and produced an immigration card. "Cheer up, Monsieur Duran," he said, handing the card to Gabriel. "Sometimes, in Argentina, it pays to use the same underhanded tactics as the men in charge. There's only one copier in that building, and the girl runs it. She would have made one copy for me and another for her superior."

"And Otto Krebs, if he's still in Argentina and still alive, might very well have been told we were looking for him."

"Exactly."

Gabriel held up the card. "Where was it?"

"Nineteen forty-nine. I suppose Chela stuck one in the wrong box."

Gabriel looked down and began to read. Otto Krebs arrived in Buenos Aires in December 1963 on a boat bound from Athens. Ramirez pointed to a number written in hand at the bottom: 245276/62.

"That's the number of his landing permit. It was probably issued by the Argentine consulate in Damascus. The 'sixty-two' at the end of the line is the year the permit was granted."

"Now what?"

"We know he arrived in Argentina." Ramirez shrugged his heavy shoulders. "Let's see if we can find him."

THEY DROVE BACK to San Telmo through the wet streets and parked outside an Italianate apartment house. Like many buildings in Buenos Aires, it had been beautiful once. Now its façade was the color of Ramirez's car and streaked by pollution.

They climbed a flight of dimly lit stairs. The air inside the flat was stale and warm. Ramirez locked the door behind them and threw open the windows to the cool evening. Gabriel looked into the street and saw Chiara parked on the opposite side.

Ramirez ducked into the kitchen and came out holding two bottles of Argentine beer. He handed one to Gabriel. The glass was already sweating. Gabriel drank half of it. The alcohol took the edge off his headache.

Ramirez led him into his office. It was what Gabriel expected—big and shabby, like Ramirez himself, with books piled in the chairs and a large desk buried beneath a stack of papers that looked as though it was waiting for the match. Heavy curtains shut out the noise and the light of the street. Ramirez went to work on the telephone while Gabriel sat down and finished the last of his beer.

It took Ramirez an hour to come up with his first clue. In 1964, Otto Krebs had registered with the National Police in Bariloche in northern Patagonia. Forty-five minutes later, another piece of the puzzle: In 1972, on an application for an Argentine passport, Krebs had listed his address as Puerto Blest, a town not far from Bariloche. It took only fifteen minutes to find the next piece of information. In 1982, the passport was rescinded.

"Why?" Gabriel asked.

"Because the holder of the passport died."

THE ARGENTINE SPREAD a dog-eared roadmap over a table and, squinting through his smudged reading glasses, searched the western reaches of the country.

"Here it is," he said, jabbing at the map. "San Carlos de Bariloche, or just Bariloche for short. A resort in the northern lake district of Patagonia, founded by Swiss and German settlers in the nineteenth century. It's still known as the Switzerland of Argentina. Now it's a party town for the ski crowd, but for the Nazis and their fellow travelers, it was something of a Valhalla. Mengele adored Bariloche."

"How do I get there?"

"The quickest way is to fly. There's an airport and hourly service from Buenos Aires." He paused, then added, "It's a long way to go to see a grave."

"I want to see it with my own eyes."

Ramirez nodded. "Stay at the Hotel Edelweiss."

"The Edelweiss?"

"It's a German enclave," Ramirez said. "You'll find it hard to believe you're in Argentina."

"Why don't you come along for the ride?"

"I'm afraid I'd be something of a hindrance. I'm *persona non grata* among certain segments of the Bariloche community. I've spent a little too much time poking around there, if you know what I mean. My face is too well known."

The Argentine's demeanor turned suddenly serious.

"You should watch your back, too, Monsieur Duran. Bariloche is not a place to make careless inquiries. They don't like outsiders asking questions about certain residents. You should also know that you've come to Argentina at a tense time."

Ramirez rummaged through the pile of paper on his desk until he found what he was looking for, a two-month-old copy of the international edition of *Newsweek* magazine. He handed it to Gabriel and said, "My story is on page thirty-six." Then he went into the kitchen to fetch two more beers.

THE FIRST TO die was a man named Enrique Calderon. He was found in the bedroom of his townhouse in the Palermo Chico section of Buenos Aires. Four shots to the head, very professional. Gabriel, who could not hear of a murder without picturing the act, turned his gaze from Ramirez. "And the second?" he asked.

"Gustavo Estrada. Killed two weeks later on a business trip to Mexico City. His body was found in his hotel room after he failed to show up for a breakfast meeting. Again, four shots to the head." Ramirez paused. "Good story, no? Two prominent businessmen, killed in a strikingly similar fashion within two weeks of each other. The kind of shit Argentines love. For a while, it took everyone's mind off the fact that their life's savings were gone and their money was worthless."

"Are the murders connected?"

"We may never know for certain, but I believe they are. Enrique Calderon and Gustavo Estrada didn't know each other well, but their fathers did. Alejandro Calderon was a close aide to Juan Perón, and Martín Estrada was the chief of the Argentine national police in the years after the war."

"So why were the sons killed?"

"To be perfectly honest, I haven't a clue. In fact, I don't have a single theory that seems to make any sense. What I do know is this: Accusations are flying among the old German community. Nerves are frayed." Ramirez took a long pull at his beer. "I repeat, watch your step in Bariloche, Monsieur Duran."

They talked awhile longer as the darkness slowly gathered around them and the wet rush of the traffic filtered in from the street. Gabriel did not like many of the people he met in his work, but Alfonso Ramirez was an exception. He was only sorry he'd been forced to deceive him.

They talked of Bariloche, of Argentina, and the past. When

Ramirez asked about the crimes of Erich Radek, Gabriel told him everything he knew. This produced a long, contemplative silence in the Argentine, as if he were pained by the fact that men such as Radek might have found sanctuary in a land he so loved.

They made arrangements to speak after Gabriel's return from Bariloche, then parted in the darkened corridor. Outside, the *barrio* San Telmo was beginning to come alive in the cool of the evening. Gabriel walked for a time along the crowded pavements, until a girl on a red motorbike pulled alongside him and patted the back of her saddle.

25

BUENOS AIRES • ROME • VIENNA

THE CONSOLE OF sophisticated electronic equipment was of German manufacture. The microphones and transmitters concealed in the apartment of the target were of the highest quality—designed and built by West German intelligence at the height of the Cold War to monitor the activities of their adversaries in the east. The operator of the equipment was a native-born Argentine, though he could trace his ancestry to the Austrian village of Braunau am Inn. The fact that it was the same village where Adolf Hitler was born gave him a certain standing among his comrades. When the Jew paused in the entrance of the apartment house, the surveillance man snapped his photograph with a telephoto lens. A moment later, when the girl on the motorbike drew away from the curb, he captured her image as well, though it was of little value since her face was concealed beneath a black crash helmet. He spent a few moments reviewing the conversation that had taken place inside the target's apartment; then, satisfied, he reached for the telephone. The number he dialed was in Vienna. The sound of German, spoken with a Viennese accent, was like music to his ears.

AT THE PONTIFICIO Santa Maria dell'Anima in Rome, a novice hurried along the second-floor corridor of the dormitory and paused outside the door of the room where the visitor from Vienna was staying. He hesitated before knocking, then waited for permission before entering. A wedge of light fell upon the powerful figure stretched out on the narrow cot. His eyes shone in the darkness like black pools of oil.

"You have a telephone call." The boy spoke with his eyes averted. Everyone in the seminary had heard about the incident at the front gate the previous evening. "You can take it in the rector's office."

The man sat up and swung his feet to the floor in one fluid movement. The thick muscles in his shoulders and back rippled beneath his fair skin. He touched the bandage on his shoulder briefly, then pulled on a rollneck sweater.

The seminarian led the visitor down a stone staircase, then

across a small courtyard. The rector's office was empty. A single light burned on the desk. The receiver of the phone lay atop the blotter. The visitor picked it up. The boy slipped quietly from the room.

"We've located him."

"Where?"

The man from Vienna told him. "He's leaving for Bariloche in the morning. You'll be waiting for him when he arrives."

The Clockmaker glanced at his wristwatch and calculated the time difference. "How is that possible? There isn't a flight from Rome until the afternoon."

"Actually, there's a plane leaving in a few minutes."

"What are you talking about?"

"How quickly can you get to Fiumicino?"

THE DEMONSTRATORS WERE waiting outside the Hotel Imperial when the three-car motorcade arrived for a rally of the party faithful. Peter Metzler, seated in the back of a Mercedes limousine, looked out the window. He'd been warned, but he'd expected the usual sad-looking lot, not a brigade-strength band of marauders armed with placards and bullhorns. It was inevitable: the nearness of the election; the aura of invulnerability building around the candidate. The Austrian left was in full panic, as were their supporters in New York and Jerusalem.

Dieter Graff, seated opposite Metzler on the jump seat, looked apprehensive. And why not? Twenty years he'd toiled to transform the Austrian National Front from a moribund alliance of former SS officers and neo-fascist dreamers into a cohesive and modern conservative political force. Almost single-handedly he'd reshaped the party's ideology and airbrushed its public image. His carefully crafted message had steadily attracted Austrian voters disenfranchised by the cozy power-sharing relationship between the People's Party and the Social Democrats. Now, with Metzler as his candidate, he stood on the doorstep of the ultimate prize in Austrian politics: the chancellery. The last thing Graff wanted now, three weeks before the election, was a messy confrontation with a bunch of left-wing idiots and Jews.

"I know what you're thinking, Dieter," said Metzler. "You're thinking we should play it safe—avoid this rabble by using the back entrance."

"The thought did cross my mind. Our lead is three points and holding steady. I'd rather not squander two of those points with a nasty scene at the Imperial that can easily be avoided."

"By going in the back door?"

Graff nodded. Metzler pointed to the television cameramen and still photographers.

"And do you know what the headline will be tomorrow in *Die Presse*? Metzler beaten back by Vienna protesters! They'll say I'm a coward, Dieter, and I'm not a coward."

"No one's ever accused you of cowardice, Peter. It's just a question of timing."

"We've used the back door too long." Metzler cinched up his tie and smoothed his shirt collar. "Besides, *chancellors* don't use the back door. We go in the front, with our head up and our chin ready for battle, or we don't go in at all."

"You've become quite a speaker, Peter."

"I had a good teacher." Metzler smiled and put his hand on

Graff's shoulder. "But I'm afraid the long campaign has started to take a toll on his instincts."

"Why would you say that?"

"Look at those hooligans. Most of them aren't even Austrian. Half the signs are in English instead of German. Clearly, this little demonstration has been orchestrated by provocateurs from abroad. If I'm fortunate enough to have a confrontation with these people, our lead will be five points by morning."

"I hadn't thought of it quite that way."

"Just tell security to take it easy. It's important that the protesters come across as the Brownshirts—and not us."

Peter Metzler opened the door and stepped out. A roar of anger rose from the crowd, and the placards began to flutter.

Nazi pig!

Reichsführer Metzler!

The candidate strode forward as though oblivious to the turmoil around him. A young girl, armed with a rag soaked in red paint, broke free of the restraint. She hurled the rag toward Metzler, who avoided it so deftly that he barely seemed to break stride. The rag struck a Staatspolizei officer, to the delight of the demonstrators. The girl who had thrown it was seized by a pair of officers and hustled away.

Metzler, unruffled, entered the hotel lobby and made his way to the ballroom, where a thousand supporters had been waiting three hours for his arrival. He paused for a moment outside the doors to gather himself, then strode into the room to tumultuous cheers. Graff detached himself and watched his candidate wade into the adoring crowd. The men pressed forward to clutch his hand or slap his back. The women kissed his cheek. Metzler had definitely made it sexy to be a conservative again.

The journey to the head of the room took five minutes. As Metzler mounted the podium, a beautiful girl in a dirndl handed him a huge stein of lager. He raised it overhead and was greeted by a delirious roar of approval. He swallowed some of the beer—not a photo opportunity sip, but a good long *Austrian* pull—then stepped before the microphone.

"I want to thank all of you for coming here tonight. And I also want to thank our dear friends and supporters for arranging such a warm welcome outside the hotel." A wave of laughter swept over the room. "What these people don't seem to understand is that Austria is for *Austrians* and that we will choose our own future based on *Austrian* morals and *Austrian* standards of decency. Outsiders and critics from abroad have no say in the internal affairs of this blessed land of ours. We will forge our own future, an *Austrian* future, and that future begins three weeks from tonight!"

Pandemonium.

26

BARILOCHE, ARGENTINA

THE RECEPTIONIST AT the *Barilocher Tageblatt* eyed Gabriel with more than a passing interest as he stepped through the door and strode toward her desk. She had short dark hair and bright blue eyes set off by an attractive suntanned face. "May I help you?" she said in German, hardly surprising, since the *Tageblatt*, as the name implies, is a German-language newspaper.

Gabriel replied in the same language, though he adroitly concealed the fact that, like the woman, he spoke it fluently. He said he had come to Bariloche to conduct genealogical research. He was looking, he claimed, for a man he believed was his mother's brother, a man named Otto Krebs. He had reason to believe Herr Krebs died in Bariloche in October 1982. Would it be possible for him to search the archives of the newspaper for a death notice or an obituary?

The receptionist smiled at him, revealing two rows of bright, even teeth, then picked up her telephone and dialed a three-digit extension. Gabriel's request was put to a superior in rapid German. The woman was silent for a few seconds, then she hung up the phone and stood.

"Follow me."

She led him across a small newsroom, her heels clicking loudly over the faded linoleum floor. A half-dozen employees were lounging in their shirtsleeves in various states of relaxation, smoking cigarettes and drinking coffee. No one seemed to take notice of the visitor. The door to the archives room was ajar. The receptionist switched on the lights.

"We're computerized now, so all the articles are stored automatically in a searchable database. I'm afraid that goes back only as far as 1998. When did you say this man died?"

"I believe it was 1982."

"You're lucky. The obituaries are all indexed—by hand, of course, the old-fashioned way."

She walked over to a table and lifted the cover of a thick, leather-bound ledger book. The ruled pages were filled with tiny handwritten notations.

"What did you say his name was?"

"Otto Krebs."

"Krebs, Otto," she said, flipping forward to the *K*s. "Krebs, Otto . . . Ah, here it is. According to this, it was November 1983. Still interested in seeing the obituary?"

Gabriel nodded. The woman wrote down a reference number and walked over to a stack of cardboard boxes. She ran a forefinger along the labels and stopped when she arrived at the one she was looking for, then asked Gabriel to remove the boxes stacked on top of it. She lifted the lid, and the smell of dust and decaying paper rose from the contents. The clips were contained in brittle, yellowing file folders. The obituary for Otto Krebs had been torn. She repaired the image with a strip of transparent tape and showed it to Gabriel.

"Is that the man you're looking for?"

"I don't know," he said truthfully.

She took the clip back from Gabriel and read it quickly. "It says here that he was an only child." She looked at Gabriel. "That doesn't mean much. A lot of them had to erase their pasts to protect their families who were still in Europe. My grandfather was lucky. At least he got to keep his own name."

She looked at Gabriel, searching his eyes. "He was from Croatia," she said. There was an air of complicity in her tone. "After the war, the Communists wanted to put him on trial and hang him. Fortunately, Perón was willing to let him come here."

She carried the clip over to a photocopier and made three duplicates. Then she returned the original to its file and the file to its proper box. She gave the copies to Gabriel. He read while they walked.

"According to the obituary, he was buried in a Catholic cemetery in Puerto Blest."

The receptionist nodded. "It's just on the other side of the lake, a few miles from the Chilean border. He managed a large *estancia* up there. That's in the obituary, too."

"How do I get there?"

"Follow the highway west out of Bariloche. It won't stay a highway for long. I hope you have a good car. Follow the road along the lakeshore, then head north. You'll go straight into Puerto Blest. If you leave now, you can get there before dark."

They shook hands in the lobby. She wished him luck.

"I hope he's the man you're looking for," she said. "Or maybe not. I suppose one never knows in situations like these."

AFTER THE VISITOR was gone, the receptionist picked up her telephone and dialed.

"He just left."

"How did you handle it?"

"I did what you told me to do. I was very friendly. I showed him what he wanted to see."

"And what was that?"

She told him.

"How did he react?"

"He asked for directions to Puerto Blest."

The line went dead. The receptionist slowly replaced the receiver. She felt a sudden hollowness in her stomach. She had no doubt what awaited the man in Puerto Blest. It was the same fate that had befallen others who had come to this corner of northern Patagonia in search of men who did not want to be found. She did not feel sorry for him; indeed, she thought him something of a fool. Did he really think he would fool anyone with that clumsy story about genealogical research? Who did he think he was? It was his own fault. But then, it was always that way with the Jews. Always bringing trouble down on their own heads.

Just then the front door opened and a woman in a sundress entered the lobby. The receptionist looked up and smiled.

"May I help you?"

THEY WALKED BACK to the hotel beneath a razor-edged sun. Gabriel translated the obituary for Chiara.

"It says he was born in Upper Austria in 1913, that he was a police officer, and that he enlisted in the Wehrmacht in 1938 and took part in the campaigns against Poland and the Soviet Union. It also says he was decorated twice for bravery, once by the Führer himself. I guess that's something to brag about in Bariloche."

"And after the war?"

"Nothing until his arrival in Argentina in 1963. He worked for two years at a hotel in Bariloche, then took a job on an *estancia* near Puerto Blest. In 1972, he purchased the property from the owners and ran it until his death."

"Any family left in the area?"

"According to this, he was never married and had no surviving relatives."

They arrived back at the Hotel Edelweiss. It was a Swiss-style chalet with a sloping roof, located two streets up from the lakeshore on the Avenida San Martín. Gabriel had rented a car at the airport earlier that morning, a Toyota four-wheel drive. He asked the parking attendant to bring it up from the garage, then ducked into the lobby to find a road map of the surrounding countryside. Puerto Blest was exactly where the woman from the newspaper had said, on the opposite side of the lake, near the Chilean border.

They set out along the lakeshore. The road deteriorated by degrees as they moved farther from Bariloche. Much of the time, the water was hidden by dense forest. Then Gabriel would round a bend, or the trees would suddenly thin, and the lake would appear briefly below them, a flash of blue, only to disappear behind a wall of timber once more.

Gabriel rounded the southernmost tip of the lake and slowed briefly to watch a squadron of giant condors circling the looming peak of the Cerro López. Then he followed a one-lane dirt track across an exposed plateau covered with gray-green thorn scrub and stands of *arrayán* trees. On the high meadows, flocks of hardy Patagonian sheep grazed on the summer grasses. In the distance, toward the Chilean border, lightning flickered over the Andean peaks.

By the time they arrived in Puerto Blest, the sun was gone and the village was shadowed and quiet. Gabriel went into a café to ask directions. The bartender, a short man with a florid face, stepped into the street and, with a series of points and gestures, showed him the way.

JUST INSIDE THE CAFÉ, at a table near the door, the Clockmaker drank beer from a bottle and watched the exchange taking place in the street. The slender man with short black hair and gray temples he recognized. Seated in the passenger seat of the Toyota four-wheel drive was a woman with long dark hair. Was it possible she was the one who had put the bullet in his shoulder in Rome? It didn't much matter. Even if she wasn't, she would soon be dead.

The Israeli climbed behind the wheel of the Toyota and sped off. The bartender came back inside.

The Clockmaker, in German, asked, "Where are those two headed?"

The bartender answered him in the same language.

The Clockmaker finished the last of his beer and left money on the table. Even the smallest movement, such as fishing a few bills from his coat pocket, made his shoulder pulsate with fire. He went into the street and stood for a moment in the cool evening air, then turned and walked slowly toward the church.

THE CHURCH OF Our Lady of the Mountains stood at the western edge of the village, a small whitewashed colonial church with a bell tower to the left side of the portico. At the front of the church was a stone courtyard, shaded by a pair of broad plane trees and enclosed by an iron fence. Gabriel walked to the back of the church. The cemetery stretched down the gentle slope of a hill, toward a coppice of dense pine. A thousand headstones and memorial monuments teetered among the overgrown weeds like a ragged army in retreat. Gabriel stood there a moment, hands on hips, depressed by the prospect of wandering the graveyard in the gathering darkness looking for a marker bearing the name of Otto Krebs.

He walked back to the front of the church. Chiara was waiting for him in the shadows of the courtyard. He pulled on the heavy oaken door of the church and found it was unlocked. Chiara followed him inside. Cool air settled over his face, as did a fragrance he had not smelled since leaving Venice: the mixture of candle wax, incense, wood polish, and mildew, the unmistakable scent of a Catholic church. How different this was from the Church of San Giovanni Crisostomo in Cannaregio. No gilded altar, no marble columns or soaring apses or glorious altarpieces. A severe wooden crucifix hung over the unadorned altar, and a bank of memorial candles flickered softly before a statue of the Virgin. The stained-glass windows along the side of the nave had lost their color in the dying twilight.

Gabriel walked hesitantly up the center aisle. Just then, a dark figure emerged from the vestry and strode across the altar. He paused before the crucifix, genuflected, then turned to face Gabriel. He was small and thin, dressed in black trousers, a black short-sleeved shirt, and a Roman collar. His hair was neatly trimmed and gray at the temples, his face handsome and dark, with a hint of red across the cheeks. He did not seem surprised by the presence of two strangers in his church. Gabriel approached him slowly. The priest held out his hand and identified himself as Father Ruben Morales.

"My name is René Duran," Gabriel said. "I'm from Montreal."

At this the priest nodded, as though used to visitors from abroad.

"What can I do for you, Monsieur Duran?"

Gabriel offered the same explanation he had given to the woman at the *Barilocher Tageblatt* earlier that morning—that he had come to Patagonia looking for a man he believed was his mother's brother, a man named Otto Krebs. While Gabriel spoke, the priest folded his hands and watched him with a pair of warm and gentle eyes. How different this pastoral man seemed from Monsignor Donati, the professional Church bureaucrat, or Bishop Drexler, the acid rector of the Anima. Gabriel felt badly about misleading him.

"I knew Otto Krebs very well," Father Morales said. "And I'm sorry to say that he could not possibly be the man you're searching for. You see, Herr Krebs had no brothers or sisters. He had no family of any kind. By the time he managed to work himself into a position to support a wife and children, he was . . ." The priest's voice trailed off. "How shall I put this delicately? He was no longer such a fine catch. The years had taken their toll on him."

"Did he ever talk to you about his family?" Gabriel paused, then added, "Or the war?"

The priest raised his eyebrows. "I was his confessor and his friend, Monsieur Duran. We discussed a great many things in the years before his death. Herr Krebs, like many men of his era, had seen much death and destruction. He had also committed acts for which he was deeply ashamed and in need of absolution."

"And you granted that absolution?"

"I granted him peace of mind, Monsieur Duran. I heard his confessions, I ordered penance. Within the confines of Catholic belief, I prepared his soul to meet Christ. But do I, a simple priest from a rural parish, really possess the power to absolve such sins? Even I'm not sure about that."

"May I ask you about some of the things you discussed?"

Gabriel asked tentatively. He knew he was on shaky theological ground, and the answer was what he expected.

"Many of my discussions with Herr Krebs were conducted under the seal of confession. The rest were conducted under the seal of friendship. It would not be proper for me to relate the nature of those conversations to you now."

"But he's been dead for twenty years."

"Even the dead have a right to privacy."

Gabriel heard the voice of his mother, the opening line of her testimony: *I will not tell all the things I saw. I cannot. I owe this much to the dead.*

"It might help me determine whether this man is my uncle."

Father Morales gave a disarming smile. "I'm a simple country priest, Monsieur Duran, but I'm not a complete fool. I also know my parishioners very well. Do you really believe you're the first person to come here pretending to be looking for a lost relative? I'm quite certain that Otto Krebs could not possibly be your uncle. I'm less certain that you're really René Duran from Montreal. Now, if you'll excuse me."

He turned to leave. Gabriel touched his arm.

"Will you at least show me his grave?"

The priest sighed, then looked up at the stained-glass windows. They had turned to black.

"It's dark," he said. "Give me a moment."

He crossed the altar and disappeared into the vestry. A moment later he emerged wearing a tan windbreaker and carrying a large flashlight. He led them out a side portal, then along a gravel walkway between the church and the rectory. At the end of the path was a lych-gate. Father Morales lifted the latch, then switched on the flashlight and led the way into the cemetery. Gabriel walked at the priest's side along a narrow footpath overgrown with weeds. Chiara was a step behind.

"Did you celebrate his funeral mass, Father Morales?"

"Yes, of course. In fact, I had to see to the arrangements myself. There was no one else to do it."

A cat slipped out from behind a grave marker and paused on the footpath in front of them, its eyes reflecting like yellow beacons in the glow of the priest's flashlight. Father Morales hissed, and the cat vanished into the tall grass.

They drew nearer the trees at the bottom of the cemetery. The priest turned left and led them through knee-deep grass. Here the path was too narrow to walk side by side, so they moved single file, with Chiara holding Gabriel's hand for support.

Father Morales, nearing the end of a row of gravestones, stopped walking and shone his flashlight down at a 45-degree angle. The beam fell upon a simple headstone bearing the name OTTO KREBS. It listed the year of his birth as 1913 and the year of his death as 1983. Above the name, beneath a small oval of scratched and weathered glass, was a photograph.

GABRIEL CROUCHED AND, brushing away a layer of powdery dust, examined the face. Evidently it had been taken some years before his death, because the man it depicted was middle-aged, perhaps in his late forties. Gabriel was certain of only one thing. It was not the face of Erich Radek.

"I assume it's not your *uncle*, Monsieur Duran?"

"Are you certain the photograph is of him?"

"Yes, of course. I found it myself, in a strongbox containing a few of his private things."

"I don't suppose you'd allow me to see his things?"

"I no longer have them. And even if I did—"

Father Morales, leaving the thought unfinished, handed Gabriel the flashlight. "I'll leave you alone now. I can find my way without the light. If you would be so kind as to leave it at the rectory door on your way out. It was a pleasure meeting you, Monsieur Duran."

With that, he turned and vanished among the gravestones.

Gabriel looked up at Chiara. "It should be Radek's picture. Radek went to Rome and obtained a Red Cross passport in the name of Otto Krebs. Krebs went to Damascus in 1948, then emigrated to Argentina in 1963. Krebs registered with the Argentine police in this district. This *should* be Radek."

"Meaning?"

"Someone else went to Rome posing as Radek." Gabriel pointed at the photograph on the gravestone. "It was this man. This is the Austrian who went to the Anima seeking help from Bishop Hudal. Radek was somewhere else, probably still hiding in Europe. Why else would he go to such lengths? He wanted people to believe he was long gone. And in the event someone ever went looking for him, they would follow the trail from Rome to Damascus to Argentina and then find the wrong man—Otto Krebs, a lowly hotel worker who'd scraped together enough money to buy a few acres along the Chilean border."

"You still have one major problem," Chiara said. "You can't *prove* Ludwig Vogel is really Erich Radek."

"One step at a time," Gabriel said. "Making a man disappear

is not so simple. Radek would have needed help. Someone else has to know about this."

"Yes, but is he still alive?"

Gabriel stood and looked in the direction of the church. The bell tower appeared in silhouette. Then he noticed a figure walking toward them through the gravestones. For a moment he thought it was Father Morales; then, as the figure drew nearer, he could see that it was a different man. The priest was thin and small. This man was squat and powerfully built, with a quick, rolling gait that propelled him smoothly down the hill among the grave markers.

Gabriel raised the flashlight and shone it toward him. He glimpsed the face briefly before the man shielded it behind a large hand: bald, bespectacled, thick eyebrows of gray and black.

Gabriel heard a noise behind him. He turned and shone the flashlight toward the woods along the perimeter of the cemetery. Two men in dark clothing were coming out of the trees at a run, compact submachine guns in their hands.

Gabriel trained the beam once again on the man coming down through the headstones and saw that he was drawing a weapon from the inside of his jacket. Then, suddenly, the gunman stopped walking. His eyes were fixed not on Gabriel and Chiara but on the two men coming out of the trees. He stood motionless for no more than a second—then abruptly he put the gun away, turned, and ran in the other direction.

By the time Gabriel turned again, the two men with the submachine guns were a few feet away and coming hard on the run. The first collided with Gabriel, driving him down into the hard soil of the graveyard. Chiara managed to shield her face as the second gunman knocked her to the ground, too. Gabriel felt a gloved hand clamp across his mouth, then the hot breath of his attacker in his ear.

"Relax, Allon, you're among friends." He spoke English with an American accent. "Don't make this difficult for us."

Gabriel pulled the hand off his mouth and looked into his attacker's eyes. "Who are you?"

"Think of us as your guardian angels. That man walking toward you was a professional assassin, and he was about to kill you both."

"And what are you going to do with us?"

The gunmen pulled Gabriel and Chiara to their feet and led them out of the cemetery into the trees.

PART THREE

THE RIVER OF ASHES

27

PUERTO BLEST, ARGENTINA

THE FOREST FELL away sharply from the edge of the cemetery into the void of a blackened ravine. They clambered down the steep slope, picking their way through the trees. The evening was moonless, the darkness absolute. They walked single file, one American in front, followed by Gabriel and Chiara, another American at the back. The Americans wore night-vision goggles. They moved, in Gabriel's opinion, like elite soldiers.

They came to a small, well-concealed encampment: black tent, black sleeping bags, no sign of a fire or stove for cooking. Gabriel wondered how long they'd been here, watching the cemetery. Not long, judging from the growth on their cheeks. Forty-eight hours, maybe less.

The Americans started packing up. Gabriel tried for a second time to determine who they were and whom they worked for. He was met by weary smiles and stony silence.

It took them a matter of minutes to break down the camp and obliterate any last trace of their presence. Gabriel volunteered to shoulder one of the packs. The Americans refused.

They started walking again. Ten minutes later, they were standing at the bottom of the ravine in a rocky streambed. A vehicle awaited them, concealed beneath a camouflage tarpaulin and pine branches. It was an old Rover with a spare tire mounted on the hood and jerry cans of extra fuel on the back.

The Americans chose the seating arrangements, Chiara in front, Gabriel in back, with a gun aimed at his stomach in the event he suddenly lost faith in the intentions of his rescuers. They lurched along the streambed for a few miles, splashing through the shallow water, before turning onto a dirt track. Several miles farther on, they came to the highway leading out of Puerto Blest. The American turned right, toward the Andes.

"You're heading toward Chile," Gabriel pointed out.

The Americans laughed.

Ten minutes later, the border: one guard, shivering in a brick blockhouse. The Rover shot across the frontier without slowing and headed down the Andes toward the Pacific.

AT THE NORTHERN END of the Gulf of Ancud lies Porto Montt, a resort town and cruise-ship port of call. Just outside the town is an airport with a runway long enough to accommodate a Gulfstream G500 executive jet. It was waiting on the tarmac, engines whining, when the Rover arrived. A gray-haired American stood in the doorway. He welcomed Gabriel and Chiara aboard and introduced himself with little conviction as "Mr. Alexander." Gabriel, before settling himself into a comfortable leather seat, asked where they were going. "We're going home, Mr. Allon. I suggest you and your friend try to get some rest. It's a long flight."

THE CLOCKMAKER DIALED the number in Vienna from his hotel room in Bariloche.

"Are they dead?"

"I'm afraid not."

"What happened?"

"To be perfectly honest," said the Clockmaker, "I don't have a fucking clue."

28

THE PLAINS, VIRGINIA

THE SAFE HOUSE is located in a corner of the Virginia horse country where wealth and privilege meet the hard reality of rural southern life. It is reached by way of a twisting, rolling roadway lined with tumbledown barns and clapboard bungalows with broken cars in the yards. There is a gate; it warns that the property is private, but omits the fact that, technically speaking, it is a government facility. The drive is gravel and nearly a mile in length. To the right is a thick wood; to the left, a pasture surrounded by a split-rail fence. The fence caused something of a scandal among the local craftsmen when the "owner" hired an outside firm to handle the construction. Two bay horses reside in the pasture. According to Agency wits, they are subjected, like all other employees, to annual polygraphs to make certain they haven't gone over to the other side, whatever side that might be.

The Colonial-style house is located at the top of the property and surrounded by towering shade trees. It has a copper roof and a double porch. The furnishings are rustic and comfortable, inviting cooperation and camaraderie. Delegations from friendly services have stayed there. So have men who have betrayed their country. The last was an Iraqi who helped Saddam try to build a nuclear bomb. His wife was hoping for an apartment in the famous Watergate and complained bitterly throughout her stay. His sons set fire to the barn. Management was pleased to see them leave.

On that afternoon, new snowfall covered the pasture. The landscape, drained of all color by the heavily tinted windows of the hulking Suburban, appeared to Gabriel as a charcoal sketch. Alexander, reclining in the front seat with his eyes closed, came suddenly awake. He yawned elaborately and squinted at his wristwatch, then frowned when he realized it was set to the wrong time.

It was Chiara, seated at Gabriel's side, who noticed the bald, sentinel-like figure standing at the balustrade on the upper porch. Gabriel leaned across the back seat and peered up at him. Shamron raised his hand and held it aloft for a moment before turning and disappearing into the house.

He greeted them in the entrance hall. Standing at his side,

dressed in corduroy trousers and a cardigan sweater, was a slight man with a halo of gray curls and a gray mustache. His brown eyes were tranquil, his handshake cool and brief. He seemed a college professor, or perhaps a clinical psychologist. He was neither. Indeed, he was the deputy director for operations of the Central Intelligence Agency, and his name was Adrian Carter. He did not look pleased, but then, given the current state of global affairs, he rarely did.

They greeted each other carefully, as men of the secret world are prone to do. They used real names, since they were all known to each other and the use of work names would have lent a farcical air to the affair. Carter's serene gaze settled briefly on Chiara, as though she were an uninvited guest for whom an extra place would have to be set. He made no attempt to suppress his frown.

"I was hoping to keep this at a very senior level," Carter said. His voice was underpowered; to hear him, one had to remain still and listen carefully. "I was also hoping to limit distribution of the material I'm about to share with you."

"She's my partner," Gabriel said. "She knows everything, and she's not leaving the room."

Carter's eyes moved slowly from Chiara to Gabriel "We've been watching you for some time—ever since your arrival in Vienna, to be precise. We especially enjoyed your visit to Café Central. Confronting Vogel face to face like that was a fine piece of theater."

"Actually, it was Vogel who confronted *me*."

"That's Vogel's way."

"Who is he?"

"You're the one who's been digging. Why don't you tell me?"

"I believe he's an SS murderer named Erich Radek, and for some reason, you're protecting him. If I had to guess why, I'd say he was one of your agents."

Carter placed a hand on Gabriel's shoulder. "Come," he said. "Obviously, it's time we had a talk."

THE LIVING ROOM was lamplit and shadowed. A large fire burned in the hearth, an institutional metal urn of coffee stood on the sideboard. Carter helped himself to some before settling with donnish detachment into a wingchair. Gabriel and Chiara shared the couch while Shamron paced the perimeter, a sentry with a long night ahead of him.

"I want to tell you a story, Gabriel," Carter began. "It's a story about a country that was drawn into a war it didn't want to fight, a country that defeated the greatest army the world had ever known, only to find itself, within a matter of months, in an armed standoff with its former ally, the Soviet Union. In all honesty, we were scared shitless. You see, before the war, we had no intelligence service—not a *real* one, anyway. Hell, your service is as old as ours. Before the war, our intelligence operation inside the Soviet Union consisted of a couple of guys from Harvard and a teletype machine. When we suddenly found ourselves nose to nose with the Russian bogeyman, we didn't know shit about him. His strengths, his weaknesses, his intentions. And what's more, we didn't know how to find out. That another war was imminent was a foregone conclusion. And what did we have? Fuck all. No networks, no agents. Nothing. We were lost, wandering in the desert. We needed help. Then a Moses appeared on the horizon, a man to lead us across Sinai, into the Promised Land."

Shamron went still for a moment in order to supply the name of this Moses: General Reinhard Gehlen, head of the German General Staff's Foreign Armies East branch, Hitler's chief spy on the Russian front.

"Buy that man a cigar." Carter inclined his head toward Shamron. "Gehlen was one of the few men who had the balls to tell Hitler the truth about the Russian campaign. Hitler used to get so pissed at him, he threatened to have him committed to an insane asylum. As the end was drawing near, Gehlen decided to save his own skin. He ordered his staff to microfilm the General Staff's archives on the Soviet Union and seal the material in watertight drums. The drums were buried in the mountains of Bavaria and Austria, then Gehlen and his senior staff surrendered to a Counterintelligence Corps team."

"And you welcomed him with open arms," Shamron said.

"You would have done the same thing, Ari." Carter folded his hands and spent a moment staring into the fire. Gabriel could almost hear him counting to ten to check his anger. "Gehlen was the answer to our prayers. The man had spent a career spying on the Soviet Union, and now he was going to show us the way. We brought him into this country and put him up a few miles from here at Fort Hunt. He had the entire American security establishment eating out of his hand. He told us what we wanted to hear. Stalinism was an evil unparalleled in human history. Stalin intended to subvert the countries of western Europe from within and then move against them militarily. Stalin had global ambitions. Be not afraid, Gehlen told us. I have networks, I have sleepers and stay-behind cells. I know everything there is to know about Stalin and his henchmen. Together, we will crush him."

Carter stood and went to the sideboard to warm his coffee.

"Gehlen held court at Fort Hunt for ten months. He drove a hard bargain, and my predecessors were so hypnotized that they agreed to all his demands. Organization Gehlen was born. He moved into a walled compound near Pullach, Germany. We financed him, we gave him directives. He ran the Org and hired the agents. Ultimately, the Org became a virtual extension of the Agency."

Carter carried his coffee back to his chair.

"Obviously, since the primary target of the Organization Gehlen was the Soviet Union, the general hired men who had some experience there. One of the men he wanted was a bright, energetic young man named Erich Radek, an Austrian who'd been chief of the SD in the Reichskommissariat Ukraine. At the time, Radek was being held by us in a detention camp in Mannheim. He was released to Gehlen and was soon behind the walls of Org headquarters at Pullach, reactivating his old networks inside the Ukraine."

"Radek was SD," Gabriel said. "The SS, SD, and the Gestapo were all declared criminal organizations after the war and all members were subject to immediate arrest, and yet you allowed Gehlen to hire him."

Carter nodded slowly, as if the pupil had answered the question correctly but missed the larger, more important point. "At Fort Hunt, Gehlen pledged that he would not hire former SS,

SD, or Gestapo officers, but it was a paper promise and one that we never expected him to keep."

"Did you know that Radek was linked to Einsatzgruppen activities in the Ukraine?" Gabriel asked. "Did you know that this bright, energetic young man had tried to conceal the greatest crime in history?"

Carter shook his head. "The scale of the German atrocities wasn't known then. As for *Aktion* 1005, no one had heard the term yet, and Radek's SS file never reflected his transfer from the Ukraine. *Aktion* 1005 was a top-secret Reich matter, and top-secret Reich matters weren't put to paper."

"But surely, Mr. Carter," Chiara said, "General Gehlen must have known about Radek's work?"

Carter raised his eyebrows, as though surprised by Chiara's ability to speak. "He might have, but then, I doubt it would have made much difference to Gehlen. Radek wasn't the only former SS man who ended up working for the Org. At least fifty others found work there, including some, like Radek, who were linked to the Final Solution."

"I'm afraid it wouldn't have made much of a difference to Gehlen's controllers either," Shamron said. "Any bastard, as long as he's anti-Communist. Wasn't that one of the Agency's guiding principles when it came to the recruitment of Cold War agents?"

"In the infamous words of Richard Helms, 'We're not in the Boy Scouts. If we'd wanted to be in the Boy Scouts, we would have joined the Boy Scouts.'"

Gabriel said, "You don't sound terribly distressed, Adrian."

"Histrionics are not my way, Gabriel. I'm a professional, like you and your legendary boss over there. I deal with the real world, not the world as I would like it to be. I make no apologies for the actions of my predecessors, just as you and Shamron make no apologies for yours. Sometimes, intelligence services must utilize the services of evil men to achieve results that are good: a more stable world, the security of the homeland, the protection of valued friends. The men who decided to employ Reinhard Gehlen and Erich Radek were playing a game as old as time itself, the game of Realpolitik, and they played it well. I won't run from their actions, and I sure as hell won't let *you* of all people sit in judgment of them."

Gabriel leaned forward, his hands folded, his elbows on his knees. He could feel the heat of the fire on his face. It only fueled his anger.

"There's a difference between using evil individuals as sources and hiring them as intelligence officers. And Erich Radek was no run-of-the-mill killer. He was a mass murderer."

"Radek wasn't directly involved in the extermination of the Jews. His involvement came after the fact."

Chiara was shaking her head, even before Carter had completed his answer. He frowned. Clearly, he was beginning to regret her inclusion in the proceedings.

"You wish to take issue with something I said, Miss Zolli?"

"Yes, I do," she said. "Obviously you don't know much about *Aktion* 1005. Whom do you think Radek used to open those mass graves and destroy the bodies? What do you think he did with them when the work was done?" Greeted by silence, she announced her verdict. "Erich Radek was a mass murderer, and you hired him as a spy."

Carter nodded slowly, as if conceding the match on points. Shamron reached over the back of the couch and placed a restraining hand on Chiara's shoulder. Then he looked at Carter and asked for an explanation of Radek's false escape from Europe. Carter seemed relieved by the prospect of virgin territory. "Ah, yes," he said, "the flight from Europe. This is where it gets interesting."

ERICH RADEK QUICKLY became General Gehlen's most important deputy. Eager to protect his star protégé from arrest and prosecution, Gehlen and his American handlers created a new identity for him: Ludwig Vogel, an Austrian who had been drafted in the Wehrmacht and had gone missing in the final days of the war. For two years, Radek lived in Pullach as Vogel, and his new identity seemed airtight. That changed in the autumn of 1947, with the beginning of Case No. 9 of the subsequent Nuremburg proceedings, the Einsatzgruppen trial. Radek's name surfaced repeatedly during the trial, as did the code name of the secret operation to destroy the evidence of the Einsatzgruppen killings: *Aktion* 1005.

"Gehlen became alarmed," Carter said. "Radek was officially listed as missing and unaccounted for, and Gehlen was eager that he remain that way."

"So you sent a man to Rome posing as Radek," Gabriel said, "and made sure you left enough clues behind so that anyone who went looking for him would follow the wrong trail."

"Precisely."

Shamron, still pacing, said, "Why did you use the Vatican route instead of your own Ratline?"

"You're referring to the Counterintelligence Corps Ratline?"

Shamron closed his eyes briefly and nodded.

"The CIC Ratline was used mainly for Russian defectors. If we'd sent Radek down the line, it would have betrayed the fact he was working for us. We used the Vatican route to enhance his credentials as a Nazi war criminal on the run from Allied justice."

"How clever of you, Adrian. Pardon my interruption. Please continue."

"*Radek* disappeared," Carter said. "Occasionally, the Org fed the story of his escape by slipping false sightings to the various Nazi hunters, claiming that Radek was in hiding in various South American capitals. He was living in Pullach, of course, working for Gehlen under the name Ludwig Vogel."

"Pathetic," Chiara murmured.

"It was 1948," Carter said. "Things were different by then. The Nuremberg process had run its course, and all sides had lost interest in further prosecutions. Nazi doctors had returned to practice. Nazi theoreticians were lecturing again in the universities. Nazi judges were back on the bench."

"And a Nazi mass murderer named Erich Radek was now an important American agent who needed protection," Gabriel said. "When did he return to Vienna?"

"In 1956, Konrad Adenauer made the Org the official West German intelligence service: the Bundesnachrichtendienst, better known as the BND. Erich Radek, now known as Ludwig Vogel, was once again working for the German government. In

1965, he returned to Vienna to build a network and make certain the new Austrian government's official neutrality remained tilted firmly toward NATO and the West. Vogel was a joint BND–CIA project. We worked together on his cover. We cleaned up the files in the Staatsarchiv. We created a company for him to run, Danube Valley Trade and Investment, and funneled enough business his way to make certain the firm was a success. Vogel was a shrewd businessman, and before long, profits from DVTI were funding all of our Austrian nets. In short, Vogel was our most important asset in Austria—and one of our most valuable in Europe. He was a master spy. When the Wall came down, his work was done. He was also getting on in years. We severed our relationship, thanked him for a job well done, and parted company." Carter held up his hands. "And that, I'm afraid, is where the story ends."

"But that's not true, Adrian," Gabriel said. "Otherwise, we wouldn't be here."

"You're referring to the allegations made against Vogel by Max Klein?"

"You knew?"

"Vogel alerted us to the fact that we might have a situation in Vienna. He asked us to intercede and make the allegations go away. We informed him that we couldn't do that."

"So he took matters into his own hands."

"You're suggesting Vogel ordered the bombing at Wartime Claims and Inquiries?"

"I'm also suggesting he had Max Klein murdered in order to silence him."

Carter took a moment before answering. "If Vogel is involved, he's worked through so many cutouts and front men you'll never be able to pin a charge on him. Besides, the bombing and Max Klein's death are Austrian matters, not Israeli, and no Austrian prosecutor is going to open a murder investigation into Ludwig Vogel. It's a dead end."

"His name is Radek, Adrian, not Vogel, and the question is *why*. Why was Radek so concerned about Eli Lavon's investigation that he would resort to murder? Even if Eli and Max Klein were able to prove conclusively that Vogel was really Erich Radek, he would have never been brought to trial by the Austrian state prosecutor. He's too old. Too much time had elapsed. There were no witnesses left, none except Klein, and there's no way Radek would have been convicted in Austria on the word of one old Jew. So why resort to violence?"

"It sounds to me as if you have a theory."

Gabriel looked over his shoulder and murmured a few words in Hebrew to Shamron. Shamron handed Gabriel a file containing all the material he had gathered in the course of the investigation. Gabriel opened it and removed a single item: the photograph he had taken from Radek's house in the Salzkammergut, Radek with a woman and a teen-aged boy. He laid it on the table and turned it so Carter could see. Carter's eyes moved to the photo, then back to Gabriel.

"Who is she?" Gabriel asked.

"His wife, Monica."

"When did he marry her?"

"During the war," said Carter, "in Berlin."

"There was never a mention of an SS-approved marriage in his file."

"There were many things that didn't make it into Radek's SS file."

"And after the war?"

"She settled in Pullach under her real name. The child was born in 1949. When Vogel moved back to Vienna, General Gehlen didn't think it would be safe for Monica and the son to go with him openly—and neither did the Agency. A marriage was arranged for her to a man employed in Vogel's net. She lived in Vienna, in the house behind Vogel's. He visited them in the evening. Eventually, we constructed a passage between the houses, so that Monica and the boy could move freely between the two residences without fear of detection. We never knew who was watching. The Russians would have dearly loved to compromise him and turn him around."

"What was the boy's name?"

"Peter."

"And the agent that Monica Radek married? Please tell us his name, Adrian."

"I think you already know his name, Gabriel." Carter hesitated, then said, "His name was Metzler."

"Peter Metzler, the man who is about to be chancellor of Austria, is the son of a Nazi war criminal named Erich Radek, and Eli Lavon was going to expose that fact."

"So it would seem."

"That sounds like a motive for murder to me, Adrian."

"Bravo, Gabriel," Carter said. "But what can you do about it? Convince the Austrians to bring charges against Radek? Good luck. Expose Peter Metzler as Radek's son? If you do that, you'll also expose the fact that Radek was our man in Vienna. It will cause the Agency much public embarrassment at a time when it is locked in a global campaign against forces that wish to destroy my country *and* yours. It will also plunge relations between your service and mine into the deep freeze at a time when you desperately need our support."

"That sounds like a threat to me, Adrian."

"No, it's just sound advice," Carter said. "It's Realpolitik. Drop it. Look the other way. Wait for him to die and forget it ever happened."

"No," Shamron said.

Carter's gaze moved from Gabriel to Shamron. "Why did I know that was going to be your answer?"

"Because I'm Shamron, and I never forget."

"Then I suppose we need to come up with some way to deal with this situation that doesn't drag my service through the cesspool of history." Carter looked at his watch. "It's getting late. I'm hungry. Let's eat, shall we?"

FOR THE NEXT hour, over a meal of roast duckling and wild rice in the candlelit dining room, Erich Radek's name was not spoken. There was a ritual about affairs such as these, Shamron always said, a rhythm that could not be broken or rushed. There was a time for hard-nosed negotiation, a time to sit back and enjoy the company of a fellow traveler who, when all is said and done, usually has your best interests at heart.

And so, with only the gentlest prod from Carter, Shamron

volunteered to serve as the evening's entertainment. For a time, he played the role expected of him. He told stories of night crossings into hostile lands; of secrets stolen and enemies vanquished; of the fiascos and calamities that accompany any career, especially one as long and volatile as Shamron's. Carter, spellbound, laid down his fork and warmed his hands against Shamron's fire. Gabriel watched the encounter silently from his outpost at the end of the table. He knew that he was witnessing a recruitment—and a perfect recruitment, Shamron always said, is at its heart a perfect seduction. It begins with a bit of flirtation, a confession of feelings better left unspoken. Only when the ground has been thoroughly plowed does one plant the seed of betrayal.

Shamron, over the hot apple crisp and coffee, began to talk not about his exploits but about himself: his childhood in Poland; the sting of Poland's violent anti-Semitism; the gathering storm clouds across the border in Nazi Germany. "In 1936, my mother and father decided that I would leave Poland for Palestine," Shamron said. "They would remain behind, with my two older sisters, and wait to see if things got any better. Like so many others, they waited too long. In September 1939, we heard on the radio that the Germans had invaded. I knew I would never see my family again."

Shamron sat silently for a moment. His hands, when he lit his cigarette, were trembling slightly. His crop had been sown. His demand, though never spoken, was clear. He was not leaving this house without Erich Radek in his pocket, and Adrian Carter was going to help him do it.

WHEN THEY RETURNED to the sitting room for the night session, a tape player stood on the coffee table in front of the couch. Carter, back in his chair next to the fire, loaded English tobacco into the bowl of a pipe. He struck a match and, with the stem between his teeth, nodded toward the tape machine and asked Gabriel to do the honors. Gabriel pressed the Play button. Two men began conversing in German, one with the accent of a Swiss from Zurich, the other a Viennese. Gabriel knew the voice of the man from Vienna. He had heard it a week earlier, in the Café Central. The voice belonged to Erich Radek.

"As of this morning, the total value of the account stands at two and a half billion dollars. Roughly one billion of that is cash, equally divided between dollars and euros. The rest of the money is invested—the usual fare, securities and bonds, along with a substantial amount of real estate. . . ."

TEN MINUTES LATER, Gabriel reached down and pressed the Stop button. Carter emptied the contents of his pipe into the fireplace and slowly loaded another bowl.

"That conversation took place in Vienna last week," Carter said. "The banker is a man named Konrad Becker. He's from Zurich."

"And the account?" Gabriel asked.

"After the war, thousands of fleeing Nazis went into hiding in Austria. They brought several hundred million dollars' worth of looted Nazi assets with them: gold, cash, artwork, jewelry, household silver, rugs, and tapestries. The stuff was stashed all through the Alps. Many of those Nazis wanted to resurrect the Reich, and they wanted to use their looted assets to help accomplish that goal. A small cadre understood that Hitler's crimes were so enormous that it would take at least a generation or more before National Socialism would be politically viable again. They decided to place a large sum of money in a Zurich bank and attach a rather unique set of instructions to the account. It could only be activated by a letter from the Austrian chancellor. You see, they believed that revolution had begun in Austria with Hitler and that Austria would be the fountain of its revival. Five men were initially entrusted with the account number and password. Four of them died. When the fifth took ill, he sought out someone to become the trustee."

"Erich Radek."

Carter nodded and paused a moment to ignite his pipe. "Radek is about to get his chancellor, but he'll never see a drop of that money. We found out about the account a few years ago. Overlooking his past in 1945 was one thing, but we weren't about to allow him to unlock an account filled with two and a half billion in Holocaust loot. We quietly moved against Herr Becker and his bank. Radek doesn't know it yet, but he's never going to see a penny of that money."

Gabriel reached down, pressed REWIND, then STOP, then PLAY:

"Your comrades provided generously for those who assisted them in this endeavor. But I'm afraid there have been some unexpected . . . complications."

"What sort of complications?"

"It seems that several of those who were to receive money have died recently under mysterious circumstances. . . ."

STOP.

Gabriel looked up at Carter for an explanation.

"The men who created the account wanted to reward those individuals and institutions who had helped fleeing Nazis after the war. Radek thought this was sentimental horseshit. He wasn't about to start a benevolent aid association. He couldn't change the covenant, so he changed the circumstances on the ground."

"Were Enrique Calderon and Gustavo Estrada supposed to receive money from the account?"

"I see you learned a great deal during your time with Alfonso Ramirez." Carter gave a guilty smile. "We were following you in Buenos Aires."

"Radek is a wealthy man who doesn't have long to live," Gabriel said. "The last thing he needs is money."

"Apparently, he plans to give a large portion of the account to his son."

"And the rest?"

"He's going to turn it over to his most important agent to carry out the original intentions of the men who created the account." Carter paused. "I believe you and he are acquainted. His name is Manfred Kruz."

Carter's pipe had gone dead. He stared into the bowl, frowned, and relit it.

"Which brings us back to our original problem." Carter blew a puff of smoke toward Gabriel. "What do we do about Erich

Radek? If you ask the Austrians to prosecute him, they'll take their time about it and wait for him to die. If you kidnap an elderly Austrian from the streets of Vienna and cart him back to Israel for trial, the shit will rain down on you from on high. If you think you have trouble in the European Community now, your problems will be multiplied tenfold if you snatch him. And if he's placed on trial, his defense will undoubtedly involve exposing our links to him. So what do we do, gentlemen?"

"Perhaps there's a third way," Gabriel said.

"What's that?"

"Convince Radek to come to Israel voluntarily."

Carter gazed at Gabriel skeptically over the bowl of his pipe.

"And how would you suppose we could convince a first-class shit like Erich Radek to do that?"

THEY TALKED THROUGH the night. It was Gabriel's plan, and therefore his to outline and defend. Shamron added a few valuable suggestions. Carter, resistant at first, soon crossed over to Gabriel's camp. The very audacity of the plan appealed to him. His own service would have probably shot an officer for putting forward so unorthodox an idea.

Every man had a weakness, Gabriel said. Radek, through his actions, had shown he possessed two: his lust for the money hidden in the Zurich account, and his desire to see his son become chancellor of Austria. Gabriel maintained that it was the second that had led Radek to move against Eli Lavon and Max

Klein. Radek didn't want his son tarred by the brush of his previous life, and he had proven that he would take almost any step to protect him. It involved swallowing a bitter pill—making a deal with a man who had no right to demand concessions—but it was morally just and produced the desired result: Erich Radek behind bars for crimes he committed against the Jewish people. Time was the critical factor. The election was less than three weeks away. Radek needed to be in Israeli hands before the first vote was cast in Austria. Otherwise their leverage over him would be lost.

As dawn drew near, Carter posed the question that had been gnawing at him from the moment the first report of Gabriel's investigation crossed his desk: *Why?* Why was Gabriel, an Office assassin, so determined that Radek be brought to justice after so many years?

"I want to tell you a story, Adrian," Gabriel said, his voice suddenly distant, as was his gaze. "Actually, maybe it would be better if she told you the story herself."

He handed Carter a copy of his mother's testimony. Carter, seated next to the dying fire, read it from beginning to end without uttering a word. When finally he looked up from the last page, his eyes were damp.

"I take it Irene Allon is your mother?"

"She *was* my mother. She died a long time ago."

"How can you be sure the SS man in the woods was Radek?"

Gabriel told him about his mother's paintings.

"So I take it you'll be the one who'll handle the negotiations with Radek. And if he refuses to cooperate? What then, Gabriel?"

"His choices will be limited, Adrian. One way or another, Erich Radek is never setting foot in Vienna again."

Carter handed the testimony back to Gabriel. "It's an excellent plan," he said. "But will your prime minister go for it?"

"I'm certain there will be voices raised in opposition," Shamron said.

"Lev?"

Shamron nodded. "My involvement will give him all the grounds he needs to veto it. But I believe Gabriel will be able to bring the prime minister around to our way of thinking."

"Me? Who said I was going to brief the prime minister?"

"I did," Shamron said. "Besides, if you can convince Carter to put Radek on a platter, surely you can convince the prime minister to partake in the feast. He's a man of enormous appetites."

Carter stood and stretched, then walked slowly toward the window, a doctor who has spent the entire night in surgery only to achieve a questionable outcome. He opened the drapes. Gray light filtered into the room.

"There's one last item we need to discuss before leaving for Israel," Shamron said.

Carter turned around, a silhouette against the glass. "The money?"

"What exactly were you planning to do with it?"

"We haven't reached a final decision."

"I have. Two and a half billion dollars is the price you pay for using a man like Erich Radek when you knew he was a murderer and a war criminal. It was stolen from Jews on the way to the gas chambers, and I want it back."

Carter turned once more and looked out at the snow-covered pasture.

"You're a two-bit blackmail artist, Ari Shamron."

Shamron stood and pulled on his overcoat. "It was a pleasure doing business with you, Adrian. If all goes according to plan in Jerusalem, we'll meet again in Zurich in forty-eight hours."

29

JERUSALEM

THE MEETING WAS called for ten o'clock that evening. Shamron, Gabriel, and Chiara, delayed by weather, arrived with two minutes to spare after a white-knuckle car ride from Ben-Gurion Airport, only to be told by an aide that the prime minister was running late. Evidently, there was yet another crisis in his brittle governing coalition, because the anteroom outside his office had taken on the air of a temporary shelter after a disaster. Gabriel counted no fewer than five cabinet officials, each surrounded by a retinue of acolytes and apparatchiks. They were all shouting at each other like quarreling relatives at a family wedding, and a fog bank of tobacco smoke hung on the air.

The aide escorted them into a room reserved for security and intelligence personnel, and closed the door. Gabriel shook his head.

"Israeli democracy in action."

"Believe it or not, it's quiet tonight. Usually, it's worse."

Gabriel collapsed into a chair. He realized suddenly that he had not showered or changed his clothing in two days. Indeed, his trousers were soiled by the dust of the graveyard in Puerto Blest. When he shared this with Shamron, the old man smiled. "To be covered with the dirt of Argentina only adds to the credibility of your message," Shamron said. "The prime minister is a man who will appreciate such a thing."

"I've never briefed a prime minister before, Ari. I would have liked to at least had a shower."

"You're actually nervous." This seemed to amuse Shamron. "I don't think I've ever seen you nervous about anything before in my life. You're human after all."

"Of course I'm nervous. He's a madman."

"Actually, he and I are quite similar in temperament."

"Is that supposed to be reassuring?"

"May I give you a piece of advice?"

"If you must."

"He likes stories. Tell him a good story."

Chiara perched herself on the arm of Gabriel's chair. "Tell it to the prime minister the way you told it to me in Rome," she said *sotto voce.*

"You were in my arms at the time," Gabriel replied. "Something tells me tonight's briefing will be a bit more formal." He smiled, then added, "At least I hope so."

It was nearing midnight by the time the prime minister's aide poked his head into the waiting room and announced that the great man was finally ready to see them. Gabriel and Shamron stood and moved toward the open door. Chiara remained seated. Shamron stopped and turned to face her.

"What are you waiting for? The prime minister is ready to see us."

Chiara's eyes opened wide. "I'm just a *bat leveyha*," she protested. "I'm not going in there to brief the prime minister. My God, I'm not even Israeli."

"You've risked your life in defense of this country," Shamron said calmly. "You have every right to be in his presence."

They entered the prime minister's office. It was large and unexpectedly plain, dark except for an area of illumination around the desk. Lev somehow had managed to slip in ahead of them. His bald, bony skull shone in the recessed lighting, and his long hands were folded beneath a defiant chin. He made a halfhearted effort to stand and shook their hands without enthusiasm. Shamron, Gabriel, and Chiara sat down. The worn leather chairs were still hot from other bodies.

The prime minister was in his shirtsleeves and looked fatigued after his long night of political combat. He was, like Shamron, an uncompromising warrior. How he managed to rule a roost as diverse and disobedient as Israel was something of a miracle. His hooded gaze fell instantly upon Gabriel. Shamron was used to this. Gabriel's striking appearance was the one thing that had given Shamron cause for concern when he recruited him for the Wrath of God operation. People *looked* at Gabriel.

They had met once before, Gabriel and the prime minister, though under very different circumstances. The prime minister had been chief of staff of the Israel Defense Forces in April 1988 when Gabriel, accompanied by a team of commandos, had broken into a villa in Tunis and assassinated Abu Jihad, the second-in-command of the PLO, in front of his wife and children. The prime minister had been aboard the special communications plane, orbiting above the Mediterranean Sea, with Shamron at his side. He had heard the assassination through Gabriel's lip microphone. He had also listened to Gabriel, after the killing, use precious seconds to console Abu Jihad's hysterical wife and daughter. Gabriel had refused the commendation awarded him. Now, the prime minister wanted to know why.

"I didn't feel it was appropriate, Prime Minister, given the circumstances."

"Abu Jihad had a great deal of Jewish blood on his hands. He deserved to die."

"Yes, but not in front of his wife and children."

"He chose the life he led," the prime minister said. "His family shouldn't have been there with him." And then, as if suddenly realizing that he had strayed into a minefield, he attempted to tiptoe out. His girth and natural brusqueness would not permit a graceful exit. He opted for a rapid change of subject instead. "So, Shamron tells me you want to kidnap a Nazi," the prime minister said.

"Yes, Prime Minister."

He held up his palms—*Let's hear it.*

GABRIEL, IF HE was nervous, did not reveal it. His presentation was crisp and concise and full of confidence. The prime minister, notorious for his rough treatment of briefers, sat transfixed throughout. Hearing Gabriel's description of the attempt on his life in Rome, he leaned forward, his face tense. Adrian Carter's confession of American involvement made him visibly irate. Gabriel, when it came time to present his documentary evidence, stood next to the prime minister and placed it piece by piece on the lamplit desk. Shamron sat quietly, his hands squeezing the arms of the chair like a man struggling to maintain a vow of silence. Lev seemed locked in a staring contest with the large portrait of Theodor Herzl that hung on the wall behind the prime minister's desk. He made notes with a gold fountain pen and once took a ponderous look at his wristwatch.

"Can we get him?" the prime minister asked, then added, "Without all hell breaking loose?"

"Yes, sir, I believe we can."

"Tell me how you intend to do it."

Gabriel's briefing spared no detail. The prime minister sat silently with his plump hands folded on the desk, listening intently. When Gabriel finished, the prime minister nodded once and turned his gaze toward Lev—*I assume this is where you part company?*

Lev, ever the technocrat, took a moment to organize his thoughts before answering. His response, when it finally came, was passionless and methodical. Had there been some way to plot it on a flow chart or actuarial table, Lev would surely have stood, pointer in hand, and droned on until dawn. As it was, he remained seated and soon reduced his audience to painful boredom. His speech was punctuated by pauses, during which he made a steeple of his forefingers and pressed them against his bloodless lips.

An impressive piece of investigatory work, Lev said in a back-handed compliment to Gabriel, but now is not the time to waste precious time and political capital settling scores with aged Nazis. The founders, except in the case of Eichmann, resisted the urge to hunt down the perpetrators of the Shoah because they knew it would detract from the primary purpose of the Office, the protection of the State. The same principles apply today. Arresting Radek in Vienna would lead to backlash in Europe, where support for Israel was hanging by a thread. It would also endanger the small, defenseless Jewish community in Austria, where the currents of anti-Semitism run strong and deep. *What will we do when Jews are attacked on the streets? Do you think the Austrian authorities will lift a finger to stop it?* Finally, his trump card: why is it Israel's responsibility to prosecute Radek? Leave it to the Austrians. As for the Americans, let them lie in a bed of their own making. Expose Radek and Metzler, and walk away from it. The point will have been made, and the consequences will be less severe than a kidnapping operation.

The prime minister spent a moment in quiet deliberation, then looked at Gabriel. "There's no doubt this man Ludwig Vogel is really Radek?"

"None whatsoever, Prime Minister."

He turned to Shamron. "And we're certain the Americans aren't going to get cold feet?"

"The Americans are anxious to resolve this matter as well."

The prime minister looked down at the documents before rendering his decision.

"I made the rounds in Europe last month," he said. "While I was in Paris, I visited a synagogue that had been torched a few weeks earlier. The next morning there was an editorial in one of the French newspapers that accused me of picking the scabs of anti-Semitism and the Holocaust whenever it suited my political purposes. Perhaps it's time to remind the world why we inhabit this strip of land, surrounded by a sea of enemies, fighting for our survival. Bring Radek here. Let him tell the world about the crimes he committed in order to hide the Shoah. Maybe it will silence, once and for all, those who contend that it was a conspiracy, invented by men like Ari and myself to justify our existence."

Gabriel cleared his throat. "This isn't about politics, Prime Minister. It's about justice."

The prime minister smiled at the unexpected challenge. "True, Gabriel, it *is* about justice, but justice and politics often go hand in hand, and when justice can serve the needs of politics, there is nothing immoral about it."

Lev, having lost in the first round, attempted to snatch victory in the second by seizing control of the operation. Shamron knew his aim remained the same: killing it. Unfortunately for Lev, so did the prime minister.

"It was Gabriel who brought us to this point. Let Gabriel bring it home."

"With all due respect, Prime Minister, Gabriel is a *kidon*, the best ever, but he is not an operational planner, which is exactly what we need."

"His operational plan sounds fine to me."

"Yes, but can he prepare and execute it?"

"He'll have Shamron looking over his shoulder the entire time."

"That's what I'm afraid of," Lev said acidly.

The prime minister stood; the others followed suit.

"Bring Radek back here. And whatever you do, don't even think about making a mess in Vienna. Get him cleanly, no blood, no heart attacks." He turned to Lev. "Make certain they have every resource they need to get the job done. Don't think you'll be safe from the shit because you voted against the plan. If Gabriel and Shamron go down in flames, you'll go down with them. So no bureaucratic bullshit. You're all in this together. *Shalom.*"

THE PRIME MINISTER seized Shamron's elbow on the way out the door and backed him into a corner. He placed one hand on the wall, above Shamron's shoulder, and blocked any possible route of escape.

"Is the boy up to it, Ari?"

"He's not a boy, Prime Minister, not anymore."

"I know, but can he do it? Can he truly convince Radek to come here?"

"Have you read his mother's testimony?"

"I have, and I know what I'd do in his position. I'm afraid I'd put a bullet in the bastard's brain, like Radek did to so many others, and call it a day."

"Would such an action be just, in your opinion?"

"There's the justice of civilized men, the kind of justice that is dispensed in courtrooms by men in robes, and then there is the justice of the Prophets. *God's* justice. How can one render justice for crimes so enormous? What punishment would be appropriate? Life in prison? A painless execution?"

"The truth, Prime Minister. Sometimes, the best revenge is the truth."

"And if Radek doesn't accept the deal?"

Shamron shrugged. "Are you giving me instructions?"

"I don't need another Demjanuk affair. I don't need a Holocaust show trial that turns into an international media circus. It would be better if Radek simply faded away."

"Faded away, Prime Minister?"

The prime minister exhaled heavily into Shamron's face.

"Are you certain it's *him*, Ari?"

"Of this, there is no doubt."

"Then, if the need arises, put him down."

Shamron looked toward his feet but saw only the bulging midsection of the prime minister. "He shoulders a heavy burden, our Gabriel. I'm afraid I put it there back in '72. He's not up for an assassination job."

"Erich Radek put that burden on Gabriel long before you came along, Ari. Now Gabriel has an opportunity to lose some of it. Let me make my wishes plain. If Radek doesn't agree to come here, tell the prince of fire to put him down and let the dogs lap up his blood."

30

VIENNA

MIDNIGHT IN THE First District, a dead calm, a silence only Vienna can produce, a stately emptiness. Kruz found it reassuring. The feeling didn't last long. It was rare that the old man telephoned him at home, and never had Kruz been dragged from bed in the middle of the night for a meeting. He doubted the news would be good.

He looked down the length of the street and saw nothing out of the ordinary. A glance into his rearview mirror confirmed that he had not been followed. He climbed out and walked to the gate of the old man's imposing graystone house. On the ground floor, lights burned behind drawn curtains. A single light glowed on the second level. Kruz rang the bell. He had the feeling of being watched, something almost imperceptible, like a breath on the back of his neck. He glanced over his shoulder. Nothing.

He reached out toward the bell again, but before he could press it, a buzzer sounded and the deadbolt lock snapped back. He pushed open the gate and crossed the forecourt. By the time he reached the portico, the door was swinging open and a man was standing in the threshold with his suit jacket open and his tie loose. He made no effort to conceal the black leather shoulder holster containing a Glock pistol. Kruz was not alarmed by the sight; he knew the man well. He was a former Staatspolizei officer named Klaus Halder. It was Kruz who had hired him to serve as the old man's bodyguard. Halder usually accompanied the old man only when he went out or was expecting visitors to the house. His presence at midnight was, like the telephone call to Kruz's house, not a good sign.

"Where is he?"

Halder looked wordlessly toward the floor. Kruz loosened the belt of his raincoat and entered the old man's study. The false wall was moved aside. The small, capsulelike lift was waiting. He stepped inside and, with a press of a button, sent it slowly downward. The doors opened a few seconds later, revealing a small subterranean chamber decorated in the soft yellow and gilt of the old man's baroque tastes. The Americans had built it for him so that he could conduct important meetings without fear the Russians were listening in. They'd built the passage, too, the one reached by way of a stainless-steel blast door with a combination lock. Kruz was one of the few people in Vienna who knew where the passage led and who had lived in the house at the other end.

The old man was seated at a small table, a drink before him. Kruz could tell he was uneasy, because he was twisting the glass, two turns to the right, two to the left. Right, right, left, left. A strange habit, thought Kruz. Menacing as hell. He reckoned the old man had picked it up in a previous life, in another world. An image took shape in Kruz's mind: a Russian commissar chained to an interrogation table, the old man seated on the other side, dressed head to toe in black, twisting his drink and gazing at his quarry with those bottomless blue eyes. Kruz felt his heart lurch. The poor bastards were probably shitting themselves even before things got rough.

The old man looked up, the twisting stopped. His cool gaze settled on Kruz's shirtfront. Kruz looked down and saw that his buttons were misaligned. He had dressed in the dark so as not to wake his wife. The old man pointed toward an empty chair. Kruz fixed his shirt and sat down. The twisting started again, two turns to the right, two to the left. Right, right, left, left.

He spoke without greeting or preamble. It was as if they were resuming a conversation interrupted by a knock at the door. During the past seventy-two hours, the old man said, two attempts had been mounted against the life of the Israeli, the first in Rome, the second in Argentina. Unfortunately, the Israeli survived both. In Rome, he apparently was saved by the intervention of a colleague from Israeli intelligence. In Argentina, things were more complicated. There was evidence to suggest that the Americans were now involved.

Kruz, naturally, had questions. Under normal circumstances he would have held his tongue and waited for the old man to say his piece. Now, thirty minutes removed from his bed, he showed none of his usual forbearance.

"What was the Israeli doing in Argentina?"

The old man's face seemed to freeze, and his hand went still. Kruz had strayed over the line, the line that separated what he knew about the old man's past and what he never would. He felt his chest tighten under the pressure of the steady gaze. It was not every day one managed to anger a man capable of orchestrating two assassination attempts on two continents in seventy-two hours.

"It's not necessary you know *why* the Israeli was in Argentina, or even that he was there at all. What you need to know is that this affair has taken a dangerous turn." The twisting resumed. "As you might expect, the Americans know everything. My real identity, what I did during the war. There was no hiding it from them. We were allies. We worked together in the great crusade against the Communists. In the past, I've always counted on their discretion, not out of any sense of loyalty to me, but out of a simple fear of embarrassment. I am under no illusions, Manfred. I am like a whore to them. They turned to me when they were lonely and in need, but now that the Cold War is over, I am like a woman they would rather forget. And if they are now cooperating with the Israelis in some fashion . . ." He left the thought unfinished. "Do you see my point, Manfred?"

Kruz nodded. "I assume they know about Peter?"

"They know *everything*. They possess the power to destroy me, and my son, but only if they are willing to endure the pain of a self-inflicted wound. I used to be quite certain they would never move against me. Now, I'm not so sure."

"What do you want me to do?"

"Keep the Israeli and American embassies under constant watch. Assign physical surveillance to all known intelligence personnel. Keep an eye on the airports and the train stations. Also, contact your informants at the newspapers. They might resort to a damaging press leak. I don't want to be caught off-guard."

Kruz looked down at the table and saw his own reflection in the polished surface. "And when the minister asks me why I'm devoting so many resources to the Americans and the Israelis? What do I tell him?"

"Do I need to remind you what's at stake, Manfred? What you say to your minister is your business. Just get it done. I will not let Peter lose this election. Do you understand me?"

Kruz looked up into the pitiless blue eyes and saw once again the man dressed head to toe in black. He closed his eyes and nodded once.

The old man raised his glass to his lips and, before drinking, smiled. It was about as pleasant as a sudden crack in a pane of glass. He reached into the breast pocket of his blazer, produced a slip of paper, and dealt it onto the tabletop. Kruz glanced at it as it spun his way, then looked up.

"What's this?"

"It's a telephone number."

Kruz left the paper untouched. "A telephone number?"

"One never knows how a situation like this might resolve itself. It might be necessary to resort to violence. It's quite possible I might not be in a position to order such measures. In that case, Manfred, the responsibility will fall to you."

Kruz picked up the slip of paper and held it aloft between his first two fingers. "If I dial this number, who's going to answer?"

The old man smiled. "Violence."

31

ZURICH

HERR CHRISTIAN ZIGERLI, special events coordinator at the Dolder Grand Hotel, was a good deal like the hotel itself—dignified and pompous, resolute and understated, a man who enjoyed his lofty perch in life because it allowed him to look down his nose at others. He was also a man who did not care for surprises. As a rule, he required seventy-two hours advance notice for special bookings and conferences, but when Heller Enterprises and Systech Wireless expressed a desire to conduct their final merger negotiations at the Dolder, Herr Zigerli agreed to waive the seventy-two-hour provision in exchange for a 15-percent surcharge. He could be accommodating when he chose to be, but accommodation, like everything else at the Dolder, came at a steep price.

Heller Enterprises was the suitor, so Heller handled the booking arrangements—not old man Rudolf Heller himself, of course, but a glossy Italian personal assistant who called herself Elena. Herr Zigerli tended to form opinions about people quickly. He would tell you that any hotelier worth his weight in sand did. He did not care for Italians in general, and the aggressive and demanding Elena quickly earned a high ranking on his long list of unpopular clients. She spoke loudly on the telephone, a capital crime in his estimation, and seemed to believe that the mere act of spending vast amounts of her master's money entitled her to special privileges. She *did* seem to know the hotel well—odd, since Herr Zigerli, who had a memory like a file cabinet, could not recall her ever being a guest at the Dolder—and she was excruciatingly specific in her demands. She wanted four adjoining suites near the terrace overlooking the golf course, with good views of the lake. When Zigerli informed her that this was not possible—two and two, or three and one, but not four in a row—she asked whether guests could be moved to accommodate her. Sorry, said the hotelier, but the Dolder Grand is not in the habit of turning guests into refugees. She settled for three adjoining suites and a fourth farther down the hall. "The delegations will arrive at two o'clock tomorrow afternoon," she said. "They'd like a light working lunch." There followed ten more minutes of bickering over what constituted a "light working lunch."

When the menu was complete, Elena lobbed one more demand his way. She would arrive four hours before the delegations, accompanied by Heller's chief of security, in order to inspect the rooms. Once the inspections were complete, no hotel personnel would be allowed inside unless accompanied by Heller security. Herr Zigerli sighed heavily and agreed, then hung up the phone and, with his office door closed and locked, performed a series of deep-breathing exercises to calm his nerves.

The morning of the negotiations dawned gray and cold. The stately old turrets of the Dolder poked into the blanket of freezing fog, and the perfect asphalt in the front drive shone like polished black granite. Herr Zigerli stood watch in the lobby, just inside the sparkling glass doors, feet shoulder-width apart, hands at his sides, girded for battle. She'll be late, he thought. They always are. She'll need more suites. She'll want to change the menu. She'll be perfectly horrible.

A black Mercedes sedan glided into the drive and stopped outside the entrance. Herr Zigerli cast a discreet glance at his wristwatch. Ten o'clock precisely. Impressive. The bellman opened the rear door, and a sleek black boot emerged—Bruno Magli, noted Zigerli—followed by a shapely knee and thigh. Herr Zigerli rocked forward onto the balls of his feet and smoothed his hair over his bald spot. He had seen many beautiful women float through the famous doorway of the Dolder Grand, yet few had done it with any more grace or style than the lovely Elena of Heller Enterprises. She had a mane of chestnut hair, held in place by a clasp at the nape of her neck, and skin the color of honey. Her brown eyes were flecked with gold, and they seemed to grow lighter when she shook his hand. Her voice, so loud and demanding over the telephone line, was now soft and thrilling, as was her Italian accent. She released his hand and turned to an unsmiling companion. "Herr Zigerli, this is Oskar. Oskar does security."

Apparently, Oskar had no last name. None needed, thought Zigerli. He was built like a wrestler, with strawberry-blond hair and faint freckles across his broad cheeks. Herr Zigerli, trained observer of the human condition, saw something he recognized in Oskar. A fellow tribesman, if you will. He could picture him, two centuries earlier, in the clothing of a woodsman, pounding along a pathway through the Black Forest. Like all good security men, Oskar let his eyes do the talking, and his eyes told Herr Zigerli he was anxious to get to work. "I'll show you to your rooms," said the hotelier. "Please, follow me."

Herr Zigerli decided to take them up the stairs rather than the elevator. They were one of the Dolder's finest attributes, and Oskar the woodsman didn't look like the type who enjoyed waiting for lifts when there was a flight of steps to be scaled. The rooms were on the fourth floor. On the landing, Oskar held out his hand for the electronic cardkeys. "We'll take it from here, if you don't mind. No need to show us the inside of the rooms. We've all been in hotels before." A knowing wink, a genial pat on the arm. "Just point us the way. We'll be fine."

Indeed, you will, thought Zigerli. Oskar was a man who inspired confidence in other men. Women too, Zigerli suspected. He wondered whether the delectable Elena—he was already beginning to think of her as *his* Elena—was one of Oskar's conquests. He placed the cardkeys in Oskar's upturned palm and showed them the way.

Herr Zigerli was a man of many maxims—*"A quiet customer is a contented customer"* was among his most cherished—and therefore he interpreted the ensuing silence on the fourth floor as proof that Elena and her friend Oskar were pleased with the accommodations. This in turn pleased Herr Zigerli. He now liked making Elena happy. As he went about the rest of his morning, she remained on his mind, like the trace of her scent that had attached itself to his hand. He found himself longing for some problem, some silly complaint that would require a consultation with her. But there was nothing, only the silence of contentment. She had her Oskar now. She had no need for the special events coordinator of Europe's finest hotel. Herr Zigerli, once again, had done his job *too* well.

He did not hear from them, or even see them, until two o'clock that afternoon, when they congregated in the lobby and formed an unlikely welcoming party for the arriving delegations. There was snow swirling in the front court now. Zigerli believed the foul weather only heightened the appeal of the old hotel—a safe haven from the storm, like Switzerland itself.

The first limousine pulled into the drive and disgorged two passengers. One was Herr Rudolf Heller himself, a small, elderly man, dressed in an expensive dark suit and silver necktie. His slightly tinted spectacles suggested an eye condition; his brisk, impatient walk left the impression that, in spite of his advanced years, he was a man who could take care of himself. Herr Zigerli welcomed him to the Dolder and shook the proffered hand. It seemed to be made of stone.

He was accompanied by the grim-faced Herr Keppelmann. He was perhaps twenty-five years younger than Heller, short-cropped hair, gray at the temples, very green eyes. Herr Zigerli had seen his fair share of bodyguards at the Dolder, and Herr Keppelmann certainly seemed the type. Calm but vigilant, silent as a church mouse, sure-footed and strong. The emerald-colored eyes were placid but in constant motion. Herr Zigerli looked at Elena and saw that her gaze was trained on Herr Keppelmann. Perhaps he was wrong about Oskar. Perhaps the taciturn Keppelmann was the luckiest man in the world.

The Americans came next: Brad Cantwell and Shelby Somerset, the CEO and COO of Systech Communications, Inc., of Reston, Virginia. There was a quiet sophistication about them that Zigerli was not used to seeing in Americans. They were not overly friendly, nor were they bellowing into cell phones as they came into the lobby. Cantwell spoke German as well as Herr Zigerli and avoided eye contact. Somerset was the more affable of the two. The well-traveled blue blazer and slightly crumpled striped tie identified him as an Eastern preppy, as did his upper-class drawl.

Herr Zigerli made a few welcoming remarks, then receded quietly into the background. It was something he did exceptionally well. As Elena led the group toward the staircase, he slipped into his office and closed the door. An impressive group of men, he thought. He expected great things to come of this venture. His own role in the affair, however minor, had been carried off with precision and quiet competence. In today's world, such attributes were of little value, but they were the coin of Herr Zigerli's miniature realm. He suspected the men of Heller Enterprises and Systech Communications probably felt exactly the same way.

IN CENTRAL ZURICH, on the quiet street near the spot where the heavy green waters of the Limmat River flow into the lake, Konrad Becker was in the process of buttoning up his private bank for the evening when the telephone on his desk purred softly. Technically, it was five minutes before the close of business, but he was tempted to let the machine get it. In Becker's experience, only problem clients telephoned so late in the afternoon, and his day had been difficult enough already. Instead, like a good Swiss banker, he reached for the receiver and brought it robotically to his ear.

"Becker and Puhl."

"Konrad, it's Shelby Somerset. How the hell are you?"

Becker swallowed hard. Somerset was the name of the American from the CIA—at least, Somerset is what he called himself. Becker doubted very much it was his real name.

"What can I do for you, Mr. Somerset?"

"You can drop the formalities for starters, Konrad."

"And for the main course?"

"You can walk downstairs to the Talstrasse and climb in the back seat of the silver Mercedes that's waiting there."

"Why would I want to do that?"

"We need to see you."

"Where is this Mercedes going to take me?"

"Somewhere pleasant, I assure you."

"What's the dress code?"

"Business attire will be fine. And, Konrad?"

"Yes, Mr. Somerset?"

"Don't think about playing hard to get. This is the real deal. Go downstairs. Get in the car. We're watching you. We're always watching you."

"How reassuring, Mr. Somerset," the banker said, but the line had already gone dead.

TWENTY MINUTES LATER, Herr Zigerli was standing at reception when he noticed one of the Americans, Shelby Somerset, pacing anxiously outside in the drive. A moment later, a silver Mercedes eased into the circle, and a small, bald figure alighted from the back seat. Polished Bally loafers, a blast-proof attaché case. *A banker*, thought Zigerli. He'd bet his paycheck on it. Somerset gave the new arrival a hail-fellow smile and a firm clap on the shoulder. The small man, despite the warm greeting, looked as though he were being led to his execution. Still, Herr Zigerli reckoned the talks were going well. The moneyman had arrived.

"GOOD AFTERNOON, HERR BECKER. Such a pleasure to see you. I'm Heller. Rudolf Heller. This is my associate, Mr. Keppelmann. That man over there is our American partner, Brad Cantwell. Obviously, you and Mr. Somerset are already acquainted."

The banker blinked rapidly several times, then settled his cunning little gaze on Shamron, as if he were trying to arrive at a calculation of his net worth. He held his attaché over his genitals, in anticipation of an imminent assault.

"My associates and I are about to embark on a joint venture. The problem is, we can't do it without your help. That's what bankers do, isn't it, Herr Becker? Help launch great endeavors? Help people realize their dreams and their potential?"

"It depends on the venture, Herr Heller."

"I see," Shamron said, smiling. "For example, many years ago, a group of men came to you. German and Austrian men. They wanted to launch a great endeavor as well. They entrusted you with a large sum of money and granted you the power to turn it into an even larger sum. You did extraordinarily well. You turned it into a mountain of money. I assume you remember these gentlemen? I also assume you know where they got their money?"

The Swiss banker's gaze hardened. He had arrived at his calculation of Shamron's worth.

"You're Israeli, aren't you?"

"I prefer to think of myself as a citizen of the world," replied Shamron. "I reside in many places, speak the languages of many lands. My loyalty, like my business interests, knows no national boundaries. As a Swiss, I'm sure you can understand my point of view."

"I understand it," Becker said, "but I don't believe you for a minute."

"And if I *were* from Israel?" Shamron asked. "Would this have some impact on your decision?"

"It would."

"How so?"

"I don't care for Israelis," Becker said forthrightly. "Or Jews, for that matter."

"I'm sorry to hear that, Herr Becker, but a man is entitled to his opinions, and I won't hold it against you. I never allow politics to get in the way of business. I need help for my endeavor, and you're the only person who can help me."

Becker raised his eyebrows quizzically. "What exactly is the nature of this endeavor, Herr Heller?"

"It's quite simple, really. I want you to help me kidnap one of your clients."

"I believe, Herr Heller, that the *endeavor* you're suggesting would be a violation of Swiss banking secrecy laws—and several other Swiss laws as well."

"Then I suppose we'll have to keep your involvement secret."

"And if I refuse to cooperate?"

"Then we'll be forced to tell the world that you were the murderers' banker, that you're sitting on two and a half billion dollars of Holocaust loot. We'll unleash the bloodhounds of the World Jewish Congress on you. You and your bank will be in tatters by the time they're finished with you."

The Swiss banker cast a pleading look at Shelby Somerset. "We had a deal."

"We still do," the lanky American drawled, "but the outlines of the deal have changed. Your client is a very dangerous man. Steps need to be taken to neutralize him. We need you, Konrad. Help us clean up a mess. Let's do some good together."

The banker drummed his fingers against the attaché case. "You're right. He *is* a dangerous man, and if I help you kidnap him, I might as well dig my own grave."

"We'll be there for you, Konrad. We'll protect you."

"And what if the 'outlines of the deal' change again? Who'll protect me then?"

Shamron interceded. "You were to receive one hundred million dollars upon final dispersal of the account. Now, there will be no final dispersal of the account, because you're going to give all the money to me. If you cooperate, I'll let you keep half of what you were supposed to receive. I assume you can do the math, Herr Becker?"

"I can."

"Fifty million dollars is more than you deserve, but I'm willing to let you have it in order to gain your cooperation in this matter. A man can buy a lot of security with fifty million."

"I want it in writing, a letter of guarantee."

Shamron shook his head sadly, as if to say there were some things—*And you should know this better than anyone, my dear fellow*—that one does not put in writing.

"What do you need from me?" Becker asked.

"You're going to help us get into his home."

"How?"

"You'll need to see him rather urgently concerning some aspect of the account. Perhaps some papers need to be signed, some final details in preparation for liquidation and dispersal of the assets."

"And once I'm inside the house?"

"Your job is finished. Your new assistant will handle matters after that."

"My new assistant?"

Shamron looked at Gabriel. "Perhaps it's time we introduced Herr Becker to his new partner."

HE WAS A MAN of many names and personalities. Herr Zigerli knew him as Oskar, the chief of Heller security. The landlord of his pied-à-terre in Paris knew him as Vincent Laffont, a free-lance travel writer of Breton descent who spent most of his time living out of a suitcase. In London, he was known as Clyde Bridges, European marketing director of an obscure Canadian business software firm. In Madrid, he was a German of independent means and a restless soul who idled away the hours in cafés and bars, and traveled to relieve the boredom.

His real name was Uzi Navot. In the Hebrew-based lexicon of the Israeli secret intelligence service, Navot was a *katsa*, an undercover field operative and case officer. His territory was western Europe. Armed with an array of languages, a roguish charm, and fatalistic arrogance, Navot had penetrated Palestinian terrorist cells and recruited agents in Arab embassies scattered across the continent. He had sources in nearly all the European security and intelligence services and oversaw a vast network of *sayanim*, volunteer helpers recruited from local Jewish communities. He could always count on getting the best table in the grill room at the Ritz in Paris because the maître d' hôtel was a paid informant, as was the chief of the maid staff.

"Konrad Becker, meet Oskar Lange."

The banker sat motionless for a long moment, as though he had been suddenly bronzed. Then his clever little eyes settled on Shamron, and he raised his hands in an inquiring gesture.

"What am I supposed to do with him?"

"You tell us. He's very good, our Oskar."

"Can he impersonate a lawyer?"

"With the right preparation, he could impersonate your mother."

"How long does this charade have to last?"

"Five minutes, maybe less."

"When you're with Ludwig Vogel, five minutes can seem like an eternity."

"So I've heard," Shamron said.

"What about Klaus?"

"Klaus?"

"Vogel's bodyguard."

Shamron smiled. Resistance had ended. The Swiss banker had joined the team. He now swore allegiance to the flag of Herr Heller and his noble endeavor.

"He's very professional," Becker said. "I've been to the house a half-dozen times, but he always gives me a thorough search and asks me to open my briefcase. So, if you're thinking about trying to get a weapon into the house—"

Shamron cut him off. "We have no intention of bringing weapons in the house."

"Klaus is always armed."

"You're sure?"

"A Glock, I'd say." The banker patted the left side of his chest. "Wears it right there. Doesn't make much of an effort to hide it."

"A lovely piece of detail, Herr Becker."

The banker accepted the compliment with a tilt of his head—*Details are my business, Herr Heller.*

"Forgive my insolence, Herr Heller, but how does one actually kidnap someone who's protected by a bodyguard if the bodyguard is armed and the kidnapper isn't?"

"Herr Vogel is going to leave his house voluntarily."

"A voluntary kidnapping?" Becker's tone was incredulous. "How unique. And how does one convince a man to allow himself to be kidnapped *voluntarily*?"

Shamron folded his arms. "Just get Oskar inside the house and leave the rest to us."

32

MUNICH

IT WAS AN OLD apartment house in the pretty little Munich district of Lehel, with a gate on the street and the main entrance off a tidy courtyard. The lift was fickle and indecisive, and more often than not, they simply climbed the spiral staircase to the third floor. The furnishings had a hotel room anonymity. There were two beds in the bedroom, and the sitting room couch was a davenport. In the storage closet were four extra cots. The pantry was stocked with nonperishable goods, and the cabinets contained place settings for eight. The sitting-room windows overlooked the street, but the blackout shades remained drawn at all times, so that inside the flat it seemed a perpetual evening. The telephones had no ringers. Instead, they were fitted with red lights that flashed to indicate incoming calls.

The walls of the sitting room were hung with maps: central Vienna, metropolitan Vienna, eastern Austria, Poland. On the wall opposite the windows hung a very large map of central Europe, which showed the entire escape route, stretching from Vienna to the Baltic coast. Shamron and Gabriel had quarreled briefly over the color before settling on red. From a distance it seemed a river of blood, which is precisely how Shamron wanted it to appear, the river of blood that had flowed through the hands of Erich Radek.

They spoke only German in the flat. Shamron had decreed it. Radek was referred to as Radek and only Radek; Shamron would not call him by the name he'd bought from the Americans. Shamron laid down other edicts as well. It was Gabriel's operation, and therefore it was Gabriel's show to run. It was Gabriel, in the Berlin accent of his mother, who briefed the teams, Gabriel who reviewed the watch reports from Vienna, and Gabriel who made all final operational decisions.

For the first few days, Shamron struggled to fit into his supporting role, but as his confidence in Gabriel grew, he found it easier to slide into the background. Still, every agent who passed through the safe flat took note of the dark pall that had settled over him. He seemed never to sleep. He would stand before the maps at all hours, or sit at the kitchen table in the dark, chain-smoking like a man wrestling with a guilty conscience.

"He's like a terminal patient who's planning his own funeral," remarked Oded, a veteran German-speaking agent whom Gabriel had chosen to drive the escape car. "And if it goes to hell, they'll chisel it on his tombstone, right below the Star of David."

Under perfect circumstances, such an operation would involve weeks of planning. Gabriel had only days. The Wrath of God operation had prepared him well. The terrorists of Black September had been constantly on the move, appearing and disappearing with maddening frequency. When one was located and positively identified, the hit team would swing into action at light speed. Surveillance teams would swoop into place, vehicles and safe flats would be rented, escape routes would be planned. That reservoir of experience and knowledge served Gabriel well in Munich. Few intelligence officers knew more about rapid planning and quick strikes than he and Shamron.

In the evenings, they watched the news on German television. The election in neighboring Austria had captured the attention of German viewers. Metzler was rolling forward. The crowds at his campaign stops, like his lead in the polls, grew larger by the day. Austria, it seemed, was on the verge of doing the unthinkable, electing a chancellor from the far right. Inside the Munich safe flat, Gabriel and his team found themselves in the odd position of cheering Metzler's ascent in the polls, for without Metzler, their doorway to Radek would close.

Invariably, soon after the news ended, Lev would check in from King Saul Boulevard and subject Gabriel to a tedious cross-examination of the day's events. It was the one time Shamron was relieved not to bear the burden of operational command. Gabriel would pace the floor with a phone against his ear, patiently answering each of Lev's questions. And sometimes, if the light was right, Shamron would see Gabriel's mother, pacing beside him. She was the one member of the team that no one ever mentioned.

ONCE EACH DAY, usually in late afternoon, Gabriel and Shamron escaped the safe flat to walk in the English Gardens. Eichmann's shadow hung over them. Gabriel reckoned he had been there from the beginning. He had come that night in Vienna, when Max Klein had told Gabriel the story of the SS officer who had murdered a dozen prisoners at Birkenau and now enjoyed coffee every afternoon at the Café Central. Still, Shamron had diligently avoided even speaking his name, until now.

Gabriel had heard the story of Eichmann's capture many times before. Indeed, Shamron had used it in September 1972 to prod Gabriel into joining the Wrath of God team. The version Shamron told during those walks along the tree-lined footpaths of the English Gardens was more detailed than any Gabriel had heard before. Gabriel knew these were not merely the ramblings of an old man trying to relive past glories. Shamron was never one to trumpet his own successes, and the publishers would wait in vain for his memoirs. Gabriel knew Shamron was telling him about Eichmann for a reason. *I've taken the journey you're about to make*, Shamron was saying. *In another time, in another place, in the company of another man, but there are things you should know.* Gabriel, at times, could not shake the sense that he was walking with history.

"Waiting for the escape plane was the hardest part. We were

trapped in the safe house with this rat of a man. Some of the team couldn't bear to look at him. I had to sit in his room night after night and keep watch over him. He was chained to the iron bed, dressed in pajamas with opaque goggles over his eyes. We were strictly forbidden to engage him in conversation. Only the interrogator was allowed to speak to him. I couldn't obey those orders. You see, I had to know. How had this man who was sickened by the sight of blood killed six million of my people? My mother and father? My two sisters? I asked him why he had done it. And do you know what he said? He told me he did it because it was his job—his job, Gabriel—as if he were nothing more than a bank clerk or a railroad conductor."

And later, standing at the balustrade of a humpbacked bridge overlooking a stream:

"Only once did I want to kill him, Gabriel—when he tried to tell me that he did not hate the Jewish people, that he actually liked and admired the Jewish people. To show me how much he cared for the Jews, he began to recite our words: *Shema, Yisrael, Adonai Eloheinu, Adonai Echad!* I could not bear to hear those words coming out of that mouth, the mouth that had given the orders to murder six million. I clamped my hand over his face until he shut up. He began to shake and convulse. I thought I'd caused him to have a heart attack. He asked me if I was going to kill him. He pleaded with me not to harm his son. This man who had torn children from the arms of their parents and thrown them into the fire was concerned about his own child, as if we would act like him, as if we would murder children."

And at a scarred wooden table, in a deserted beer garden:

"We wanted him to agree to return with us voluntarily to Israel. He, of course, did not want to go. He wanted to stand trial in Argentina or Germany. I told him this was not possible. One way or another, he was going to stand trial in Israel. I risked my career by allowing him to have a bit of red wine and a cigarette. I did not drink with the murderer. I could not. I assured him that he would be given a chance to tell his side of the story, that he would be given a proper trial with a proper defense. He was under no illusions about the outcome, but the notion of explaining himself to the world somehow appealed to him. I also pointed out the fact that he would have the dignity of knowing he was about to die, something he denied to the millions who marched into the disrobing rooms and the gas chambers while Max Klein serenaded them. He signed the paper, dated it like a good German bureaucrat, and it was done."

Gabriel listened intently, his coat collar around his ears, his hands crammed into his pockets. Shamron shifted the focus from Adolf Eichmann to Erich Radek.

"You have an advantage because you've seen him face to face once already, at the Café Central. I'd seen Eichmann only from afar, while we were watching his house and planning the snatch, but I had never actually spoken to him or even stood next to him. I knew exactly how tall he was, but couldn't picture it. I had a sense of how his voice would sound, but I didn't *really* know. You know Radek, but unfortunately he knows a bit about you, too, thanks to Manfred Kruz. He'll want to know more. He'll feel exposed and vulnerable. He'll try to level the playing field by asking you questions. He'll want to know why you are pursuing him. Under no circumstances are you to engage him in anything like normal conversation. Remember, Erich

Radek was no camp guard or gas chamber operator. He was SD, a skilled interrogator. He'll try to bring those skills to bear one final time to avoid his fate. Don't play into his hands. You're the one in charge now. He'll find the reversal a shock to the system."

Gabriel cast his eyes downward, as if he were reading the words carved into the table.

"So why do Eichmann and Radek deserve the trappings of justice," he said finally, "but the Palestinians from Black September only vengeance?"

"You would have made a fine Talmudic scholar, Gabriel."

"And you're avoiding my question."

"Obviously, there was a measure of pure vengeance in our decision to target the Black September terrorists, but it was more than that. They posed a continuing threat. If we didn't kill them, they would kill us. It was war."

"Why not arrest them, put them on trial?"

"So they could spout their propaganda from an Israeli court?" Shamron shook his head slowly. "They already did that"—he raised his hand and pointed to the tower rising over the Olympic Park—"right here in this city, in front of all the world's cameras. It wasn't our job to give them another opportunity to justify the massacre of innocents."

He lowered his hand and leaned across the table. It was then that he told Gabriel of the prime minister's wishes. His breath froze before him as he spoke.

"I don't want to kill an old man," Gabriel said.

"He's not an old man. He wears an old man's clothing and hides behind an old man's face, but he's still Erich Radek, the monster who killed a dozen men at Auschwitz because they couldn't identify a piece of Brahms. The monster who killed two girls by the side of a Polish road because they wouldn't deny the atrocities of Birkenau. The monster who opened the graves of millions and subjected their corpses to one final humiliation. Infirmity does not forgive such sins."

Gabriel looked up and held Shamron's insistent gaze. "I know he's a monster. I just don't want to kill him. I want the world to know what this man did."

"Then you'd better be ready to do battle with him." Shamron glared at his wristwatch. "I'm bringing in someone to help you prepare. In fact, he should be arriving shortly."

"Why am I being told about this now? I thought I was the one making all the operational decisions."

"You are," Shamron said. "But sometimes I have to show you the way. That's what old men are for."

NEITHER GABRIEL NOR Shamron believed in harbingers or omens. If they had, the operation that brought Moshe Rivlin from Yad Vashem to the safe house in Munich would have cast doubt on the team's ability to carry out the task before them.

Shamron wanted Rivlin approached quietly. Unfortunately, King Saul Boulevard entrusted the job to a pair of apprentices fresh from the Academy, both markedly Sephardic in appearance. They decided to contact Rivlin while he walked home from Yad Vashem to his apartment near the Yehuda Market. Rivlin, who had grown up in the Bensonhurst section of Brooklyn and was still vigilant when walking the streets, quickly noticed that he was being followed by two men in a car. He assumed them to be Hamas suicide bombers or a pair of street criminals. When the car pulled alongside him and the passenger asked for a word, Rivlin broke into a lopsided run. To everyone's surprise, the tubby archivist proved himself to be an elusive prey, and he evaded his captors for several minutes before finally being cornered by the two Office agents in Ben Yehuda Street.

He arrived at the safe flat in Lehel late that evening, bearing two suitcases filled with research material and a chip on his shoulder over the way his summons had been handled. "How do you expect to snatch a man like Erich Radek if you can't grab one fat archivist? Come on," he said, pulling Gabriel into the privacy of the back bedroom. "We have a lot of ground to cover and not much time to do it."

ON THE SEVENTH DAY, Adrian Carter came to Munich. It was a Wednesday; he arrived at the safe flat in the late afternoon, as the dusk was turning to dark. The passport in the pocket of his Burberry overcoat still said Brad Cantwell. Gabriel and Shamron were just returning from an outing in the English Gardens and were bundled in their hats and scarves. Gabriel had dispatched the rest of the team members to their final staging positions, so the safe flat was empty of Office personnel. Only Rivlin remained. He greeted the deputy director of the CIA with his shirttail out and his shoes off and called himself Yaacov. The archivist had adapted well to the discipline of the operation.

Gabriel made the tea. Carter unbuttoned his coat and led himself on a preoccupied tour of the flat. He spent a long time in front of the maps. Carter believed in maps. Maps never lied to you. Maps never told you what they thought you *wanted* to hear.

"I like what you've done with the place, Herr Heller." Carter finally removed his overcoat. "Neocontemporary squalor. And the smell. I'm sure I know it. Carry-out from the Wienerwald down the block, if I'm not mistaken."

Gabriel handed him a mug of tea with the string from the bag still dangling over the edge of the rim. "Why are you here, Adrian?"

"I thought I'd pop over to see if I could be of help."

"Bullshit."

Carter cleared a spot on the couch and sat down heavily, a salesman at the end of a long and fruitless road trip. "Truth be told, I'm here at the behest of my director. It seems he's getting a serious case of preoperative jitters. He feels we're out on a limb together and you boys are the ones holding the chainsaw. He wants the Agency to be brought into the picture."

"Meaning?"

"He wants to know the game plan."

"You know the game plan, Adrian. I told you the game plan in Virginia. It hasn't changed."

"I know the broad strokes of the plan," Carter said. "Now I'd like to see the fine print."

"What you're saying is that your director wants to review the plan and sign off on it."

"Something like that. He also wants me standing on the sidelines with Ari when it goes down."

"And if we tell him to go to hell?"

"I'd say there's a fifty-fifty chance someone will whisper a warning in Erich Radek's ear, and you'll lose him. Play ball with the director, Gabriel. It's the only way you'll get Radek."

"We're ready to move, Adrian. Now is not the time for helpful suggestions from the seventh floor."

Shamron sat down next to Carter. "If your director had an ounce of brains, he'd stay as far away from this as possible."

"I tried to explain that to him—not in those terms, mind you, but something close. He'd have none of it. He came from Wall Street, our director. He likes to think of himself as a hands-on, take-charge sort of fellow. Always knew what every division of the company was doing. Tries to run the Agency the same way. And as you know, he's also a friend of the president. If you cross him, he'll call the White House, and it'll be over."

Gabriel looked to Shamron, who gritted his teeth and nodded. Carter got his briefing. Shamron remained seated for a few minutes, but soon he was up and pacing the room, a chef whose secret recipes are being given to a competitor up the street. When it was finished, Carter took a long time loading the bowl of his pipe with tobacco.

"Sounds to me as if you gentlemen are ready," he said. "What are you waiting for? If I were you, I'd put it in motion before my hands-on director decides he wants to be part of the snatch team."

Gabriel agreed. He picked up the telephone and dialed Uzi Navot in Zurich.

33

VIENNA • MUNICH

KLAUS HALDER KNOCKED softly on the door of the study. The voice on the other side granted permission for him to enter. He pushed open the door and saw the old man seated in the half-light, his eyes fixed on the flickering screen of the television: a Metzler rally that afternoon in Graz, adoring crowds, talk already turning to the composition of the Metzler cabinet. The old man killed the image by remote and turned his blue eyes on the bodyguard.

Halder glanced toward the telephone. A green light was winking.

"Who is it?"

"Herr Becker, calling from Zurich."

The old man picked up the receiver. "Good evening, Konrad."

"Good evening, Herr Vogel. I'm sorry to bother you so late, but I'm afraid it couldn't wait."

"Is something wrong?"

"Oh, no, quite the contrary. Given the recent election news from Vienna, I've decided to quicken the pace of my preparations and proceed as though Peter Metzler's victory is a fait accompli."

"A wise course of action, Konrad."

"I thought you'd agree. I have several documents that require your signature. I thought it would be best for us to start that process now rather than waiting until the last moment."

"What sort of documents?"

"My lawyer will be able to explain them better than I can. If it's all right with you, I'd like to come to Vienna for a meeting. It won't take more than a few minutes."

"How does Friday sound?"

"Friday would be fine, as long as it's late afternoon. I have an appointment in the morning that can't be moved."

"Shall we say four o'clock?"

"Five would be better for me, Herr Vogel."

"All right, Friday at five o'clock."

"I'll see you then."

"Konrad?"

"Yes, Herr Vogel."

"This lawyer—tell me his name, please."

"Oskar Lange, Herr Vogel. He's a very talented man. I've used him many times in the past."

"I assume he's a fellow who understands the meaning of the word 'discretion'?"

"Discreet doesn't even begin to describe him. You're in very capable hands."

"Goodbye, Konrad."

The old man hung up the phone and looked at Halder.

"He's bringing someone with him?"

A slow nod.

"He's always come alone in the past. Why is he suddenly bringing along a helper?"

"Herr Becker is about to receive one hundred million dollars, Klaus. If there's one man in the world we can trust, it's the gnome from Zurich."

The bodyguard moved toward the door.

"Klaus?"

"Yes, Herr Vogel?"

"Perhaps you're right. Call some of our friends in Zurich. See if anyone's heard of a lawyer named Oskar Lange."

ONE HOUR LATER, a recording of Becker's telephone call was sent by secure transmission from the offices of Becker & Puhl in Zurich to the safe flat in Munich. They listened to it once, then again, then a third time. Adrian Carter did not like what he heard.

"You realize that as soon as Radek put down the phone, he made a second phone call to Zurich to check out Oskar Lange. I hope you've accounted for that."

Shamron seemed disappointed in Carter. "What do you think, Adrian? We've never done this sort of thing before? We're children who need to be shown the way?"

Carter put a match to his pipe and puffed smoke, awaiting his answer.

"Have you ever heard of the term *sayan*?" Shamron said. "Or *sayanim*?"

Carter nodded with the pipe between his teeth. "Your little volunteer helpers," he said. "The hotel clerks who give you rooms without checking in. The rental car agents who give you cars that can't be traced. The doctors who treat your agents when they have wounds that might raise difficult questions. The bankers who give you emergency loans."

Shamron nodded. "We're a small intelligence service, twelve hundred full-time employees, that's all. We couldn't do what we do without the help of the *sayanim*. They're one of the few benefits of the Diaspora, my private army of little volunteer helpers."

"And Oskar Lange?"

"He's a Zurich tax and estate lawyer. He also happens to be Jewish. It's something that he doesn't advertise in Zurich. A few years ago, I took Oskar to dinner in a quiet little restaurant on the lake and added him to my list of helpers. Last week, I asked him for a favor. I wanted to borrow his passport and his office, and I wanted him to disappear for a couple of weeks. When I told him why, he was all too willing to help.

In fact, he wanted to go to Vienna himself and help capture Radek."

"I hope he's in a secure location."

"You might say so, Adrian. He's in a safe flat in Jerusalem at the moment."

Shamron reached down toward the tape player, pressed REWIND, STOP, then PLAY:

"How does Friday sound?"

"Friday would be fine, as long as it's late afternoon. I have an appointment in the morning that can't be moved."

"Shall we say four o'clock?"

"Five would be better for me, Herr Vogel."

"All right, Friday at five o'clock."

STOP.

MOSHE RIVLIN LEFT the safe flat the following morning and returned to Israel on an El Al flight, with an Office minder in the seat next to him. Gabriel remained until seven o'clock Thursday evening, when a Volkswagen van with two pairs of skis mounted to the roof pulled up outside the flat and honked its horn twice. He slipped his Beretta into the waist of his trousers. Carter wished him luck; Shamron kissed his cheek and sent him down.

Shamron opened the curtains and peered into the darkened street. Gabriel emerged from the passageway and went to the driver's side window. After a moment of discussion, the door opened and Chiara emerged. She walked around the front of the van and was briefly illuminated by the glow of the headlights before climbing into the passenger seat.

The van eased away from the curb. Shamron followed its progress until the crimson taillights disappeared around a corner. He did not move. The waiting. Always the waiting. His lighter flared, a cloud of smoke gathered against the glass.

34

ZURICH

KONRAD BECKER AND Uzi Navot emerged from the offices of Becker & Puhl at precisely four minutes past one o'clock on Friday afternoon. An Office watcher called Zalman, posted on the opposite side of the Talstrasse in a gray Fiat sedan, recorded the time as well as the weather, a drenching downpour, then flashed the news to Shamron in the Munich safe flat. Becker was dressed for a funeral, in a gray pinstripe suit and charcoal-colored tie. Navot, mimicking Oskar Lange's stylish attire, wore an Armani blazer with matching electric blue shirt and tie. Becker had ordered a taxi to take him to the airport. Shamron would have preferred a private car, with an Office driver, but Becker always traveled to the airport by taxi and Gabriel wanted his routine left undisturbed. So it was an ordinary city taxi, driven by a Turkish immigrant, that bore them out of central Zurich and across a fogbound river valley to Kloten Airport, with Gabriel's watcher in tow.

They were soon confronted with the first glitch. A cold front had moved over Zurich, turning the rain to sleet and ice and forcing Kloten Airport authorities to briefly suspend operations. Swiss International Airlines Flight 1578, bound for Vienna, boarded on time, then sat motionless on the tarmac. Shamron and Adrian Carter, monitoring the situation on the computers in the Munich safe flat, debated their next move. Should they instruct Becker to call Radek and warn him about the delay? What if Radek had other plans and decided to cancel the meeting and reschedule it for another time? The teams and vehicles were at final staging positions. A temporary stand-down would jeopardize operational security. Wait, counseled Shamron, and wait is what they did.

By 2:30, weather conditions had improved. Kloten reopened and Flight 1578 took its place in the queue at the end of the runway. Shamron made the calculations. The flight to Vienna took less than ninety minutes. If they got off the ground soon, they could still make it to Vienna in time.

At 2:45, the plane was airborne, and disaster was averted. Shamron flashed the reception team at Schwechat Airport in Vienna that their package was on its way.

The storm over the Alps made the flight to Vienna a good deal more turbulent than Becker would have preferred. To settle his nerves he consumed three miniature bottles of Stolichnaya and visited the toilet twice, all of which was recorded by Zalman, who was seated three rows behind. Navot, a picture of concentration and serenity, stared out the window at the sea of black cloud, his sparkling water untouched.

They touched down at Schwechat a few minutes after four o'clock in a dirty gray twilight. Zalman shadowed them through the terminal toward passport control. Becker made one more visit to the toilet. Navot, with an almost imperceptible movement of his eyes, commanded Zalman to go with him. After availing himself of the facilities, the banker spent three minutes primping in front of the mirror—an inordinate amount of time, thought Zalman, for a man with virtually no hair. The watcher considered giving Becker a kick in the ankle to move him along, then decided to let him have the reins instead. He was, after all, an amateur acting under duress.

After clearing passport control, Becker and Navot made their way into the arrivals hall. There, standing amid the crowds, was a tall, reedy surveillance specialist called Mordecai. He wore a drab black suit and held a cardboard sign that read BAUER. His car, a large black Mercedes sedan, was waiting in short-term parking. Two spaces away was a silver Audi hatchback. The keys were in Zalman's pocket.

Zalman gave them wide berth during the drive into Vienna. He dialed the Munich safe flat, and with a few carefully chosen words let Shamron know that Navot and Becker were on time and proceeding toward the target. By 4:45, Mordecai had reached the Danube Canal. By 4:50, he had crossed the line into the First District and was making his way through the rush-hour traffic along the Ringstrasse. He turned right, into a narrow cobblestone street, then made the first left. A moment later, he drew to a stop in front of Erich Radek's ornate iron gate. Zalman slipped past on the left and kept driving.

"FLASH THE LIGHTS," Becker said, "and the bodyguard will admit you."

Mordecai did as he was told. The gate remained motionless for several tense seconds; then there was a sharp metallic clank, followed by the grind of a motor engaging. As the gate swung slowly open, Radek's bodyguard appeared at the front door, the intense light of a chandelier blazing around his head and shoulders like a halo. Mordecai waited until the gate was fully open before easing forward into the small horseshoe drive.

Navot climbed out first, then Becker. The banker shook the bodyguard's hand and introduced "my associate from Zurich, Herr Oskar Lange." The bodyguard nodded and gestured for them to come inside. The front door closed.

Mordecai looked at his watch: 4:58. He picked up his cell phone and dialed a Vienna number.

"I'm going to be late for dinner," he said.

"Is everything all right?"

"Yes," he said. "Everything's fine."

A FEW SECONDS LATER, in Munich, the signal flashed across Shamron's computer screen. Shamron looked at his watch.

"How long are you going to give them?" Carter asked.

"Five minutes," Shamron said, "and not a second more."

THE BLACK AUDI sedan with a tall antenna mounted to the trunk was parked a few streets over. Zalman pulled in behind it, then climbed out and walked to the passenger door. Oded was seated behind the wheel, a compact man with soft brown eyes and a pugilist's flattened nose. Zalman, settling in next to him, could smell tension on his breath. Zalman had had the advantage of activity that afternoon; Oded had been trapped in the Vienna safe flat with nothing to do but daydream about the consequences of failure. A cell phone lay on the seat, the connection already open to Munich. Zalman could hear Shamron's steady breathing. A picture formed in his mind—a younger version of Shamron marching through a drenching Argentine rain, Eichmann stepping off a city bus and walking toward him from the opposite direction. Oded started the car engine. Zalman was hauled back to the present. He glanced at the dashboard clock: *5:03* . . .

THE E461, BETTER known to Austrians as the Brünnerstrasse, is a two-lane road that runs north from Vienna through the rolling hills of the *Weinviertel*, Austria's wine country. It is fifty miles to the Czech border. There is a crossing, sheltered by a high arching canopy, usually manned by two guards who are reluctant to leave the comfort of their aluminum and glass hut to carry out even the most cursory inspection of outgoing vehicles. On the Czech side of the crossing, the examination of travel documents typically takes a bit longer, though traffic from Austria is generally welcomed with open arms.

One mile across the border, anchored to the hills of South Moravia, stands the ancient town of Mikulov. It is a border town, with a border town's siege mentality. It suited Gabriel's mood. He stood behind the brick parapet of a medieval castle, high above the red-tile roofs of the old city, beneath a pair of wind-bent pine. The cold rain beaded like tears on the surface of his oilskin coat. His gaze was down the hillside, toward the border. In the blackness, only the lights of the traffic along the highway were visible, white lights rising toward him, red lights receding toward the Austrian border.

He looked at his watch. They would be inside Radek's villa now. Gabriel could picture briefcases opening, coffee and drinks being poured. And then another image appeared, a line of women dressed in gray, making their way along a snowy road drenched in blood. His mother, shedding tears of ice.

"What will you tell your child about the war, Jew?"

"The truth, Herr Sturmbannführer. I'll tell my child the truth."

"No one will believe you."

She had not told him the truth, of course. Instead, she had set the truth to paper and locked it away in the file rooms of Yad Vashem. Perhaps Yad Vashem was the best place for it. Perhaps there are some truths so appalling they are better left confined to an archive of horrors, quarantined from the uninfected. She had been unable to tell him she was Radek's victim, just as

Gabriel could never tell her he was Shamron's executioner. She always knew, though. She knew the face of death, and she had seen death in Gabriel's eyes.

The telephone in his coat pocket vibrated silently against his hip. He brought it slowly to his ear and heard the voice of Shamron. He dropped the telephone into his pocket and stood for a moment, watching the headlights floating toward him across the black Austrian plain.

"What will you say to him when you see him?" Chiara had asked.

The truth, Gabriel thought now. *I'll tell him the truth.*

He started walking, down the narrow stone streets of the ancient town, into the darkness.

35

VIENNA

UZI NAVOT KNEW a thing or two about body searches. Klaus Halder was very good at his job. He started with Navot's shirt collar and ended with the cuffs of his Armani trousers. Next he turned his attention to the attaché case. He worked slowly, like a man with all the time in the world, and with a monkish attention to detail. When the search was finally over, he straightened the contents carefully and snapped the latches back into place. "Herr Vogel will see you now," he said. "Follow me, please."

They walked the length of the central corridor, then passed through a pair of double doors and entered a drawing room. Erich Radek, in a herringbone jacket and rust-colored tie, was seated near the fireplace. He acknowledged his guests with a single nod of his narrow head but made no attempt to rise. Radek, Navot gathered, was a man used to receiving visitors seated.

The bodyguard slipped quietly from the room and closed the doors behind him. Becker, smiling, stepped forward and shook Radek's hand. Navot did not wish to touch the murderer, but given the circumstances he had no choice. The proffered hand was cool and dry, the grip firm and without a tremor. It was a testing handshake. Navot sensed that he had passed.

Radek flicked his fingers toward the empty chairs, then his hand returned to the drink resting on the arm of his chair. He began twisting it back and forth, two twists to the right, two to the left. Something about the movement made acid pour into Navot's stomach.

"I hear very good things about your work, Herr Lange," Radek said suddenly. "You have a fine reputation among your colleagues in Zurich."

"All lies, I assure you, Herr Vogel."

"You're too modest." He twisted his drink. "You did some work for a friend of mine a few years back, a gentleman named Helmut Schneider."

And you're trying to lead me into a trap, thought Navot. He had prepared himself for a ploy like this. The real Oskar Lange had provided a list of his clients for the last ten years for Navot to memorize. The name Helmut Schneider had not appeared on it.

"I've handled a good many clients over the last few years, but I'm afraid the name Schneider was not among them. Perhaps your friend has me confused with someone else."

Navot looked down, opened the latches of his attaché case, and lifted the lid. When he looked up again, Radek's blue eyes were boring into his, and his drink was rotating on the arm of the chair. There was a frightening stillness about his eyes. It was like being studied by a portrait.

"Perhaps you're right." Radek's conciliatory tone did not match his expression. "Konrad said you required my signature on some documents concerning the liquidation of the assets in the account."

"Yes, that's correct."

Navot removed a file from his attaché and placed the attaché on the floor at his feet. Radek followed the progress of the briefcase downward, then returned his gaze to Navot's face. Navot lifted the lid of the file folder and looked up. He opened his mouth to speak but was interrupted by the ringing of the telephone. Sharp and electronic, it sounded to Navot's sensitive ears like a scream in a cemetery.

Radek made no movement. Navot glanced toward the Biedermeier desk, and the telephone rang a second time. It started to ring a third time, then went suddenly silent, as though it had been muzzled midscream. Navot could hear Halder, the bodyguard, speaking on an extension in the corridor.

"Good evening. . . . No, I'm sorry, but Herr Vogel is in a meeting at the moment."

Navot removed the first document from the file. Radek was now visibly distracted, his gaze distant. He was listening to the sound of his bodyguard's voice. Navot inched forward in his chair and held the paper at an angle so Radek could see it.

"This is the first document that requires—"

Radek lifted his hand, demanding silence. Navot heard footfalls in the corridor, followed by the sound of the doors opening. The bodyguard stepped into the room and walked to Radek's side.

"It's Manfred Kruz," he said in a chapel murmur. "He'd like a word. He says it's urgent and can't wait."

ERICH RADEK ROSE slowly from his chair and walked to the telephone.

"What is it, Manfred?"

"The Israelis."

"What about them?"

"I have intelligence to suggest that during the past few days a large team of operatives has assembled in Vienna in order to kidnap you."

"How certain are you of your intelligence?"

"Certain enough to conclude it's no longer safe for you to remain in your home. I've dispatched a Staatspolizei unit to collect you and take you to a safe location."

"No one can get inside here, Manfred. Just put an armed guard outside the house."

"We're dealing with the *Israelis,* Herr Vogel. I want you out of the house."

"All right, if you insist, but tell your unit to stand down. Klaus can handle it."

"One bodyguard isn't enough. I'm responsible for your security, and I want you under police protection. I'm afraid I have to insist. The intelligence I have is very specific."

"When will your officers be here?"

"Any minute. Get ready to move."

He hung up the telephone and looked at the two men seated next to the fire. "I'm sorry, gentlemen, but I'm afraid I have something of an emergency. We'll have to finish this another time." He turned to his bodyguard. "Open the gates, Klaus, and get me a coat. *Now.*"

THE MOTORS OF the front gates engaged. Mordecai, seated behind the wheel of the Mercedes, looked into his rearview mirror and saw a car turning into the drive from the street, a blue light whirling on the dash. It pulled up behind him and braked hard. Two men piled out and bounded up the front steps. Mordecai reached down and slowly turned the ignition.

ERICH RADEK WENT into the corridor. Navot packed his attaché case and stood. Becker remained frozen in place. Navot hooked his fingers beneath the banker's armpit and lifted him to his feet.

They followed Radek into the corridor. Blue emergency lights flashed across the walls and ceilings. Radek was next to his bodyguard, speaking quietly into his ear. The bodyguard was holding an overcoat and looked tense. As he helped Radek into the coat, his eyes were on Navot.

There was a knock at the door, two sharp reports that echoed from the high ceiling and marble floor of the corridor. The bodyguard released Radek's overcoat and turned the latch. Two men in plainclothes pushed past and entered the house.

"Are you ready, Herr Vogel?"

Radek nodded, then turned and looked once more at Navot and Becker. "Again, please accept my apologies, gentlemen. I'm terribly sorry for the inconvenience."

Radek turned toward the door, Klaus at his shoulder. One of the officers blocked his path and put a hand on the bodyguard's chest. The bodyguard swatted it away.

"What do you think you're doing?"

"Herr Kruz gave us very specific instructions. We were to take only Herr Vogel into protective custody."

"Kruz would have never given an order like that. He knows that I go wherever *he* goes. That's the way it's always been."

"I'm sorry, but those were our orders."

"Let me see your badge and identification."

"There isn't time. Please, Herr Vogel. Come with us."

The bodyguard took a step back and reached inside his jacket. As the gun came into view, Navot lunged forward. With his left hand, he seized the bodyguard's wrist and pinned the gun against his abdomen. With his right, he delivered two vicious open-handed blows to the back of the neck. The first blow staggered Halder; the second caused his knees to buckle. His hand relaxed, and the Glock clattered to the marble floor.

Radek looked at the gun and for an instant thought about trying to pick it up. Instead, he turned and lunged toward the open door of his study and slammed it shut.

Navot tried the latch. Locked.

He took a few steps back and drove his shoulder into the door. The wood splintered and he tumbled into the darkened room. He scrambled to his feet and saw that Radek had already moved away the false front of a bookcase and was standing inside a small, phone-booth–sized lift.

Navot sprang forward as the elevator door started to close. He managed to get both his arms inside and grab Radek by the lapels of his overcoat. As the door slammed against Navot's left shoulder, Radek seized his wrists and tried to break free. Navot held firm.

Oded and Zalman came to his aid. Zalman, the taller of the two, reached over Navot's head and pulled against the door. Oded slithered between Navot's legs and applied pressure from below. Under the onslaught, the door finally slid open again.

Navot dragged Radek out of the elevator. There was no time for subterfuge or deception now. Navot clamped a hand over the old man's mouth, Zalman took hold of his legs and lifted him off the floor. Oded found the light switch and doused the chandelier.

Navot glanced at Becker. "Get in the car. Move, you idiot."

They bundled Radek down the steps toward the Audi. Radek was pulling at Navot's hand, trying to break the vise grip over his mouth, and kicking hard with his legs. Navot could hear Zalman swearing under his breath. Somehow, even in the heat of battle, he managed to swear in German.

Oded threw open the rear door before running around the back of the car and climbing behind the wheel. Navot pushed

Radek headfirst into the back and pinned him to the seat. Zalman forced his way inside and closed the door. Becker climbed into the back of the Mercedes. Mordecai accelerated hard, and the car lurched into the street, the Audi following closely.

RADEK'S BODY WENT suddenly still. Navot removed his hand from Radek's mouth, and the Austrian gulped greedily of the air.

"You're hurting me," he said. "I can't breathe."

"I'll let you up, but you have to promise to behave yourself. No more escape attempts. Do you promise?"

"Just let me up. You're crushing me, you fool."

"I will, old man. Just do me a favor first. Tell me your name, please."

"You know my name. My name is Vogel. Ludwig Vogel."

"No, no, not that name. Your *real* name."

"That is my real name."

"Do you want to sit up and leave Vienna like a man, or am I going to have to sit on you the whole way?"

"I want to sit up. You're hurting me, damn it!"

"Just tell me your name."

He was silent for a moment, then he murmured, "My name is Radek."

"I'm sorry, but I couldn't hear you. Can you say your name again, please? Loudly this time."

He drew a deep breath of air and his body went rigid, as though he were standing at attention instead of lying across the back seat of a car.

"My—name—is—Sturmbannführer—Erich—*Radek!*"

IN THE MUNICH safe flat, the message flashed across Shamron's computer screen: PACKAGE HAS BEEN RECEIVED.

Carter clapped him on the back. "I'll be goddamned! They got him. They actually got him."

Shamron stood and walked to the map. "Getting him was always the easiest part of the operation, Adrian. Getting him out is quite another thing."

He gazed at the map. Fifty miles to the Czech border. *Drive, Oded,* he thought. *Drive like you've never driven before in your life.*

36

VIENNA

ODED HAD MADE the drive a dozen times but never like this—never with the siren screaming and the blue light whirling on the dash, and never with Erich Radek's eyes in the rearview mirror, staring back into his own. Their flight from the city center had gone better than expected. The evening traffic had been persistent, but never so heavy that it didn't part for his siren and flashing light. Twice, Radek rebelled. Each uprising was ruthlessly put down by Navot and Zalman.

They were racing north now on the E461. The Vienna traffic was gone, the rain was falling steadily and freezing at the edges of the windshield. A sign flashed past: CZECH REPUBLIC 42 KM. Navot took a long look over his shoulder, then, in Hebrew, instructed Oded to kill the siren and the lights.

"Where are we going?" Radek asked, his breathing labored. "Where are you taking me? *Where*?"

Navot said nothing, just as Gabriel had instructed. *"Let him ask questions till he's blue in the face,"* Gabriel had said. *"Just don't give him the satisfaction of an answer. Let the uncertainty prey on his mind. That's what he would do if the roles were reversed."*

So Navot watched the villages flashing past his window—Mistelbach, Wilfersdorf, Erdberg—and thought of only one thing, the bodyguard he had left unconscious in the entranceway of Radek's house on the Stöbbergasse.

Poysdorf appeared before them. Oded sped through the village, then turned into a two-lane road and followed it eastward through snow-covered pine.

"Where are we going? Where are you taking me?"

Navot could endure his questions in silence no longer.

"We're going home," he snapped. "And you're coming with us."

Radek managed a glacial smile. "You made only one mistake tonight, Herr Lange. You should have killed my bodyguard when you had the chance."

KLAUS HALDER OPENED one eye, then the other. The darkness was absolute. He lay very still for a moment, trying to determine the position of his body. He had fallen forward, with his arms at his sides, and his right cheek was pressed against cold marble. He tried to lift his head, a bolt of thunderous pain shot down his neck. He remembered it now, the instant it had happened. He'd been reaching for his gun when he'd been clubbed twice from behind. It was the lawyer from Zurich, Oskar Lange. Obviously, Lange was no mere lawyer. He'd been in on it, just as Halder had feared from the beginning.

He pushed himself onto his knees and sat back against the wall. He closed his eyes and waited until the room stopped spinning, then rubbed the back of his head. It was swollen the size of an apple. He raised his left wrist and squinted at the luminous dial of his wristwatch: 5:57. When had it happened? A few minutes after five, 5:10 at the latest. Unless they'd had a helicopter waiting on the Stephansplatz, chances were they were still in Austria.

He patted the right front pocket of his sport jacket and found that his cell phone was still there. He fished it out and dialed. Two rings. A familiar voice.

"This is Kruz."

THIRTY SECONDS LATER, Manfred Kruz slammed down the phone and considered his options. The most obvious response would be to sound the alarm Klaxons, alert every police unit in the country that the old man had been seized by Israeli agents, close the borders and shut down the airport. Obvious, yes, but very dangerous. A move like that would raise many uncomfortable questions. *Why was Herr Vogel kidnapped? Who is he really?* Peter Metzler's candidacy would be swept away, and so too would

Kruz's career. Even in Austria, such affairs had a way of taking on a life of their own, and Kruz had seen enough of them to know that the inquiry would not end at Vogel's doorstep.

The Israelis had known he would be hamstrung, and they had chosen their moment well. Kruz had to think of some subtle way to intervene, some way to impede the Israelis without destroying everything in the process. He picked up the telephone and dialed.

"This is Kruz. The Americans have informed us that they believe an al-Qaeda team may be transiting the country by automobile this evening. They suspect the al-Qaeda members might be traveling with European sympathizers in order to better blend into their surroundings. As of this moment, I'm activating the terrorism alert network. Raise security at the borders, airports, and train stations to Category Two status."

He rang off and gazed out the window. He had thrown the old man a lifeline. He wondered whether he would be in any condition to grab it. Kruz knew that if he succeeded, he would soon be confronted with yet another problem—what to do with the Israeli snatch team. He reached into the breast pocket of his suit jacket and removed a slip of paper.

"If I dial this number, who's going to answer?"

"Violence."

Manfred Kruz reached for his telephone.

THE CLOCKMAKER, SINCE his return to Vienna, had scarcely found cause to leave the sanctuary of his little shop in the Stephansdom Quarter. His frequent travels had left him with a large backlog of pieces requiring his attention, including a Vienna Biedermeier regulator clock, built by the renowned Vienna clockmaker Ignaz Marenzeller in 1840. The mahogany case was in pristine condition, though the one-piece silvered dial had required many hours of restoration. The original handmade Biedermeier movement, with its 75-day runner, lay in several carefully arranged pieces on the surface of his worktable.

The telephone rang. He lowered the volume on his portable CD player, and Bach's Brandenburg Concerto No. 4 in G faded to a whisper. A prosaic choice, Bach, but then the Clockmaker found the precision of Bach a perfect accompaniment to the task of dismantling and rebuilding the movement of an antique timepiece. He reached out for the telephone with his left hand. A shock wave of pain shot down the length of his arm, a reminder of his exploits in Rome and Argentina. He brought the receiver to his right ear and cradled it against his shoulder. "Yes," he said inattentively. His hands were already at work again.

"I was given your number by a mutual friend."

"I see," the Clockmaker said noncommittally. "How can I help you?"

"It's not me who requires help. It's our friend."

The Clockmaker laid down his tools. "Our friend?" he asked.

"You did some work for him in Rome and Argentina. I assume you know the man I am referring to?"

The Clockmaker did indeed. So, the old man had misled him and twice put him in compromising situations in the field. Now he had committed the mortal operational sin of giving his name to a stranger. Obviously he was in trouble. The Clockmaker suspected it had something to do with the Israelis. He decided that now would be an excellent moment to sever their relationship. "I'm sorry," he said, "but I believe you have me confused with someone else."

The man at the other end of the line tried to object. The Clockmaker hung up the phone and turned up the volume on his CD player, until the sound of Bach filled his workshop.

IN THE MUNICH safe flat, Carter hung up the telephone and looked at Shamron, who was still standing before the map, as if imagining Radek's progress northward toward the Czech border.

"That was from our Vienna station. They're monitoring the Austrian communications net. It seems Manfred Kruz has taken their terror alert readiness to Category Two."

"Category Two? What does that mean?"

"It means you're likely to have a bit of trouble at the border."

THE TURNOUT LAY in a hollow at the edge of a frozen streambed. There were two vehicles, an Opel sedan and a Volkswagen van. Chiara sat behind the wheel of the Volkswagen, headlights doused, engine silent, the comforting weight of a Beretta across her lap. There was no other sign of life, no lights from the village, no grumble of traffic along the highway, only the rattle of sleet on the roof of the van and the whistle of the wind through the spires of the fir trees.

She glanced over her shoulder and peered into the rear compartment of the Volkswagen. It had been prepared for Radek's arrival. The rear foldout bed was deployed. Beneath the bed was the specially constructed compartment where he would be hidden for the border crossing. He would be comfortable there, more comfortable than he deserved.

She looked out the windshield. Not much to see, the narrow road rising into the gloom toward a crest in the distance. Then, suddenly, there was light, a clean white glow that lit the horizon and turned the trees to black minarets. For a few seconds, it was possible to see the sleet, swirling like a cloud of insects on the windswept air. Then the headlamps appeared. The car breasted the hill, and the lights bore into her, throwing the shadows of the trees one way, then another. Chiara wrapped her hand around the Beretta and slipped her forefinger inside the trigger guard.

The car skidded to a stop next to the van. She peered into the back seat and saw the murderer, seated between Navot and Zalman, rigid as a commissar waiting for the blood purge. She crawled into the rear compartment and made one final check.

"TAKE OFF YOUR OVERCOAT," Navot commanded.

"Why?"

"Because I told you to."

"I have a right to know why."

"You have no rights! Just do as I say."

Radek sat motionless. Zalman pulled at the lapel of his coat, but the old man folded his arms tightly across his chest. Navot sighed heavily. If the old bastard wanted one final wrestling match, he was going to get it. Navot pried open his arms while Zalman pulled off the right sleeve, then the left. The herringbone jacket came next, then Zalman tore open his shirtsleeve and exposed the sagging bare skin of his arm. Navot produced a syringe, loaded with the sedative.

"This is for your own good," Navot said. "It's mild and very short in duration. It will make your journey much more bearable. No claustrophobia."

"I've never been claustrophobic."

"I don't care."

Navot plunged the needle into Radek's arm and depressed the plunger. After a few seconds, Radek's body relaxed, then his head fell to one side and his jaw went slack. Navot opened the door and climbed out. He took hold of Radek's limp body beneath the armpits and dragged him out of the car.

Zalman picked him up by the legs, and together they carried him like war dead to the side of the Volkswagen. Chiara was crouched inside, holding an oxygen bottle and a clear plastic mask. Navot and Zalman laid Radek on the floor of the Volkswagen, then Chiara placed the mask over his nose and mouth. The plastic fogged immediately, indicating that Radek was breathing well. She checked his pulse. Steady and strong. They maneuvered him into the compartment and closed the lid.

Chiara climbed behind the wheel and started the engine. Oded slid the side door shut and rapped his palm against the glass. Chiara slipped the Volkswagen into gear and headed back toward the highway. The others climbed into the Opel and followed after her.

FIVE MINUTES LATER, the lights of the border appeared like beacons on the horizon. As Chiara drew nearer, she could see a short line of traffic, about six vehicles in length, waiting to make the crossing. There were two border policeman in evidence. They had their flashlights out and were checking passports and looking through windows. She glanced over her shoulder. The doors over the compartment remained closed. Radek was silent.

The car in front of her passed inspection and was released to the Czech side. The border policeman waved her forward. She lowered her window and managed a smile.

"Passport, please."

She handed it over. The second officer had maneuvered his way around to the passenger side of the van, and she could see the beam of his flashlight flickering around the interior.

"Is something wrong?"

The border policeman kept his eyes down on her photograph and said nothing.

"When did you enter Austria?"

"Earlier today."

"Where?"

"From Italy, at Tarvísio."

He spent a moment comparing her face to the photo in the passport. Then he pulled open the front door and motioned for her to get out of the van.

UZI NAVOT WATCHED the scene from his vantage point in the front passenger seat of the Opel. He looked at Oded and swore softly under his breath. Then he dialed the Munich safe flat on his cell phone. Shamron answered on the first ring.

"We've got a problem," Navot said.

HE ORDERED HER to stand in front of the van and shone a light in her face. Through the glare she could see the second border policeman pulling open the side door of the Volkswagen. She forced herself to look at her interrogator. She tried not to think of the Beretta pressing against her spine. Or of Gabriel, waiting on the other side of the border in Mikulov. Or Navot, Oded, and Zalman, watching helplessly from the Opel.

"Where are you traveling to this evening?"

"Prague," she said.

"Why are you going to Prague?"

She shot him a look—*None of your business.* Then she said, "I'm going to see my boyfriend."

"Boyfriend," he repeated. "What does your boyfriend do in Prague?"

"He teaches Italian," Gabriel had said.

She answered the question.

"Where does he teach?"

"At the Prague Institute of Language Studies," Gabriel had said.

Again, she answered as Gabriel had instructed.

"And how long has he been a teacher at the Prague Institute of Language Studies?"

"Three years."

"And do you see him often?"

"Once a month, sometimes twice."

The second officer had climbed inside the van. An image of Radek flashed through her mind, eyes closed, oxygen mask over his face. *Don't wake*, she thought. Don't stir. Don't make a sound. Do the decent thing, for once in your wretched life.

"And when did you enter Austria?"

"I've told you that already."

"Tell me again, please."

"Earlier today."

"What time?"

"I don't remember the time."

"Was it the morning? Was it the afternoon?"

"Afternoon."

"Early afternoon? Late afternoon?"

"Early."

"So it was still light?"

She hesitated; he pressed her. "Yes? It was still light?"

She nodded. From inside the van came the sound of cabinet doors being opened. She forced herself to look directly into the eyes of her questioner. His face, obscured by the harsh flashlight, began to take on the appearance of Erich Radek—not the pathetic version of Radek that lay unconscious in the back of the van, but the Radek who pulled a child named Irene Frankel from the ranks of the Birkenau death march in 1945 and led her into a Polish forest for one final moment of torment.

"Say the words, Jew! You were transferred to the east. You had plenty of food and proper medical care. The gas chambers and the crematoria are Bolshevik-Jewish lies."

I can be as strong as you, Irene, she thought. I can get through this. For you.

"Did you stop anywhere in Austria?"

"No."

"You didn't take the opportunity to visit Vienna?"

"I've been to Vienna," she said. "I don't like it."

He spent a moment examining her face.

"You are Italian, yes?"

"You have my passport in your hand."

"I'm not referring to your passport. I'm talking about your ethnicity. Your blood. Are you of Italian descent, or are you an immigrant, from, say, the Middle East or North Africa?"

"I'm Italian," she assured him.

The second officer climbed out of the Volkswagen and shook his head. Her interrogator handed over the passport. "I'm sorry for the delay," he said. "Have a pleasant journey."

Chiara climbed behind the wheel of the Volkswagen, slipped the van into gear, and eased over the border. The tears came, tears of relief, tears of anger. At first she tried to stop them, but it was no use. The road blurred, the taillights turned to red streamers, and still they came.

"For you, Irene," she said aloud. "I did it for you."

THE MIKULOV TRAIN station lies below the old town, where the hillside meets the plain. There is a single platform that endures a near-constant assault of wind pouring down out of the Carpathian Mountains, and a melancholy gravel car park that tends to pond over when it rains. Near the ticket office is a graffiti-scarred bus shelter, and it was there, pressed against the leeward side, where Gabriel waited, hands plunged into the pockets of his oilskin jacket.

He looked up as the van turned into the car park and

crunched over the gravel. He waited until it came to a stop before stepping from the bus shelter into the rain. Chiara reached across and opened the door to him. When the overhead light came on, he could see her face was wet.

"Are you all right?"

"I'm fine."

"Do you want me to drive?"

"No, I can do it."

"Are you sure?"

"Just get in, Gabriel. I can't stand being alone with him."

He climbed in and closed the door. Chiara turned around and headed back to the highway. A moment later, they were racing north, into the Carpathians.

IT TOOK A HALF-HOUR to reach Brno, another hour to get to Ostrava. Twice Gabriel opened the doors of the compartment to check on Radek. It was nearly eight o'clock when they reached the Polish border. No security checks this time, no line of traffic, just a hand poking from the brick bunker, waving them across the frontier.

Gabriel crawled to the back of the van and pulled Radek from the compartment. Then he opened a storage drawer and removed a syringe. This time it was filled with a mild dosing of stimulant, just enough to raise him gently back to the surface of consciousness. Gabriel inserted the needle into Radek's arm, injected the drug, then removed the needle and swabbed the wound with alcohol. Radek's eyes opened slowly. He surveyed his surroundings for a moment before settling on Gabriel's face.

"Allon?" he murmured through the oxygen mask.

Gabriel nodded slowly.

"Where are you taking me?"

Gabriel said nothing.

"Am I going to die?" he asked, but before Gabriel could answer, he slipped below the surface once more.

37

EASTERN POLAND

THE BARRIER BETWEEN consciousness and coma was like a stage curtain, through which he could pass at will. How many times he slipped through this curtain he did not know. Time, like his old life, was lost to him. His beautiful house in Vienna seemed another man's house, in another man's city. Something had happened when he'd shouted out his real name at the Israelis. Ludwig Vogel was a stranger to him now, an acquaintance whom he had not seen in many years. He was Radek again. Unfortunately, time had not been kind to him. The towering, beautiful man in black was now imprisoned in a weak, failing body.

The Jew had placed him on the foldout bed. His hands and ankles were bound by thick silver packing tape, and he was belted into place like a mental patient. His wrists served as the portal between his two worlds. He had only to twist them at a certain angle, so that the tape dug painfully into his skin, and he would pass through the curtain from a dreamscape to the realm of the real. Dreams? Is it proper to call such visions dreams? No, they were too accurate, too telling. They were memories, over which he had no control, only the power to interrupt them for a few moments by hurting himself with the Jew's packing tape.

His face was near the window, and the glass was unobstructed. He was able, when he was awake, to see the endless black countryside and the dreary, darkened villages. He was also able to read the road signs. He did not need the signs to know where he was. Once, in another lifetime, he had ruled the night in this land. He remembered this road: Dachnow, Zukow, Narol. . . . He knew the name of the next village, even before it slid past his window: *Belzec* . . .

He closed his eyes. Why now, after so many years? After the war, no one had been terribly interested in a mere SD officer who had served in the Ukraine—no one but the Russians, of course—and by the time his name surfaced in connection with the Final Solution, General Gehlen had arranged for his escape and disappearance. His old life was safely behind him. He had been forgiven by God and his Church and even by his enemies, who had greedily availed themselves of his services when they too felt threatened by Jewish-Bolshevism. The governments soon lost interest in prosecuting the so-called war criminals, and the amateurs like Wiesenthal focused on the big fish like Eichmann and Mengele, unwittingly helping smaller fish like himself find sanctuary in sheltered waters. There had been one serious scare. In the mid-seventies, an American journalist, a Jew, of course, had come to Vienna and asked too many questions. On the road leading south from Salzburg he had plunged into a ravine, and the threat was eliminated. He had acted without hesitation then. Perhaps he should have hurled Max Klein into a ravine at the first sign of trouble. He'd noticed him that day at the Café Central, as well as the days that followed. His instincts had told him Klein was trouble. He'd hesitated. Then Klein had taken his story to the Jew Lavon, and it was too late.

He passed through the curtain again. He was in Berlin, sitting in the office of Gruppenführer Heinrich Müller, chief of the Gestapo. Müller is scraping a bit of lunch from his teeth and waving a letter he'd just received from Luther in the Foreign Office. It is 1942.

"It seems that rumors of our activities in the east have started to reach the ears of our enemies. We've also got a problem with one of the sites in the Warthegau region. Complaints about contamination of some kind."

"If I may ask the obvious question, Herr Gruppenführer, what difference does it make if rumors reach the West? Who would believe that such a thing was truly possible?"

"Rumors are one thing, Erich. Evidence is quite another."

"Who's going to discover evidence? Some half-witted Polish serf? A slant-eyed Ukrainian ditchdigger?"

"Maybe the Ivans."

"The Russians? How would they ever find—"

Müller held up a bricklayer's hand. Discussion over. And then he understood. The Führer's Russian adventure was not going according to plan. Victory in the east was no longer assured.

Müller leaned forward at the waist. "I'm sending you to hell, Erich. I'm going to stick that Nordic face of yours so deep in the shit you'll never see daylight again."

"How can I ever thank you, Herr Gruppenführer?"

"Clean up the mess. All of it. Everywhere. It's your job to make sure it remains only a rumor. And when the operation is done, I want you to be the only man standing."

He awakened. Müller's face withdrew into the Polish night. Strange, isn't it? His real contribution to the Final Solution was not killing but concealment and security, and yet he was in trouble now, sixty years on, because of a foolish game he'd played one drunken Sunday at Auschwitz. *Aktion* 1005? Yes, it had been his show, but no Jewish survivor would ever testify to his presence at the edge of a killing pit, because there *were* no survivors. He'd run a tight operation. Eichmann and Himmler would have been advised to do the same. They'd been fools to allow so many to survive.

A memory rose, January 1945, a chain of ragged Jews straggling along a road very much like this one. The road from Birkenau. Thousands of Jews, each with a story to tell, each a witness. He'd argued for liquidation of the entire camp population before evacuation. No, he'd been told. Slave labor was urgently needed inside the Reich. Labor? Most of the Jews he'd seen leaving Birkenau could barely walk, let alone wield a pickax or a shovel. They weren't fit for labor, only slaughter, and he'd killed quite a few himself. Why in God's name did they order him to clean out the pits and then allow thousands of witnesses to walk out of a place like Birkenau?

He forced open his eyes and stared out the window. They were driving along the banks of a river, near the Ukrainian border. He knew this river, a river of ashes, a river of bone. He wondered how many hundreds of thousands were down there, silt on the bed of the River Bug.

A shuttered village: Uhrusk. He thought of Peter. He had warned this would happen. "If I ever become a serious threat to win the chancellery," Peter had said, "someone will try to expose us." He had known Peter was right, but he had also believed he could deal with any threat. He had been mistaken, and now his son faced an unimaginable electoral humiliation, all because of him. It was as if the Jews had led Peter to the edge of a killing pit and pointed a gun at his head. He wondered whether he possessed the power to prevent them from pulling the trigger, whether he could broker one more deal, engineer one final escape.

And this Jew who stares at me now with those unforgiving green eyes? What does he expect me to do? Apologize? Break down and weep and spew sentimentalities? What this Jew does not understand is that I feel no guilt for what was done. I was compelled by the hand of God and the teachings of my Church. Did the priests not tell us the Jews were the murderers of God? Did the Holy Father and his cardinals not remain silent when they knew full well what we were doing in the east? Does this Jew expect me now to suddenly recant and say it was all a terrible mistake? And why does he look at me like that? They were familiar, those eyes. He'd seen them somewhere before. Maybe it was just the drugs they'd given him. He couldn't be certain of anything. He wasn't sure he was even alive. Perhaps he was already dead. Perhaps it was his soul making this journey up the River Bug. Perhaps he was in hell.

Another hamlet: Wola Uhruska. He knew the next village. *Sobibor*...

He closed his eyes, the velvet of the curtain enveloped him. It is the spring of 1942, he is driving out of Kiev on the Zhitomir road with the commander of an Einsatzgruppen unit at his side. They are on their way to inspect a ravine that's become something of a security problem, a place the Ukrainians call Babi Yar. By the time they arrive, the sun is kissing the horizon and it is nearly dusk. Still, there is just enough light to see the strange phenomenon taking place at the bottom of the ravine. The earth seems to be in the grips of an epileptic fit. The soil is convulsing, gas is shooting into the air, along with geysers of putrid liquid. The stench! Jesus, the stench. He can smell it now.

"When did it start?"

"Not long after winter ended. The ground thawed, then the bodies thawed. They decomposed very rapidly."

"How many are down there?"

"Thirty-three thousand Jews, a few Gypsies and Soviet prisoners for good measure."

"Put a cordon around the entire ravine. We'll get to this one as soon as we can, but at the moment other sites have priority."

"What other sites?"

"Places you've never heard of: Birkenau, Belzec, Sobibor,

Treblinka. Our work is done here. At the others, they're expecting imminent new arrivals."

"What are you going to do with this place?"

"We'll open the pits and burn the bodies, then we'll crush the bones and scatter the fragments in the forests and the rivers."

"Burn thirty thousand corpses? We tried it during the killing operations. We used flamethrowers, for God's sake. Mass open-air cremations do not work."

"That's because you never constructed a proper pyre. At Chelmno, I proved it can be done. Trust me, Kurt, one day this place called Babi Yar will be only a rumor, just like the Jews who used to live here."

He twisted his wrists. This time, the pain was not enough to wake him. The curtain refused to part. He remained locked in a prison of memories, wading across a river of ashes.

THEY PLUNGED ON through the night. Time was a memory. The tape had cut off his circulation. He could no longer feel his hands and feet. He was feverishly hot one minute, and shivering with cold the next. He had the impression of stopping once. He had smelled gasoline. Were they filling the tank? Or was it just the memory of fuel-soaked railroad ties?

The effects of the drug finally wore off. He was awake now, alert and cognizant and quite certain he was not dead. Something in the determined posture of the Jew told him they were nearing the end of their journey. They passed through Siedlce, then, at Sokołow Podlaski, they turned onto a smaller country road. Dybow came next, then Kosow Lacki.

They turned off the main road, onto a dirt track. The van shuddered: *thump-thump . . . thump-thump.* The old rail line, he thought—it was still here, of course. They followed the track into a stand of dense fir and birch trees and came to a stop a moment later in a small, paved carpark.

A second car entered the clearing with its headlights doused. Three men climbed out and approached the van. He recognized them. They were the ones who had taken him from Vienna. The Jew stood over him and carefully cut away the packing tape and loosened the leather straps. "Come," he said pleasantly. "Let's take a walk."

38

TREBLINKA, POLAND

THEY FOLLOWED A footpath into the trees. It had begun to snow. The flakes fell softly through the still air and settled on their shoulders like the cinders of a distant bonfire. Gabriel held Radek by the elbow. His steps were unsteady at first, but soon the blood began flowing to his feet again and he insisted on walking without Gabriel's support. His labored breath froze on the air. It smelled sour and fearful.

They moved deeper into the forest. The pathway was sandy and covered by a fine bed of pine needles. Oded was several paces ahead, barely visible through the snowfall. Zalman and Navot walked in formation behind them. Chiara had remained behind in the clearing, standing watch over the vehicles.

They paused. A break in the trees, approximately five yards wide, stretched into the gloom. Gabriel illuminated it with the beam of a flashlight. Down the center of the lane, at equidistant intervals, stood several large upright stones. The stones marked the old fence line. They had reached the perimeter of the camp. Gabriel switched off the flashlight and pulled Radek by the elbow. Radek tried to resist, then stumbled forward.

"Just do as I say, Radek, and everything will be fine. Don't try to run, because there's no way to escape. Don't bother calling for help. No one will hear your cries."

"Does it give you pleasure to see me afraid?"

"It sickens me, actually. I don't like touching you. I don't like the sound of your voice."

"So why are we here?"

"I just want you to see some things."

"There's nothing to see here, Allon. Just a Polish memorial."

"Precisely." Gabriel jerked at his elbow. "Come on, Radek. Faster. You have to walk faster. We haven't got much time. It will be morning soon."

A moment later, they stopped again before a trackless rail line, the old spur that had carried the transports from Treblinka station into the camp itself. The ties were recreated in stone and frosted over by new snow. They followed the tracks into the camp and stopped at the place where the platform had been. It too was represented in stone.

"Do you remember it, Radek?"

He stood silently, his jaw slack, his breathing ragged.

"Come on, Radek. We know who you are, we know what you did. You're not going to escape this time. There's no use playing games or trying to deny any of it. There isn't time, not if you want to save your son."

Radek's head swiveled slowly around. His mouth became a tight line and his gaze very hard.

"You would harm my son?"

"Actually, you would do it for us. All we would have to do is tell the world who his father is, and it would destroy him. That's why you planted that bomb in Eli Lavon's office—to protect Peter. No one could touch you, not in a place like Austria. The window had closed for you a long time ago. You were safe. The only person who could pay a price for your crimes is your son. That's why you tried to kill Eli Lavon. That's why you murdered Max Klein."

He turned away from Gabriel and peered into the darkness.

"What is it that you want? What do you want to know?"

"Tell me about it, Radek. I've read about it, I can see the memorial, but I can't picture how it could really work. How was it possible to turn a trainload of people into smoke in only forty-five minutes? Forty-five minutes, door to door, isn't that what the SS staff used to boast about here? They could turn a Jew into smoke in forty-five minutes. Twelve thousand Jews a day. Eight hundred thousand in all."

Radek emitted a mirthless chuckle, an interrogator who did not believe the statement of his prisoner. Gabriel felt as though a stone had been laid over his heart.

"Eight hundred thousand? Where did you get a number like that?"

"That's the official estimate from the Polish government."

"And you expect a bunch of subhumans like the Poles to be able to know what happened here in these woods?" His voice seemed suddenly different, more youthful and commanding. "Please, Allon, if we are going to have this discussion, let us deal with facts, and not Polish idiocy. Eight hundred thousand?" He shook his head and actually smiled. "No, it wasn't eight hundred thousand. The actual number was much higher than that."

A GUST OF sudden wind stirred the treetops. To Gabriel it sounded like the rushing of whitewater. Radek held out his hand and asked for the flashlight. Gabriel hesitated.

"You don't think I'm going to attack you with it, do you?"

"I know some of the things you've done."

"That was a long time ago."

Gabriel handed him the flashlight. Radek pointed the beam to the left, illuminating a stand of evergreens.

"They called this area the lower camp. The SS quarters were right over there. The perimeter fence ran behind them. In front, there was a paved road with shrubbery and flowers in spring and summer. You might find this hard to believe, but it was really very pleasant. There weren't so many trees, of course. We planted the trees after razing the camp. They were just saplings then. Now, they're fully mature, quite beautiful."

"How many SS?"

"Usually around forty. Jewish girls cleaned for them, but they had Poles to do the cooking, three local girls who came from the surrounding villages."

"And the Ukrainians?"

"They were quartered on the opposite side of the road, in five barracks. Stangl's house was in between, at the intersection of two roads. He had a lovely garden. It was designed for him by a man from Vienna."

"But the arrivals never saw that part of the camp?"

"No, no, each part of the camp was carefully concealed from the other by fences interlaced with pine branches. When they arrived at the camp, they saw what appeared to be an ordinary country rail station, complete with a false timetable for departing trains. There were no departures from Treblinka, of course. Only empty trains left this platform."

"There was a building here, was there not?"

"It was made up to look like an ordinary stationhouse, but in fact it was filled with valuables that had been taken from previous arrivals. That section over there they referred to as Station Square. Over there was Reception Square, or the Sorting Square."

"Did you ever see the transports arrive?"

"I had nothing to do with that sort of business, but yes, I saw them arrive."

"There were two different arrival procedures? One for Jews from western Europe, and another for Jews from the east?"

"Yes, that's correct. Western European Jews were treated with great deception and fakery. There were no whips, no shouting.

They were asked politely to disembark the train. Medical personnel in white uniforms were waiting in Reception Square to care for the infirm."

"It was all a ruse, though. The old and the sick were taken off immediately and shot."

He nodded.

"And the eastern Jews? How were they greeted at the platform?"

"They were met by Ukrainian whips."

"And then?"

Radek raised the flashlight and followed the beam a short distance across the clearing.

"There was a barbed-wire enclosure here. Behind the wire were two buildings. One was the disrobing barracks. In the second building, work Jews cut the hair off the women. When they were finished, they went that way." Radek used the flashlight to illuminate the path. "There was a passage here, rather like a cattle chute, a few feet wide, barbed wire and pine branches. It was called the tube."

"But the SS had a special name for it, didn't they?"

Radek nodded. "They called it the Road to Heaven."

"And where did the Road to Heaven lead?"

Radek raised the beam of his light. "The upper camp," he said. "The death camp."

THEY WALKED FORWARD into a large clearing strewn with hundreds of boulders, each stone representing a Jewish community destroyed at Treblinka. The largest stone bore the name Warsaw. Gabriel looked beyond the stones, toward the sky in the east. It was beginning to grow faintly lighter.

"The Road to Heaven led directly into a brick building housing the gas chambers," Radek said, breaking the silence. He seemed suddenly eager to talk. "Each chamber was four meters by four meters. Initially, there were only three, but they soon discovered that they needed more capacity to keep up with demand. Ten more were added. A diesel engine pumped carbon monoxide fumes into the chambers. Asphyxiation resulted in less than thirty minutes. After that, the bodies were removed."

"What was done to them?"

"For several months, they were buried out there, in large pits. But very quickly, the pits overflowed, and the decomposition of the bodies contaminated the camp."

"Which is when you arrived?"

"Not immediately. Treblinka was the fourth camp on our list. We cleaned the pits at Birkenau first, then Belzec and Sobibor. We didn't get to Treblinka until March of 1943. When I arrived . . ." His voice trailed off. "Terrible."

"What did you do?"

"We opened the pits, of course, and removed the bodies."

"By hand?"

He shook his head. "We had a mechanical shovel. It made the work go much faster."

"The claw, isn't that what you called it?"

"Yes, that's right."

"And after the bodies were removed?"

"They were incinerated on large iron racks."

"You had a special name for the racks, did you not?"

"Roasts," Radek said. "We called them roasts."

"And after the bodies were burned?"

"We crushed the bones and reburied them in the pits or carted them off to the Bug and dumped them in the river."

"And when the old pits were all emptied?"

"After that, the bodies were taken straight from the gas chambers to the roasts. It worked that way until October of that year, when the camp was shut down and all traces of it were obliterated. It operated for a little more than a year."

"And yet they still managed to murder eight hundred thousand."

"Not eight hundred thousand."

"How many then?"

"More than a million. That's quite a thing, isn't it? More than a million people, in a tiny place like this, in the middle of a Polish forest."

GABRIEL TOOK BACK the flashlight and drew his Beretta. He prodded Radek forward. They walked along a footpath, through the field of stones. Zalman and Navot remained behind in the upper camp. Gabriel could hear the sound of Oded's footsteps in the gravel behind him.

"Congratulations, Radek. Because of you, it's only a symbolic cemetery."

"Are you going to kill me now? Have I not told you what you wanted to hear?"

Gabriel pushed him along the path. "You may take a certain

pride in this place, but for us, it is sacred ground. Do you really think I would pollute it with your blood?"

"Then what is the point of this? Why did you bring me here?"

"You needed to see it one more time. You needed to visit the scene of the crime to refresh your memory and prepare for your upcoming testimony. That's how you're going to save your son the humiliation of having a man like you as a father. You're going to come back to Israel and pay for your crimes."

"It wasn't *my* crime! I didn't kill them! I just did what Müller ordered me to do. I cleaned up the mess!"

"You did your fair share of killing, Radek. Remember your little game with Max Klein in Birkenau? And what about the death march? You were there too, weren't you, Radek?"

Radek slowed and turned his head. Gabriel gave him a push between the shoulder blades. They came to a large, rectangular depression where the cremation pit had been. It was filled now with pieces of black basalt.

"Kill me now, damn it! Don't take me to Israel! Just do it now, and get it over with. Besides, that's what you're good at, isn't it, Allon?"

"Not here," Gabriel said. "Not in this place. You don't deserve to even set foot here, let alone die here."

Radek fell to his knees before the pit.

"And if I agree to come with you? What fate awaits me?"

"The truth awaits you, Radek. You'll stand before the Israeli people and confess your crimes. Your role in *Aktion* 1005. The murders of prisoners at Birkenau. The killings you carried out during the death march from Birkenau. Do you even remember the girls you murdered, Radek?"

Radek's head twisted round. "How do you—"

Gabriel cut him off. "You won't face trial for your crimes, but you'll spend the rest of your life behind bars. While you're in prison, you'll work with a team of Holocaust scholars from Yad Vashem to compile a thorough history of *Aktion* 1005. You'll tell the deniers and the doubters exactly what you did to conceal the greatest case of mass murder in history. You'll tell the truth for the first time in your life."

"Whose truth, yours or mine?"

"There's only one truth, Radek. Treblinka is the truth."

"And what do I get in return?"

"More than you deserve," Gabriel said. "We'll say nothing about Metzler's dubious parentage."

"You're willing to stomach an Austrian chancellor of the far right in order to get to me?"

"Something tells me Peter Metzler is going to become a great friend of Israel and the Jews. He'll want to do nothing to anger us. After all, we'll hold the keys to his destruction long after you're dead."

"How did you convince the Americans to betray me? Blackmail, I suppose—that's the Jewish way. But there must have been more. Surely you vowed that you would never give me an opportunity to discuss my affiliation with Organization Gehlen or the CIA. I suppose your dedication to the truth goes only so far."

"Give me your answer, Radek."

"How can I trust you, a Jew, to live up to your end of the bargain?"

"Have you been reading *Der Stürmer* again? You'll trust me because you have no other choice."

"And what good will it do? Will it bring back even one person who died in this place?"

"No," Gabriel conceded, "but the world will know the truth, and you'll spend the last years of your life where you belong. Take the deal, Radek. Take it for your son. Think of it as one last escape."

"It won't stay secret forever. Someday, the truth of this affair will come out."

"Eventually," Gabriel said. "I suppose you can't hide the truth forever."

Radek's head pivoted slowly around and he stared at Gabriel contemptuously. "If you were a real man, you'd do it yourself." He managed a mocking smile. "As for the truth, no one cared while this place was in operation, and no one will care now."

He turned and looked into the pit. Gabriel pocketed the Beretta and walked away. Oded, Zalman, and Navot stood motionless on the footpath behind him. Gabriel brushed past them without a word and headed down through the camp to the rail platform. Before turning into the trees, he paused briefly to look over his shoulder and saw Radek, clinging to the arm of Oded, rising slowly to his feet.

PART FOUR

THE PRISONER OF ABU KABIR

39

JAFFA, ISRAEL

THERE WAS CONSIDERABLE debate over where to put him. Lev thought him a security risk and wanted him kept permanently under Office care. Shamron, as usual, took the opposite position, if for no other reason than he did not want his beloved service in the business of running jails. The prime minister, only half-jokingly, suggested that Radek be force-marched into the Negev to be picked over by the scorpions and the vultures. It was Gabriel, eventually, who carried the day. The worst punishment for a man like Radek,

Gabriel argued, was to be treated like a common criminal. They searched for a suitable place to lock him away and settled on a police detention facility, originally built by the British during the Mandate, in a seedy quarter of Jaffa still known by its Arab name, Abu Kabir.

A period of seventy-two hours passed before Radek's capture was made public. The prime minister's communiqué was terse and deliberately misleading. Great care was taken to avoid needlessly embarrassing the Austrians. Radek, the prime minister said, was discovered living under a false identity in an unspecified country. After a period of negotiation, he had consented to come to Israel voluntarily. Under the terms of the agreement, he would not face trial, since, under Israeli law, the only possible sentence was death. Instead he would remain under permanent administrative detention and would effectively "plead guilty" to his crimes against humanity by working with a team of historians at Yad Vashem and Hebrew University to produce a definitive history of *Aktion* 1005.

There was little fanfare and none of the excitement that accompanied news of Eichmann's kidnapping. Indeed, word of Radek's capture was overshadowed within hours by a suicide bomber who murdered twenty-five people in a Jerusalem market. Lev derived a certain crude satisfaction from the development, for it seemed to prove his point that the State had more important things to worry about than chasing down old Nazis. He began referring to the affair as "Shamron's folly," though he quickly found himself out of step with the rank and file of his own service. Within King Saul Boulevard, Radek's capture seemed to rekindle old fires. Lev adjusted his stance to meet the prevailing mood, but it was too late. Everyone knew that Radek's apprehension had been engineered by the *Memuneh* and Gabriel, and that Lev had tried to block it at every turn. Lev's standing among the foot soldiers fell to dangerously low levels.

The half-hearted attempt to keep secret Radek's Austrian identity was undone by the videotape of his arrival at Abu Kabir. The Vienna press quickly and correctly identified the prisoner as Ludwig Vogel, an Austrian businessman of some note. Did he truly agree to leave Vienna voluntarily? Or was he in fact kidnapped from his fortresslike home in the First District? In the days that followed, the newspapers were filled with speculative accounts of Vogel's mystifying career and political connections. The press investigations strayed perilously close to Peter Metzler. Renate Hoffmann of the Coalition for a Better Austria called for an official inquiry into the affair and suggested that Radek may have been linked to the bombing of Wartime Claims and Inquiries and the mysterious death of an elderly Jew named Max Klein. Her demands fell largely on deaf ears. The bombing was the work of Islamic terrorists, the government said. And as for the unfortunate death of Max Klein, it was a suicide. Further investigation, said the minister of justice, was pointless.

The next chapter in the Radek affair would take place not in Vienna but in Paris, where a mossy former KGB man popped up on French television to suggest Radek was Moscow's man in Vienna. A former Stasi spymaster who'd become something of a literary sensation in the new Germany laid claim to Radek as well. Shamron first suspected the claims were part of a coordinated campaign of disinformation designed to inoculate the

CIA from the Radek virus—which is exactly how he would have played it had he been in their shoes. Then he learned that inside the Agency, the suggestions that Radek may have been plying his trade on both sides of the street had caused something of a panic. Files were being hauled out of the deep freeze; a team of elderly Soviet hands was being hastily assembled. Shamron secretly reveled in the anxiety of his colleagues from Langley. Were it to turn out that Radek was a double agent, Shamron said, it would be profoundly just. Adrian Carter requested permission to put Radek under the lights when the Israeli historians were finished with him. Shamron promised to give the matter thorough consideration.

THE PRISONER OF Abu Kabir was largely oblivious to the storm swirling around him. His confinement was solitary, though not unduly harsh. He kept his cell and his clothing neat, he took food and complained little. His guards, though they longed to hate him, could not. He was a policeman at his core, and his jailors seemed to see something in him they recognized. He treated them courteously and was treated courteously in return. He was something of a curiosity. They had read about men like him at school, and they wandered past his cell at all hours just to have a look. Radek began to feel increasingly as though he were an exhibit in a museum.

He made only one request, that he be granted a newspaper each day so he could keep abreast of current affairs. The question was taken all the way to Shamron, who gave his consent, so long as it was an Israeli newspaper and not some German publication. Each morning, a *Jerusalem Post* arrived with his breakfast tray. He usually skipped the stories about himself—they were largely inaccurate in any case—and turned straight to the foreign news section to read about developments in the Austrian election.

Moshe Rivlin paid Radek several visits to prepare for his upcoming testimony. It was decided that the sessions would be videotaped and broadcast nightly on Israeli television. Radek seemed to grow more agitated as the day of his first public appearance drew nearer. Rivlin quietly asked the chief of the detention facility to keep the prisoner under a suicide watch. A guard was posted in the corridor, just beyond the bars of Radek's cell. Radek chafed under the added surveillance at first, but was soon glad for the company.

On the day before Radek's testimony, Rivlin came one final time. They spent an hour together; Radek was preoccupied and, for the first time, largely uncooperative. Rivlin packed away his documents and notes and asked the guard to open the cell door.

"I want to see him," Radek said suddenly. "Ask him whether he would do me the honor of paying me a visit. Tell him I have a few questions I'd like to ask him."

"I can't make any promises," Rivlin said. "I'm not connected to—"

"Just ask him," Radek said. "The worst he can do is say no."

SHAMRON IMPOSED ON Gabriel to remain in Israel until the opening day of Radek's testimony, and Gabriel, though he was anxious to return to Venice, reluctantly agreed. He stayed in the safe flat near the Zion Gate and woke each morning to the sound of church bells in the Armenian Quarter. He would sit on the shadowed terrace overlooking the walls of the Old City and linger over coffee and the newspapers. He followed the Radek affair closely. He was pleased that Shamron's name was linked to the capture and not his. Gabriel lived abroad, under an assumed identity, and he did not need his real name splashed about in the press. Besides, after all Shamron had done for his country, he deserved one final day in the sun.

As the days eased slowly past, Gabriel found that Radek seemed more and more a stranger to him. Though blessed with a near-photographic memory, Gabriel struggled to clearly recall Radek's face or the sound of his voice. Treblinka seemed something from a nightmare. He wondered whether it had been this way for his mother. Did Radek remain in the rooms of her memory like an uninvited guest, or did she force herself to recall him in order to render his image on canvas? Had it been like this for all those who had encountered so perfect an evil? Perhaps it explained the silence that descended on those who had survived. Perhaps they had been mercifully released from the pain of their memories as a means of self-preservation. One idea turned ceaselessly in his thoughts: If Radek had murdered his mother that day in Poland instead of two other girls, he would have never existed. He, too, began to feel the guilt of survival.

He was certain of only one thing—he was not ready to forget. And so he was pleased when one of Lev's acolytes telephoned one afternoon and wondered whether he would be willing to write an official history of the affair. Gabriel accepted, on the condition that he also produce a sanitized version of the events to be kept in the archives at Yad Vashem. There was a good deal of back and forth about when such a document could be made public. A release date of forty years hence was set, and Gabriel went to work.

He wrote at the kitchen table, on a notebook computer supplied by the Office. Each evening he locked the computer in a floor safe concealed beneath the living room couch. He had no experience writing, so, instinctively, he approached the project as though it were a painting. He started with an underdrawing, broad and amorphous, then slowly added layers of paint. He used a simple palette, and his brush technique was careful. As the days wore on, Radek's face returned to him, as clearly as it had been rendered by the hand of his mother.

He would work until the early afternoon, then take a break and walk over to the Hadassah University Hospital, where, after a month of unconsciousness, Eli Lavon was showing signs that he might be emerging from his coma. Gabriel would sit with Lavon for an hour or so and talk to him about the case. Then he would return to the flat and work until dark.

On the day he completed the report, he lingered at the hospital until early evening and happened to be there when Lavon's eyes opened. Lavon stared blankly into space for a moment, then the old inquisitiveness returned to his gaze, and it flickered around the unfamiliar surroundings of the hospital room before finally settling on Gabriel's face.

"Where are we? Vienna?"

"Jerusalem."

"What are you doing here?"

"I'm working on a report for the Office."

"About what?"

"The capture of a Nazi war criminal named Erich Radek."

"Radek?"

"He was living in Vienna under the name Ludwig Vogel."

Lavon smiled. "Tell me everything," he murmured, but before Gabriel could say another word he was gone again.

WHEN GABRIEL RETURNED to the flat that evening, the light was winking on the answering machine. He pressed the Play button and heard the voice of Moshe Rivlin.

"The prisoner of Abu Kabir would like a word. I'd tell him to go to hell. It's your call."

40

JAFFA, ISRAEL

THE DETENTION CENTER was surrounded by a high wall the color of sandstone topped by coils of razor wire. Gabriel presented himself at the outer entrance early the following morning and was admitted without delay. To reach the interior, he had to travel a narrow, fenced passage that reminded him too much of the Road to Heaven at Treblinka. A warder awaited him at the other end. He led Gabriel silently into the secure lockup, then into a windowless interrogation room with bare cinderblock walls. Radek was seated statuelike at the table, dressed for his testimony in a dark suit and tie. His hands were cuffed and folded on the table. He acknowledged Gabriel with an almost imperceptible nod of his head but remained seated.

"Remove the handcuffs," Gabriel said to the warder.

"It's against policy."

Gabriel glared at the warder, and a moment later, the cuffs were gone.

"You do that very well," Radek said. "Was that another psychological ploy on your part? Are you trying to demonstrate your dominion over me?"

Gabriel pulled out the crude iron chair and sat down. "I wouldn't think that under these conditions a demonstration like that would be necessary."

"I suppose you're right," Radek said. "Still, I do admire the way you handled the entire affair. I would like to think I would have done as well."

"For whom?" Gabriel asked. "The Americans or the Russians?"

"You're referring to the allegations made in Paris by that idiot Belov?"

"Are they true?"

Radek regarded Gabriel in silence, and for just a few seconds some of the old steel returned to his blue eyes. "When one plays the game as long as I did, one makes so many alliances, and engages in so much deception, that in the end it's sometimes difficult to know where the truth and the lies part company."

"Belov seems certain he knows the truth."

"Yes, but I'm afraid it's the certainty of a fool. You see, Belov was in no position to know the truth." Radek changed the subject. "I assume you've seen the papers this morning?"

Gabriel nodded.

"His margin of victory was larger than expected. Apparently, my arrest had something to do with it. Austrians have never liked outsiders meddling in their affairs."

"You're not gloating, are you?"

"Of course not," Radek said. "I'm only sorry I didn't drive a harder bargain at Treblinka. Perhaps I shouldn't have agreed so easily. I'm not so certain Peter's campaign would have been derailed by the revelations about my past."

"There are some things that are politically unpalatable, even in a country like Austria."

"You underestimate us, Allon."

Gabriel permitted a silence to fall between them. He was already beginning to regret his decision to come. "Moshe Rivlin said you wanted to see me," he said dismissively. "I don't have much time."

Radek sat a little straighter in his chair. "I was wondering whether you might do me the professional courtesy of answering a couple of questions."

"That depends on the questions. You and I are in different professions, Radek."

"Yes," Radek said. "I was an agent of American intelligence, and you are an assassin."

Gabriel stood to leave. Radek put up a hand. "Wait," he said. "Sit down. Please."

Gabriel returned to his seat.

"The man who telephoned my house the night of the kidnapping—"

"You mean your arrest?"

Radek dipped his head. "All right, my *arrest.* I assume he was an imposter?"

Gabriel nodded.

"He was very good. How did he manage to impersonate Kruz so well?"

"You don't expect me to answer that, do you, Radek?" Gabriel looked at his watch. "I hope you didn't bring me all the way to Jaffa to ask me one question."

"No," Radek said. "There is one other thing I'd like to know. When we were at Treblinka, you mentioned that I had taken part in the evacuation of prisoners from Birkenau."

Gabriel interrupted him. "Can we please, at long last, drop the euphemisms, Radek? It wasn't an *evacuation.* It was a death march."

Radek was silent for a moment. "You also mentioned that I personally killed some of the prisoners."

"I know you murdered at least two girls," Gabriel said. "I'm sure there were more."

Radek closed his eyes and nodded slowly. "There *were* more," he said distantly. "*Many* more. I remember that day as though it were last week. I had known the end was coming for some time, but seeing that line of prisoners marching toward the Reich . . . I knew then that it was Götterdämmerung. It was truly the Twilight of the Gods."

"And so you started killing them?"

He nodded again. "They had entrusted me with the task of

protecting their terrible secret, and then they let several thousand witnesses walk out of Birkenau alive. I'm sure you can imagine how I felt."

"No," Gabriel said truthfully. "I can't begin to imagine how you felt."

"There was a girl," Radek said. "I remember asking her what she would say to her children, about the war. She answered that she would tell them the truth. I ordered her to lie. She refused. I killed two other girls and still she defied me. For some reason, I let her walk away. I stopped killing the prisoners after that. I knew after looking into her eyes that it was pointless."

Gabriel looked down at his hands, refusing to rise to Radek's bait.

"I assume this woman was your witness?" Radek asked.

"Yes, she was."

"It's funny," Radek said, "but she has your eyes."

Gabriel looked up. He hesitated, then said, "So they tell me."

"She's your mother?"

Another hesitation, then the truth.

"I would tell you that I'm sorry," Radek said, "but I know my apology would mean nothing to you."

"You're right," Gabriel said. "Don't say it."

"So it was for her that you did this?"

"No," said Gabriel. "It was for all of them."

The door opened. The warder stepped into the room and announced that it was time to leave for Yad Vashem. Radek rose slowly to his feet and held out his hands. His eyes remained fastened to Gabriel's face as the cuffs were ratcheted around his wrists. Gabriel accompanied him as far as the entrance, then watched him make his way through the fenced-in passage, into the back of a waiting van. He had seen enough. Now he wanted only to forget.

AFTER LEAVING ABU KABIR, Gabriel drove up to Safed to see Tziona. They ate lunch in a small kebab café in the Artists' Quarter. She tried to engage him in conversation about the Radek affair, but Gabriel, only two hours removed from the murderer's presence, was in no mood to discuss him further. He swore Tziona to secrecy about his involvement in the case, then hastily changed the subject.

They spoke of art for a time, then politics, and finally the state of Gabriel's life. Tziona knew of an empty flat a few streets over from her own. It was large enough to house a studio and was blessed with some of the most gorgeous light in the Upper Galilee. Gabriel promised he would think about it, but Tziona knew that he was merely placating her. The restlessness had returned to his eyes. He was ready to leave.

Over coffee, he told her that he had found a place for some of his mother's work.

"Where?"

"The Museum of Holocaust Art at Yad Vashem."

Tziona's eyes welled over with tears. "How perfect," she said.

After lunch they climbed the cobblestone stairs to Tziona's apartment. She unlocked the storage closet and carefully removed the paintings. They spent an hour selecting twenty of the best pieces for Yad Vashem. Tziona had discovered two more canvases bearing the image of Erich Radek. She asked Gabriel what he wanted her to do with them.

"Burn them," he replied.

"But they're probably worth a great deal of money now."

"I don't care what they're worth," Gabriel said. "I never want to see his face again."

Tziona helped him load the paintings into his car. He set out for Jerusalem beneath a sky heavy with cloud. He went first to Yad Vashem. A curator took possession of the paintings, then hurried back inside to watch the beginning of Erich Radek's testimony. So it seemed did the rest of the country. Gabriel drove through silent streets to the Mount of Olives. He laid a stone on his mother's grave and recited the words of the mourner's Kaddish for her. He did the same at the grave of his father. Then he drove to the airport and caught the evening flight for Rome.

41

VENICE • VIENNA

THE FOLLOWING MORNING, in the *sestière* of Cannaregio, Francesco Tiepolo entered the Church of San Giovanni Crisostomo and made his way slowly across the nave. He peered into the Chapel of Saint Jerome and saw lights burning behind the shrouded work platform. He crept forward, seized the scaffolding in his bearlike paw, and shook it once violently. The restorer raised his magnifying visor and peered down at him like a gargoyle.

"Welcome home, Mario," Tiepolo called up. "I was beginning to worry about you. Where have you been?"

The restorer lowered his visor and turned his gaze once more to the Bellini.

"I've been gathering sparks, Francesco."

Gathering sparks? Tiepolo knew better than to ask. He only cared that the restorer was finally back in Venice.

"How long before you finish?"

"Three months," said the restorer. "Maybe four."

"Three would be better."

"Yes, Francesco, I know three months would be better. But if you keep shaking my platform, I'll never finish."

"You're not planning on running any more errands, are you, Mario?"

"Just one," he said, his brush poised before the canvas. "But it won't take long. I promise."

"That's what you always say."

THE PACKAGE ARRIVED at the clock shop in Vienna's First District via motorcycle courier exactly three weeks later. The Clockmaker took delivery personally. He affixed his signature to the courier's clipboard and gave him a small gratuity for his trouble. Then he carried the parcel into his workshop and placed it on the table.

The courier climbed back on the motorbike and sped away, slowing briefly at the end of the street, just long enough to signal the woman seated behind the wheel of a Renault sedan.

The woman punched in a number on her cell phone and pressed the Send button. A moment later, the Clockmaker answered.

"I just sent you a clock," she said. "Did you receive it?"

"Who is this?"

"I'm a friend of Max Klein," she whispered. "And Eli Lavon. And Reveka Gazit. And Sarah Greenberg."

She lowered the phone and pressed four numbers in quick succession, then turned her head in time to see the bright red ball of fire erupt from the front of the Clockmaker's shop.

She eased away from the curb, her hands trembling on the wheel, and headed toward the Ringstrasse. Gabriel had abandoned his motorcycle and was waiting on the corner. She stopped long enough for him to climb in, then turned onto the broad boulevard and vanished into the evening traffic. A Staatspolizei car sped past in the opposite direction. Chiara kept her eyes on the road.

"Are you all right?"

"I think I'm going to be sick."

"Yes, I know. Do you want me to drive?"

"No, I can do it."

"You should have let me send the detonation signal."

"I didn't want you to feel responsible for another death in Vienna." She punched a tear from her cheek. "Did you think of them when you heard the explosion? Did you think of Leah and Dani?"

He hesitated, then shook his head.

"What did you think of?"

He reached out and brushed away another tear. "You, Chiara," he said softly. "I thought only of you."

AUTHOR'S NOTE

A Death in Vienna completes a cycle of three novels dealing with the unfinished business of the Holocaust. Nazi art looting and the collaboration of Swiss banks served as the backdrop for *The English Assassin.* The role of the Catholic Church in the Holocaust and the silence of Pope Pius XII inspired *The Confessor.*

A Death in Vienna, like its predecessors, is based loosely on actual events. Heinrich Gross was indeed a physician at the notorious Spiegelgrund clinic during the war, and the description of the halfhearted Austrian attempt to try him in 2000 is entirely accurate. That same year, Austria was rocked by allegations that officers of the police and security services were working on behalf of Jörg Haider and his far-right Freedom Party to help discredit critics and political opponents.

Aktion 1005 was the real code name of the Nazi program to conceal evidence of the Holocaust and destroy the remains of millions of Jewish dead. The leader of the operation, an Austrian named Paul Blobel, was convicted at Nuremberg for his role in the Einsatzgruppen mass murders and sentenced to death. Hanged at Landsberg Prison in June 1951, he was never questioned in detail about his role as commander of *Aktion* 1005.

Bishop Aloïs Hudal was indeed the rector of the Pontificio Santa Maria dell'Anima, and helped hundreds of Nazi war criminals flee Europe, including Treblinka commandant Franz Stangl. The Vatican maintains that Bishop Hudal was acting without the approval or knowledge of the pope or other senior Curial officials.

Argentina, of course, was the final destination for thousands of wanted war criminals. It is possible that a small number may still reside there today. In 1994, former SS officer Erich Priebke was discovered living openly in Bariloche by an ABC News team. Evidently Priebke felt so secure in Bariloche that, under questioning by ABC correspondent Sam Donaldson, he freely admitted his central role in the Ardeatine Caves massacre of March 1944. Priebke was extradited to Italy, tried, and sentenced to life in prison, though he was permitted to serve his term under "house arrest." During several years of legal maneuverings and appeals, the Catholic Church allowed Priebke to live at a monastery outside Rome.

Olga Lengyel, in her landmark 1947 mémoire of survival at Auschwitz, wrote: "Certainly everyone whose hands were directly, or indirectly stained with our blood must pay for his or her crimes. Less than that would be an outrage against the millions of innocent dead." Her impassioned plea for justice, however, went largely unheeded. Only a tiny percentage of those who carried out the Final Solution or served in an ancillary or collaborationist role ever faced punishment for their crimes. Tens of thousands found sanctuary in foreign lands, including the United States; others simply returned home and carried on with their lives. Some found employment in the CIA-sponsored intelligence network of General Reinhard Gehlen. What impact did men such as these have on the conduct of American foreign policy during the early years of the Cold War? The answer may never fully be known.

ACKNOWLEDGMENTS

A Death in Vienna, like the previous books in the Gabriel Allon series, could not have been written without the support, wisdom, and friendship of David Bull. David is truly one of the world's finest art restorers and historians, and our consultations, usually conducted over a hastily prepared pasta and a bottle of red wine, have enriched my life.

In Vienna, I was assisted by a number of remarkable individuals who are working to combat Austria's newest outbreak of anti-Semitism. Unfortunately, because of the seriousness of the situation, I cannot thank them by name, though their spirit and courage have certainly found their way onto the pages of this story.

In Jerusalem, I made Gabriel's journey through the memorials of Yad Vashem at the side of Dina Shefet, a Holocaust historian who has recorded the memories of numerous survivors. To demonstrate how one can locate and print the Pages of Testimony stored in the Hall of Names, she used as an example her grandparents, who were murdered at Treblinka in 1942. The staff at the Yad Vashem Archives, especially Karin Dengler, could not have been more helpful. Gabriel Motskin, Dean of the Faculty of Humanities at the Hebrew University of Jerusalem, and his wife, art historian and curator Emily Bilski, took good care of me and deepened my understanding of contemporary Israeli society.

A special thanks to the library staff at the U.S. Holocaust Memorial Museum; Naomi Mazin of the Anti-Defamation League in New York; Moshe Fox of the Israeli Embassy in Washington; and Dr. Ephraim Zuroff, a real-life Nazi-hunter from the Simon Wiesenthal Center in Jerusalem who, to this day, is tirelessly seeking justice for the victims of the Shoah. It goes without saying that the expertise is all theirs, the mistakes and dramatic license all mine.

My friend Louis Toscano read my manuscript and made it immeasurably better. Dorian Hastings, my copyeditor, spared me much embarrassment. Eleanor Pelta, though she didn't always know it, helped me to better understand what it means to be the child of survivors. Marilyn Goldhammer, head of the Temple Sinai religious school in Washington, D.C., taught me and my children the lesson of the Midrash of the Broken Vessel. Dan Raviv, author of the groundbreaking history of the Mossad, *Every Spy a Prince*, and his wife, Dori Phaff, were an indispensable resource on all things Israeli. The actor and entertainer Mike Burstyn opened many doors for me, and his wife, Cyona, allowed me to borrow the Hebrew version of her beautiful name.

I consulted hundreds of books, articles, and Web sites during preparation of this manuscript, far too many to name individually, but I would be remiss if I did not mention Christopher Simpson's groundbreaking *Blowback*, which documented the use of Nazi war criminals by American intelligence in the years after the Second World War, and *The Real Odessa*, by Uki Goni, who has almost single-handedly forced Argentina to reexamine its past. Many survivors of Auschwitz-Birkenau summoned the courage later in life to record their experiences—in book form, on videotape, or in depositions given to Yad Vashem and other repositories of Holocaust memory—and I borrowed from them to create the fictional testimony of Irene Allon. Two works were particularly helpful: *Five Chimneys*, by Olga Lengyel, and *Rena's Promise*, by Rena Kornreich Gelissen, both of which documented the journeys of young women through the horrors of Birkenau and the death march.

None of this would have been possible without the friendship and support of my literary agent, Esther Newberg of International Creative Management. Also, a heartfelt thanks to the remarkable team at Penguin Putnam: Carole Baron, Daniel Harvey, Marilyn Ducksworth, and especially my editor, Neil Nyren, who quietly helped me turn a few random notions into a novel.

If you enjoyed A DEATH IN VIENNA
look out for

THE CONFESSOR

by Daniel Silva

Penguin Books £6.99

Art restorer Gabriel Allon is trying to put his secret service past behind him. But when his friend Benjamin Stern is murdered in Munich, he's called into action once more.

Police in Germany are certain that Stern, a professor well known for his work on the Holocaust, was killed by right-wing extremists. But Allon is far from convinced. Not least because all trace of the new book he was researching has now mysteriously disappeared . . .

Meanwhile in Rome, the new Pope paces around his garden, thinking about the perilous plan he's about to set in motion. If successful he will revolutionize the Church. If not, he could very well destroy it . . .

In the dramatic weeks to come, the journeys of these two men will intersect. Long-buried secrets and unthinkable deeds will come to light, and both their lives will be changed for ever . . .

"One of those rare books that sweep you into forgetting to eat or sleep. Daniel Silva has now indisputably joined the ranks of Graham Greene and John Le Carré" *The Washingtonian*

Read on for a taster . . .

✦1✦

MUNICH

THE APARTMENT HOUSE at Adalbertstrasse 68 was one of the few in the fashionable district of Schwabing yet to be overrun by Munich's noisy and growing professional elite. Wedged between two red brick buildings that exuded prewar charm, No. 68 seemed rather like an ugly younger stepsister. Her façade was a cracked beige stucco, her form squat and graceless. As a result her suitors were a tenuous community of students, artists, anarchists, and unrepentant punk rockers, all presided over by an authoritarian caretaker named Frau Ratzinger, who, it was rumored, had been living in the original apartment house at No. 68 when it was leveled by an Allied bomb. Neighborhood activists derided the building as an eyesore in need of gentrification. Defenders said it exemplified the very sort of Bohemian arrogance that had once made Schwabing the Montmartre of Germany—the Schwabing of Hesse and Mann and Lenin. And Adolf Hitler, the professor working in the second-floor window might have been tempted to add, but few in the old neighborhood liked to be reminded of the fact that the young Austrian outcast had once found inspiration in these quiet tree-lined streets too.

To his students and colleagues, he was Herr Doktorprofessor Stern. To friends in the neighborhood he was just Benjamin; to the occasional visitor from home, he was Binyamin. In an anonymous stone-and-glass office complex in the north of Tel Aviv, where a file of his youthful exploits still resided despite his pleas to have it burned, he would always be known as Beni, youngest of Ari Shamron's wayward sons. Officially, Benjamin Stern remained a member of the faculty at Hebrew University in Jerusalem, though for the past four years he had served as visiting professor of European studies at Munich's prestigious Ludwig-Maximilian University. It had become something of a permanent loan, which was fine with Professor Stern. In an odd twist of historical fate, life was more pleasant for a Jew these days in Germany than in Jerusalem or Tel Aviv.

The fact that his mother had survived the horrors of the Riga ghetto gave Professor Stern a certain dubious standing among the other tenants of No. 68. He was a curiosity. He was their conscience. They railed at him about the plight of the Palestinians. They gently asked him questions they dared not put to their parents and grandparents. He was their guidance counselor and trusted sage. They came to him for advice on their studies. They poured out their heart to him when they'd been dumped by a lover. They raided his fridge when they were hungry and pillaged his wallet when they were broke. Most importantly, he served as tenant spokesman in all disputes involving the dreaded Frau Ratzinger. Professor Stern was the only one in the building who did not fear her. They seemed to have a special relationship. A kinship. "It's

Stockholm Syndrome," claimed Alex, a psychology student who lived on the top floor. "Prisoner and camp guard. Master and servant." But it was more than that. The professor and the old woman seemed to speak the same language.

The previous year, when his book on the Wannsee Conference had become an international bestseller, Professor Stern had flirted with the idea of moving to a more stylish building—perhaps one with proper security and a view of the English Gardens. A place where the other tenants didn't treat his flat as if it were an annex to their own. This had incited panic among the others. One evening they came to him en masse and petitioned him to stay. Promises were made. They would not steal his food, nor would they ask for loans when there was no hope of repayment. They would be more respectful of his need for quiet. They would come to him for advice only when it was absolutely necessary. The professor acquiesced, but within a month his flat was once again the de facto common room of Adalbertstrasse 68. Secretly, he was glad they were back. The rebellious children of No. 68 were the only family Benjamin Stern had left.

The clatter of a passing streetcar broke his concentration. He looked up in time to see it disappear behind the canopy of a chestnut tree, then glanced at his watch. Eleven-thirty. He'd been at it since five that morning. He removed his glasses and spent a long moment rubbing his eyes. What was it Orwell had said about writing a book? *A horrible, exhausting struggle, like a long bout of some painful illness.* Sometimes, Benjamin Stern felt as though this book might be fatal.

The red light on his telephone answering machine was blinking. He made a habit of muting the ringers to avoid unwanted interruptions. Hesitantly, like a bomb handler deciding which wire to cut, he reached out and pressed the button. The little speaker emitted a blast of heavy metal music, followed by a warlike yelp.

"I have some good news, Herr Doktorprofessor. By the end of the day, there will be one less filthy Jew on the planet! Wiedersehen, Herr Doktorprofessor."

CLICK.

Professor Stern erased the message. He was used to them by now. He received two a week these days; sometimes more, depending on whether he had made an appearance on television or taken part in some public debate. He knew them by voice; assigned each a trivial, unthreatening nickname to lessen their impact on his nerves. This fellow called at least twice each month. Professor Stern had dubbed him *Wolfie*. Sometimes he told the police. Most of the time he didn't bother. There was nothing they could do anyway.

He locked his manuscript and notes in the floor safe tucked beneath his desk. Then he pulled on a pair of shoes and a woolen jacket and collected the rubbish bag from the kitchen. The old building had no elevator, which meant he had to walk down two flights of stairs to reach the ground floor. As he entered the lobby, a chemical stench greeted him. The building was home to a small but thriving *kosmetik*. The professor detested the beauty shop. When it was busy, the rancid smell of nail-polish remover rose through the ventilation system and enveloped his flat. It also made the building less secure than he would have preferred. Because the *kosmetik* had no separate street entrance, the lobby was constantly cluttered with beautiful Schwabinians arriving for their pedicures, facials, and waxings.

He turned right, toward a doorway that gave onto the tiny courtyard, and hesitated in the threshold, checking to see if the cats were about. Last night he'd been awakened at midnight by a skirmish over some morsel of garbage. There were no cats this morning, only a pair of bored beauticians in spotless white tunics smoking cigarettes against the wall. He padded across the sooty bricks and tossed his bag into the bin.

Returning to the entrance hall, he found Frau Ratzinger punishing the linoleum floor with a worn straw broom. "Good morning, Herr Doktorprofessor," the old woman snapped; then she added accusingly: "Going out for your morning coffee?"

Professor Stern nodded and murmured, *"Ja, ja, Frau Ratzinger."* She glared at two messy stacks of fliers, one advertising a free concert in the park, the other a holistic massage clinic on the Schellingstrasse. "No matter how many times I ask them not to leave these things here, they do it anyway. It's that drama student in 4B. He lets anyone into the building."

The professor shrugged his shoulders, as if mystified by the lawless ways of the young, and smiled kindly at the old woman. Frau Ratzinger picked up the fliers and marched them into the courtyard. A moment later, he could hear her berating the beauticians for tossing their cigarette butts on the ground.

He stepped outside and paused to take stock of the weather. Not too cold for early March, the sun peering through a gauzy layer of cloud. He pushed his hands into his coat pockets and set out. Entering the English Gardens, he followed a tree-lined path along the banks of a rain-swollen canal. He liked the park. It gave his mind a quiet place to rest after the morning's exertions on the computer. More importantly, it gave him an opportunity to see if today they were following him. He stopped walking and beat his coat pockets dramatically to indicate he had forgotten something. Then he doubled back and retraced his steps, scanning faces, checking to see if they matched any of the ones stored in the database of his prodigious memory. He paused on a humpbacked footbridge, as if admiring the rush of the water over a short fall. A drug dealer with spiders tattooed on his face offered him heroin. The professor mumbled something incoherent and walked quickly away. Two minutes later he ducked into a public telephone and pretended to place a call while carefully surveying the surroundings. He hung up the receiver.

Wiedersehen, Herr Doktorprofessor.

He turned onto the Ludwigstrasse and hurried across the university district, head down, hoping to avoid being spotted by any students or colleagues. Earlier that week, he had received a rather nasty letter from Dr. Helmut Berger, the pompous chairman of his department, wondering when the book might be finished and when he could be expected to resume his lecturing obligations. Professor Stern did not like Helmut Berger—their well-publicized feud was both personal and academic—and conveniently he had not found the time to respond.

The bustle of the Viktualienmarkt pushed thoughts of work from his mind. He moved past mounds of brightly colored fruit and vegetables, past flower stalls and open-air butchers. He picked out a few things for his supper, then crossed the street to Café Bar Eduscho for coffee and a *Dinkelbrot*. Forty-five minutes later, as he set out for Schwabing, he felt refreshed, his mind light, ready for one more wrestling match with his book. His illness, as Orwell would have called it.

As he arrived at the apartment house, a gust of wind chased him into the lobby and scattered a fresh stack of salmon-colored fliers. The professor twisted his head so he could read one. A new curry takeaway had opened around the corner. He liked a good curry. He scooped up one of the fliers and stuffed it into his coat pocket.

The wind had carried a few of the leaflets toward the courtyard.

Frau Ratzinger would be furious. As he trod softly up the stairs, she poked her head from her foxhole of a flat and spotted the mess. Predictably appalled, she glared at him with inquisitor's eyes. Slipping the key into his door lock, he could hear the old woman cursing as she dealt with this latest outrage.

In the kitchen, he put away the food and brewed himself a cup of tea. Then he walked down the hallway to his study. A man was standing at his desk, casually leafing through a stack of research. He wore a white tunic, like the ones worn by the beauticians at the *kosmetik,* and was very tall with athletic shoulders. His hair was blond and streaked with gray. Hearing the professor enter the room, the intruder looked up. His eyes were gray too, cold as a glacier.

"Open the safe, Herr Doktorprofessor."

The voice was calm, almost flirtatious. The German was accented. It wasn't Wolfie—Professor Stern was sure of that. He had a flair for languages and an ear for local dialects. The man in the tunic was Swiss, and his *Schwyzerdütsch* had the broad singsong accent of a man from the mountain valleys.

"Who in the hell do you think you are?"

"Open the safe," the intruder repeated as the eyes returned to the papers on the desk.

"There's nothing in the safe of any value. If it's money you're—"

Professor Stern wasn't permitted to finish the sentence. In a swift motion, the intruder reached beneath the tunic, produced a silenced handgun. The professor knew weapons as well as accents. The gun was a Russian-made Stechkin. The bullet tore through the professor's right kneecap. He fell to the floor, hands clutching the wound, blood pumping between his fingers.

"I suppose you'll just have to give me the combination now," the Swiss said calmly.

The pain was like nothing Benjamin Stern had ever experienced. He was panting, struggling to catch his breath, his mind a maelstrom. *The combination?* God, but he could barely remember his name.

"I'm waiting, Herr Doktorprofessor."

He forced himself to take a series of deep breaths. This supplied his brain with enough oxygen to permit him to access the combination to the safe. He recited the numbers, his jaw trembling with shock. The intruder knelt in front of the safe and deftly worked the tumbler. A moment later, the door swung open.

The intruder looked inside, then at the professor.

"You have backup disks. Where do you keep them?"

"I don't know what you're talking about."

"As it stands right now, you'll be able to walk with the use of a cane." He raised the gun. "If I shoot you in the other knee, you'll spend the rest of your life on crutches."

The professor was slipping from consciousness. His jaw was trembling. *Don't shiver, damn you! Don't give him the pleasure of seeing your fear!*

"In the refrigerator."

"The refrigerator?"

"In case"—a burst of pain shot through him—"of a fire."

The intruder raised an eyebrow. *Clever boy*. He'd brought a bag along with him, a black nylon duffel, about three feet in length. He reached inside and withdrew a cylindrical object: a can of spray paint. He removed the cap, and with a skilled hand he began to paint symbols on the wall of the study. Symbols of violence. Symbols of hate. Ludicrously, the professor found himself wondering what Frau Ratzinger would say when she saw this. In his delirium, he must have murmured something aloud, because the intruder paused for a moment to examine him with a vacant stare.

When he was finished with his graffiti, the intruder returned the spray can to his duffel, then stood over the professor. The pain from the shattered bones was making Benjamin Stern hot with fever. Blackness was closing in at the edges of his vision, so that the intruder seemed to be standing at the end of a tunnel. The professor searched the ashen eyes for some sign of lunacy, but he found nothing at all but cool intelligence. This man was no racist fanatic, he thought. He was a professional.

The intruder stooped over him. "Would you like to make a last confession, Professor Stern?"

"What are you"—he grimaced in pain—"talking about?"

"It's very simple. Do you wish to confess your sins?"

"*You're* the murderer," Benjamin Stern said deliriously.

The assassin smiled. The gun swung up again, and he fired two shots into the professor's chest. Benjamin Stern felt his body convulse but was spared further pain. He remained conscious for a few seconds, long enough to see his killer kneel down at his side and to feel the cool touch of his thumb against his damp forehead. He was mumbling something. *Latin?* Yes, the professor was certain of it.

"*Ego te absolvo a peccatis tuis, in nomine Patris et Filii et Spiritus Sancti. Amen.*"

The professor looked into his killer's eyes. "But I'm a Jew," he murmured.

"It doesn't matter," the assassin said.

Then he placed the Stechkin against the side of Benjamin Stern's head and fired one last shot.

✦ 2 ✦

VATICAN CITY

FOUR HUNDRED MILES to the south, on a hillside in the heart of Rome, an old man strolled through the cold shadows of a walled garden, dressed in an ivory cassock and cloak. At seventy-two years of age, he no longer moved quickly, though he came to the gardens each morning and made a point of walking for at least an hour along the pine-scented footpaths. Some of his predecessors had cleared the gardens so they could meditate undisturbed. The man in the ivory cassock liked to see people—*real* people, not just the fawning Curial cardinals and foreign dignitaries who came to kiss his fisherman's ring each day. A Swiss Guard always hovered a few paces behind him, more for company than protection, and he enjoyed stopping for a brief chat with the Vatican gardeners. He was a naturally curious man and considered himself something of a botanist. Occasionally, he borrowed a pair of pruning shears and helped trim the roses. Once, a Swiss Guard had found him on his hands and knees in the garden. Assuming the worst, the guard had summoned an ambulance and rushed to his side, only to find that the Supreme Pontiff of the Roman Catholic Church had decided to do a bit of weeding.

Those closest to the Holy Father could see that something was troubling him. He had lost much of the good humor and easy charm that had seemed like a breath of spring breeze after the dour final days of the Pole. Sister Teresa, the iron-willed nun from Venice who ran his papal household, had noticed a distinct loss of appetite. Even the sweet biscotti she left with his afternoon coffee went untouched lately. She often entered the papal study on the third floor of the Apostolic Palace and found him lying face-down on the floor, deep in prayer, eyes closed as though he were in agony. Karl Brunner, the head of his Swiss Guard detail, had noticed the Holy Father frequently standing at the Vatican walls, gazing across the Tiber, seemingly lost in thought. Brunner had protected the Pole for many years and had seen the toll the papacy had taken on him. It was part of the job, he counseled Sister Teresa, the crushing burden of responsibility that falls on every pope. "It is enough to make even the holiest of men lose their temper from time to time. I'm certain God will give him the strength to overcome it. The old Pietro will be back soon."

Sister Teresa was not so sure. She was among the handful of people inside the Vatican who knew how much Pietro Lucchesi had not wanted this job. When he had arrived in Rome for the funeral of John Paul II, and the conclave that would choose his successor, the elfin, soft-spoken patriarch of Venice was not considered remotely *papabile,* a man possessed with the qualities necessary to be pope. Nor did he give even the slightest indication that he was interested. The fifteen years he had spent working in the Roman Curia were the unhappiest of his career, and he had no desire to return to the back-biting village on the Tiber, even as its lord high mayor. Lucchesi had intended to cast his vote for the archbishop of Buenos Aires, whom he had befriended during a tour of Latin America, and return quietly to Venice.

But inside the conclave, things did not go as intended. As their predecessors had done time and time again over the centuries, Lucchesi and his fellow princes of the church, one hundred thirty in all, entered the Sistine Chapel in solemn procession while singing the Latin hymn *Veni Creator Spiritus.* They gathered beneath Michelangelo's *Last Judgment,* with its humbling depiction of tormented souls rising toward heaven to face the wrath of Christ, and prayed for the Holy Spirit to guide their hand. Then each cardinal stepped forward individually, placed his hand atop the Holy Gospels, and swore an oath binding him to irrevocable silence. When this task was complete, the master of papal liturgical ceremonies commanded, *"Extra Omnes"*—Everyone out—and the conclave began in earnest.

The Pole had not been content to leave matters solely in the hands of the Holy Spirit. He had stacked the College of Cardinals with prelates like himself, doctrinaire hardliners determined to preserve ecclesiastical discipline and the power of Rome over all else. Their candidate was an Italian, a consummate creature of the Roman Curia: Cardinal Secretary of State Marco Brindisi.

The moderates had other ideas. They pleaded for a truly pastoral papacy. They wanted the occupant of the throne of St. Peter to be a gentle and pious man; a man who would be willing to share power with the bishops and limit the influence of the Curia; a man who could reach across the lines of geography and faith to heal those corners of the globe torn by war and poverty. Only a non-European was suitable to the moderates. They believed the time had come for a Third World pope.

The first ballots revealed the conclave to be hopelessly divided, and soon both factions were searching for a way out of the impasse. On the final ballot of the day, a new name surfaced. Pietro Lucchesi, the patriarch of Venice, received five votes. Hearing his name read five times inside the sacred chamber of the Sistine Chapel, Lucchesi closed his eyes and blanched visibly. A moment later, when the ballots were placed into the *nero* for burning, several cardinals noticed that Lucchesi was praying.

That evening, Pietro Lucchesi politely refused an invitation to dine with a group of fellow cardinals, adjourning to his room at the Dormitory of St. Martha instead to meditate and pray. He knew how conclaves worked and could see what was coming. Like Christ in the Garden of Gethsemane, he pleaded with God to lift this burden from his shoulders—to choose someone else.

But the following morning, Lucchesi's support built, rising steadily toward the two-thirds majority necessary to be elected pope. On the final ballot taken before lunch, he was just ten votes short. Too anxious to take food, he prayed in his room before returning to the Sistine Chapel for the ballot that he knew would make him pope. He watched silently as each cardinal advanced and placed a twice-folded slip of paper into the golden chalice that served as a ballot box, each uttering the same solemn oath: "I call as my witness Christ the Lord, who will be my judge that my vote is given to the one whom before God I think should be elected."

The ballots were checked and rechecked before the tally was announced. One hundred fifteen votes had been cast for Lucchesi. The *camerlengo* approached Lucchesi and posed the same question that had been put to hundreds of newly elected popes over two millennia. "Do you accept your canonical election as Supreme Pontiff?" After a lengthy silence that produced much tension in the chapel, Pietro Lucchesi responded: "My shoulders are not broad enough to bear the burden you have given me, but with the help of Christ the Savior, I will try. *Accepto*."

"By what name do you wish to be called?"

"Paul the Seventh," Lucchesi replied.

The cardinals filed forward to embrace the new pontiff and offer obedience and loyalty to him. Lucchesi was then escorted to the scarlet chamber known as the *camera lacrimatoria*—the crying room—for a few minutes of solitude before being fitted with a white cassock by the Gammarelli brothers, the pontifical tailors. He chose the smallest of the three ready-made cassocks, and even then he seemed like a small boy wearing his father's shirt. As he filed onto the great loggia of St. Peter's to greet Rome and the world, his head was barely visible above the balustrade. A Swiss Guard brought forth a footstool, and a great roar rose from the stunned crowd in the square below. A commentator for Italian television breathlessly declared the new pope "Pietro the Improbable." Cardinal Marco Brindisi, the head of the hard-line Curial cardinals, privately christened him Pope Accidental I.

The *Vaticanisti* said the message of the divisive conclave was clear. Pietro Lucchesi was a compromise pope. His mandate was to run the Church in a competent fashion but launch no grand initiatives. The battle for the heart and soul of the Church, said the *Vaticanisti,* had effectively been postponed for another day.

But Catholic reactionaries, religious and lay alike, did not take such a benign view of Lucchesi's election. To militants, the new pope bore an uncomfortable resemblance to a tubby Venetian named Roncalli who'd inflicted the doctrinal calamity of the Second Vatican Council. Within hours of the conclave's conclusion, the websites and cyber-confessionals of the hardliners were bristling with warnings and dire predictions about what lay ahead. Lucchesi's sermons and public statements were scoured for evidence of unorthodoxy. The reactionaries did not like what they discovered. Lucchesi was trouble, they concluded. Lucchesi would have to be kept under watch. Tightly scripted. It would be up to the mandarins of the Curia to make certain Pietro Lucchesi became nothing more than a caretaker pope.

But Lucchesi believed there were far too many problems confronting the Church for a papacy to be wasted, even the papacy of an unwilling pope. The Church he inherited from the Pole was a Church in crisis. In Western Europe, the epicenter of Catholicism, the situation had grown so dire that a recent synod of bishops declared that Europeans were living as though God did not exist. Fewer babies were being baptized; fewer couples were choosing to be married in the Church; vocations had plummeted to a point where nearly half the parishes in Western Europe would soon have no full-time priest. Lucchesi had to look no further than his own diocese to see the problems the Church faced. Seventy percent of Rome's two and a half million Catholics believed in divorce, birth control, and premarital sex—all officially forbidden by the Church. Fewer than ten percent bothered to attend mass on a regular basis. In France, the so-called "First Daughter" of the Church, the statistics were even worse. In North America, most Catholics didn't even bother to read his encyclicals before flouting them, and only a third attended Mass. Seventy percent of Catholics lived in the Third World, yet most of them rarely saw a priest. In Brazil alone, six hundred thousand people left the Church each year to become evangelical Protestants.

Lucchesi wanted to stem the bleeding before it was too late. He longed to make his beloved Church more relevant in the lives of its adherents, to make his flock Catholic in more than name only. But there was something else that had preoccupied him, a single question that had run ceaselessly around his head since the moment the conclave elected him pope. *Why?* Why had the Holy Spirit chosen him to lead the Church? What special gift, what sliver of knowledge, did he possess that made him the right pontiff for this moment in history? Lucchesi believed he knew the answer, and he had set in motion a perilous stratagem that would shake the Roman Catholic Church to its foundations. If his gambit proved successful, it would revolutionize the Church. If it failed, it might very well destroy it.

Daniel Silva

THE ENGLISH ASSASSIN

Art restorer and sometime spy Gabriel Allon is asked to visit Zurich, to clean the work of an Old Master for a millionaire banker. But when he gets there he finds the corpse of his client in a pool of blood beneath the masterpiece, and discovers that a secret collection of priceless paintings – stolen by Nazis in the war – is missing.

With the Swiss authorities trying to pin the murder on Allon and a powerful cabal determined to make sure this wartime secret remains buried, the art restorer must use all his former spy skills to find out the truth. And with an assassin that he helped to train also on the loose, Allon will need all his wits just to stay alive …

'An exceptionally readable, sophisticated thriller' *Washington Post*

'Silva excitingly delivers his story's twists and turns' *New York Times*

'Rich, multilayered, compelling' *Denver Post*